A Philosophy of Stars

"Evoking Kurt Vonnegut and Philip K. Dick, F. P. Dorchak works his storytelling magic to ponder the social, philosophical, political, and existential questions that have followed humanity through the ages: How did we get here and where exactly are we all heading? Like all good science fiction, it seamlessly blends technology, humanity, and a healthy dose of adventure to offer a telling critique of the mess we humans have been getting ourselves into since time immemorial."

Marc Schuster

Author of *The Greatest Show in the Galaxy: The Discerning Fan's Guide to Doctor Who* and *Frankie Lumlit's Janky Drumkit*

"There are science fiction writers and then there is F. P. Dorchak. In *A Philosophy of Stars*, Dorchak takes us on a wild ride through space and time (not necessarily in that order). This thought-provoking, mind-bending novel ingeniously weaves together chapters, each feeling like its own novella that come full circle to a satisfying climax that will have you thinking about mankind in a new light."

Lon Kirschner

Cover Designer

"A courageous and creative study of the many iterations of humanity. Dorchak's intense philosophical and sci-fi underpinnings set us up for the tense action that follows. Protocols are distrusted, amnesia is engineered, and cautionary tales are deadly.

"This is a challenging masterwork of hypotheticals, contradictions, and uncountable futures. What can a pod full of saved technology, people, and memories teach us about today's corruption and conundrums?

"May the best rook win."

Karen Albright Lin

Author of *American Moon: A Chinese Immigrant Story* and *Mu Shu Mac & Cheese*

"A Philosophy of Stars is a brilliant series of vignettes, in the same style as Ray Bradbury, written by F. P. Dorchak. Follow along through a deeply philosophical and psychological exploration of who we are, how we LIVE, and where we truly exist, as humans, in this vast Universe we live in. Five stars!"

Lou J. Berger

Author and Editor

"Philosophical, surreal, political, and insidious, A Philosophy of Stars illustrates the secrets and corruption of new beginnings burdened with old luggage and repeated patterns in a cerebral exodus into space."

Shannon Lawrence

Author, *Myth Stalker: Wendigo Nights and The Business of Short Stories*

"A Philosophy of Stars is not a cute, fun beach read. Beware this book. It will force you to think, to reevaluate. Beware this book."

Pat LoBrutto

Editor

"Science fiction, at its best, entertains us as it explores the eternal questions of life. It stretches our imagination, pulling us into another time and place while inviting us to ponder the mysteries that lie beyond the world we can see and touch. Easier said than done, of course, but F. P. Dorchak, in A Philosophy of Stars, pulls off this difficult feat with a deft and witty touch. It's a fun, fascinating read. Fans of Ray Bradbury will definitely want to check it out"

Paul Gallagher

Writer/Editor
Blogger, *Shadow & Substance*

Also by F. P. Dorchak

Novels

Sleepwalkers (2001)
The Uninvited (2013)
ERO (2013)
Psychic (2014)

Short Stories

"Clowns" (2016)
"Broken Windows" (2017)

Anthologies

Do The Dead Dream? (2017)
An Anthology of the Weird and the Peculiar

"Tail Gunner":
The You Belong Collective—Writing and Illustrations by Longmont Area Residents (2012)

"Broken Windows":
You Belong 2016—Words and Images from Longmont Area Residents (2016)

F. P. Dorchak

A Philosophy of Stars

Colorado Springs, Colorado

Copyright 2024 by F. P. Dorchak

Published by Wailing Loon, 2024

Cover design by Kirschner • Caroff Design Inc.

Print formatting by Class Clown Publications

All rights reserved. No part of this book, except in the case of brief quotations embodied in critical articles or reviews, may be reproduced in any form by any means, including information storage and retrieval systems, without prior written permission from the author.

This book is a work of fiction. Names, characters, places, and incidents are either products of the author's imagination or are used fictitiously. Any resemblance to actual events, locales, business establishments, or persons living or dead, is entirely coincidental.

The scanning, uploading, and distributing of this book via the Internet or via any other means without the permission of the copyright owner is illegal and punishable by law. Please purchase only authorized print and electronic editions, and do not participate in or encourage piracy of copyrighted materials. Your support of the author's rights is appreciated.

ISBN: 979-8-218-38599-6

I thank the following people for their assistance in this story: first and foremost, Ray Bradbury for his inspirational work, *The Martian Chronicles*. Mr. Bradbury's imagination was peerless! I loved where his mind went and how playful, vast, and exploratory it was. This is my homage to Mr. Bradbury, his imagination, and *The Martian Chronicles*. I cannot thank Joyce Combs enough for her ever watchful and editorial eye! She has been indispensable. My brother, Greg Dorchak, for his formatting wizardry and patience. Jane Roberts, Rob Butts, and the Seth material. My first violin instructor, Autumn Deppa. My dad, Frank P. Dorchak, Jr., a retired NYS Forest Ranger who passed away in February of 2022 at 85 years of age. I miss you, Dad. Scott van Laer, also a retired NYS Forest Ranger, who was instrumental in getting me to these two gentlemen: David R. Weise, Ph.D., Research Forester, USDA Forest Service, Pacific Southwest Research Station, Riverside, California, and Professor Guillermo Rein, Ph.D., Professor of Fire Science, Faculty of Engineering, Department of Mechanical Engineering, Imperial College, London. Both assisted me in the details of ground-fire combustion, which, of course, I fictionalized.

To my agent and friend, who insisted on believing in my work when no one else did. She fought for me and did her best over many years. I can not thank her enough. She is a force for good. *I revere and respect you beyond words.*

And, finally, a nostalgic, well-deserved, and respectful nod to Professor Emeritus William F. Nietmann, late of Northern Arizona University's Philosophy Department. I studied under him from 1979 to 1983. Dr. Nietmann taught me the history of philosophy, the art of philosophy, the thinkers of philosophy, and the importance of philosophy. He also taught me the virtuosity of questioning and showed me how asking questions could be done with composure and elegance. How people with differing ideas could actually carry on respectful conversations, agree to disagree, and learn from each other. And, yes, he actually did write the thought-provoking work mentioned herein, *The Unmaking of God*.

I thank the following people for their assistance in this story: first and foremost, Ray Bradbury for his inspirational work, *The Martian Chronicles*. Mr. Bradbury's imagination was peerless! I loved where his mind went and how playful, vast, and exploratory it was. This is my homage to Mr. Bradbury, his imagination, and *The Martian Chronicles*. I cannot thank Joyce Combs enough for her ever watchful and editorial eye! She has been indispensable. My brother, Greg Dorchak, for his formatting wizardry and patience. Jane Roberts, Rob Butts, and the Seth material. My first violin instructor, Autumn Deppa. My dad, Frank P. Dorchak, Jr., a retired NYS Forest Ranger who passed away in February of 2022 at 85 years of age. I miss you, Dad. Scott van Laer, also a retired NYS Forest Ranger, who was instrumental in getting me to these two gentlemen: David R. Weise, Ph.D., Research Forester, USDA Forest Service, Pacific Southwest Research Station, Riverside, California, and Professor Guillermo Rein, Ph.D., Professor of Fire Science, Faculty of Engineering, Department of Mechanical Engineering, Imperial College, London. Both assisted me in the details of ground-fire combustion, which, of course, I fictionalized.

To my agent and friend, who insisted on believing in my work when no one else did. She fought for me and did her best over many years. I can not thank her enough. She is a force for good. *I revere and respect you beyond words.*

And, finally, a nostalgic, well-deserved, and respectful nod to Professor Emeritus William F. Nietmann, late of Northern Arizona University's Philosophy Department. I studied under him from 1979 to 1983. Dr. Nietmann taught me the history of philosophy, the art of philosophy, the thinkers of philosophy, and the importance of philosophy. He also taught me the virtuosity of questioning and showed me how asking questions could be done with composure and elegance. How people with differing ideas could actually carry on respectful conversations, agree to disagree, and learn from each other. And, yes, he actually did write the thought-provoking work mentioned herein, *The Unmaking of God*.

For Laura

OUT THERE IS NOTHING	5
THE WHISPERERS	90
PLANETFALL	92
BECK AND CALL	100
IF AT FIRST YOU DON'T SUCCEED	103
FRACTAL THEORY	115
CREEPY TOWN	119
THE OTHER SIDE OF THE TREES	130
THE LIAR'S BRIGADE	163
IN THE NAME OF PROGRESS	167
THERE GOES THE NEIGHBORHOOD	170
A STUDY OF RUINS	180
INTO THE DARKNESS	202

THE EXTINCTION SAMARITANS	219
SOMETHING'S IN THE AIR TONIGHT	227
FROM WHENCE COME THY BREEZES	247
PAYIN' CUSTOMERS ONLY, PLEASE	251
UNPEACE	262
TWELVE	264
YOU CAN ALL GO TO HELL	279
THE TRAVELER	290
ANÓNYMOS	292
THE HOUSE OF SINS	294
SOMETIMES A FLOWER IS JUST A FLOWER	325
LET'S NOT GO THERE, MY FRIEND	328
A PHILOSOPHY OF STARS	345
GEDANKENEXPERIMENT	354
ANTECEDENT	356

Life is far more philosophical than we give it credit. As in the Socratic path to enlightenment, so, too, Humanity's.
FPD

Out there is nothing.
I know this, I do . . . but nobody else does.

OUT THERE IS NOTHING
Year 2073 Current Era (C.E.)

1

The stars . . . were different.
We were—all of us—onboard a ship . . . heading out into them—the stars.
We'd headed for another Earth-type planet out there. A planet a certain privileged sector of our population . . . "Earthly Nobility," I called them . . . believed was our best destination . . . into orbit about another star much like our own. We found ourselves out among the stars because of stories and goals that I now know are myths and legends and lies, and I desperately need to set the record straight. Not continue to perpetuate inaccuracies masquerading as fact.
Again . . . nobody knows this but me.
But they will.
Our ships—for there are several of them—are immense. The size of our largest Earth towns. Built in orbit. I am not a scientist nor an

engineer, but am part of the non-technical, non-essential system of classification, called "corps."

In the creation of Earth's global space exploration strategy, the planners created my position almost as an afterthought. Yes, they had thought of everything else that belonged to the mind, body, and spirit of space travelers, including the theological, but after much deliberation and my continued lobbying, finally decided upon another corps that included—and once included were amazed they hadn't considered it earlier—

Philosophers.

The Philosophy Corps.

I am a philosopher.

After all, was it not the spirit of philosophy that drove men and women to explore?

Gave rise to the very sciences themselves?

Philosophy *is* the exploration of the unknown. The probing, questioning, critical thought, and systematic presentation of reason to those considerations that haunt Humankind in its quest for knowledge and placement within the universe.

It is exactly what we are doing right now.

It had been the very origins of philosophy that had given birth to the sciences, upon which Humanity had relied far too heavily . . . forgetting its humble roots in the natural, moral, and metaphysical *gedankenexperimenten* that had given everything else birth. These very same philosophical organics that have become more important now than, arguably, any other period of history.

All sciences *had* emerged from philosophy.

And nothing could or should become more germane in the discovery of the universe about *us* than to return to those very roots . . . those philosophies . . . about which the entirety of Humanity revolves.

What else is out there?
Are we alone?
Can we survive?
Is what we are doing right?
Is there a God?

Do machines have a soul?
Should they?
What is to become of us?
While sciences built this ship . . . philosophy built the *sciences*.
Ergo . . .
Philosophy built this ship.
We've come full circle. The reduction of all Humankind's advancement *is* philosophy.

And it was within the hubris of Humankind that the original spark of questioning found its mark. It's poignancy.

Found its way.

Life had found its way.

And Life *always* finds a way.

Things had gone south amazingly—stupidly—fast.

When the hubris of arrogant and spiritually adolescent minds were given no checks, no balances . . . when the results of said hubris had been intentionally ignored and had exacted their toll upon the Earth and its inhabitants . . . well, they (those Earthly nobilities)—those who claimed all manner of entitlements in performing their ever-expanding God-like behaviors—had no choice but to reveal their hands. And they had plenty of cardboard shoved up into their dirty little sleeves.

We had torn holes in our skies, driven species of plant and animal into oblivion, reduced weather to algorithms, overpopulated our stay, and became masters at genetic manipulation.

Machines.

Machines . . . oh, the *machines!*

We were so proud of our damned *machines!*

We'd created tools upon which we'd assigned . . . souls.

Sentience?

Tools to help us, they told us . . . yet which turned out to be our undoing.

Implanted technologies into our bodies.

Had forgotten who we were . . . had become something more—or less than?—human.

And in so doing, had lost all respect for life . . . *organic* life.

If we killed something off . . . or lost a body part . . . we merely replicated its DNA and reproduced it.

Duplicated it.

Replaced it.

Our wars . . . originally fought by people . . . had become a chess game of mechanistic pawns and rooks—machines . . . then went back to people when we'd discovered it was cheaper for us to replicate the deceaseds' DNA . . . then turn *them* into machines with implants . . . to continue to do our dirty work.

It had become our bread and circuses.

All of this had come out much later, of course, but we had all turned blind eyes away from reading between the lines, most of us, long ago . . . until it was too late. We had all been so enamored with our iPhones, iWatches, and iLives. But all the secret government and industrial experimentations and projects had continued . . . and the Earthly Nobility had *thrived* . . .

Then came the earthquakes.

Murderous weather.

Depleted ozone.

Pandemics.

War.

Whole populations killed off.

It had become a perfect storm of all the wrong things: genetically manipulated food, strain-resistant disease, godlike technological advancements, the if-we-don't-do-it-someone-else-will mentalities . . . and the politics of utter corruption.

Oh, how *they* thrived!

Then the real atrocities had begun.

The destroyed regions of the world had been *recreated* . . . gene . . . by *gene*.

Only to *again* be wiped out.

So we just created more!

We called them Cemetery Cities, also known as "Creepy Towns." That is what they were. Heinous experiments that went beyond all reason and ethos.

All decency.

Humankind had finally created . . . Humankind.

Recreated it.

Was there no limit to our conceit?

But the last straw had been the volcanic eruptions that had torn open the Earth's mantle and seemed to vastly out-perform even the earthquakes in their absolute destruction of our planet.

The damage had become truly extraordinary.

After years of taunting behavior, years of pushing the limits of tectonic manipulation and penetrating our Earth's mantle deeper, ever deeper, Yellowstone Caldera, Mauna Loa, Grímsvötn, and more had blown. And these caused chain reactions across our world on an unimaginable scale.

People had finally revolted.

The Bright and Shiny of their addictive technologies had no longer been enough.

But it was too late.

Corruption had been complete . . . destruction . . . absolute.

Secret technologies had already stacked their decks. Shown their hands.

Marches and protests had surfaced across the planet . . . but where there had suddenly been revolts and riots and marches . . . suddenly there weren't.

They had all been . . . snuffed out.

The Nobility had simply broadcast one of their highly secretive algorithms and the results were immediate and astounding.

All opposition . . . terminated.

All those bright-and-shiny phones? . . . those implanted chips and cyborgian enhancements? . . . had taken over our minds. Our bodies.

The Nobility had seen to that.

But by then, their hidden projects on the moon had also begun taking their toll on our planet. Since no one any longer cared what was being done—not just on the Dark Side, but in plain view of any Earth-based telescope—The Nobility had begun modifying the moon's very orbit. Experiments had been stepped up on the moon that had greatly affected Earth's condition.

The earthquakes . . . the volcanic activity . . . the murderous weather had increased into unbelievable magnitude.

It truly appeared as if Earth was tearing itself apart.

That was when The Nobility showed their final hand, their exit strategy: *it was time to leave.*

So the chosen few . . . the families, all powerful, all wealthy, and their support staffs, who had been prepared and bred and pre-selected down through the ages . . . left Earth. They had all been quietly ferried onto the moon.

Nothing drew attention.

Everyone had been programmed to ignore their disappearances. To focus on only that which was fun or important to each individual. Anyone and everyone who had anything to do with entertainment—movies, books, gaming—all had been manipulated into making those things the public wanted . . . directed into making everyone feel safe and cozy. To employ a more biblical term, the Earth had become a veritable Sodom and Gomorrah. Messages had been subliminally inserted into all-things viewed . . . listened to . . . played. As with the entertainment industry, the pharmaceutical industry skyrocketed. As the blissfully ignorant masses watched their shows, read their books, obsessed over their ASMRotica, and immersed themselves into their virtual and streamed realities, they also heavily ingested their pharmaceuticals. And, oh, how Humanity loved its pharmaceuticals—they were a close second to their Bright and Shiny!

Other, lesser exodus plans had been allowed to grow and expand, if for nothing else than to divert attention away from The Nobility and their plans. And it is one such program of which I am a part: the lesser ships with their lesser population, their lesser crews.

Do you really think a Philosophy Corps would exist on the main ship? The Flag Ship's mission?

Everything had been planned for centuries. Vetted by the greatest minds to ever grace the planet. *And these plans had been hatched and developed and carried out over the entire history of Humankind.*

Everything The Nobility had done—everything—had a purpose and had been done in preparation for this moment. It had all been carefully funded and orchestrated and staged across the ages, since the dawn of civilization. For just this eventuality.

An exodus to the stars.
To leave Earth behind to its global annihilation.
Nothing had been left untouched.
And we had done it. All of it.
Our hubris. Our arrogance. Our sense of entitlement.
Our warped sense of right and wrong.
Our underdeveloped sense of spirit.

Then came a feat of irony that went unmatched in all of humor's history as it fell upon deaf ears: our Earthly Nobility had the notion that the move into space had been *their* idea.

Their idea to continue the Human race . . . to leave behind the damaged world that they had wrought . . . for the distant reaches of the

(*Bright and Shiny*)

interstellar.

Yes . . . *our* idea to leave Earth for space . . . The Nobility had so declared to its chosen.

But had it been their idea?

I say "their," but in all reality I am every bit a part of that nobility by my presence aboard this ship.

In the madness of it all, no one really understood that it had never been our decision to leave. It had been a far more insidious and powerful force. One by which The Nobility had absolutely no control. No idea.

It had been under our noses the entire time. Right in front of our faces.

There for all to see.

But we had been too blind by our power . . . overly enamored with ourselves and our arrogant logic.

Life.

The most profound and far-reaching of four-letter words.

Life . . . had found a way and had forcibly expelled us.

But they, The Nobility, had not seen that. Not at first. No, that would be my doing. Much later. And they fought me. Tried to silence me. My words. My epiphanies. My message to the world—well, as it existed upon the *Renaissance*.

I had . . . uncovered . . . that we had lost our respect for our home, our people, our planet, our *lives* . . . so *we* had been the ones expelled into extinction, just like all of the animal and plant life we had "choked out" of existence. Again, the lesson here was that *we* had not forced flora and fauna into extinction . . .

Flora and fauna had left us.

Forced *us* out.

In our imperiousness we had forgotten our place.

Our *participation.*

We had not been here to exploit. To destroy. We had been here to *participate*. And if we no longer participated . . . we were no longer welcome.

So, *we* had been expelled.

You see, all who look at extinction look at it from the wrong perspective. It is truly not us who wiped out whole genera and phyla.

Entire genera and phyla had left us, *because we were no longer worthy of them.*

Their existence.

Their souls, *their* participation.

So, no, Nobility, make no mistake, the decision to leave Mother Earth was not *your* decision. Not in the least.

Life had found a way and it had rejected *us.*

Life always finds a way.

Yet, no one had really seen that.

No one seemed to know this . . . understand this . . . but me.

And, in all truth, neither had *I* known this when our journey had begun.

It had only been after many long days and weeks and months (and what did "day" or "night" mean anymore?) of staring off into the cold, dark depths of the space between the stars that I'd had my epiphany. An epiphany that had had me lock and seal myself off from the rest of my spaceborne kind as I'd cried and wept and wailed my own, personal penance in my own personal living space. For all I had done . . . allowed to happen. Not taken a stand against. The shipboard doctors had tried to assuage my anguish with all manner of technology and medication, and I stared blankly at them as they worked their best. But I knew . . . *knew* that once their methods had worn off, I'd be right back to where I'd been as I had before they'd begun injecting me with their technological ameliorations. That I'd have to find some way to cope . . . or lose my sanity to the unfathomable abyss of space.

So I sat and thought and meditated.

Pulled out my Stradivarius (yes one of the original remaining few, my previous Earthly station had wonderfully afforded me the luxury of acquiring) and played Chopin's *Nocturne in C-sharp minor*.

And, in time (again, what does "Time" mean out here, in the farthest reaches of an immortal universe?), I did come to be at peace with myself. If I'd pretended hard enough, I could still imagine I was back on Earth . . . lying on the ground and gazing up into a brilliant night sky . . . as I had on many an occasion before the calamities hit, for I was of an age to remember the slightly better times.

But, instead of looking up, now I was looking . . . horizontally.

Out of a spaceship's view port.

And in time, I even came to return to my more jovial self. Came to again smile and be pleasant to my kind aboard this ark into perpetual darkness. But such was always measured. With an eye to a questionable future that only I knew existed.

So, while we thought ourselves ever so noble and high-minded and heroic amidst the Bright and Shiny of our incredibly advanced technologically and scientifically designed and built ships . . . what we actually were were the chaff and castoff of our very existence.

We were the garbage of our planet.

And were speeding faster and faster and farther and farther, into *Nothing*.

There was nothing out here.

2

At the time I didn't know if what had begun to happen to me had happened to others onboard the *Renaissance*, but I had begun to notice odd things beginning to occur. Occur to me. Within me.

To the Space and Time around me.

And the more I noticed it, the more pronounced it had become.

I had begun to . . . lose touch . . . yes . . . actually *lose touch* with reality.

Or perhaps a better way to put it is to say that I had become *more aware* of the incredible depth of what was *happening*. Of reality. It's multiple layers and textures and probabilities.

No . . . I did not so much as "lose touch" with reality . . . as I had become *more aware of it.*

I'd discovered that when I'd begun to consider things . . . mull over the quandaries of our new existence, our daily lives . . . that I'd seemed to be doing more than just thinking about them. I'd seemed—and you'll surely think me mad for saying this—to become more deeply *immersed* in them . . . become more a *part* of . . . whatever it was I was thinking about.

Again, you'll think me crazy for what I'm about to relate, *but I seemed to actually* live *the issues that I'd ruminated about!*

By this I mean that as I thought and considered and pondered a problem, a daydream, *gedankenexperiment*, whatever you'd like to call it . . . it was as if I'd gone into a dream state and became an active part of whatever it was I was thinking about . . . actively "there," actively acting it out . . . *participating* . . . in the thought.

It was like when you're so tired and you nod off to sleep—only for but a moment—and are in this temporary sleep state. And let's say in this sleep state you reach out for a glass of water. So, for all intents and purposes *you* . . . *are* . . . *there.* And you reach out for the water, but instead of actually grabbing the glass—for this is, in reality, all in your mind—your entire body jerks and you are jarred awake back to your present, waking consciousness . . . and in doing so you find that your physical hand and arm are actually extended out before you, and the non-existent glass of water gone. And you marvel—even laugh—at yourself for how real, how totally and completely *life-like* that temporary hypnogogic experience had been!

Only now I wasn't laughing.

This was becoming a common occurrence for me.

My entire awake state was becoming confused with this new altered state of awareness.

It continued to get so bad that almost every time I closed my eyes, I didn't know if when I opened them I was going to actually be awake and conscious... or again thrown into that conscious/unconsciousness/awake/hypnogogic/dream state.

And I didn't care!

I'd found my new state of mind far more to my liking!

You see, it didn't just happen with thought-experiments or problem-solving, it began to infiltrate my every consideration!

My music!

If I thought of a lake I'd known on Earth and imagined myself standing there, on its shores, my bare feet and toes pressed into the cool grains of sand that no longer existed for me—

I was there.

If I thought of myself meandering through a thickly treed and cool northern hemisphere forest—

I was there.

If I wistfully remembered a lost love... holding her in my arms—

I was there.

As one becomes one with one's music... it is hard to convey... but I could smell... and taste... and feel... each note in brilliant multidimensional resonances.

Before I'd realized it, I'd been spending more time in my head than

(... *sitting against a tree... soaking up the late afternoon rays of the sun...*)

in my... reality?... in my spaceship's quarters...

(... *hiking through a hillside meadow...*)

(... *hands brushing the tops of tall grasses...*)

(... *inhaling deeply of fresh air... looking up to the sun...*)

under artificial illumination... looking outside into an endless darkness peppered with intense, crisp pinholes of brilliant light.

Yes, I had truly gone mad—or, at the very least, had begun my descent into the spiraling, delusional depths of insanity.

I was losing my mind.

But was I?

I would be walking down the corridors of our ship, a stray thought of reading *The Unmaking of God*

(... *reading the book late at night... in my dorm...*)

(... *highlighting passages...*)

(. . . taking notes . . .)
would enter my mind—and I'd *be* there. In my university years . . . reading Professor Nietmann's classic work on the connections between philosophy and religion and how those connections impacted the philosophical considerations of God.

Believe me when I tell you, it wasn't that I *remembered* reading it, it wasn't *remembering* what it felt like to be nineteen and back in the university reading Nietmann's seminal work, it wasn't at all like what "remembering" is usually all about—

I'm telling you . . . I . . . was . . . there . . .

(. . . flipping through pages in the book . . .)

(. . . late at night in my university dorm room . . .)

in Space and Time.

(. . . pondering . . . writing . . .)

Passers-by, I'd come to determine, would not see me blink in and out of existence or perceive anything so dramatic.

No.

They would not see what I was seeing—nor *experience* what I was *experiencing*—and I would not go catatonic. No, these . . . participations . . . of mine . . . no matter how long they lasted . . . or where they took me—no matter how long I was subjectively experiencing them—only occurred for but fractions of a *moment* within the Objective Time of the spaceship. *Objective Time* . . . that is what I need to call my time, here, on this ship. I can't call it anything else to better communicate what I desperately need to communicate, here . . . before I cannot do so anymore . . . and fall into and get lost within the cracks and fissures and crevasses of folding and unfolding multidimensional Time . . . .

I could have spent two years reliving a lost love . . . re-experiencing my university years one-for-one . . . then would "pop out" of those experiences back to the exact moment I went *in* to them, while doing whatever I'd been doing in OT, before I became immersed into the mental experience . . . and even *realized* all of the above upon my return! But even if I'd never physically experienced something . . . in these participations *I'd experienced it*. Sure . . . I'd be slightly confused, but no more so than had I temporarily slipped into some intense, whimsical, and short-lived daydream.

I never lost sense of my OT upon my returns . . . yet never considered it when I re-lived those mental, metaphysical moments of displaced participation. There was never a thought given to Future Me (which was, actually, my *Objective Time/Present Day* me). Only the "me" I was—am?—during those Timeless events. *I was in the very moment I was experiencing.* Nothing else mattered.

And when you are truly "in the moment," there is no past, no future, only *now.*

I lived them as fully and in-the-moment as I did the first time through, in Chronological Life's timeline.

But things became even more fantastical.

There were several instances where I'd emerge from one such conscious/unconscious experience . . . *only to find that I was "awakening" into yet another conscious/unconscious experience!*

I'd be

(. . . *making love with a woman* . . .)

dreaming of making love with a woman I knew . . . then would "wake up" into OT—only this wouldn't *be* OT. Instead

(. . . *falling asleep . . . eyes flashing open* . . .)

(. . . *sitting upright in a high school English class* . . .)

(. . . *looking around as if just waking up* . . .)

I'd awaken to find myself a sixteen-year-old student daydreaming in an Earth English class!

Or

(. . . *sitting in a movie, laughing and looking to the girl beside me* . . .)

sitting in a movie theater watching a movie.

Performing

(. . . *being instructed in violin vibrato technique* . . .)

violin lessons.

Or lazily

(. . . *on a hill, staring up at billowy clouds floating overhead* . . .)

watching billowy clouds drifting across a brilliant blue sky.

And it would all be exactly as real and unnerving as when I awoke to my shipboard OT reality!

What was going on in my head became *wholly and just as real as* what was going on outside it.

I'd think: *Wow, what'd just happened?*
Am I really here? Or
(. . . *sitting in sophomore English class* . . .)
(. . . *looking away from the teacher and out the classroom window* . . .)
am I really just/still that sixteen-year-old back in Mrs. Dougall's second-period English class, and my entire life after that class has just been one intense, immense daydream?

Then I began to get bleed-throughs of my future in my *past* experiences.

I'd feel that I was still daydreaming, only it was about all the experiences and memories that I *currently* have—from my spaceship Objective Time—*but I'd be*
(. . . *writing at a dorm-room desk when assaulted by mental images of*—)
(—*the* Renaissance—)
(—*walking throughout the* Renaissance—)
(—*looking out a port hole into interstellar space*—)
sitting in Mrs. Dougall's English class.
My points-of-view had excruciatingly flip-flopped!

And it wasn't that I was simply conscious of any present-day self from the spaceship's OT—no, this was truly me receiving future bleed throughs *while I was that sixteen year old.*

And it got so that several times I'd have a
(. . . *waking up in English class*—)
(. . . *waking up in the middle of a* Renaissance *mission briefing*—)
third such—*and on two occasions a* fourth such—awakening.

I began to lose all track of Time. Location. Sense of place.
Sense of *self.*

This would go on for (apparently) days . . . weeks . . . months . . . on end.

Or did it?

Time and location began to lose all meaning for me, let alone bearing.

And I began to hear about others on our ship whispering about their similar experiences in private. Others who said it had made their thinking . . . slower? faster? . . . they didn't really know. Just that their thinking had become . . . more creepy . . . more dimensional . . . more—

Hyper dimensional?

More possessive of depth and density and dimension.

Others began to talk, their eyes taking on faraway stares, speaking about aspects of their pasts as if they, too, were still there . . . or had yet to experience them.

And that was where I'd gotten my epiphany.

That instead of running away from our problems, the loneliness of space brought us closer to them.

Our personal issues.

Every one of us.

The farther away you travel from your problems . . . the closer to them you actually become.

In hurtling ourselves away from Earth . . . out into the stars . . . I'd realized that we were all actually and directly confronting our issues like never before. That . . . space—outer space, interstellar space—*did* something to you when you left the confines of Earth, the *gravity* (which had been scientifically proven to alter Space and Time) of Earth. It didn't behave as it had around the safe orbit of our home planet, the only planet we'd ever intimately known. No. The physics of Life seemed to have changed the farther away from it we traveled . . . or maybe this was exactly how physics worked all along, but we never discovered it, because this was our first time traveling so far away from Earth ourselves, instead of by proxy with space probes.

And, it seemed, all these perfect, pre-chosen, elite nobility from Earth seemed to have quite the baggage they'd been hauling around within the folds of their existences.

(. . . *men and women having affairs* . . .)

Remembering them.

(. . . *men and women impeding others from positions they took* . . .)

Reliving them.

(. . . *a man killed by poison* . . .)

(. . . *a woman strangled after sex* . . .)

(. . . *a man getting onto a passenger plane* . . . *that plane blown out the sky* . . .)

So, they began to seek me out, rather than ship psychologists . . . they needed to talk to someone . . . someone who trucked in the abstract . . . the philosophical . . . the metaphysical . . . but not someone who would have to—by law—log all of their problems into an historical medical and psychiatric repository, for part of our mission's protocol was to report all psychological sessions for the benefit of Humankind . . . or any other "kind" we met out here. This was, after all, an historic moment for Humankind, and as much as possible every aspect of life and living need be recorded for archival—and forensic—matters of record.

However, the Philosophy Corps appeared exempt from said decree.

Apparently we had slid between the cracks, as a last-minute addition to mission requirements.

These people had all done all manner of things to get and remain where they were and they were—now—not very proud of what they'd done . . . floating around out here with all the Time in the Universe to think and ponder and grow increasingly penitent about their actions in the past. About everything being thrown into intense perspective by the brutal enormity of it all and our relative physical insignificance within it. Well, at least those who actually had a conscience, a soul, and sought me out, anyway.

All of those people, the ones with souls—down to the last man and woman—all felt that they could now start over.

But that was not what was happening.

They were *re-living*.

Expanding upon what had already been enacted.

And it was as I sat before the port holes of our ship, the decks, my quarters, and stared out into the stars and blackness and infinity of Life that I realized this.

That the stars to which I stared out at were not *out* there . . . outside me . . . they were *within* me.

Within *all* of us.

We had not left the Earth.

We had not done anything of the sort.

We were not flying through deep space, heading through uncharted star fields for a new life . . .

No, we were where we were . . .

Little individual moments in Time . . . as brilliant or brighter than any such distant star.

We had left *nothing* . . . for . . . *nothing*.

And it seemed I was the only one who knew this.

So, I attempted to educate.

3

The farther away you travel from your problems . . . the closer to them you actually become.

As I walked the halls of our deceptively massive ship things looked so . . . deceptively . . . beautiful. So bright and shiny. So . . . sterile. Everything was of course new. Well-kept. The best of everything. No spared expense. Now I know where all the funneled money went and why our governments had always been so in the red.

But as I walked the decks, one aspect of the ship really hit me: how polished and clean everything was!

What else had you to do out in deep space?

We all pitched in.

There were schedules that rotated through every individual onboard. We all had a stake in our voyage, so we all contributed to the well-being of not only our individual lives, but the condition of our ship—except the captain of our vessel. He had far more pressing duties to be concerned with 24/7 (again, what did "24/7" mean out here?) Even our "*Nouveau* Nobility," I now called them, the remaining Earthly nobility out here, onboard the *Renaissance*. We all performed cleaning and polishing of our environment, since to have a fully and properly staffed Janitorial Corps that huge (though we did have a core group) would have taken up precious space and resources from our whole "saving the best, brightest, and the most entitled from Earth" mission.

Well, to begin with.

It didn't take long for our more-entitled to realize they could get other, lesser-entitleds to do their cleaning for them.

It was Langster who first sub-contracted out, so to speak.

Captain Talbot was the captain of the ship, but Stephen Langster captained the mission. He was also the head of our *Nouveau* Nobility . . . and he wasted no time in hiring out for others to perform his menial tasks.

Others soon followed. It was only a matter of
(*objective*)
time.

I found it increasingly difficult to maintain focus in shipboard OT. I was constantly . . . daydreaming . . . for lack of a better term. Skipping? Maybe that's the better term. Skipping. Yes. I found myself "skipping" all the time—

Isn't it funny how and how frequently we employ the term "time" in our language? Even as I now (another Time derivative) use it, I find its meaning diluted . . . diminished. There have even been times (there I go again) I've used the word and had to stop. Dead stop. And ask myself   the

                                                             meaning
             of the
                       word.

Had I used the most correct version of the term?
What does it mean?

But I also found myself asking even more penetrating considerations, such as . . . is the proper word correctly placed within Time and Space? Upon the written screen or paper sentence location . . . in multidimensional coordinates? Should this word actually be better placed here . . .

                                . . . or *here?*

Should more white space be employed around *this* version of the word used
         here . . .
rather than this version of it
                                     over here?

I found this increasingly disturbing.

Was I the only one this was happening to? And if so, why?

I began to ask those who sought me out a series of questions:

How frequently do you find yourself skipping?

Do you find yourself skipping more or less during certain times of the day?

How do you feel during them?

How do you feel when you've returned?

Do you find yourself forgetting the meanings of words? Concepts?

Do you find yourself discovering deeper, more layered meanings to words and concepts?

Do you see any changes in yourself?

Do you lose track of reality?

Do you . . . .

Then I compiled the results.

Most of those I'd interviewed had said they felt no change in themselves . . . which I found odd. But was that because they were going crazy themselves and just couldn't see it? The so-called "Catch-22"?

So I quietly began to follow my crew mates around. Observe them. Take notes on their behavior, that kind of thing. I even skipped on some of them, pondering their conditions, their lives, their—

In short . . . I began spying upon my companions.

I found all manner of information . . . most of which I wish I hadn't discovered . . . affairs . . . stealing . . . lying . . . and the general elitist and unnerving ruminations of an entitled segment of our earthly population, with whom I shared an inescapable and confined existence.

It sickened me.

But I did not find that they'd all experienced the same reality warping and bending I experienced.

I found that even eternally separated from the lives they had lived back on Earth, they, this entitled Nobility, maintained the same mentalities that they had employed while there. Only here, out in the depths of space, they seemed more . . . *intense*. Their mindsets continued to ponder what to do if and when we made planetfall. If and when we found . . . life. Who would do what . . . who would lead . . . who . . .

Was expendable.

I had found their list. A rack-and-stacked list of who would be culled, for whatever reason, in specific order.

And I was highly placed upon that list.

But I knew this. I was only important while I was important—needed. Useful. A smoke screen for diversity and included Humanity and critical thought—or maybe they just liked me and wanted to shut me up with my incessant lobbying. After all, I was the only one on this ship part of the Philosophy Corps! So, I suppose I couldn't hold it against them that once everyone had become adjusted to the rigors of space travel, I would no longer be useful and would be the first to go, should such a situation arose.

Go where?

Do . . . what?

But still . . . I found no metaphysically important irregularities among all those with whom I'd researched.

Spied upon.

So I went to the theologians.

And spied upon them as well. Though at this point I didn't really need to talk with them, since I easily found all I'd needed from skipping, I was becoming increasingly concerned with my sanity and just needed to *talk* . . . if nothing else to maintain my focus in OT. I was finding that my grip on OT—on reality, or reality as I thought I knew it—was quickly becoming increasingly tenuous. Maintaining physical contact with the people I was with . . . doing the shipboard cleaning . . . *eating* . . . talking . . . all helped maintain my needed corporeal focus.

But I found time continued to warp. It was a weird metaphysical perversion of the Red Shift/Blue Shift principle. As I was expecting, thinking about some activity that would seem to be a comfortable amount of time in my OT future, an activity that fit into the OT world view of which I was *presently* a part of—once I was there, in *that* OT future I'd been earlier contemplating and doing *that* OT future activity I'd been early imagining in my OT's *past* . . . it was as if I was screaming through the now-*present* OT experience of the event and was screaming past all that I was doing . . . *now, in my OT future* . . . and once past this *Now,* the future OT event, I was somehow continually screaming faster and faster and ever *farther* away from that which

I

Was.

In my OT future.

It was a metaphysical sling-shot effect around my corporeal OT Future-Present moment.

My earlier self's pondering of my future-OT's-present-moment soon became something so far "in the distant past" from me that I began to question whether or not it had ever occurred at all!

Yet I could skip it and re-experience it like everything else.

It was maddening!

And, yes, you may find all this difficult to understand, but try explaining it!

OT had now become hideously warped. Elongated and contracted in ways I still find hard to convey, because our physical communication is so heavily rooted in Time, and Time was quickly losing all meaning to me. *Focus.*

As I spied and talked with the theological on our ship (who were, curiously, not as high on the expendable list as I was) I found that they were also not having the same problems I was experiencing with reality and Time and placement and sense of self.

But I found them entirely frightful just the same.

In truth, *more* so.

Most of them would not even talk with me, for they saw me as a Godless heathen who couldn't make up his mind and kept questioning his own questions and answers and was one who would never arrive at a solution that was—to them—as plain as the nose on my face. Was one who used his own methods as an excuse against faith of whatever denomination I contacted. Only the Buddhists gave me any measure of respect. Or the Lutherans. I came to really like the Lutherans.

But as I sat back and pondered all that I was experiencing, I became aware of the trend . . . the method to this space madness, this sickness I was experiencing and experienced another reality changing epiphany: *our worldviews, our beliefs* shaped *our madnesses.*

Those entrenched in the religious believed that the end was actually here, now, and that the Rapture had occurred (though they couldn't quite reconcile how others not of their beliefs were also resident upon this Rapture platform with them) . . . that their variously believed devils were also nipping at their heels, and that they were well on their way to the Second Coming.

How could I argue?

Was not, indeed, the Book of Revelations coming to its terrified conclusion?

Those elitists of a corporate mindset were continuing with their conspiracy constructions and implementations. Already creating sub-elitist groups. Ways of handling those on the ship who they defined as being future complications to their master plans. Growing and reshuffling their expendables lists. Finding new ways of expanding their lost Earthly powers in the Black Sea of space. As I'd skipped these people and their concepts, I'd even found their securely hidden shipboard files detailing their master plans . . . how this ship was actually sent out toward a planet they believed was their historical quest, their own "holy" destination. A planet that they believed was heading our way—Earth's way. *A planet they believed was the bringer of Life to Earth.*

So I'd skipped that concept . . . and discovered it was a myth upon which the entirety of generations extending back into the earliest mists of Earthly history had based their lives. A dream based upon and fueled by awake and somnolent fears and anxieties of the day. One could hardly fault them, given the turbulent times in which they lived. Everything that this *Nouveau* Elite had done while on Earth was for just this reason. And it was all based upon a misconception . . . a misinterpretation.

A *dream.*

But they believed it.

So all that they did, had done, and thought and planned was and had been focused to that end.

It was here that I must confess to the beginnings of a slowly burning rage building up inside me: that the entirety of our being here, out in the vast distances between the stars was based upon a misinterpreted *dream?*

I know, it wasn't that simple—*but wasn't it?*

The more I thought about it, the more it got under my skin.

Throughout the entire and various ages of Humankind, all that had ever been done in secret . . . all the weather and environmental manipulation, all the scientific and technological advancements . . . the accumulation of wealth and power and waging of war . . . had all been done on the misguided, parochial interpretations of an unconscious collective fantasy, interpreted as a *vision*. A dream one or more persons had had about a fictitious end-of-life scenario that could have been caused by a bit of undigested beef from the night before. And because of that, those who controlled life on Earth had made plans that tore apart not only the heart and soul of Earth's population . . . but also that of the very planet upon which we'd all *lived* and walked and *breathed*.

The ludicrousness of it all was utterly staggering and it enraged me.

We were all out here . . . *for* nothing.

Absolutely *nothing!*

For no goddamned reason!

All of Earth . . . the comforts of home we had known could all have still been there if not for the overzealous mental sicknesses of those running history! The beauty of our lives were gone: the grasses growing beneath our feet . . . the sparkling, crystal clear waters of our seas, lakes, and brooks . . . the nurturing rays of our sun's energy entering our lives . . . warming our skin and the very air that we breathed—

Gone.

And we were *way* the hell out here!

For absolutely no good reason at all!

Had destroyed our planet—our home—for absolutely *no* reason!

But before I could delve much more into my growing fury of this revelation, the shipboard separations had begun.

Various segments of the ship had begun to avoid each other. Began creating sub-strata upon sub-strata.

Castes.

People began to only associate with their own kind . . . their own "clubs."

Those who had come to me for answers had begun to stop doing so. Had subtly and not so subtly asked me where I stood on various topics trying to gauge where I stood to either get me to come to their side or weed me out.

Until they all stopped coming to me altogether.

But I just didn't care!

Nothing mattered anymore!

As I wandered the hollow decks and corridors during the empty hours, I soon found certain areas locked and closed off. Initially notices had been posted declaring "maintenance activity," but the notices never came down. Increased in postings. Until those unknowingly in the lower echelons of this new caste system began to take notice and complain about, *Hey, what was going on?*

And these were people used to getting their own way back on Earth . . . suddenly finding themselves on the *outside* of their own lifetime of privileges.

The unrest grew . . . and it grew swiftly. Swept throughout the ship. Other sections began to retaliate by closing off "their" sections . . . claimed in their own retaliatory right.

And then the Enforcers made their entrance.

Of course there were stores of weaponry onboard. One never knew who or what we'd come across out here, and as we've done throughout the course of Human history, we've always gone into the unknown heavily armed and more than ready to employ it. This voyage was no different. We've always defended ourselves from enemies, both foreign and domestic. And while many on board had been trained in their effective usage only an even-more select few had been tapped as the actual employers of said force. It was easy to spot them as they patrolled the ship brandishing all the finest hardware our armory had to offer. There had been a few scuffles, but so far no one had been

(*killed*)

hurt.

But even I—who was so ensconced into what this space sickness had been doing to my mind—began to worry.

It was only a matter of time!

(*Ha!*)

(*I laughed.* Time!)

Then the ship's captain, Captain Talbot, had become ill.

That wasn't supposed to happen.

All harmful pathogens had been filtered out from our environment and people weeded out who had any such illnesses, so that only the superiorly healthy (all genetically engineered) had been brought aboard. Nothing was being divulged to the rest of us . . . so I perfunctorily skipped his illness, I saw that it wasn't a physical illness to which Talbot had succumbed, but the space sickness.

Simply put, he had gone mad.

A mind and life so heavily rooted in protocols and rules and order had suddenly and unexpectedly unraveled. Became unstructured.

He had glimpsed into the other side and seen how nothing he had ever done had ever, really mattered.

How nothing he was *doing* mattered.

He had glimpsed—just like me—into the nothingness that was out here.

That everything he had been told had been a lie that even the *liars* believed . . . and had been forced upon the rest of us!

But he had seen more, so much more . . . and just couldn't handle it.

Perhaps was even brave enough to do what I could not—go over to the Darkside. Succumb to these alternate realities and simply leave our physical existence behind.

When you've discovered that the entirety of your life had been based upon lies . . . that the present and the future of your life were based upon even *more* lies . . . .

Talbot died a week later—by his own hand, I'd skipped—the first such shipboard casualty.

Langster, the civilian mission commander, stepped in, as was the protocol. But when Langster also homesteaded permanent captaincy of our *ship*—that violated the protocol of the separation of mission from ship command. No matter that he physically couldn't perform both jobs—he kept the title, designating everything else.

Something foul was afoot.

But when confronted about his takeover, Langster claimed that once a new captain was identified, she or he would take over—but that had never materialized in my lifetime. There was already an established protocol of who would succeed who for all command positions, but Langster claimed that mission objectives had so drastically transformed (Transformed? How "transformed," we'd cried?) and that this change hadn't been foreseen by our existing protocols and had to be thoughtfully considered. If the so-called perfect candidate couldn't handle the rigors of the job, who's to say any lesser-qualified candidate could do better?

He was challenged.

Her name was Eleanor Faramount and she had publicly taken issue with Langster's claims. She was the ship's librarian, though in her Earthly existence had been the most powerful captain of the publishing industry. Knew all the protocols and maintained that there existed no-such citations. Instead *she'd* cited all the pertinent indices and paragraphs that disallowed his permanency. Stood up to Langster in the Town Meetings, as we'd called them. Langster conceded and declared that she and he would talk more at a side meeting. To which she agreed.

They'd had their meetings.

Continued to disagree.

A few of us had taken on the rolls of reporters, and it was a news cycle that kept us all riveted to our screens and made us forget our whereabouts.

Had us all pretending we were all still back on *Earth*.

Then . . . several weeks later . . . Eleanor had had a sudden change of heart.

Backed off. Conceded that there had been a subparagraph that she had overlooked in all the thousands of protocols that had declared exactly what Langster had been promoting all along.

And that . . . was that.

But I knew better.

I'd skipped the situation and discovered that Langster had indeed hacked the code and had
(. . . *raped . . . beaten . . .*)
intimidated Eleanor. Had done the same to her family members. Eleanor backed off.
Knew her place . . . the game . . . and had done similar in her old life back on Earth. There was a new structure forming and she (apparently, and much to her dismay) was no longer one of the chosen.
Now I was concerned.
The farther away you travel from your problems . . . the closer to them you actually become.

4

This was when I began to detail all that was happening, not only to me, but our ship, our lives. I began recording all that I knew into my personal logs, my shipboard recordings.
And I began sending them out into space.
Sent them out in all directions in the hopes the misguided intention of someone out there, perhaps on one of the other ships or even Earth itself, would find them . . . learn from them.
I'm an optimist that way.
Despite all our seemingly important problems, something strange . . . and wonderful . . . was happening to us. And I'd hoped that my intentions could be sent . . . backward . . . in *time*, Objective or otherwise . . . to help others before they found . . . ourselves.
I'd essentially become a hermit.
Why would I need the comfort of others, when I could skip to wherever and see whomever I wanted?
Then throw in recording all that I'd experienced, well, it took up a lot of OT.
Then something that should have been so obvious finally occurred to me: *why not skip to our ship's destination?*
With all the journeys I'd taken, this had just never occurred to me! I guess I was so busy with the trees
(. . . *let's go see what's . . .*)
for the forest . . . or the stars for the universe.

But dare I do such a thing?

I picked up my violin and began to play and allowed my mind to wander....

(... *arrival... exploration... colonization—suburbs?*)

What if doing so showed no hope for us?

(... *thriving... ruins?... exploitation...*)

What if it showed a painful

(... *war... war... a haunted house? A butler? a flower?... destruction...*)

and protracted end?

But the more I thought about it... the more those didn't make sense. And just thinking about thinking about it brought images—albeit disjointed images—to my mind. But if I'd learned anything with my version of this space sickness... with all my skipping... it's that there are unlimited probable realities out there!

That there was no one, hard-and-fast "end"... to *anything*.

Everything had multiple options... possibilities....

So, how all these renderings fit into Life, the Universe, and Everything Else... that, well, that I had no idea.

I had no idea how these different versions of Life were chosen and experienced. Came about. Materialized. Fanned out. What happened to each of us... on the soul level... with all of this. If we died in certain versions, but lived in others... how did that work at the God level? Sure, I'm alive now... out in the reaches of interstellar space... but what did that *mean*?

Is the me, here, now, the real, rock-bed me? Or am I just a casual spin-off of *another* me, elsewhere? A recreational version of the Real Me still alive and back on an Earth not yet destroyed by hubris and greed and entitlement?

Or is another Real Me entirely somewhere else?

Some*time* else?

On another planet?

Another universe?

Am I just a dream of a dream of a dead person in a Cemetery City?

It... vapor-locks... all reason... the mind.

And how would such knowledge change me? Affect my mental state?

If I knew there was no hope for us . . . that we are all eternally lost and destined to die floating out among effectively lifeless stars . . . how would that affect me?

Could I go on? Could any of us?

I mean, really, what would be the point for This Me to continue living if I knew that there was nothing in store for Future Me, but continued isolation from all of life as we know it? That we found no livable planet? Or that perhaps we do find something, but it isn't welcoming. Or that we get sucked up into a Black Hole? What if all of our alternatives are bleak or unbeneficial?

But what if they're not?

I am, by nature, an optimist . . . and, largely, life has borne itself out to me as being supportive and good, despite my birth into this Earthly Royalty . . . even if I'd gotten caught up in this spaceborne conspiracy theory of planet hunting. I was merely in the right place at the right time, of the correct and proper required pedigree to *be* here . . . to be the needed scapegoat.

That doesn't make me a bad person.

Yet I am useful enough to be expendable when the requirements are called for.

But part of my philosophy is that everything *does* happen for a reason.

So . . . though I do not know my course . . . my destination . . . I must trust in my *life*. Go in the directions that it guides me.

And the totality of it has, indeed, guided me to here, this very . . . *moment*.

I set down my violin.

So, yes, I took that leap. Skipped to our destination . . . and saw our end.

5

What I'd experienced, I hadn't been prepared for.

Once I'd returned, though it was but a moment "away"—actually it was less!—when I'd returned, I'd actually returned to just *prior* to performing the skip, which further blew my mind.

It had taken me better than a week to record all that I had experienced up to this point, then also send it out into space with all my other transmissions.

What I'd seen had not disappointed . . . but it had also saddened. I felt it my duty to let my compatriots know what was in store for them. And I knew if I'd only gone to Langster, nothing would get accomplished. My skipping had shown me that if I was to change the course of Humanity—at least our little oasis of it—I had to let them know what was in store for them, so *they* could change it, not just Langster.

Go in with their eyes, as well as their minds, their perspectives, wide open.

Don't let Langster dominate—win.

I began contacting those who had deserted me and labeled me as expendable. I sat down with them in little groups . . . careful not to omit anyone. Careful to fully disclose all that I had seen and learned. And, of course, there were many, many questions.

Why had none of them seen any of this?

Why was I so special?

How did they know any of this was true and accurate? Talbot had gone crazy . . . how did we know I wasn't heading down that same path?

All I could tell them was that whether or not I was going crazy—like Talbot—wasn't it best they were at least aware of what *might* . . . very well *could* . . . transpire? And if my knowledge really was corrupt and contaminated by this space sickness, then nothing would come of it and none of what I had to say would bear itself out. No harm, no foul, as they used to say. But if I was correct—if even the smallest detail that I had relayed had even the tiniest ounce of truth to it—wasn't it worth hearing me out? Documenting all I had to say?

As to why it only appeared to myself and no one else, I tried in my best, most politically correct manner, to inform them that what I had also learned was that space . . . deep, interstellar space . . . seems to affect each of us in our own ways. That whatever is . . . out here . . . seems to amplify our predilections . . . our mindsets . . . as they already exist. If we believe in something, that something will be amplified, expanded upon, maybe even distorted. If we have fears, those fears are magnified. Expanded. Experienced. If we do not believe in something, those things are ignored.

That actually brought up more questions than my intended discussion had.

How did I know this?

What made me the expert?

And again, not in so many words, but . . . *why* was *I so damned special?*

Not intentionally, but in the back of my mind, I began to envision my name on the expendables list moving ever so slightly *downward*, toward the bottom. How odd I thought.

I reminded them that they—all of them, many of whom I was currently talking with this very moment—had come to *me*. Had sought *me* out for *my* advice . . . that because I was nondenominational, because I was of the intellectually investigative mindset (yes, the Philosophy Corps—I was the targeted *professional* here) I had been the one from whom they had sought answers. Asked questions. Requested discussion. And as such—in my professional capacity—I had, indeed, investigated *their* concerns and observed them and the rest of our crew . . . when in fact I had actually done all this prior to them ever having taken note of my existence, let alone my professional investigative capacity.

That seemed to pique their attention. They grew silent, introspective . . . pondered all that I'd relayed.

Okay, they'd said, nodding and giving me grave expressions of frightful wonder. But the more I thought about how they'd looked at me, the more I began to wonder if their looks had been more suspicious than accepting.

They'd asked me if I'd intended to tell everyone.

Yes, I told them, that is my intention.

Langster?

Yes. *Everybody* needs to know.

Then why didn't I do it all at once? In the auditorium?

Because I wanted to do it in small groups, so people didn't feel intimidated or overwhelmed. People would already feel overwhelmed by the information . . . I didn't want them to feel further intimidated by their peers or Langster. People are more apt to be open and vocalize questions or concerns in smaller settings. And with the way things were going with Langster and the others who were all posturing for power . . . well, this was going to b—

How was I determining who I spoke to first? Who already knew about this? Didn't I think that people would grow angry over my picking certain groups first? Showing favoritism?

They really had me there. But I gave them the same answer I'd given myself: there was no way I could please everybody, but I was starting with those who had sought me out.

Then the question came: *could I hold off a day or two in telling the others?*

I stared at the man who'd asked that question. Fariss Rothchild.

I looked to those who stood with him. There were twelve others in addition to him.

And why would I do that? I'd asked, unblinkingly holding his gaze. *How would that be fair?*

We're not talking "fair," we're talking life and death. How others who get this might subvert my efforts—

I again held his gaze.

Subvert?

Your efforts?

Fariss nodded slowly, also holding my scrutiny.

Who's to say you wouldn't be doing exactly that with your *request?* I said.

With that, a wry smile crept across Fariss's face, and he broke out into a chuckle.

Well, Fariss said, casually getting to his feet and pouring himself another cup of coffee, *who* is *to say . . . if they don't know?*

He turned back around and took a sip from his mug. Returned to the table and sat back down.

"Look," Fariss said, "Langster's already got people on this ship segregating and taking sides to something that shouldn't *have* 'sides.' We're all from the elite on Earth . . . were all hand selected. We all have our own special superpowers, if you will. Yet he's done just that. Has your skipping shown you any probable outcomes to his gaining this knowledge? What he would do with it?"

I sat there, my hands folded before me.

All eyes were on me.

"Yes," I said sullenly.

There were collective expressions of surprise.

Fariss sat back in his chair, again taking further sips of coffee, a look of considered surprise on his own face.

"And what have you seen?"

I held my tongue.

"Are you holding out on us?"

"*Everything* . . . everything I've experienced is why I'm here before you—all of you—doing what I'm doing. There is no one, solitary precursor. There are so man—"

"Have you discovered that Langster has secretly created an Intelligence Corps?"

Now it was my turn to express surprise.

Had I missed something?

Forgotten it because of the overall importance of everything else clearly overshadowing such mundane and prosaic concerns?

I did not like the turn things were taking.

How could I have missed such a thing, if it was important enough an occurrence?

And if I hadn't seen it did that mean it wasn't important in the overall probability timeline?

"Have you?" Fariss again asked, pulling me out of my thoughts.

"I have not."

Those three words felt universes apart.

The people before me looked to each other.

"Well, if you haven't seen such an important development . . . how can we, then, believe that all that *you* have seen—or purported to have seen—really happened? Will happen? How is it that no one else has corroborated your account of events? Has anyone?"

Still lost in thought, I slowly shook my head.

"No . . . to date . . . I've found not one person who has experienced the same events that I've experienced."

I was . . . stunned.

Maybe *I* was wrong.

Maybe I had been too much in my own head.

Maybe . . . maybe I wasn't too far behind Talbot and would soon join him.

Fariss said, "Do not mistake our questions for a personal attack on you. We do not mean that." Fariss returned to a more relaxed state. "We have skipped other scenarios—

"*Skipped?* So you *are* able to skip?" I said.

"Yes, but nowhere near the degree you're able to go, to the intensities you're experiencing. Anyway, you are not alone in your exploratory investigations. And it was through one of our own, here, I will not say who, that we discovered Langster's secret unit. We do, however, regret to inform that we have not skipped into the future. We have—much unlike yourself—grown myopically shortsighted, which is not good, given our predicament. And . . . we *doubt*," Fariss said, emphasizing the last word as he looked about the group, "that Langster is similarly flawed. We are sure he has already skipped to . . . our destination, as you called it . . . and already has his plans set into motion. Reality. And if you are not with him . . . you are not in those plans."

Now Fariss sat back and looked concerned . . . dare I say, frightened?

He forced his hands through his hair and leaned forward on his elbows, momentarily closing his eyes, as the others about us took a moment to release their tensions as well.

Another in the group, Miranda Murdock, spoke up. She was Fariss's significo.

"We have purposely taken you into our confidence, because we did skip you coming to us . . . and your intent."

Miranda looked to her husband, as did the rest of the group. Fariss raised his head and again looked to me.

"And that's why we ask that you . . . hold off . . . in making any more . . . pronouncements . . . to the rest of the crew—"

"But I've already tol—"

"We know. And we've already made . . . provisions . . . about those you've already discussed this with."

"Provisions?"

Fariss got to his feet.

"Unlike you, our focus is far more . . . parochial. While your *weltanschauung* is fascinating and, indeed, thought-provoking and concerning . . . if we don't survive the voyage itself . . . well . . . your view of events are then merely pipedreams and hallucinations. Will never come to pass.

"First . . . we have to survive this voyage.

"That is why we ask you to temporarily suspend your mission until we can figure things out a bit more. Come up with a better course of action . . . and if that action is to continue on the path you are forging . . . then, well, so be it. We don't ask this lightly. We know exactly what we are asking. Know how it must appear to you . . . but we mean no malice to you, Langster, or the rest of the Humanity encapsulated within this ship."

Fariss suddenly looked exhausted. Spent beyond his years.

And I felt he was telling me the truth, for, you see, one of the side effects of my developing and refining my abilities was in knowing if someone was telling me the truth.

"Okay," I said. "I'll do as you ask."

Fariss, looking bleary eyed, said, "*thank* you." He turned to his wife and smiled wearily. She smiled back, then reached out and grasped one of his hands. The rest of the group also seemed as though some massive weight had been lifted from their collective shoulders.

Miranda said, "We'd seen various—strong and possible—scenarios to telling you this. We just couldn't be sure how you would actually react . . . and all versions of your reactions propelled us into uniquely different situations . . . not all of them beneficial to our cause."

Our cause?

What had I gotten myself into?

6

I returned to my cabin confused.

Had I just become my own conspiracy theory?

And further . . . what if I was wrong? Fariss had said so himself.

Why was I so special?
Who had made me the expert?
I could very well be my own kind of crazy.

If what I'd discovered about this space sickness was true . . . who's to say that my version of everything was more right than *anyone else's* versions? I could very well become the next Talbot.

I did not want this.

Didn't want to become the forefront of any kind of movement . . . some predictive guru—*any* kind of guru, for that matter.

As I look back on my life . . . how I got here . . . I feel this is all some crazy dream, and I'm still back on Earth, and there are no earthquakes nor felonious weather. No power-mongers-run-amok. That everything is as it was in the Old Books . . . happy, ignorant, and unrestricted. Where people could go wherever and whenever they wanted. Lived the lives they lived directly in front of their faces without any technologies plugged into them. No one reading their thoughts or directing and tracking their movements. Where everything had had a *natural* order to it—or so it appeared, anyway.

Sometimes appearances were everything.

But as I think these thoughts I wonder if they're from my actual experiences, or are those I'd skipped.

As I sat in my cabin and looked about me . . . looked out my portal into the dark unknown . . . I grew sad . . . outright despondent. I knew what awaited us . . . or the various versions of what awaited us. Or my *perceived* various versions of what awaited us—

Or I could be totally wrong!

What if the gravity of our planet was also the gravity of our Time, senses, and reality? And once we slip those surly bonds, everything freewheels, everything warps? Becomes

(*temporally*)

temporarily unhinged?

That space travel was a state of mind, not of *body*?

What if the power of interstellar space so messed with all of our minds that nothing we perceived was correct? Or became a new kind of Time . . . a new kind of "correct"?

That it was all the product of loneliness, guilt, and homesickness? That all there is is a well-crafted ship of high technology loaded full with the debatably best minds and the decidedly most corrupt from Earth, flung far out into the nothingness of endless space?

Being shot out into and among the stars?

And for *what*?

To escape *what*?

Some perceived manufactured, future threat?

The annihilation of our home—our planet? A destruction of our own making?

Why should we be allowed to depart our home and go find *another* one . . . only to again destroy *that* one, sometime in our far-flung future?

If Life—okay, call it God—always "finds a way" . . . *why would It allow us to do such a thing?*

And how far does Its reach extend?

Did this mysterious "Life" extend beyond Earth? Is It actually a part of the universe?

When we lived and breathed and walked the Earth, that was, essentially, the extent of our knowledge, our perceptions. We threw our weight around with concepts like religion and God and Life . . . but we were doing so through an essentially Earth-based point of view. Once we left Earth, all of our concepts took on a different point of view . . . which essentially made our Earth-based ones comically parochial.

If . . . if I were Life Incarnate . . . I would not allow us to leave Earth and perpetuate our kind. No, I would not allow us to find anything else out here, so we could mess that up. Destroy it. Corrupt it.

I might . . . indeed . . . mess with the *minds* of Humankind . . . to allow them to *think* that there was more out here . . . Earth-like planets . . . extraterrestrial souls . . . but then I'd slap 'em back with calamities and glitches to wipe out any advancement that got too ahead of themselves, but I would leave them with some elements of hope, because Humanity does thrive on hope and what-ifs and discovery. That's what keeps us going, however misguided we may be along the way. We do always try to do more . . . never happy with what we have . . . until we lose it. Or break it.

So, yes, were *I* Life . . . I would indeed mess with the minds of Humankind and give them false hope, or send them far, far away in the wrong direction if they did leave Earth—any civilization—to be alone and leave the rest of the universe—Life—*alone*.

I would keep them to themselves until-and-IF—*big* "if"—they learned their lessons. Then I would direct them to a better place where they could start over again, if that were in the cards.

But . . . I . . . have . . . seen . . . our . . . *future*.

Or not.

So I *know*.

Or not.

Because I would mess with each and every mind on board this ship to keep them all off-balance, guessing, to see what they do and if they learn from My misdirection.

And if they—again—killed themselves off . . . well, how, tragic—but *bonus!* They wiped their own scourge from the slate of Life without Me having to lift a finger!

And other things could now take over.

Like flowers and birds and animals and *nature*.

Like other things that I can't even imagine are out there that are every bit as beautiful and pure and organic and *not* trying to bully or kill each other off.

But I understand Life is more than just birds and animals and nature. At least in this probability. So, since we do have us in the picture, I would instill all manner of personal guilt into each Human to get them to understand their failings and have pity on their ways and means. To desperately try to get them to never do what they had already done.

To learn.

As Life, I would continue to send them on wild

(*planet?*)

goose chases into the wrong direction of an immensely empty part of the universe all the while . . . until they either got it . . . or again destroyed themselves.

A flower is more important than we are.

And I know this because I have seen our future.

7

"Captain Robert Mitchell Talbot was loved by all who knew him," the Reverend Mikael Roszky declared from his podium at Niagara Park, our ship's largest park. The park's miniaturized waterfall comfortably crashed its water behind the reverend, its ghostly spray hanging in the air and reminding us about Earthly humidity. I stood in the audience with everyone else. A big screen was positioned above the reverend, with several smaller ones spaced throughout the crowd. On the screen above the Good Reverend a montage of Captain Talbot's life was on display. Talbot had been a handsome man, tall and confident. Had held many commands and had led a distinguished naval career before becoming an astronaut. He'd married one of his science officers 23 years ago, and she, Tiffindee Talbot, stood beside the reverend now. Captain Talbot's beautifully and hypnotically multicolored casket sat before us (its rainbow of colors moved and swirled and intermixed before our eyes), on a platform between the audience and the reverend, raised to waist height. It was adorned with an Australian flag and a host of colorful flowers. A handsome image of him in his uniform rested upon a small table nearby.

"He, like the rest of us," continued the Reverend, "made the decision to go on this voyage and leave all that he knew forever behind . . . ."

I looked among the crowd as the reverend continued speaking. The park had been packed solid, with those of the ship's crew, who could depart their duty stations, up front. Video feeds throughout the ship provided complete coverage. Everyone had taken time to attend his service in one way or the other . . . Captain Bob Talbot . . . our first casualty in our journey out into the stars.

Several members of his immediate staff had gone to the podium to speak and had given glowing praise for the man who had gotten us safely this far, as well as glowing praise for his past achievements. His second-in-command . . . the woman who should be, by all rights, the new ship's captain . . . also spoke, bringing tears to many eyes. All mourned his passage.

Tiffindee took the stage.

She was tall and statuesque and possessed an intense gaze. She appeared to handle her grief well, and bravely held it in check. She, too, had spoken glowingly of his accomplishments, talked about how they'd met, married, and lived. Worked together. What a great man he'd been. How much he will be missed not only by her, but also those he worked with. As she left the stage, Tiffindee was escorted by Stephen Langster.

I was surprised at her restrained composure, military bearing or not.

The reverend continued with a few more words . . . several prayers for various denominations, and one multi-cultural prayer meant for all.

As Tiffindee was escorted from the stage the lights were dimmed and Talbot's kinetically colored casket lowered into the floor. The overhead ceiling became transparent and positively glowed as the stars now came into better view.

"And now . . . ," the reverend said, "Captain Talbot so loved his work, this mission, and all that was this wonderful universe that this was the end he chose."

Roszky paused, looking up into the space-hardened glass above us, then continued.

"He also believed that death was not the end. And with that he did not want to leave us all on such a dour note. His last words and wishes are this, and I will now play a recording from the Captain himself," the reverend said, making a selection.

As Talbot's message played, a projectile shot out from the *Renaissance* and into space for all to see, which displayed on all the ship's monitors. The projectile left a fiery tale trailing behind.

Talbot's casket.

This was not my idea of a send-off. Though I am out here among the stars . . . I do not like the idea of my body being sent out into the vast nothingness of space like that for all eternity. Just incinerate me on board, thank you very much, among people. People I know, from an imperfect but peopled Earth I once knew.

Talbot's prepared recording continued.

" . . . know, my crew and all who watch this, that the wonders of the universe are many and varied, and death—or our perception of it—is but one of the many wonders we know little-to-nothing about. I knew the risks we were undertaking and I accepted them, as all of you have also done. I have devoted my entire life to the risky and the dangerous to help advance Humankind, in the various methods of exploration I have participated in over the course of my life. I regret nothing! As I have given my life, I ask that you continue to give yours in this brave new endeavor we are all undertaking. Fair winds and following seas, the Old Navy used to say and I now say to you, my fellow travelers! I will forever be with you in spirit!"

The fiery trail to Talbot's casket faded . . . and when Talbot completed speaking, the reverend again turned and lifted his gaze to the glass dome above us—when it was suddenly filled with a mini-nova of multicolored, showering lights exploding from where Talbot's casket had been.

The crowd erupted into absolute awe and amazement. We actually had to shade our eyes from the explosion's brightness.

Now, *that* was more like it!

There were sorrowful sighs and murmurs as the display faded, and many held onto their significant others. I looked to Tiffindee. She was being comforted by Stephen Langster.

A little *too* comforted.

While all eyes had been focused upon Talbot's dazzling and fiery end, Langster and Tiffindee shared an ever-so-briefly kiss during their extended hug, hidden among their cheeks and chins.

8

It wasn't long before Langster showed up.

And he hadn't arrived alone. Had his enforcers, one stationed outside my quarters, another inside. I recognized both of them—Ted Simon and Kam Clark—of course, never really thought of them as "enforcers." But life was much different now . . . we needed structure, different and new . . . and weapons and power magnify one's abilities . . . one's confidence . . . one's insecurities.

Our ship was a small new world, after all.

I stood in the middle of my cabin.

"I hear you've been telling stories," Langster said. No introduction, no handshakes. One moment I was alone in my quarters, and the next I was not.

I said nothing.

Langster casually wandered about my quarters, exhibiting faux curiosity about my décor, my books, my awards.

Me.

"Wild . . . fantastic tales . . . but you'd stopped," he said.

He paused before a bookcase, hands clasped behind his back. Tilted his face upward as he read spine titles.

"Why?"

He turned to me.

Equally as casually, I went over to one of my port windows and stared out into the blackness.

He pensively pulled one of my books out by its spine.

"When were you going to get to me?" he said without looking up. He then cracked open the book, calmly turning its pages. *The Pride and the Prejudice* was its title.

I was growing weary with his wasting of my time, OT or not.

Without turning to directly address him, I said, "*Don't you sense it?*"

I paused.

"Don't you feel what *I'm* feeling? What *others* are feeling?"

"And what would that be?" he said, twisting in my direction. He swung his gaze directly to mine like a repositioning weapon. Held my gaze unblinkingly as he closed my book. Perfectly replaced it without looking to what he was doing. Clearly, he was developing his own superpowers with this space sickness. "Loneliness? Guilt? Insignificance?"

I turned around to face him.

"No . . . I don't," he said.

He continued to faux survey my room.

He meandered over to a display case of mine, where I had had various awards from my Earthly profession, my multiple degrees

. . . including some from high school, like a "Most Improved Student" award from my pre-university junior year. He picked it up.

Surprised by my own reaction . . . I tensed.

Langster examined the award as he turned back to me—when, I know not how, the award suddenly launched from his grasp.

It rotated through the air like a circus performer.

As it came back down toward his other hand, Langster made a grab for it—but instead knocked it back into the air.

Again, the wild circus tumbling.

Now, despite his initial . . . "clumsiness" . . . Langster suddenly snatched the trophy from the air with theatrical flair.

Eyed me as he did so.

Undamaged.

"Wow!" he said, chuckling as he completed his turn to me, the award safely cupped in his hands. "*That* would have been unfortunate!"

A wolfish grin.

He replaced it back in the display case, chuckling.

I glared at him.

"Would you please get to the point, Stephen."

Langster came to a stop before my desk, smiled, and turned to Kam, who stood at my door.

"Would you mind waiting outside, Kam, please? Thank you."

Kam began to object, but Langster quickly flashed him a fierce expression. He departed.

Langster waited for the door to close.

"Some people," Langster began, "in this life, feel their position to be more elevated than it actually is." He took a seat in my chair behind the desk. "So there must be an adjustment period. He'll learn."

"And if he doesn't?" I asked.

"Start talking," he said to me.

"What would you like me to say?"

"Whatever you've been telling everyone else."

"It appears to me you don't need me to tell you anything. It's no secret. We're all experiencing it in our own way."

"What?"

"A space sickness."

Langster chuckled.

"Then you know," he said.

We looked at each other. This, I didn't expect. *He* knows what's going on with the sickness? Of all people who shouldn't have this ability, *Langster* has it?

"I do," I said.

"And what are you prepared to do about it?"

"I'm certainly not going to rape my way through this ship."

He looked at me with a predatory glint.

"Then you'll perish like the rest of them. The meek shall not inherit *this* Earth."

"Will I?"

"You said yourself . . . you've seen the future. Our future. I would think you'd be quite keen on survival."

"Nothing's set."

"Perhaps . . . but if you've seen what you've claimed to have seen, you know that things don't look very good on-the-whole. Probabilities considered."

So he had seen what I've seen . . . or versions thereof. Knows of the inherent uncertainties—

"Look," Langster continued, "who do you think you are—we all are? The people on this ship—you and your crewmates—we were all *hand selected* . . . have held prime stations in life. We're all highly intelligent . . . highly . . . *cultivated* . . . for this life, this moment. We've used subterfuge and intimidation and all of its tools to get what we wanted out of life to some degree or another—even you. Don't think I don't know about your past, *my friend*."

Langster held my gaze.

My past.

Yes, it was true . . . I had wielded some academic influence back on Earth . . . but I didn't always like that I had, once I got more and more into my chosen area of expertise. My family, however, was no laughing matter. They were ruthless in the conduct of their everyday existence, to which I'd turned a blind eye once I'd gotten into Oxford. And just now, as I thought about all this, their—and my—practices flooded back to me like repressed memories. I was embarrassed at all I had done or allowed to have been done in my name.

"What's your point," I asked.

"As you yourself have discovered . . . this . . . 'illness' . . . for lack of a better term . . . we all have it to one degree or the other. It amplifies . . . capabilities. We're all smart people . . . have intimidated and manipulated everyone we came into contact with to get what we wanted . . . so, when they came to you . . . what makes you think that everyone was telling you the truth? *What makes you think you were not being manipulated for their own ends?*"

I had not considered that.

"And as for Ms. Elaine Faramount . . ."

I shot a look back to him.

"*She,*" he said chuckling, "was no saint either! You think she did everything she did out of some sense of moral purity? Out of some newly discovered sense of altruism and societal conscience? Hell, no! *She wanted my position!*"

"Am I to believe all that *you're* telling me?"

"I came to see her, much like I am here with you, now, and she attempted to seduce *me*. I had no issues getting all fleshy with her, I jumped at the chance—or, I should say, *on* her—but when she tried to use me—shisst me over, if you will—I showed her just who was actually going to get 'shissted' in the process. I didn't get to where I am by being nice, just like she didn't get to where she was by being nice. But she wasn't in charge of our ship's mission, was she? She was—*is*—just a frigging *librarian.* So, yeah, I roughed her up a bit, I admit it. But she also roughed me up a bit. I just happened to come out on top.

"You think leopards change their spots? You think we all got God or something once we left Earth? *Art thou that naïve?*"

"Of course not," I said.

"No. We didn't. None of us."

Langster bore into me.

"So, this being the case—my *friend*—I suggest you choose wisely with whom you align. Fariss and his crew are no different. They're using you just like I'm looking to use you. Thing is . . . he who has the most power . . . is the most likely to succeed, no? Keep an eye on things. I will show you just how much power each of us has and who will remain or emerge at the top in this little dog fight."

Langster got up and walked past me as I stood there. I stared into the floor before me.

"By the way? When I leave here I'm going over to see Elaine. And it's not for polite conversation."

9

Damn him.

Am I being played?

How had I not seen any of this?

Is it because I just choose not to? That I focus only on what I want to see . . . and I want to see the good in our crew? That I'd hoped that those on this ship might want to start over . . . reinvent themselves in a more positive manner?

Or is it more that Langster—and possibly others, if what he says is true—are only focusing on the dark? The negative. The same lives that they'd come from.

Or are we both different outcomes—probabilities—to the same set of personalities?

Or he's just flat-out lying to me. Trying to get me to do what he wants.

And what has made me so damned important that people need me on their team?

Maybe I'm just an upstart, an instigator, and people want me to shut the hell up. Or want me on their team for my more-advanced abilities.

Things are getting out of hand.

I try to focus *on what is actually going on* . . . and I'm thrown into a psychic vortex.

Events flash far too fast in and around me . . . interleave and fold within themselves. Even though I've become better at discerning multiple events . . . rapidly flashing events . . . even these are beyond my abilities.

I can only make of this that things are changing. Not yet set. Or there are yet too many probabilities that are even now, or have been, set into motion . . . and until I make a decision . . . take a physical step . . . nothing has solidified.

And what had he meant about "*keep an eye on things*"? That he would show me just how much power each of us actually wields? How much *he* wields?

I can't believe this is happening. I should have kept to myself. I don't want to be a part of any of this. To be honest . . . I'm not even sure how I got on this ship. The more I've thought about it, the more confused I grow.

Is what I remember correct?
Was I really a part of some ruling class or had I just made it all up? Conveniently forgot about it?
Had my parents thought they were doing me a favor?
Had some other forces oh so subtly groomed me for this journey?
It hurts to think about it all.

I have some vague recollection of being tapped for the position. Of . . . looking into things? The ship . . . the company building it . . . the leadership. But it all seems so, *so* far away. In another
(*oh, the irony in this statement!*)
land . . . another *me*.

It all seems too dreamlike to be real.

That all I have lived before this *has* been a dream.

But to *what* am I waking up? What *is* my Objective Reality?

I am—most assuredly—*here*. Wherever that is or however I'd arrived.

It ultimately doesn't matter how I got here . . . only that I . . . in this moment . . . am aboard this ship . . . and am being flung out into the farthest and darkest reaches of space toward some (initially, anyway, before the accident) predetermined destination . . . with a ship full of *Nouveau* royalty . . . heading toward a destiny entirely of our own making.

And, to further complicate matters, as I have roundly maintained, I have seen our future.

It is not a future I want to be a part of. But it is also not a future that is entirely set in stone.

It is as if some unknown, massive entity is at work here. Manipulating chess pieces into position and trying to checkmate some additionally elusive opponent.

But I don't feel that this is a game . . . no . . . it is very real and affects us all.

And things out here, in the spaces between the stars, feels much more . . . malleable? Flexible? Things don't feel as "set" out here as they did back on Earth. I don't know if the proper term *is* space *sickness*. Maybe . . . out here . . . away from our Earth . . . away from our sandbox, if you will . . . we are now out in the very real realm of the Creator-or-Creators of this playground that contains the sandbox of our lives. We are out and about the realm of the *gods* . . . God! . . . who created the universe, the firmament, but broke the Fourth Wall . . . the glass ceiling. I feel a definite difference in the air I now breathe . . . in the "physical" space I now maintain and maneuver within . . . and the darkness I now look out into . . . and *through*.

That last part seems to take on a special, eerie significance to me.

Even my thoughts feel different. Feel more real to me, which sounds so utterly inane.

Seem to employ more destiny.

More *vector*, if I may?

When I think and observe and look around, I truly feel as if I'm employing an extended metaphysical beam directed out from the center of my head—my mind—to everything I look at. I feel that everything I look at . . . everything I think about . . . takes on the form of invisible clay. *And I am molding it moment to moment.* Setting into motion. No thought is wasted. Each thought is *life*.

Given life.

No . . . existing out here . . . between the stars . . . is vastly different. Nothing like back on Earth.

And it is driving me mad.

I can see why Talbot had taken his life.

But I have no intention of taking mine!

For all that I've seen—and I've seen far too much—I have seen that my life is not to take . . . but to give. That there is much for me to learn . . . and that there are unclear areas in my life . . . probabilities . . . far too many for my conscious mind to focus upon as yet.

I need to live my life.

I need to return to some semblance of Humanity.

I have been inside my head for far too long and far too much. If people were meant to live inside their heads as much as I have, they would not have need of the corporeal . . . of their bodies.

10

I still have not heard back from Fariss or Miranda.

But I have taken to spending more time outside my cabin. I would take reading material and go to the common areas and just hang out. People watch. Carry on casual conversations with those I didn't know or who didn't know me. Or would take walks throughout our massive ship. Our walkways or "trails" have been designed as Möbius strips, so there would be no end. You could walk continuously, forever, if so desired. But now and again I would see someone from Fariss's group go by . . . or even Langster himself—Eleanor, even. They would look at me just long enough to let me know intentional eye contact.

Weeks go by.

Town meetings had been held. All the usual discussions, good and bad. And Langster and Eleanor went to every one of them. Both remained polite but kept their distances from each other. One or the other occasionally spoke up when something interested them, but never were they seen together. If they passed each other, they simply ignored each other without so much as a nod.

It was about three weeks later when Fariss sent me a message, delivered by a woman I had slept with. I had seen the woman, named Lydia, around, but not initially at Fariss and Miranda's meeting, and she had more than once held my gaze and was quite easy on the eyes. The long and the short of it was that after we'd been together, she'd told me that Fariss and Miranda were her friends . . . and that they were ready to talk with me again. That they had some rather important news. That if I was open-minded enough . . . would I join them? They were holding another of their Town Meetings this Tuesday, after which they would like to speak with me.

I try to make Tuesday mean something.

Lydia then gave me a passionate kiss . . . turned away . . . and just before she left—with an ever so slight turn of her head and a wry smile—said that this was not why she'd slept with me.

She left.

I smiled.

I arrived at the appointed time and location of Fariss and company's Town Meeting, at our Niagara Park. There was a good showing. People from all across the ship poured in. Banners everywhere proclaimed:

"Elect your Legislature!"

"Elect your Executives!"

"Elect your Judiciaries!"

Fariss was proposing a reimagining of our Earthly government.

And really, who could argue with him?

Our old form of government had, really, worked quite well on Earth—at least in theory . . . and definitely better than dictatorships, which was, essentially, where we were currently headed, benign or otherwise—and it was time to create a better form of self-government.

But, still, it shocked me. It shouldn't have, but it did.

Something felt wrong. I couldn't put my finger on it, but something big was about to happen. Fariss and Miranda . . . were about to put their names down in the *nouveau* history books as being part of the parentage of our government. With all the preplanning that had gone into our voyage, this had, surprisingly, been absent—

Or had it?

That was an interesting thought.

Was this really a surprise? *Should* it have been a surprise?

If the global leadership of our mass exodus had really put any thought into how our individual ships would govern themselves, this should have arisen organically. Sure, to start, there would need to be appointed positions . . . like Langster's Mission Directorship or Talbot's Captaincy . . . that makes sense. These people already know how to do what we need them to do and had been appointed by the Smart People planning this voyage, under the governorship we'd used in our Earthly lives. But once out there—*here*—and in cruise mode in more than one way . . . we should be able to then elect those better suited to structuring and running our

(*for lack of a better term?*)

world.

Everything can't just be one big, winged, free-for-all.

But how do you get an incorruptible government from corrupted individuals?

So, Fariss and Miranda had hit upon something. Probably the first big something of this voyage, and it had nothing to do with star travel or the extraterrestrial.

Unless this had been planned. Planned all along to *appear* to emerge organically, but actually preplanned to emerge when the time was right.

Authoritarianism.

Neither of them had ever spoken the word, but I'd skipped them—their intents, actually—so, yes . . . that was the term. Rule by a small group of individuals that allows people to basically go about lives. But still . . . rule by a privileged few.

Miranda was first to the podium. She spoke at length about government, the people, their inalienable rights, and privileges . . . about the power of determining one's own actions. Independence . . . self-government . . . self rule. It all seemed like word play to me. Criminal, insidious, word play. As I looked around, more and more people filtered into the crowd. She reminded us about our heritage from a world that all felt more and more like a dream, well, to *me*, anyway. And if I thought this way, you could be sure others did, too. People were people . . . even all of us over-privileged, eminently entitled space travelers.

Yes, Fariss would be the voice and face, the name in the office . . . but in the background it wouldn't be advisors, it'd be *rulers*. Sure, they meant well. This was their solution, partly and largely because they realized no one among them really had the ability, skill, or experience to run a government, and one person, one corrupt person, has far too much authority, especially if enabled by a corrupt staff. Who knows if this would be any better than a single president or chancellor, everyone on this ship is a corrupt individual, but, at least they're trying.

I was just about to return my attention to the podium, when I caught sight of Langster in the sea of faces in the still-gathering assembly.

He stared at me.

Yeah, if anyone could possibly have had any issues with what was happening here, it would be him. He wanted to rule, all right, just not with Fariss and Miranda.

Let's just call it what it was he wanted: a dictatorship.

Miranda continued on with our Earthly history lesson. Proudly reviewing where we had come from and how far we had yet to go. Of course, she never pointed out how everyone in this structure—absolutely every one of us—had grown up and prospered outside of the more pedestrian confines of Earthly government. That we had all, in some way, been the Earthly Elite. The *Nouveau* Royalty. Had flaunted our manipulation of rules and government. That was how we found ourselves here, instead of back on an Earth that was consuming itself—because of *us*. *Our* hubris and greed.

That would not have served any purpose here. Instead, she intoned, we needed to grow as a race. Grow *up*.

Behind her was a screen that flashed a montage of all the good Earthly leaders. Scenes of the *good* Earth we had destroyed. Scenes of various global congresses-in-action.

Yes, how quickly we forgot.

But at least now we were starting from the ground up and could (theoretically) learn from our mistakes. Or it would take a similarly long time for the same problems to occur, so we would still have the honeymoon period for some extended portion of . . . time . . . and since we knew of our shortcomings, we could easily modify things as we went, because that is how we would structure our new government.

This time, she proclaimed, we would get it right. Learn from our mistakes.

Thunderous applause and cheers arose from the crowd, and for a moment—just a moment—I actually forgot where I was and grew temporally confused . . . overcome by an ever-so-slight vertigo. I'd closed my eyes, and when I'd opened them, could have sworn I was in the actual Earthly halls of *Congress*.

I blinked and again opened my eyes and was back in the *Renaissance's* Niagara Park. I looked for Langster.

Nowhere.

" . . . and with that," Miranda declared, " I offer you our first official candidate for President . . . *Fariss Rothchild!*"

I'd been so overwhelmed with my own philosophical dilemmas that I'd never given this any thought . . . Fariss and Miranda had been planning this from the very beginning.

How far back?

Before leaving Earth, my new ability just informed me.

And who would be their competition?

Eleanor Faramount?

Stephen Langster?

Of course.

Fariss took the stage.

While there was largely applause—clearly close friends and family of our new candidate—many in the crowd were rightly taken aback. Didn't know how to respond. Here were the most elite of the Earthly secret-and-not-so-secret societies, chosen precisely because they were above the common people . . . above the law . . . politics . . . and suddenly they'd all been *re*-segregated into groups . . . and now even further segregated into old-Earth political factions!

"I am sure most of you are surprised," Fariss began from the podium, hand gesturing down the surprise and clamor, "at the recent turn of events aboard this ship . . . but . . . I am here to tell you . . . we are *not* here to make things worse—to repeat the past!"

While there was immediate applause . . . it was thin and sporadic.

"We did not mean to blindside with this decision—"

"Then why did you do it in secret? Haven't we had enough of things being done in secret?"

Melvin Vanderbuilt. I actually know the man well.

Fariss paused and turned to Miranda. I actually felt for them when I saw the emotion that transferred between them both. Yes . . . they indeed looked as if they meant no real harm, had only our best interests in mind . . . knew no matter how they handled it, how they did it, things would upset some. But I'd also sensed another undercurrent exchange between them . . . something not quite so innocent.

Fariss looked back to his audience, nodded knowingly, and again displayed calming hands just above the podium's airspace.

"Mel," Fariss began . . . when a look of concern abruptly washed over his face. He blinked, then shot another concerned glance back at Miranda, who returned the same.

"Mel . . . as we've said . . . ," Fariss tried to continue, but he instead gripped the podium with both hands. Paused . . . and not in a good way.

White knuckled, not only could I see this, but I felt his nauseating energy radiate out in powerful waves.

"Um . . . I . . . *we* . . . we . . . *never* plu . . . plu-*annned* . . . ."

He collapsed.

Fariss fell heavily onto the stage behind the podium.

Gasps and outcries erupted. Miranda and those on stage rushed to him.

As I watched those onstage converge and shield Fariss's body from the crowd, I looked around . . . and found him.

Langster.

He stood beside a broad oak, its leaves lightly rustling in our artificial breeze. Stared at me.

I suggest you choose wisely with whom you align.

And the very last thing Langster had said to me on his way out had been: *I will show you just how much power each of us has and who will remain or emerge at the top in this dog fight.*

Langster.

I turned away and looked back to the stage. Medical staff had somehow already appeared on-scene. People were cleared from the hasty exit, as the team whisked Fariss away.

I looked back over to Langster—gone.

The well-behaved crowd had now broken up into mini-groups all no-doubt expressing concern—in more than one way—about what had just transpired.

Langster had shown his hand.

He had not only shown it to Fariss and his group, but to the rest of us. Except for myself and Fariss's contingent, others would certainly speculate about what had just happened and who might have done what, but there was no real reason to immediately suspect Stephen Langster.

That wouldn't last forever.

Fariss wasn't supposed to have collapsed, you see, because people on board this ship just weren't *supposed* to collapse.

Accidents, sure, skin a knee here, trip down some stairs there, but to have what might appear to be a heart attack? Stroke? No. Everyone on board this ship had been given the most thorough physical, mental, and spiritual evaluations ever devised. Had been born and *bred* to be in perfect health. *No one* was ever projected to get sick for a lifetime—a *lifetime*—given our advanced genetic engineering. That said, most everyone on this ship wouldn't have immediately thought this, but since I had re-experienced the past, I knew.

So . . . for someone to die . . . well, that certainly would raise eyebrows.

As I stood there amongst the chaos, I watched as the groups of attendees were double-whammied with not only the re-emergence of political parties and an in-place candidate . . . but also a serious medical condition befalling one of their own, the first-ever, new world candidate.

You see, these people also know quite well that coincidences do not exist.

11

I arrived at the medical center and found Fariss in the ICU. He had survived the apparent heart attack. So he wasn't to be taken out . . . just made an example of.

I was allowed to see him—though I had to be escorted, given his new position as a Presidential candidate. He was surrounded by Miranda and his closest associates. He was far from deterred and quite happy to see me. Miranda and he both told me this was exactly why such politics were necessary. To not let those who would be tyrants to again take over. Fariss also said that now having been shot out into space had cleared their—his—minds, they'd all seen the error of their Earthly ways of deception, manipulation, and treachery. That they'd actually had the epiphany that they needed to clean up their collective acts, if Humanity was ever to survive itself.

As I stood bedside and listened, he reached out and grasped my hand.

Looked deeply into my eyes and swore to me that he and his group meant only good for this ship and its crew members and hoped I would join their cause. He sensed good within me and wanted to help bring that to bear in their campaign. He also apologized to me for all that he'd done—directly and indirectly—to me and the rest of Humanity, while having lived the life of unlimited privilege and power back on Earth. But what ended up causing a lump in my throat, and actually brought me visibly to tears was when I turned to leave and absolutely everyone in that room—and there were perhaps fifteen or twenty or so crammed in there—all made the same apologetic gestures to me!

Lydia, she was the first . . . she'd come up and hugged me so passionately—*kissed* me! Then they each had taken turns grasping my hands or out-and-out hugging me and proclaiming their guilt and apologies!

And I believed them!

I stood before the door in tears, trembling with emotion that had emerged from deep within me . . . and it was the most profound and powerful love and respect I'd ever felt for any other human. I was moved beyond comprehension. They all looked at me as if they were each my mother, expressing her love for me!

I had no choice but to—*wanted* to—apologize for my *own* part in the same conspiracy and power plays back on Earth!

Yes, though I was part of the fabric of the conspiracy machine, I was a very low-level element of it . . . but, yes, I still had actively taken part in all I had been instructed to do, reaped all the entitlements and every other benefit.

But as I stood there . . . at that door . . . I felt no greater love for Humanity than I did at that moment . . . and no greater guilt for my part in misdirecting all of Humanity, no matter how miniscule (I again rationalized) my part in the Earthly subversions (if only lying by omission) had all led to this moment.

I couldn't return to my cabin fast enough.

I broke down into an horrendous emotional paroxysm on the floor. The beckoning stars outside my viewports the only witness to my apopletic outburst.

My, God—what have we done?
What have we done to sentence ourselves to this . . . this quest?
This voyage into nothingness?

We had all needlessly sentenced ourselves into a self-fulfilling prophecy of our own creation. Sent ourselves out into an endless night of ineffective hope, toward a *destination* of our own mythical creation.

A destination of despair and angst and vagary!

Of *illusions!*

Was it truly not better to have remained on Earth and organically perished within the logical conclusions of our hubris?

We were heading out into the middle of *nowhere* . . . to a destination I have glimpsed. Toward several probable scenarios, none of which I'd ever confer upon *anybody*.

I *know* this.

A place . . . a Möbius of irony and destruction! . . . with a timeline whose sole purpose was to draw out the pain and inevitable conclusions, so that we, as a race, reimburse for our sins against ourselves, our planet, and Life itself.

When another consideration slammed my emotional rampage to a halt.

Langster.

Langster must be privy to his own versions of this, himself—and was trying to get his own foot into that door first.

Fariss and his crew appear oblivious to our bleak futures . . . or are ignoring them for the present moment, or—far better—are actually trying to change things, directions, intents *for* the better. Instead constructing affairs enhancingly ameliorated for what time we have left. Maybe their actions are why events are still so in flux and not yet set.

And that is honorable.

This first good deeds out of a ship full of sinners.

To give us all something to better . . . aspire . . . *toward*. Become engrossed *within*.

Take the sting away for the present moment, however long that ends up being . . . until the inevitable befell us all.

Yes, theirs is truly an honorable quest, and they have transmogrified into honorable souls. And if he has the will . . . the heart and soul . . . to do what is honorable, then I, too, must also do what is honorable. Even if I know . . . *know* . . . what is to be our inevitable outcome. I must do what is right, what is ethical.

I, too, must step up, take the torch, and light the way as Fariss and Miranda and Lydia are doing.

But I am afraid!

The Human in me, the frail, physical, flesh-and-blood composition that I am is afraid of what is to come—*for I have also seen my end!*—yet the questioning, ever philosophically oriented exploration of the soul of which I am a part . . . is *not* afraid. That part of me is *excited*. Excited to discover what comes next.

What the new probabilities are.

For what I have witnessed is about to manifest—

Discovery.

Complacency.

War.

Redemption.

War

Redemption.

War—

And I can take an active role in this . . . or a passive, fearful one . . . here, alone . . . in my cabin. It would be so easy to side with Fariss—or Langster—but neither of those is my logical conclusion.

I know my logical conclusion, and it is wholly my own.

My . . . end . . . my most probable destination . . . is a far more difficult journey than what any of these people will experience.

I pick up my

(*suburbia*)

(*Samaritans*)
(*iced tea*)
violin.
And *played* . . . .

12

As I strode the decks and halls toward Langster's offices, I recounted all that I'd set into motion . . . and I truly felt a sense of elation well up within me!

A renewed sense of purpose! Though how could I ever compare this to what I was about to compare it to? I felt as one would feel at the termination of one's lifelong efforts . . . one who'd experienced a life *well-lived*. Harboring no regrets . . . met and made all penances. One who could smile in the face of adversity . . . because she or he had made peace not only with themselves, but with the world . . . in all its glory *and* denigration.

Perhaps not a saint . . . but no longer a sinner.

As I continued along the hall . . . which was surprisingly empty except for myself . . . I felt . . . another presence.

I felt watched.

Guided?

The image I held in my mind's eye was that of an immensely gigantic face.

Faces.

The images filled my mind in proportions that were too difficult to wrap my head around . . . but which I imagined were but a small infinitesimal aspect of an overall gargantuan *whole* . . . filling the hallway before and around me. The face or faces (for it/they seemed at once singular yet many) seemed simultaneously infinitesimal but *immense*. Neutral in tone. Emotion? Did it/they even possess emotion? It/they appeared . . . felt . . . somewhat detached . . . yet very much godlike.

Observant.

Yes, that's what it/they were—interestingly observant—and, curiously, it/they seemed to keep my skipping at bay, which I'd never before experienced.

They'd kept me from doing it.

As I strode toward my Objective Time's probability, I felt as if I strode through not only Space and Time . . . but this entity's *face*. Or an ever so small portion of it as it hung before me.

A watcher?

Yes.

Then . . . as quickly as I'd become aware of it . . . it—they—were gone.

I was so overtaken by it, I had to reach out to a wall for support.

It was like being offered a chair after a difficult run—then having had that chair abruptly yanked out from under you.

Had I imagined it?

I tried to reach out to it . . . but felt an incredible distance . . . so much more distancing than physical measurements could ever seemingly define. Almost a taunting—as if dangling a cosmic carrot before me that it knew I could never grab. Metaphysically—dare I say *amusingly?*—batting away my feeble attempts at definition and contact.

Something so very beyond our ken—that the more one tried to contact it, the more impossible that contact became, not because it was evading, but because of its incorporeal, Godlike, composition.

I got the ever-so-slight feeling that it wasn't so much keeping its distance from me . . . but that what was happening was simply a part of what it was.

Then it was all gone.

All the weirdness.

Except for me.

I continued on.

I entered the command sector of our ship. There had been many times where I'd actually forgotten that we were, indeed, racing through cold, desolate, and empty space on a Human-created vessel constructed in the orbit between our dear, long-departed planet Earth and its ever-watchful moon. The dynamics of our shipboard life had become so very much like—*exactly* like—life had been on Earth.

Which had been the whole intent.

A life our kind—and by that I mean our *privileged* kind, here onboard this ship—had somehow planned to get away from, from the beginnings of time on Earth, as we knew it. This massive ship . . . at least by our adolescent standards . . . was built in such a way that had we never, ever attained planetfall, we could blissfully continue to live out the entirety of our lives aboard this vessel in relative ease.

I'd chuckled at that thought!

In fact, just before making the offices, I'd actually broken into all-out *laughter* in the corridor on my way there, so hard that I'd again had to stop and support myself with a hand to the wall, until I could calm down and wipe the tears from my eyes.

How hard I'd laughed!

Now, of course, others had suddenly appeared in the corridor and had stopped and asked me if I'd been okay. I'd just waved them away, saying, *Yes, Yes! I am quite fine, thank you!* using the backs of my hands to wipe the tears from my eyes.

I knew the medics would soon search me out once my odd behavior had been reported . . . but I'd be beyond their reach.

I approached the rather attractive receptionist and told her I was here to see Stephen Langster. That he was expecting me. I looked about me at the magnificence of the office within which I stood. We Humans had so many wonderful and amazing qualities . . . one of which was the creation of *things*. We build beautiful monuments . . . everything from (at last count) our ancient pyramids on a planet that may or may not still exist as we'd last known it . . . to great and wonderful and awe-inspiring interstellar spaceships.

To the beautiful and engaging artwork that adorned its walls.

It's contemporary furniture and office décor.

To the exquisite fashion the receptionist before me wore . . . her tastefully—and dare I say suggestive—hair style, makeup, and form-fitting apparel. The effective exposure of just enough skin and form to tastefully *entice*—

"Please, go right in," the receptionist—whose name was Daniella, according to the nameplate upon her desk—said. She flashed me a pleasant, if flirtatious, smile.

I entered Langster's office, the door automatically opening upon my arrival. It was a most expansive office, with large windows open to our voyage into space. There was no hiding from it in here. Many of the walls' panels were actually floor-to-ceiling windows. Office lighting was subdued. Comfortable.

"So good to see you again," he said coming to his feet and out from around the back of his massive, highly polished cherrywood desk. Made from trees that knew soil and water and air and rain . . . now flying out here with the rest of us and just as alien and out of place as we were.

Langster was crisply and sharply attired, his hand outstretched toward me immaculate and well-manicured.

I took it.

"Thank you," I said, firmly shaking his hand. Firm handshakes can be so comfortable . . . especially now, out in the voids of the interstellar.

Langster, now back in his "public mode," motioned me toward a well-designed and comfortable seat, off to the side and away from his desk, in a cozy reception area you'd see only in high-end executive offices. On the center coffee table were flutes of water and a selection of alcoholic beverages . . . just enough to give the aura of an inviting appearance.

I sat.

Langster looked at me for a moment without saying a word. He was gauging my body language.

I knew what he was doing.

He gestured toward the beverage arrangement before us, which I politely waved off.

"You have arrived at a decision," he said.

"I have."

"And it's not to my benefit."

"It is not."

"I see."

"I don't think you do," I responded calmly . . . neutrally. I was amazed at my composure.

Confidence.

Langster nodded.

"Fariss?"

I smiled, then ever-so slightly shook my head.

"No. It's not about siding with anyone."

"Curious. I assumed your presence here—"

"Understandable."

We both sat in silence. I allowed that for just enough effect before continuing.

"There is no disrespect in anything I do or am about to say, but in being Human, we must employ the physical expression of communication—words—of our race . . . and sometimes said expression is difficult in its employment . . . or framing . . . the preciseness of our thoughts. And I am a philosopher, you would be good to remember. Am one of the first and most expendable on your disposable list."

Langster chuckled mightily.

"And quite intuitive, indeed," he said. He did nothing to hide the predatory look that now overtook his face.

"Don't worry . . . I will be long gone before the employment of your expendables list."

Langster stopped laughing and unblinkingly held my look.

"Being oriented toward the philosophical," I continued, "seems to invite the popular view that we're somehow . . . foolish . . . perhaps even flighty. But I would also remind that it was the study of philosophy that gave rise to all of *this*," I said, making a casual, sweeping gesture to the ship.

Langster again chuckled and nodded. Returning to his more "public" profile.

"Point taken," he said.

He regarded me most curiously . . . as I would have done to a "me" sitting before a man such as him.

"We are more oriented toward the processes and effects of thinking . . . employing the subjective and objective . . . an employment, if you will, of logical argumentation . . . of observation and reasoning rather than the output of discrete fabricated products. Philosophers create through *thought* . . . discussion, consideration, internally or otherwise. There is nothing 'good' nor 'bad' about any outcome. Just knowledge. Things just *are*."

"Okay."

"I have experienced your words, concepts, and deception and the same of Fariss and his following. And while both of you would seem to have your own versions of merits... they are both flawed... to the extent that anything Humans do can be so-called 'flawed.' I do not pass judgement on either of you. I *understand*. But I also understand that we have become no better than the Earthy existences we'd left. The struggles we have claimed to have forsaken. For some strange, optimistic reason, I guess I'd hoped that we could transcend our petty power struggles and come together, see the errors of our ways, and try to do things better."

Langster reached down, poured himself a brandy, and sat back. Took a pensive sip. His attention remained intensely focused on my every word.

I, however, was compelled to my feet. I paced. Walked over to a window beautifully displaying the incalculable reaches of space and stood there.

"This... frightens me," I said, taking in the innumerable points of brilliance against an utterly dark background. "It frightens me on a purely Human level. On a philosophical level, however, it *excites* me. I am frightened because of the all-too-real unknown corporeal ramifications, possible destruction to my flesh. Of the lack of comfort. Black holes! It also frightens me because of *us*. Those of us who believe in certain things upon which we not only gamble the entirety of our lives... but the lives of others.

"And what we will do to attain—maintain—our so-called 'certainties of cause'... *at* the expense of others."

I turned around and looked at Langster.

He sat comfortably, brandy on the table before him, one leg crossed over the other.

"And what makes you think," he said, "such certainty to be ill-founded? What makes you so full of confide—"

"Another term for such expressions," I said, interrupting, "is zealotry."

"And what makes you so All Knowing? So sure of yourself... so certain that everyone else is wrong?"

I returned to Langster and took my seat across from him.

"For me . . . it is not a case of who's wrong, Stephen. I do respect your—and Fariss's—opinions. I just do not agree with all that goes into them. I ultimately and truly *do* believe that you both feel you are doing the best that you can in our situation. But just as you and he are both adamant on your courses of action, I, through my ethical imperative, need to pursue my own course of action."

"And would you not also cite yourself a 'zealot'?"

I smiled.

"It would be easy to do so. And I obviously cannot make that case against your argument to yourself . . . because if you knew what I did . . . you would not ask that question."

This time it was me who bore into and held the gaze.

"The old adage is," Langster said, "how can one know if one is crazy, if one is, indeed, crazy?"

My own words used against me.

I chuckled . . . and felt that earlier gigantic face once again present with me.

I comfortably and casually shifted in my seat. I didn't know where it came from, but I felt a definite transformation overcome and flow throughout me. My expression must surely have changed, for I detected in Langster's countenance a sudden shift as well. What I'd seen come across his face just then . . . was a look of *fear*.

What if I am wrong?

What if this guy who sat before me did, indeed, know something I didn't?

These were not *my* thoughts, but the considerations I suddenly felt consumed Langster's mind.

I felt a renewed confidence in my being that swelled in experience like a massive, cosmic balloon of righteousness.

Call it "zealotry," if you must.

"Stephen," I said, again getting to my feet, and feeling the totality of my height—my presence—to be far greater than its corporeal composition, "*I do not mean you—nor Fariss—any ill will.* This I truly hope you comprehend—assimilate—but I cannot, in all good conscience and ethical consideration align myself with either of you.

I graciously thank you for your offer and for hearing me out."

I reached out a hand to him, which he surprisingly took and shook—I'm sure, all in a haze of confusion.

"What . . . what are you going to do?" he asked.

In that moment I perceived Stephen Langster as the revealed and penitent bully purely and only because he'd been "caught."

I made my way away from his shrinking presence and paused.

"You'll see," I said.

With a wry, unnerving grin . . . *I* left *him*.

13

I'd scheduled my presentation long before walking into Langster's office. It was now time to address what was happening to all of us. I'd scheduled the Stardust Amphitheater. The booking went out to everyone's calendar.

I calmly paced the stage as the theater—and video teleconferencing equipment—filled. I smiled to and acknowledged people I'd recognized, but largely kept to my thoughts. I'd employed theater security, but, admittedly, wasn't sure of their loyalty. Like most everything, Langster had his hands-up-to-his-elbows in everything beyond his allowed professional considerations.

Everything had become polarized.

I turned to the audience then back to the ship's windows behind me.

Stared out into the depths of space that displayed behind me by the massive floor-to-ceiling panel windows, much like those in Langster's office. Such large panels of glass might unnerve you . . . but this was *space*-formed glass, glass that ended up being far stronger than even the structural rigidity of diamonds.

While a part of me felt small and insignificant, another part of me felt as excited as I felt small, in terms of the philosophy of our journey. I was about to impart all that I'd experienced upon those who were filling the stadium behind me. As I closed my eyes, it was easy to lapse into the meditative me and blank out all that was going on behind me. Or even begin to feel myself lapse into the skipping mode. In fact, as I did so, I again felt that humongous observing face make itself known. But this time there were multiple faces . . . all observing me. From so indescribably far away—yet they still appeared indescribably massive even from that "distance."

Yes, in quotes.

I felt them not only come to me from the ends of the universe, but from *outside* it.

How was such a thing possible?

If something was outside the universe . . . that meant there was more than everything that existed. That meant *something else* was buoying up the universe, supporting it—and what was supporting *that?*

How can you have something outside . . . of *everything?*

Even more, how can you have an infinite *anything?* Does not that also imply something containing that "everything," which usually means defined parameters for any such "containment"? Each containment is therefore being contained by some *higher order* of containment.

It blew one's mind!

But that is exactly where these gigantic, unknown faces appeared to originate, exist . . . at least my grasping of their concept.

Yet I felt as if they were right up into my face . . . and what I experienced was but a miniscule percentage of a cell of their skin, as I stood upon this stage, the entirety of this ship's attention focused upon me, both in-person and by video feeds.

Langster was certainly out there.

Fariss and Miranda. Lydia.

I turned around.

Performed a mic check.

The controlled roar of small talk quieted.

I smiled.

Folded my hands before me.

"Good evening," I said. "*I have seen my death . . . and the end of our voyage.*"

I had begun by introducing myself, my association with the Philosophy Corps, and related the events of the recent past. My skipping experiences. How people had begun coming to me for advice and as a sounding board. Philosophical discussions.

I brought up the lists.

At that, my audience grew visibly upset and there was much shifting and shouting and side conversations. I was actually surprised that Langster hadn't had me immediately removed from the stage at this point . . . even though I had seen that that wouldn't happen.

Probabilities being fluid.

Calmly I paced the stage as I talked. If anything was to get me forcibly removed from this stage, what I was about to launch into next, would. Or wouldn't. But I was prepared to take whatever my logical conclusion, based upon the myriad of probabilities. If I'd learned anything from my experiences . . . it was that things were not what they seemed. Our mission . . . our lives . . . our thoughts. Our probabilities are endless . . . and we are only physically focusing on just one miniscule portion of an infinitesimal range of what's really going on with our lives.

So I faced them all and just said it:

"Out there . . . is nothing."

I surveyed my audience. Many just looked at me. Pockets-of-people turned to their neighbors and again began whispered micro-conversations.

"We've been told . . . by our leadership . . . Captain Talbot . . . Stephen Langster . . . Miriam Rockefeller, and all the others . . . that there *is* life out here. That there is a target at the end of our destination awaiting our return.

"Our *return*.

"And we believed them. Believed them all. Believed we were the cream of Humanity's crop.

"All of us were raised in our secret little world for this supposed secret little eventuality. We Embraced it. That's why we're all here. But now . . . actually here . . . headed toward our murky objective . . . we've come to experience something else: I'll call it . . . a 'sickness' . . . a 'space sickness.' We've all noticed it. All talked about it amongst ourselves. And it has caused us . . . to *see* things, maybe even develop new . . . talents."

I again paused and allowed what I'd said to sink in.

"Now . . . those of us who've theoretically had some professional truck in the mysterious . . . the religious . . . the most metaphysical . . . feel we know what it is, what we're seeing. We all believe we're right. But within our so-called objectivity is infinite subjectivity. Not everything that we see is as we *think* it is—"

"So what *is* it?" someone in front called out.

Lydia.

I looked at her and smiled . . . a pleasant, if surely exhausted smile.

"None of us really knows, Lydia. We each *think* we do . . . using our own personal filters and beliefs . . . methods of interpretation . . . but—as you know—I've spoken with many of you," I said, making direct and momentary eye contact with those whom I'd recognized in the audience and had, in fact, discussed this with. "But since no one's been willing to openly talk about it and air out our fears and concerns and interpretations . . . I thought *I* would. Instead . . . we've all resorted to what we know best—secrecy. Compartmentalization. It worked before . . . why shouldn't it continue to work? We do this because it's all we know. Has been our conditioning. Some have even begun to act on our interpretations . . . for both the good and the ill of our futures."

I cast a poignant glare at Langster. Some in the crowd noticed that and looked in the direction I was looking.

"I'm not here to cast judgement nor castigate. I am here to bring this discussion . . . *in lucem* . . . out into the open and do something we are not used to doing, and that is to openly discuss this situation amongst all of us. No more creating compartmentalized conspiracy groups—

"Haven't we had enough of that already?"

I looked to Lydia . . . Langster, members of Fariss's group.

"*When is enough going to be enough?*"

"When are we going to treat each other as equals . . . as the Human Beings that we are? For all we know—we're *it*. There are no others . . . and for all practical purposes—for *our* purposes—this is true. We'll never see another person from Earth—or the Earth itself—ever again.

"*Ever.*

"We have outdistanced our Earthly communication feeds . . . we'll never again know their touch . . . their presences. The planet itself. And as we'd last seen, things weren't getting any better back there.

"What does it take for us to learn our lessons?

"When will we get the message?

"The point is that we need to come together as one . . . terminate all the one-upmanship. The posturing for power. We thought we *were* that power . . . we were hand-selected because we were all part of that massive machine that powered and fueled and promulgated our current state of affairs—

"And now we find a new challenge. A new monkey wrench. And we resort to our old ways?

"*Enough!*"

I realized I'd said it with far more emotional intensity than I'd intended—but what did it matter? We had to get out of our ruts. I had to collect myself some and took a deep breath before continuing.

"I don't care what denomination you are . . . what belief or political alignment . . . but we need to breed tolerance and cooperation. Respect. We need to openly discuss our situation, our feelings, and what we need to do about it. And that is why I've called this meeting. And I cannot thank you all enough for taking the time to hear me speak."

Everyone began to talk among themselves, as I turned my back to them and paced the stage. I stopped and looked out over my audience, allowing their conversations to continue for a moment. I looked for Langster, but no longer saw him.

I knew what he was doing.

"What about your death?" Lydia asked.

The crowd stopped talking.

I smiled.

"Yes, I do know the date and time of my . . . expiration. But I will not share it with you . . . *now*. I will in the very, very near future, however. If I share it now, it will influence your interpretation of it . . . and the events as a whole that are yet to transpire . . . and I cannot have that. It is critically important that you all heed my words . . .

my message . . . without any hint of me, say, giving things away . . . or giving others . . . *ideas*."

"What do you mean?" Lydia pressed. "You come here and throw all these bombshells out at us, and—"

"I know what it looks like, believe me, but let me just say that all of you will have your answers before this time tomorrow. This I *promise* . . . tomorrow, you will have your answers. I cannot be as specific as I need to be at this point in time. It does not suit the purposes."

"'*The* purposes?' *Please*," Lydia said *to me* in a low whisper that was only meant for me. Her eyes locked on mine.

I smiled warmly to her. Then I directed the following thoughts to her: *We are never alone . . . I will always be with you . . . there is nothing to fear.*

Her jaw dropped and she stumbled backward into the people behind her, who asked if she was okay. I held her wonderfully large, stunned eyes with my own . . . and merely flashed her another warm smile.

I returned my attention to the audience, who were all now trying to get their questions noticed by me.

"I've learned that we all experience things differently. It depends on what our individual *focuses* are. If we are devoted to our religions, I've learned from the devout with whom I've spoken that those are exactly the kinds of experiences you will immerse yourselves in. They will follow the tenets and beliefs of their chosen religion. If you are into creating a new life for yourself, then you will become immersed into experiences around you that you believe may or may not transpire in your future . . . and all of these experiences will be further filtered and presented to ever-increasing granularity, based upon your deepest, darkest, most privately held beliefs that you tell only to—or keep hidden from—yourselves.

"So . . . *I* would like to start this conversation," I said, raising my hands into the air before me in a calming manner, "by sharing what I know to be true—"

"How can you claim *truth*," an observer from the video feed called out, "when you just told us that we're all subjectively interpr—"

Another also called out: "What did you mean by 'nothing is out there'?"

"Your death, what *about* your—"

Many more frenzied questions pelted me.

I again brought calming hands up before me, and said, "I don't ask that you believe me right this moment, because certain events are *about* to unfold . . . and were I to give you the specifics right now, you would all say I influenced the outcome by giving those responsible for said events 'ideas.' But by this time tomorrow . . . you will know that I have either spoken the truth . . . or am just as much off as everyone else. Please. Allow me my say . . . and you can all make up your minds tomorrow. Is that too much to ask? What else have you to do? Where else have you to be?"

The crowd grumbled . . . quieted.

"Thank you."

I inhaled . . . exhaled . . .

Paused.

"I have seen . . . multiple scenarios . . . *probable* . . . scenarios. I have actively looked for other life . . . all the different versions of what might happen to us . . . and I have not found one other form of intelligent, extra-human life out there. All I saw . . . was us. *Humanity*.

"In short, I have seen nothing out there."

I allowed a moment for my audience to grasp my words.

"All we have been told has been misinterpreted by those in control. It has all been based upon myths and legends. Dreams, perhaps—and I mean this literally. A mass dream of probable events that never . . . *physically* . . . occurred. I don't know how or why such things happened . . . but I know . . . based upon my research into this, since I first became aware of this phenomena, based upon all my interviews with many of you, that this is the Truth. We have been approaching this concept from the wrong point of view. You have all seen things you believe to be true, despite the fact that they contradict each other's visions. So, I focused on *that* concept and followed that 'trail' backward. And this is what I'd found. The further mechanics and details of all this research I have meticulously detailed in my recordings that'll be made available to each and every one of you by this time tomorrow. Those recordings have been transmitted into space, as is my current presentation. I desperately wanted to record this for all of our other ships that are possibly and hopefully out there and need to learn from our experiences . . . so no one person—" I again looked for Langster—"would ever hold us hostage again, because of a misinterpreted *idea*.

"I have also spoken of my death. I know in the exact manner, method, and hour . . . down to the second . . . of my termination in *this* world. I have logged all that as well, and you shall all know of it by this time tomorrow. This should be all the proof any of you should ever need to heed the words I am sharing . . . and better your lives—"

"*Our* lives," Lydia shouted out.

"But though there is nothing out there . . . there is . . . a planet," I said, holding Lydia's gaze.

I looked back up to the rest of the amphitheater.

"This ship will have a new beginning! A new *home*. The timelines vary and some of the details remain fluid, but I do detail them, given certain other probabilities. And most of you will be there to see it."

"*Most?*" someone called out.

"Yes," I said. "Not everyone onboard our vessel will make it. This is also detailed in my recordings. As well as the reasons for . . . all that occurs."

People again grew restless, but I continued.

"Yet . . . as grim as this may appear . . . I also want to let it be known that our deaths are not tragic! I do see life beyond death! The very fact that I—we—can see all that we are seeing should prove that there *is* an afterlife! How can something like this be possible if an afterlife didn't exist? If there truly was nothing more than what we see—here, now, in front of us—then how could any of us see any so-called future . . . or past? Alternatives? That would literally not be possib—"

"But what makes you think what we're all seeing is true?" another called out. "As you just said, you called all this a 'space *sick*ness.' What if it's exactly that? Delusional ravings of minds gone mad?"

"As I'm sure even you have experienced," I said, addressing the gentleman who'd just addressed me, "you've felt—*lived*—these strange 'visions' yourself, have you not?"

The man nodded hesitantly.

"And given all that you know about living, your life, your states of mind, your psychology . . . would you really prefer to believe that all that you have experienced was false? Delusional? Have you truly *not* revisited loved ones since coming out here? *Not* relived all manner of moments both significant and insignificant? Not again held the birth of your newborn in your arms and thought *this was not real?* Not again stood on the surface of Earth and experienced our warm sun-filled sky? Looked up into its beautiful blue skies and inhaled its fresh, clean air *and thought this was not real?*

"Remember, we have all been put through the most rigorous psychological testing and analysis before being include on this voyage—and each of us, I am sure, have tragic tales of loved ones and friends we thought surely would have been included in this passage with us, but were not admitted because of . . . *findings* . . . all things being equal."

The man remained quiet, then briefly looked away making that face that says, *Yes . . . yes I have . . . .*

"Of course you have," I said, sweeping my gaze over the crowd before me. "We have all experienced moments like this *in our own ways.* We know what we felt and lived and breathed had to be real . . . that we *had* to actually be in all these places that we are not in *now.* Out here. We don't know why or how . . . we don't know or understand what is happening to us, but something is . . . something strange and magical and upsetting *is* occurring . . . and we have no alternatives. We *are* all afraid. Apprehensive. This is the most *Unknown* to ever happen to our race . . . just as is our travels out here are . . . it is foreign and frightening and mysterious. But do not let it paralyze us . . . *no matter what happens.*

"We all signed up for this!

"We all answered the questions and we all said and penned and affirmed, *yes,* we *were* willing to go through with this. And that is exactly how we need to approach this new situation, because it is a part of the Unknown we all signed up for."

I again paused . . . walked a little way across the stage . . . then returned to where I'd started.

"We need to be brave and explore what is happening to all of us. Not allow Talbot's life to have been wasted. Learn from it and not let the same things happen to the rest of us. Not allow what happened on Earth to happen *here*. Yes, we were all part of the conspiracies . . . but that needs to stop *now*. Through an honest and a rigorous exploratory method—I am not going to use the term 'scientific method,' because that carries preconceptual baggage and prejudices with it, as we all know . . . but we need to explore *this* and better understand *this* . . . because our lives depend upon it. Literally. We have to not allow ourselves to go crazy with its discovery . . . nor go crazy from fear."

The crowds again broke off into their muted mini-conversations.

"Excuse me . . . excuse me!" came a voice over the speakers.

I turned my attention to the monitors.

"Yes?" I asked.

"But what of your death?" the voice asked. Her visage now filled the screen. I did not know her.

"What is your name?"

"Cassandra."

"Thank you, Cassandra. What about my death?"

"Aren't you scared? You seem so calm. I'm terrified for you!"

I briefly smiled, choosing my words carefully. Felt entirely outside myself, wistfully looking down at all this like a proud parent answering a child's startlingly perceptive question.

"Cassandra, yes . . . I am more than a bit terrified. But it's like . . . when you rode that Sky Ride, back home . . . You saw how far up it went, how it looked and felt like you were sitting in nothing . . . you saw all the SkyCam footage beforehand, and it looked as if you were not in any way supported by anything . . . yet you were flying through the upper atmosphere . . . through the clouds . . . all of it—but you still got on that ride. Still screamed and smiled and whooped it up . . . and then you landed. All of you . . . intact. Enriched by the mind-expanding excitement and perspective you'd just been part of.

"That . . . is how I feel . . . nervous and fearful and all those ranges of emotion . . . but I know there is no other route to take. All my visions—for lack of a better term—lead to that event. But, you see, I've also experienced what happens *afterward*."

"Afterward?"

I smiled a massive ear-to-ear grin. Held it as I continued.

"Yes—*afterward*. I have been to what will become of me following my death. And I am awestruck and amazed. There are so many probabilities that await me—us!—it's almost as if—"

"You can't *wait* to get on that SkyRide," Cassandra said.

I nodded enthusiastically. "Yes, Cassandra, *yes!*"

"Is there nothing else you can tell us before . . . before . . . before your time?"

"Oh, there is! There truly is! And I so much want and need to tell you all that I can! But . . . elements . . . of our current situation prevent me from doing so, I am afraid to say. And I have visited the probabilities for telling you all more than I have already told you . . . and they all are better suited to the probabilities themselves."

"What does that mean?" another chimed in.

"People . . . look . . . there is so much more to tell you but suffice it to say . . . no matter what I say here . . . now . . . absolutely every possible action I take . . . is . . . has been . . . will always be . . . already *done*."

"What are you saying?" Cassandra asked.

"It doesn't matter what I do or don't do now . . . what I tell you or do not tell you . . . I have already done so in a myriad of other realities—probabilities.

"You think this is the only reality? The one-and-truly rock-bed reality? Do you? Do each of you think this is your main one-and-only life . . . your *main* probability? That all the other versions of life I have spoken of are spin-offs and are secondary, lesser versions of the one you're living now?

"Dear, dear, shipmates, my friends, you're all sadly mistaken! You just don't realize the gravity of what I've told you. And that's precisely why I'm telling you *what* I'm telling you . . . in the *manner* in which I'm telling you . . . as well as the amount of data I am exposing you to . . . all that I am doing . . . and what you *think* . . . I am doing.

"It is because of all of you that I am behaving in precisely the way I am behaving.

"All of our actions have *innumerable* outcomes, despite what we think we see. Experience. There is nothing out there, there are far more probabilities to each physical act than you can imagine, and there is no death . . . yet to all of you, I will be dead this time tomorrow."

14

The good people of the *Renaissance* awoke.
Came out of their daydreams . . . their reveries . . . their catnaps . . . their slumbers.
One last time they sought me out.
Checked ship's records. Speaker's records. Convention records. The Stardust Amphitheater's event records.
The *Renaissance's* manifest.
Had I really existed?
Had I really held a conference with the entire ship?
Had it all been a dream?
Had I really spoken to *each* of them?
They'd awoken nervous, many in cold sweats, panicked.
All except for a small handful of individuals.
And, oh, yes, they'd found my name. Found me.
But I was no longer there.

∞ ∞ ∞

I had been in my cabin late that previous night, after my presentation. It's amazing how "small" . . . two-dimensional . . . everything appears when you realize it's the last you'll ever see of whatever it is you're looking at.
I awaited my visitors.
They'd just walked into my cabin. There were four heavily armed goons with Langster. These guys I did not know.
I hadn't put up a fight—not at all. I knew it was my time. He did not know what he was doing. None of them did.
But what they had *thought* they were doing was what they thought was best for all involved.
In a roundabout way.
Langster was still in the conspiracy mindset. Would always be

so. It was why he had been chosen for the position. It had all been prearranged, oh, so long ago.

I knew everything and he knew it.

I was a danger to all that he was . . . all that had been planned. Set into motion. Had been programmed into this ship. Its real mission.

And all that was *believed*.

I was a danger to everything that had been planned for as long as Humanity had existed.

That had been the real reason why Talbot had died. Talbot hadn't died of any so-called "space sickness." Had not committed suicide.

He'd been murdered.

How had I missed this? Because I'm human and all humans make mistakes? I don't know. Perhaps as I'd skipped Talbot's death I'd seen the first, most probable event and accepted that, since it fit my world view and I was just beginning to understand the whole phenomena that afflicted us, instead of properly exploring his death more thoroughly.

But Talbot had been murdered because he'd discovered Langster's true purpose. The ship's true, hidden mission. And that his wife had been working for Langster. Had been a sleeper planted with Talbot a lifetime ago, also in planning for this mission. Had Talbot just kept what he'd found to himself and gone along with the plan . . . he'd most likely (most probabilities I'd viewed pointed to this, but not all of them) still been around . . . would have still been unknowingly sharing his wife with Langster. Langster shared a lot of women this way.

The real mission of this ship and all involved—because there were literally only a handful of others among us who knew the real plan . . . and they were all keeping an ever-watchful eye on the rest of us—is so far-fetched I did not believe it . . . could not . . . for the longest Objective Time.

But I know people.

That is my profession. You think philosophy is all about concepts?

Philosophy is the study of the fundamental issues concerning all of Humanity: existence, knowledge, values, reason, mind, language.

And all of these would not exist if *we* did not exist, therefore the study of philosophy *is* about Humanity.

People.

Though I do now understand my place in things . . . originally I did not. I was amazed at how I, too, had also *all along been positioned to play the part I was now performing.*

By Life.

Because it always finds a way!

It always does . . . despite our best or worst intentions.

And I had willingly taken on that role once I'd discovered it . . . aboard this ship. Which makes no sense to OT, but perfect sense now.

The plan . . . farther back than the time of sands and pyramids . . . had always been to leave Earth.

Originally people . . . the eventual funneling down to only the most elite of the elite of each ancient-upon-ancient of societies . . . had forever planned the mass exodus of Earth. Again, I do not prefer to perpetuate the original concepts' life by continuing to speak of them—for even to think of something gives it concept and placement and therefore life, and my mission here is to set records straight, not perpetuate untruths—because they were nowhere near the truth of what actually exists out here. And in my present state, I can say I'm *not* thinking of something and actually *not be thinking* of that something.

It's one of my new superpowers.

But, in talking about all of this, it's hard to not relate these myths throughout the ages that these elite few grew and passed on to the succeeding generations of elitists in ways that no longer matter. What matters is that Talbot found them out in the ship's records simply because he was bored! There isn't much to do when you're the captain of a perfectly pre-programmed and operating starship! With his accesses, he had all the time in the . . . well, *universe* . . . to hack his way around things. Nothing is unhackable. But it cost him. I know that Talbot is now fine wherever he has chosen to explore in his incorporeal afterlife.

But I had also discovered Langster's Master Plan on my own, through my exploratory skipping. Had discovered that this ship was actually preprogrammed to head toward a certain planet that *Earthly Nobility* believed was where Earth life had originated.

Emigrated from.

But had been wholly misinterpreted.

The thing is . . . I have the luxury of perspective, whereas Langster and his following do not. They are razor-focused on that singular premise and could not and cannot see beyond it. Would not allow themselves to see any other perspective. So as soon as I discovered their view . . . I skipped to see if this was really true . . . and was presented with a rush of alternate experiences!

Alternates cannot exist to something if that something is truly all that exists.

And I explored them all!

Sent portions of myself everywhere!

I can still feel them, these alternates of me . . . exploring . . . sending me back all that they found/find/continue to find—that I can handle, because some of what is discovered is so far beyond what Humanity and myself can conceptually handle as to mortally incapacitate a still-corporally tethered individual!

But I'd discovered the secrets. And as such, become a liability to Langster.

So . . . he showed up to my cabin.

And took me away.

They knew not what they were doing.

Or did.

It really didn't matter, because the probability transpired.

He made all manner of apology to me as he set me into a casket similar to the one Talbot had been packed into. He offered to "put me out," as it were, prior to sending me out among the stars. Said it would be better that way before the self-destruction timer actuated. *Isn't it always better to die in your sleep?* he said.

But everyone will see my explosion, I told him, and I've already programmed my follow-up message to everyone onboard this ship.

Who cares? He replied. *You'd already told everyone about your imminent demise, and there will be no way anyone could physically prove who did what, despite your philosophical ramblings. It will be my word against yours—and I run this ship.* And, he added with a wry grin. *It would be well-received as a cautionary tale to others who might also think about sticking their noses where they don't belong.*

All I could do was chuckle and laugh as they stuffed me into my casket (which was actually quite comfortable) . . . and shot me out into the stars.

As soon as I left the ship, I went into my skipping mode.

"My friends . . . as I have told you all . . . I will now make good on my promises," my pre-recorded message announced as it went out to everyone onboard the *Renaissance* . . .

Yes, I was apprehensive. There is an ancient Earth saying: *where the rubber meets the road.*

So this was what death looked like!

". . . I have told you that I'd be murdered . . . and I have been . . . and the names of those responsible I've provided in the accompanying files. Their names have been provided not as any form of retribution for their roles in my so-called death . . . but as to point out the error of certain misinformed individuals who continue to promulgate their misguided agenda . . ."

There was no more thinking or philosophizing about it. No more "in the future."

The future was now.

My death—

Now.

". . . communicate with each other . . . start fresh—reinvent yourselves and learn from your mistakes . . ."

And I had to—like all of us—address it. *Face* it.

Yes, the proper terms make all the difference.

In my meditative mode I was suddenly—though not unexpectedly—*free!*

". . . if you look to the coordinates I have programmed into Navigation, you will shortly discover your new home . . . and it is not the one you think it is . . . planned all this time."

All my surface human fear evaporated!

But now, I had truly internalized—if I could use such a term anymore!—that I would no longer be returning to whence I'd come!

". . . starting over will not be easy, but each moment is a chance to begin anew . . ."

So . . . just for fun . . . I held off the explosion of my tiny corporeal encapsulation.

Because I could!

How could I do this, you ask?

Because Time is fluid! Corporeal events malleable!

". . . and though I may no longer be with you . . . I will be with you as each of you create a new beginning for Humanity at your new home. Out here is nothing . . . but within each of you . . . is everything . . ."

Oh, there was so much I could do and see that seemed somehow far more elevated than ever before, while I'd been upon the ship! It was as if, with an actual impending death, the rules of the game . . . *expanded*. I felt I could actually return to my body and remain in that illusional casket, if I'd chosen, and experience the explosion and enter the new phase of my existence that way . . . or do it the way I was currently handling it—*by simply, consciously leaving.*

I could leave this existence right now, prior to the explosion . . . leaving the detonation in limbo, so to speak, in Human OT. In other words . . . in a very real way . . . I'd have left that reality just before that event and not allowed it to materialize into my perspective. Freezing all of that reality . . . for *me*. To leave it "hanging" forever in limbo . . . for *me*.

Or, at least, that probability.

". . . so I bid you each adieu and leave you all in peace and love!"

In a deeply philosophical way, I had foiled Langster's plans.

All that would follow would simply *not be* in my version of probabilities.

Or it would be. That's the beauty of multiple realities.

And I would simply live out my remaining . . . *existence?* . . . however it will be in this new state.

I felt my consciousness, my entire existence, expand outward into the farthest and furthest reaches of the universe!

As I floated in space, I left my casket behind.

The expansion of my body . . . my soul . . . was like nothing I'd ever previously experienced with all my other skipping experiences. It almost ripped my consciousness apart just thinking about it.

I ... stood ... there was really no other ... word? ... for it. In space itself. My position felt as solid and stable as any stance on Earth I had ever taken ... yet in the middle of interstellar space was I.

Inundated by life and energy and the majesty of the corporally and incorporeally unseen!

I possessed no fear! Only wonder!

But my ... vision? ... was far more than any visions I had *ever* enjoyed!

Space ... was no longer an unknown, limitless black expanse, punctuated by the pinholes of equally distant light!

No and *lo!*

It was filled with sights and images and sounds and feelings that I cannot yet express in my old categories of sights and images and sounds and feelings and *words.*

I am moved beyond all human emotion by the Life that teems here—not even "out" here, but "*in*" here!

Oh, that Humanity could just experience but a *taste* of it all!

It moves me to tears! My consciousness explodes with emotion!

There *is* Life out here ... there *is* something.

I was wrong ... so very, so utterly, beautifully wrong.

But not in a way any of us could have ever imagined!

In my unfathomably immense consciousness, I looked back to the *Renaissance*. I watched as it shot farther and farther away from me in every illusional way possible ... yet I still felt myself walking those corridors and now began to understand what those gigantic "faces" had been all about.

I thought of all that I had wrought onboard there and what Langster and his crew would be going through right now—which suddenly felt more yesterday—or tomorrow—or never had happened at all—but did ... *in a future's distant past?*

I was intoxicated with ever mind-expanding awareness presenting Itself to me!

I wished Langster no ill ... I had never wished him ill ... not even any so-called "sense of justice."

It just didn't matter!

I reeled with the seeming contradictions!

I wanted for the people onboard the *Renaissance* to find their new home. To begin again! And all about me I saw them . . .

Planets.

Stars.

Wonder and amazement!

I was awash with excitement for them! The people of the *Renaissance* would find their home . . . they will not believe it—or have already . . . or yet *will*—but they will have their planetfall.

I reached out to one of the many stars before me! So young and bright! Planets orbiting about it!

It was much closer than it appeared . . . everything was much closer than they appeared . . . I'd felt as if I'd overreached . . . but it all easily fell into the palms of my hands!

I laughed!

I cried!

Such nostalgic familiarity once again!

A home of rock and water! Life-giving sunshine!

It was so . . . *warm* . . . so . . . *comfortable!*

I loved this star! This beautiful conglomeration of the energy of multiple dimensions, all of which near-blinded even my newfound senses! I brought and flexed and clenched my hand inside its glow and light! Swam within its limitless multiple inner dimensions! Drank its energy—which I also felt this star do with me! It was *alive*, so *alive*—and knew of and acknowledged *my* presence!

It . . . had . . . *personality* . . . .

Of course this would do!

I looked for the most suitable planet and brought it to me. My smile extended (and still does beyond my mention of it here) into the farthest reaches of whatever all this is that I was experiencing!

I cupped the chunk of rock within my hands. Smoothed my touch over it as if polishing a lake-stone.

Brought it up to even closer examination.

I laughed heartily as I inspected it!

I massaged the shell of the rock into clumps here and there . . . grappled and squeezed and formed it within my cosmic grasp.

Manipulated it with love and care.

Breathed upon it.

My breath became one with it, giving it a gloriously faint and sparkling haze about the once lump of heavy metals and collections of water.

I floated my life's work before my consciousness.

Heard the whispers of Life.

Whispered back.

Gently repositioned it back within its orbit . . . and compelled upon it emotion and intention at all that I had done and what it was now capable of!

And left a little present for them upon planetfall.

Was everything I did metaphorical? Incorporeal?

Did it matter?

I could not keep from laughing and crying and growing ever more joyful with each moment, as I expanded and left my work for the depths of whatever this new life of mine had . . . would now . . . manifest—

And became one with the stars.

THE WHISPERERS

no
they're coming
yes
inevitable
we knew they would
have already been here
would have always been
preparations are in place
have always been
good
indeed
i've always liked them
they've always been pests
they are who they are
not needed don't need them

but we do they have already been here
unfortunately
i find them amusing
i rather enjoy their antics
i don't
oh but you do
tiresome behavior rather employ energy elsewhere
you already have
don't remind me
you seem to need me to
and me
let's get this over with
here they are
had they never come we'd never exist
they've always existed
we should have killed them

PLANETFALL

Year 2073 C. E.

1

Everything is a concept.
Life . . . death . . . journeys . . .
Humanity. The universe.
Reality.
None of which excuses the other from actuality.
Nothing lasts forever . . . including—according to current scientific theories—the universe . . . which is everything.
Humanity had tried its best. Had done so on the rock it had been given. Decided it had wanted more. Had made mistakes. Branched out . . . stretched its legs . . . and had stepped off of the oblate spheroid's firmament. Had sent its emissaries out into the voids between the stars. When the first ships launched they had largely done so undetected. Whether by obfuscation, lack of interest, or whatever, didn't matter. Just that they'd been launched.

And had subsequently disappeared.

Had left all greed and murder—and every other injustice—behind.

Only nothing had been left behind.

They'd sent out ships with names like *Inspire, Renaissance, Discover,* and *Pioneer.*

Had populated them not only with the militarily and explorer minded . . . but the agronomically . . . philosophically . . . organizationally minded. The constructionally and artistically minded.

No expense had been spared. This would, after all, be the starter kit for the next iteration of Humanity. Once the global nobility . . . the entitled . . . had sat down and gotten past their egos and culture and had put their heads together it became soberingly clear: they'd needed two of *everything.* Had gone back to the ancient Greek philosophers for their solid architectural reflection for who and what would be needed. Not just intellectually . . . but in terms of wisdom, brawn, adventure, fertility, ability to think outside the box, and much, much more than money and life's station could ever provide . . . but also money and station and status and entitlement.

They had, after all, been running the show.

And money had been no object.

Every aspect of Humankind had been packed into these containers . . . all identical in construction and capability to rebuild any aspect of either the ship itself or the most complex building, mechanical, or living structures needed to populate a new world.

You know, because the one they'd already had hadn't been good enough.

Singles and couples. Families. Clones. AI. Diversity of every possible form of life below, above, and upon the Earth itself, if not in live form, then through genetics. A set of veritable and sophisticated Noah's Arks, these ships had shot out into specific sectors . . . to where the latest research had suspected the best chances for livable and hospitable environments might exist.

Planets.

Well, and one other destination never mentioned outside a chosen few, saved for the *Intrepid,* the Flag Ship of the fleet.

As they were built and filled, they were launched.

Most found nothing and continued on, for to return *was* out of the question.

There was nothing to return *to*.

For all of Humanity's best efforts, their hubris had wrought the destruction of everything.

Earth, air, and water.

Animals, trees, and people.

Life.

Specifically controlled earthquakes and engineered weather had run amok. The occasional catastrophic storm and earthquake had become the New Normal. The government pooh-poohed climate change because they had been causing climate change. Engineering and weaponizing weather, as well as everything else. Messing around with the atmosphere had torn ever-widening chasms into the ozone and magnetosphere and had drastically reshaped all of earthly existence.

What had been discovered far too late by those scientists and engineers, and never fully understood, was another variable that they simply could not control, because they ignored all acknowledgement of such a concept.

Earth's consciousness.

Life.

Life has a way of ridding itself of unwanted pests very much like the healthy human organism does.

And Life *always* finds a way.

After all those-of-privilege had received passage into space . . . after the best and brightest . . . the entitled . . . the hand-picked . . . it had become a severely controlled selection of skills—and even those selected had been run through the most rigorous refinements to cull out the mentally unstable, violent, or otherwise high-risk, undesirable behaviors or unbeneficial genetic continuations. If someone didn't apply for passage, the *Nouveau* Elite didn't want them. These people had to *want* to go. Required motivation, a drive . . . to survive.

Much of this had all been covertly put into action generations before those who had actually been preselected had been put into place. It had all been highly orchestrated. And when it had finally and blatantly been pulled out from the stink of shadows and skullduggery—put into action—it had been an effective and swiftly moving mechanization, the likes of which had never before been seen by the current crop of Humanity

Suddenly, there had been no more wars.

No more police actions.

Political strife.

All governments had worked together, if for but seconds upon the geological timeline.

Political parties.

Militaries.

And they'd brutally and effectively crushed all resistance.

Agitators.

Those who allowed the global machine to do its obscene work had been left alone to do anything they wanted . . . play with their Bright and Shiny . . . as long as they didn't impede exodus operations.

And if they had ended up getting in the way, they simply . . . disappeared.

ExOps took what it needed . . . and left the rest to fend for themselves. Even those in the military carrying out the very orders that made the others "go away," were just as effectively dealt with if discovered they were not one of the chosen, were not playing along.

In this way, Earth would start over.

In this way . . . Humanity shot out into the voids between the stars.

In this way

2

Nothing is perfect.

The ships blindly raced for the stars. While several of the ships destroyed themselves through their own internal political or psychological implosions, others survived—some on planets or moons—and some for extremely limited durations deficient to what they would have survived had they stayed aboard ship, and some in ships whose faster-than-light drives had failed less miserably than those that had disintegrated . . . creeping along at rates that guaranteed death to generations before any remote considerations of a generous nomadic planetfall.

But for those who had survived . . . of course they reverted to the
(government)
(politics)
(organizational constructs)
(entitlement)
old ways. It was what they knew.

After all . . . everything had worked before, had it not? To some degree or another?

"We," they'd vowed, "*would just not make the same mistakes we'd made in the past.*"

"We," they'd promised themselves, "*would do it* right *this time.*"

"We . . . *would start over.*"

They'd said.

And into the stars they'd made their promises.

However, the farther out the remaining ships ventured, the more members of the missions discovered a new and disquieting occurrence. There appeared to be . . . a sickness . . . a *condition* . . . that afflicted all crew members. Subtly at first . . . it had quickly manifested into an unbalanced warping of time, space, and *consciousness.*

Individuals . . . lost track of where they were . . . in some cases, *who* they were . . . and in all cases *when* they were . . . .

3

Quite by accident, and in advance of the Flag Ship, the *Renaissance* had been the first sent out into the stars . . . far in advance of all of the others. It had been testing various aspects of the ship's flight some 500,000 miles above the Earth's ecliptic, as other issues were still being tidied up back on Earth. As urgent and hurried the need to initiate ExOps and depart Earth had become, things had become ever more exacerbated when the *Intrepid* had vaporized in Earth orbit from a catastrophic faster-than-light drive malfunction that had not only taken out the *third*-designated ship as well, still early into construction, but also the better part of northern Russia. The downloaded data analysis a fraction of a second before the destruction had identified a similar flaw in the *Renaissance*, but had not caused any issues, since the *Renaissance* had not yet employed its FTL drive. The *Renaissance's* crew worked feverishly to identify and formulate workarounds and had finally felt it had devised a solution . . . tested it . . . retested it . . . then tested it again . . . until it had been deemed Operational.

But to really test it, the *Renaissance* had to kick it into FTL drive . . . which it did, indeed do—and forever disappeared from Earthly contact.

There were still a few loose ends to the whole FTL bit, not the least of which was rearward communications.

Early into the *Renaissance's* journey, its onboard operational and governmental structure was, of course, no different than what it had left behind.

Parties . . . political and otherwise.

What else did they know?

There had been its share of strife . . . crime . . . existential stress, which led to increased pharmaceutical use . . . and in turn led back to strife and crime. Even smart people do bad. But as they had developed their shipboard politics and organization . . . so had they also developed their method for self-policing. Executing laws and judging issues. Corruption again reared its ugly head, and immediately all the old, comforting ills of yore had resurfaced, the bad as well as the good, not to mention the manifestation of hidden agendas, new and old.

But new leadership had also emerged, led by the newly unopposed and overwhelmingly chosen President Rothchild, and instigated investigations . . . arrested and tried the guilty . . . and meted out swift justice to keep things sustainable, while effectively (some would say almost "magically") seeking out and crushing uprisings before any meaningful traction had yet been gained.

It was all once more comfortably familiar for those onboard the *Renaissance*.

But growing incidents of the space sickness, renamed "Holcomb's Syndrome," by the first medical professional to officially classify it, also continued. Certain official departments had tried to contain it, study it, handle it . . . but as it advanced . . . and manifested, it did so differently in each affected individual.

Then quickly became epidemic.

Mentally and spiritually affected all onboard as harshly and thoroughly as any Earthly, traditional viral pandemic.

It wasn't until the loss of several of the crew—the *murder* of multiple crew members—that things had come to light . . . a video log of one crew member's detailed investigations into the affliction, which he'd released to all onboard the *Renaissance*, truly advanced Humanity's understanding of the condition . . . not the least of which also identified his killer.

And though death sentences had never been . . . officially . . . passed, let alone a complete

(*corruption*)

(*entitlement*)

investigation, the killer and his associates, had never been heard from again.

Life continued on. Always finds a way.

4

The *Renaissance's* faster-than-light drive worked . . . until it didn't.

While their drive had not self-destructed and vaporized all onboard, it had . . . *seized* . . . and permanently destroyed any further faster-than-light operation. A complete overhaul was instituted. This, of course, occurred far outside any Earth-charted space.

The stars were completely different where they'd found themselves.

And given the ever-increasing effects of Holcomb's Syndrome, many began to doubt their own faculties . . . their own eyes.

What was real? What was imagined?

Had all that they'd experienced actually happened?

When the *Renaissance* emerged, limping, from its FTL journey . . . it was far beyond anywhere the crew'd
(*imagined?*)
projected they'd emerge.

They were alone. In the uncharted reaches of space.

The only saving grace was that they'd emerged into the neighborhood of a brightly illuminated, medium-sized star that possessed a few marbles orbiting it. Upon closer inspection the second-of-multiple planets possessed a thin, blue atmosphere.

Breathable air!

Water!

As the passengers and crew of the *Renaissance* approached this system . . . they could not be sure if what they were seeing and heading toward was real . . . or yet another . . . space-sickened . . . mirage . . . whether or not one of their own had successfully predicted this would, indeed, happen—

5

Imagined or actual, the planet reached out and gave the *Renaissance* an enthusiastic and oh-so-excited welcome.

BECK AND CALL
Year 2073 C. E.

    The *Bio-Engineered Computer, Original,* also known as "BEC00," also known as "Beck," stirred within his coffin-like confinement, a ship-to-ground deployment pod.
    And while no one on board the *Renaissance* knew about Beck's existence, Beck did.
    He knew everything.
    Much like his fellow covert operatives, the Gray Berets, but to even far greater extremes, Beck knew how to fight, hide, evade, observe, collect, and analyze.
    How to upset, influence, and obfuscate.
    How to be diplomatic, humorous, charming, and—
    Ruthless.
    Human.
    Beck knew a lot of things—information. More so than the rest of his unit. A unit composed of twelve other BECs none of whom knew of him – or of each other's – existences.

Information.

The Gray Berets were to gather as much information as possible over the course of their lives and funnel it back to (even to them) an unknown, covert database.

But unlike his gray-bereted brothers and sisters, Beck also knew the real, secret histories of Earth, and the actual and shrouded reasons behind the *Renaissance's* real journey, and all about that unknown, covert database.

He knew about Earth's devolutionary course.

Yes, he knew *everything*.

And he *knew* he knew.

Only problem was . . . he didn't. Not really.

But one thing Beck knew for certain was that he was to be awoken for one reason and one reason only.

Planetfall.

Eyes closed, and still largely in his suspended animation, Beck initiated various system start-ups in a rigidly defined protocol. Checked their statuses, the status of the other twelve BECs similarly stowed—and hidden—from the rest of the *Renaissance* crew. His protocols were such that he would be the first deployed to the surface of any new planet they intended to explore. The other BECs would deploy later . . . still under a veil of secrecy . . . just not now.

Beck accessed the ship's computers and analyzed its data. Accessed human voice communications from the *Renaissance's* Command Deck, which were (like everything else) recorded. Yes, the *Renaissance* was, indeed, achieving orbit. Yes, this world had a breathable atmosphere. Yes, this world did, indeed, seem promising.

Beck enabled all self-check protocols and prepared for departure. As soon as a stable orbit had been achieved, he would analyze his best options from the shipboard scanning data and would, based upon his own protocols and defined mission, choose his point of insertion.

Beck ejected from the *Renaissance*, masking the ship's sensors as he did so.

His deployment pod quickly rocketed down toward the alien

surface. The quicker it got to the surface, the better. Less time in orbit, less time in the air, less chance for even accidental detection.

Only Beck knew his true mission.

Only Beck knew his landing zone.

Only Beck knew of his existence.

And Beck wasn't talking.

Beck left the disintegrating remains of his pod's self-destruction to the planet's stiff winds. He crisply slung his backpack on, for even one such as Beck required tools, and simply strode away from his landing.

After several strides, he squatted down to the arid plains at his feet—his eyes ever-scrutinizing the harsh desert terrain before him—and speared a knife-like hand into the hard-packed dirt. He scooped up handfuls of the rough, stone-and-pebble-laden soil. Mixed it with the fingers of the same hand. As he continued to visually scan his environment, Beck then hefted the soil in his palm, sifted it through his fingers, and allowed some of it to flow back down to the ground. This time visually scanning the soil before him, he scooped up another handful of the dirt-and-gravel mixture and mixed it with the remaining dirt he already held. He again scanned his surroundings as he came back to his feet—

And dumped the entirety of his palm's contents into his mouth.

Continued on.

Beck headed up and into the ancient hills before him.

He was never seen nor heard from ever again by those called Humans . . . at least as far as those who never knew of his existence were concerned.

IF AT FIRST YOU DON'T SUCCEED

Year 2073 C. E.

1

The first to officially touch down upon alien soil were military.

This wasn't even a question.

Three parties had been simultaneously sent down to different regions of the planet.

The first landing craft set down uneventfully at the confluence of two rivers in, what to the humans appeared to be, virgin territory. Scans of the planet had yielded no animal life . . . no fauna. Only flora.

The multi-national force of twelve Global Alliance and Treaty Organization marines, led by Colonel William "Wild Bill" Herndon, off-loaded from their landing craft in three massive terrain-chewing armored Military All-terrain Vehicles, of four personnel each. The six-wheeled MAVs hit the ground running with their powerful, throaty roar and rumblings, digging deep ruts with their massively lugged tires that bit deeply into alien soil and spit it out the rear in huge, dirty rooster-tailed waterfalls. All sensors, weaponry, observation, and tactics honed and focused at maximum.

Their mission was clear.

Explore . . . observe . . . record.

Claim.

And they were psyched. Pumped.

Motivated.

They were Marines.

As throughout all of Earth history, Humanity had found new land and had taken it over. Made it their own. Mastered it. If others inhabited, the goal would continue to be as it had always been: explore . . . observe . . . subjugate.

Claim.

Herndon and his unit made quick time across the easy terrain of rolling hills and expansive plains, weapons at the ready, eyes peeled. And when they'd encountered forests, thick, pristine, and dense . . . they blasted through them. Barreled through two swamps, and even spent more than a little time unnecessarily messing around in some sand dunes. Captain Gina "Kick Ass" Peccadillo, Herndon's second-in-command, made an off-color comment about getting sand in places that would make date-night a bit rough without a good power-washing.

They

(explore)

(observe)

(record)

took their readings. Made their observations.

Nothing.

Not an insect, field mouse, nor chickadee—not a single life form beyond trees, brush, and grasses—but the obvious observation of a breathable nitrogen/oxygen mix and the comfortable temperatures in the low eighties were duly noted.

They went on like this for three days, three unforgiving sets-of-tracks through grasslands, woodlands, and deserts. Deep, enthusiastically cut ruts extending back to their landing craft.

IF AT FIRST YOU DON'T SUCCEED

Year 2073 C. E.

1

The first to officially touch down upon alien soil were military.

This wasn't even a question.

Three parties had been simultaneously sent down to different regions of the planet.

The first landing craft set down uneventfully at the confluence of two rivers in, what to the humans appeared to be, virgin territory. Scans of the planet had yielded no animal life . . . no fauna. Only flora.

The multi-national force of twelve Global Alliance and Treaty Organization marines, led by Colonel William "Wild Bill" Herndon, off-loaded from their landing craft in three massive terrain-chewing armored Military All-terrain Vehicles, of four personnel each. The six-wheeled MAVs hit the ground running with their powerful, throaty roar and rumblings, digging deep ruts with their massively lugged tires that bit deeply into alien soil and spit it out the rear in huge, dirty rooster-tailed waterfalls. All sensors, weaponry, observation, and tactics honed and focused at maximum.

Their mission was clear.

Explore . . . observe . . . record.

Claim.

And they were psyched. Pumped.

Motivated.

They were Marines.

As throughout all of Earth history, Humanity had found new land and had taken it over. Made it their own. Mastered it. If others inhabited, the goal would continue to be as it had always been: explore . . . observe . . . subjugate.

Claim.

Herndon and his unit made quick time across the easy terrain of rolling hills and expansive plains, weapons at the ready, eyes peeled. And when they'd encountered forests, thick, pristine, and dense . . . they blasted through them. Barreled through two swamps, and even spent more than a little time unnecessarily messing around in some sand dunes. Captain Gina "Kick Ass" Peccadillo, Herndon's second-in-command, made an off-color comment about getting sand in places that would make date-night a bit rough without a good power-washing.

They

(explore)

(observe)

(record)

took their readings. Made their observations.

Nothing.

Not an insect, field mouse, nor chickadee—not a single life form beyond trees, brush, and grasses—but the obvious observation of a breathable nitrogen/oxygen mix and the comfortable temperatures in the low eighties were duly noted.

They went on like this for three days, three unforgiving sets-of-tracks through grasslands, woodlands, and deserts. Deep, enthusiastically cut ruts extending back to their landing craft.

Peccadillo chatted on her hot mic in the front passenger seat, as Herndon consulted his tablet maps in his seat behind the driver, Sergeant Reginald Morton. Herndon kept the *Renaissance* leadership informed. He periodically picked up his digital binoculars and scanned the terrain. Took glances to the other two MAVs.

Hours of utter boredom.

"Sir," Captain Peccadillo hailed, as she turned around in her seat to address Herndon. "The boots are gettin' restless and've made a request to blow off some steam."

Without looking up, Herndon said, "And how would they like to do that?" He continued to make annotations to his tablet, occasionally glancing up and outside the MAV as he spoke.

Peccadillo grinned. "By doing what we do best, sir."

Herndon grinned. Looked up to her. He momentarily held Peccadillo's gaze. Then he glanced back down to his tablet, made a couple of keystrokes, and again looked back up to her. Again holding her gaze, his grin still enabled, he said, "Sergeant . . . pull over up there . . . at that tree line."

Peccadillo turned back around in her seat, beaming ear to ear. Herndon got on the horn.

All three MAVs sat at the edge of the forest. One marine per MAV stood in the open turret of each vehicle as sentry. The rest of the rifle squad stood at attention. Peccadillo stood off to the side, weapon ready, continually scanning the terrain.

"It has come to my attention," Herndon bellowed, pacing back and forth before the unit, "that some of you are itchin' for action. Well, I've been in contact with HQ and they tell me that there are no hostiles in sight. On this planet."

He eyed the troops.

They had the best training Earth had to offer, or they wouldn't be here, but they were a unit that was largely untested and as restless for action as they were disciplined. Their leadership was more experienced and understood the young marine's need to prove themselves. Humans are human, no matter what they wear or what they do, and with all that they had been through with Holcomb's, and now a new planet, well, even the best-trained warriors needed an outlet now and then.

And the best commanders realized this.

Herndon momentarily brought his tablet up before him, performed some actions on it, then let it again hang by his side from its sling. Indeed, no life forms registered.

"But they . . . are not *here*," the colonel continued, hands clasped rigidly behind a ramrod-straight back.

"They . . . do not have the same intel *we* have."

"They . . . are not on the *ground*."

Herndon paced right up to his marines and went nose-to-nose with several of them, all unflinching and eyes focused two-thousand-yards-front.

"*My* intel says something different.

"*My* intel tells me there *are* hostiles . . . right this moment . . . mounting an offense, fifty yards into those trees," he said, pointing without looking, "employing the very best in electromagnetic cloaking."

Herndon paused.

The troops shifted anticipatorily.

"*We* picked them up because of *our* proximity and *our* superior technological and analytical expertise. *Why?*" he said, suddenly directing his question into the face of the marine he stood before.

"*Marines*, sir!" the marine shouted back.

Herndon left that marine, continued to pace, and said, with an ever-increasing volume of his voice, "it is our sworn *mission* to take out any hostiles, alien or otherwise, to keep our objective safe . . . our *ship* safe . . . *and our charges upon that ship* safe."

Here Herndon allowed himself to crack an ever-so-slight smirk.

The marines struggled to maintain their in-place military bearing, a few grinning and snatching quick side-long glances to their comrades.

"To *that* end . . . I am ordering you to break ranks *and do what we do best*."

The rifle squad intoned: "*Ooh-RAH!*" and dispersed.

Several ran back to the MAVs, retrieving mortars, M240Cs, and one Mark VII Laser Cannon.

"Form up!" Sergeant Morton commanded.

The men and women immediately and effectively took up firefighting positions, weapons and attention directed into the forest. Those who had broken off from the main group returned with a couple of test-round mortars and heavy artillery. Peccadillo allowed them to set up, grinning as she unslung her own weapon.

"Yeah, baby," Peccadillo uttered under her breath.

Everything was ready.

Morton cast a shisst-eating grin toward Peccadillo.

Peccadillo, a smile upon her face, shouted, *"Fi-ire!"*

The squad opened a veritable Gates of Hell.

The destruction was devastating.

Herndon, Peccadillo, and the men and women of GATO's 1st Marine Space-Ground Task Force tore into trees and rocks and brush. The mortar rounds kept coming, thundering through the air and pounding the ground. The MAVs fired round after round after round into the trees.

Herndon remained stoic but focused, as he, too, channeled his frustrations.

Peccadillo quietly grunted, as an evil sneer overtook her face, and she vented unholy fire power into the once-pristine woods.

The rest of the unit yelled and hollered and were beside themselves as they annihilated what appeared to be trees very similar to pine, beech, maple, and more.

Within three minutes, a swath of alien wilderness had been obliterated into mangled, bruised, and smoking debris. Deeper inside the forest lay clumps of smoking holes left by Earth-developed ordinance and ammunition. The Mark VII.

Whoops and hollers continued to elicit from the squad as they dropped their aims and looked upon all that they had done.

High-fives. Foot stomping. Body slamming.

The twelve-person unit stood, weapons down, and stared into the still smoking and foul-smelling carnage. It smelled very much like what they were familiar with back on Earth, but with a faint hint of something else . . . there was something . . . different . . . to it all.

"*That's* what I'm talking about," one troop said under his breath as he pumped his weapon into the air, fired a round, high-fived a comrade, then turned and left his position for a vape.

Peccadillo momentarily closed her eyes and forcefully open-mouthed her breathing for a few moments, as her chest heaved mightily. Eyes closed, she took a moment to allow the adrenaline rush to wash over her.

Herndon calmly pulled a cigar from a pocket, bit off the end, forcefully spit out the piece toward the defiled region, then lit the stogey.

Inhaled satisfyingly.

The 1MSGTF left behind their damage. Continued on. Bantered excitedly about all they had done, how good it felt to again unleash such power and destruction. On a new world. The more talented among them even sketched various versions of the scene, including their grim, fierce, excited expressions.

They

(claimed)

trekked ever onward, over the extraterrestrial terrain.

More woodlands, more plains, more rolling hills, and came to rest a fourth night. Thoroughly exhausted from not only several days of driving, but the earlier massive adrenaline release, each officer or enlisted personnel said little to each other as they turned in for the night.

As each marine fell off to sleep . . . reliving the events of the day, one thought went through each person's mind:

Live by the sword . . . die by the sword . . .
Live by the sword . . . die by the sword . . .
Live by the sword . . . die by the sword . . . .

Without warning, they were all promptly shaken, rattled, and rolled as massive rifts simultaneously opened up beneath their now-distant landing craft, their encampment, and the copse of alien woods they'd decimated with their pent-up frustrations. Even the tracks their MAVs had made across the land had been wiped from the earth.

It was like they'd never been there.

2

The second attempt launched to the planet's surface was led by Dr. Marcia Philippon. Her five-person team, composed of a botanist, biologist, archeologist, and geologist, was escorted by Lieutenant Wilhelm Vost and his four-person GATO 1MSGTF. The men and women had landed in a more arid area very much like Earth's deserts.

The team's plan was to only range out as far as their boots, and later, MAVs, could take them, then return to the landing craft at the end of each day. Move on. Rinse, repeat.

The party spread out, the military contingent ever mindful of their surroundings, and explored. It wasn't too long before Lieutenant Vost slapped his face.

He stopped . . . hand still clamped to his right jaw.

His eyes went wide.

All other team members similarly stopped as if told their next step would settle on a landmine and shot looks at the lieutenant. Dr. Philippon made a startled move toward Vost and stopped.

Carefully removing his hand from his face, Vost looked at it.

Everyone looked to Vost's hand.

Philippon rushed to his side. She grabbed his hand into both of hers. Eyes wide, she squealed—then covered her mouth and shot a look toward the rest of the party.

Vost looked questioningly to her.

"Is it . . . *really?*" he said, allowing Philippon to angle and turn his hand closer to her face as she pulled out one of her instruments and hovered it over the hand. Took pictures and readings.

Philippon began to chuckle . . . then laugh. A full-on, excited laughter that brought the rest of their party in closer. She showed them all Vost's hand.

Resting at the base of Vost's middle fingers, just above the palm-proper . . . was a squashed insect.

It actually looked just like a smacked Earth mosquito would look.

"Holy To-*le*-do . . . ," the biologist said.

"You gotta be kidding me!" the geologist said.

All the scientists huddled around the find.

"Great—I left my bug dope on-ship," Vost said.

Vost began to pull his hand back in to him, when Philippon yanked it back.

"Don't you *dare!*" she said, her eyes wide with enthusiasm and smiling ear to ear. "I'm gonna scrape that off your hand, Marine!"

Vost chuckled.

"Have at it," he said.

Philippon pulled out another piece of equipment, a Mobile Quantification Unit, made some selections, and hovered it over the alien insect carcass. It was sucked up into the handheld machine.

"I could just kiss your hand full on the *mouth!*" Philippon said, absentmindedly as she looked to her instrument, making additional adjustments.

Giving Philippon a quizzical look, Vost said, "I have something else I'd rather you—"

Philippon ignored him, yanking him by that hand over to her colleagues. Vost stumbled as she shoved his hand toward the other scientists.

The squashed item on Vost's hand was—for all practical purposes—a mosquito.

"Geez," Vost said, "hope it wasn't carrying some form of alien Zika!" He wiped his hands on his uniform. Sniffed his hand.

"Well, that is a legit concern," Philippon said, "so we'd better get you checked out." She quickly motioned to the biologist. "Iris, why don't you screen the Lieutenant, here, for any infectious activity."

Iris nodded and hurried over, unslinging her gear. As the rest of the scientists discoursed about the amazing find, she took a blood sample, uploading all of Vost's data into her gear. She called out to Vost and said, "I'll let you know in just a few," and went off to be by herself, as her instrumentation ran its algorithms.

The party, psyched by its finding, hurriedly moved onward.

A mosquito!

Collected and inserted into each MQU were the incinerated lives that had been broken down into their molecular and genetic building blocks for immediate upload into the *Renaissance's* database. Handfuls of live specimens were also captured and sealed away in specimen containers.

But as the scientists continued with their scientific duties, the military contingent began to grow uneasy. Restless. While Philippon and the others were more than happy to linger wherever they'd decided to stop and collect and analyze samples, all day, every day, Vost and his group were restless to range farther and not keep camping out at each stop, where all they did was sit and observe, sit and observe, and do *nothing*.

There was no glory in that.

No exploration.

No busting down of doors.

Or blowing up of things.

The lieutenant and his folks were nothing more than a bunch of babysitters for a bunch of shissting eggheads. All this classifying and analysis could be done once the planet had been fully explored, conquered, and

(*claimed*)

controlled.

The time now was for exploration—far, wide, and aggressive.

Not sitting around counting bugs and leaves.

"I think we need to split up," Vost told Philippon one night back at the landing craft, in the galley. They both sat at one of the galley's tables.

Philippon shot him a look.

"And why would you say something like that?" she said.

"This planet needs to be explored . . . as quickly and efficiently as possible. We can't do that with you people camping out for days every three feet, 'running your numbers.'"

Philippon got to her feet. "You do know that we lost the first expedition to just such a plan of attack, don't you?" she said, looking to Vost, who remained seated at the table.

Vost shot her a clear look of disdain.

"Casualties are accepted during exploration, Doctor. It's the cost of doing business. And we really—"

"The whole point of this excursion, *Lieutenant*," Philippon said, "was to be more careful . . . more thoughtful . . . more *thorough*. The point of this expedition—"

"The point of this expedition, *Doctor*, is a military operation! You people are merely along for the ride!" Vost shot to his feet.

Philippon uttered a short, strained chuckle, shook her head once, and began to say something, when she clipped it short.

"Until things are taken over and controlled, the lands sanitized, this is a military operation with an attached scientific contingent," Vost continued. "That is how these things are done and the sooner you understand this, the better off we'll all be."

"It most certainly is *not*," Philippon said sharply. "This is a joint, *scientific* exploration, where upon the military is merely providing protec—"

"*Negative!*" Vost said, slamming a hand down to the table. "I don't know where you got your information or what you were fed up there before heading down here, but that is not how these things work, and I am tired of my squad and me babysitting to a bunch of tablet-clicking lab geeks! We are here to explore and take over this planet, so that *Humanity* can survive! *Humanity!* At this rate it'll be our great-great grandchildren who affect planetfall! Once we have taken control of this planet, you and your fellow lab rats can do as you please. But starting tomorrow we're going to do this right and push forward . . . and you and your . . . *brainboxes* can keep up or not—we're done, here!"

Vost smartly about-faced and stormed out of the room—or at least attempted to. He was met by the rest of the scientific contingent standing at the entrance to the room. Vost came to an abrupt halt.

"What's going on here?" Beaker asked, looking between Vost and Philippon.

"I'm taking control of this little outing, like I should have from the start," Vost said.

"Wait a minute—this is a joint ventu—" Thomas said.

"Wrong!" Vost interrupted. "That was never th—"

"But it *was*," I was there from the beginning," Philippon said.

"There were agreements beforehand—*protocols*," Vost said.

"Agreements? What are you talking about?" Philippon said.

At this point the rest of the troops caught up to the scientists, and everyone spilled into the galley.

"What agreements... what 'protocols'" Singer asked. "You mean where the military always takes things over and kills everything in its path?"

The sergeant took issue with Singer and made his feelings known by throwing a haymaker. Singer took it squarely on the jaw. There was an audible crack and Singer crumpled to the floor.

Vost and the rest of the uniforms picked their targets.

Attacked.

Fists flew. Chairs. Coffee mugs. Rage.

Blood spattered walls.

Things... both animate and inanimate... broke.

Philippon was on Vost before she'd realized what she was doing. In the back of her mind was the oh-so-distant thought that she would have so much rather preferred to have jumped Vost in a far different way, but the situation being what it was, that was most likely never going to happen. Instead, Philippon threw the first punch in her entire life, the rage inside her taking on such huge proportions that she had never felt before. She didn't know what was happening, knew it wasn't good, that it should be stopped—now—before things went too far... but felt totally helpless at controlling her escalating rage.

She wanted to rip him apart with her bare hands.

Vost easily absorbed her meager attempt at a punch. Wide-eyed that she'd even tried such a stunt, his expression quickly changed to one of utter hatred and disdain for her and her kind.

Scientists!

He lunged at her like a starving cheetah. They both fell to the floor, and Vost immediately began to pummel her with hardened, military-trained fists. Philippon did her best to deflect, but Vost fists continued to land and land and land upon her once beautiful face...

Military campaign!

Scientific exploration!

They all had their ways with each other, tooth, nail, and knuckle . . . .

Outside their landing craft, a storm had abruptly developed.

Embedded within this storm was, what on Earth would have been called, tornados.

Embedded within said tornados were horrendous wind speeds.

One of the tornados had quickly developed into a two-mile-wide swath that headed directly for the landing craft. The *Renaissance* had seen this development and quickly hailed the landing party, but everyone was far too busy beating the living shisst out of each other to be bothered.

The after-action report by the *Renaissance* crew had been that wind speeds had topped 500 miles per hour. Through uploads from the landing party's data-gathering equipment during the storm, *Renaissance* analysts had also determined that both people and equipment had been tossed seven miles up into the planet's atmosphere . . . when the storm had just as suddenly terminated.

FRACTAL THEORY
Year 2073 C. E.

Trees swayed and sung to warm and gentle winds that quickly grew in intensity. Rocks tall, small, and everywhere in-between were scattered far and wide. Piled upon each other. Grasses and flowers carpeted the open spaces and swayed and fluttered with the wind's passage.

(. . . *an* . . . *tici* . . . *pa* . . . *tion* . . .)
Something . . .
(. . . *anticipation* . . .)
Popped, fizzled, and *sparked!*
(ANTICIPATION)
Everywhere jetted vibrant and frenzied surges of energy—bangs and blasts and bursts—ecstatic eruptions of multidimensional fireworks and popcorn!
The rocks! The trees! The dirt!
Atomic structures! . . . vibrated! . . . rearranged! . . . transmogrified!

Things . . . *shifted*—
Wildly folding and unfolding, multicolored energies wrinkled and wove throughout the air and earth!

!ANTICIPATION!

Suddenly geometrical extrusions of all manner of form and dimension burst forth into the field and its airspace . . . shapes danced and transformed and coalesced . . . fused . . .

Spiraled and expanded!

Traced and displayed patterns from unseen blueprints . . . slid among and about each other like playful children . . .

Vivid and kinetic angles, planes, and enclosures . . . long, short, and otherwise . . . filled with stars and galaxies and space dust . . . formed from and throughout each other, expansively ballooning into existence only to silently explode and reform into every imaginable shape, value, and dimension . . . then clatter and bump and knock up against each other like building blocks moved by creative, unseen hands . . .

Within these multifaceted articulations even smaller crystalized geometrical arrangements continued to erupt, conform, and multiply, as if they were rampant viral propagations . . . spinning and tumbling . . . flying and landing and bouncing. Endless and dizzying, kaleidoscopic architectures arranged and rearranged like the most maddening and intricate of sentient schizophrenic puzzle boxes.

Mysterious and identifiable rectangles and triangles and polygons formed into walls and doors and ceilings and windows. Expanded outward, some inward. Windows in corners and floors. Doors and ceilings as ceilings and doors.

Gradually the explosion of geometry slowed until—

Whole buildings balanced on a single corner.

Erupted out of another's structure.

Upside down and inside out.

Faces and edges and bases and vertices.

Angles and planes.

Pointing this way and that. That way and this.

And the trees swayed, the leaves fluttered, the needles trembled. A warm and wonderful sun beat down upon it all, heating the winds that explored the now pristine structures that protruded and rearranged and formed into every possible architecture...

Among this town of the misshapen and confused—

Assembled a house.

Complete, upright, *and* correct.

A *home*.

And this home was composed of beautiful clapboard, painted a light shade of blue with darker blue trim and accents. Quaint window dressings displayed from inside perfectly formed panes.

Colorful flowers extruded from a thoughtfully arranged flower bed.

Mature maple trees in the front, two oaks in the back, their leaves stirring and shimmering in the warm, gentle breezes of bright afternoon sunlight.

The scent of Springtime.

The home was complete with a lush and manicured front and rear lawn. A white picket fence. Edged sidewalk.

A mailbox... within which were a utility statement, two personal letters, and a sweepstakes

(*You've won!*)

notification.

From a door—open and beckoning—wafted the aroma of just-made coffee and coffee cake.

But unique it was not... for this one-of-many-now-such-beautiful-suburban-homes occupied space and time in a mature neighborhood of other such beautiful homes fanning out behind it, all the fractal structures with their beautifully manicured lawns all similarly falling into place.

If one were here... and looked hard enough... one might see a thirty-something woman in a bathrobe, hair slightly disheveled, coming out the front door to fetch a newspaper that rested at the bottom of the driveway, down... by a street.

Or one might spy a hypothetical couple out walking their hypothetical dog, waving to another hypothetical neighbor already out and trimming his hypothetical yard, weeding his hypothetical flower bed. Or yet another neighbor taking her hypothetical coffee outside, sitting on her hypothetical porch and smiling and waving to all who hypothetically passed by.

If one looked hard enough.

And one was there.

Which, of course, one was not—

Except for a lone, stalwart fellow, who observed the entire genesis and went by the name of "Beck."

CREEPY TOWN
Year 2073 C. E.

1

Beck cautiously entered the empty, windswept town by way of the concrete sidewalk that began or ended at his feet. There was a high . . . expectation . . . in the air. The sun shone brightly and beat down upon his face and all the homes and various other structures. Beck felt their radiated heat, inhaled the fresh scent of warming wood and paint, and for but a moment . . . nostalgia . . . an intense wave of it . . . he was back on Earth . . . in the mid-western town of Williamsport, Indiana . . .

His hometown.

Yes . . . he had . . . ever so briefly . . . thought about Williamsport, as he stood and watched the absurdity of all that had unfolded before him, mere moments ago.

He paused. Took in all that was before him. Yes, if he didn't know any better, that's exactly where he'd swear he was right this moment:

in the Earth town of Williamsport, Indiana . . . a place he hadn't returned to since he'd left high school.

He closed his eyes. Analyzed his system settings and accumulated data up to this point.

No . . . all indicators pointed to . . . that he was, indeed, on a new, unnamed planet, standing at the edge of a brand-new, extraterrestrially created suburban setting that exactly mirrored his hometown—as he'd remembered it.

He opened his eyes.

Beck looked down to the concrete sidewalk (for yes, his scans told him, it really was concrete). It had also created itself during that metaphysical construction and had literally materialized up to his feet.

Apparently, his presence had not gone unnoticed.

Beck continued into the suburban domain. Though none of his scans indicated any other soul in the area, he definitely felt . . . observed.

The hum of air-conditioning units kicked on and off around him.

Sprinklers went off on the lawns at each of the . . . dwellings?—*were any of these buildings inhabited as well?*—with a powerful *sh-shhh-shhhhhhh!*

He inhaled the moisture and grass scents in the air. Just like they had smelled back on Earth.

He recorded everything.

He also picked up coffee and coffee cake aromas emanating from a house off to his immediate right. It was a beautiful, single-storied, single-family dwelling, just like the one he'd grown up in, complete with picket fence, a mailbox, and mature maples in the front yard.

In front of the home was a colorful flower garden beneath simple, unadorned windows, composed of what looked to be multicolored zinnias that stretched out in both directions along the front of the house. The term "curb appeal" entered his mind—*had he thought of that phrase, or had something else planted that in his head?*

The sprinkler systems quietly watered the lawn, with just a touch of water getting onto the concrete driveway and sidewalk. Now *that* was a feat of advanced engineering.

Beck walked over to
(*his?*)
the home's mailbox. Opened it.

Mail!

He pulled out the mail. Bent over and peered inside the box. Nothing else.

He stared into the metal box a moment longer. Swore he glimpsed just a few flashing points of light popping on and off inside it that quickly faded away.

He reached his free hand all the way inside the mailbox, until it hit the rear of the receptacle. Banged his hand around the inside the box before removing it. Closed the hatch.

Flipping through the mail he found mostly junk, addressed to "Resident." Flyers for odd jobs, lawn mowing, and a several-page flyer for a supermarket named "Martin's Super Market." Then he felt one more item stuck to the rear of the Martin's flyer, and with his fingers peeled it free from the paper's static cling. It was a "Welcome to the Neighborhood!" postcard. The postcard was high quality and sported a photograph of a neighborhood on the card. *This* neighborhood. He looked up and verified. It was the very same neighborhood he stood in, from the exact perspective where he presently stood. He looked back down to the card. Flipped it over.

It was addressed to "Beck," at 21 Elm Street. His childhood address.

He again looked to the house.

"21" was stamped on the outside of the house to the right of the door. That hadn't been there moments before.

Looked to the street sign: "Elm."

If Beck had been one prone to smiling, he would have done so now.

He returned the card to the pile and continued onto the 21 Elm Street driveway.

A rolled-up newspaper.

He picked it
(*Review Republican*)
up and continued toward the house.

As he approached the front stoop, he observed the flower bed. Inhaled the redwood mulch. Fresh, pungent. Its color bright and new.

He looked to the windows. They sported matching window boxes of still more brightly colored zinnias.

Those hadn't been there, either, when he'd first sighted the house. Nice touch.

At the front door, he continued to inhale the fresh-brewed coffee and coffee cake wafting outside. The human part of him, he surprisingly noted, wanted both, and his mouth watered—which he quickly put a stop to. He also analyzed that the aroma had increased its intense, aromatic assault.

It was as if whomever had created all this had *really* wanted him inside.

Examining the front door, Beck found it to be "tastefully ornate, yet functional," his database informed. A thick and heavy wood-and-glass door. The glass was etched. A doorbell button was off to the right.

Contemporarily designed porch lamps flanked the door.

There was quite a detailed knowledge of Earth architecture and design. No detail was spared.

Beck rang the doorbell. It
(*empty foyer*)
(*empty hallways*)
(*empty kitchen*)
reverberated inside.
Nothing.
He opened the door and stepped across the threshold.

2

The inside of the house was bright and cheery, just as he half remembered it. Most of his early life and memories were vague, partial, or outright lost. Destroyed. Came with the cyborg life.

Beck closed the door behind him and deliberately set down the mail and paper on an end table there without looking.

The aroma of coffee and cake was powerful. He looked for the kitchen. Just up ahead.

He thoughtfully made his way toward the kitchen, noting everything about the house's interior . . . from the neutral carpeting and walls to the traditionally designed furniture décor that, according to his database anyway, was still the latest style when they'd left Earth.

In the kitchen he found a family-sized coffee pot sitting on the counter, fully made, but some of its contents gone. Off to his right, on the kitchen table, he found three table settings, all with filled cups of coffee and plates of coffee cake . . . and accompanying utensils.

Two of the coffee mugs and cake appeared partially consumed, their utensils resting on their plates.

The third was untouched.

His.

Beck approached the table. Examined the table settings.

Dipped his finger into the unused coffee.

One-hundred-and-forty degrees, his sensor told him. Touched the coffee cake. Forty degrees. Yes, some distant memory hinted, he seemed to like his crumb cakes cold. Beck picked up the cake and took a closer look . . . bit into it. The powerful aroma of the cinnamon filled his olfactories as he bit down, stimulating a flood of partial, fractured memories. Reminded him of his grandmother—

Flour, baking powder, salt, sugar, vanilla, cinnamon.

Indeed, real coffee cake.

Cake still in hand, Beck gestured a toast into the air with it, before setting it back down on the table. He then brought the unused coffee up to his nose and inhaled deeply. Took a sip. With its light-to-medium body and a berry-like aftertaste, it sampled exactly like Earth's Ethiopian *Yirgacheffee* coffee. Wow. Hadn't had *Yirgacheffee* coffee since his last deployment to the African Continent—hadn't thought about that in a while . . . .

Beck performed another toast into the air with the coffee, as he also returned it to the table.

Beck went over to the refrigerator. Opened it.

Stocked with everything one would expect: milk, eggs, butter, and cheese. Peppers, celery, what looked like red-leaf lettuce . . .

Closed the door and went over to the sink. Turned on the hot water.

Hot water issued forth from the faucet.

Switched to cold water.

Cold water issued forth from the faucet.

Beck shut off the water and turned back around to face the direction he'd entered.

Scanned the rest of the house for any presences. None.

This was a perfectly normal dwelling . . . except for the lack of people.

Yet he still felt observed.

An idea grabbed him, and he went into the living room. A large-screened television adorned a wall. He looked to the two recliners and couch and spotted the remotes. He grabbed one and turned on the TV. It came to life and showed . . . himself standing in the middle of the living room with the remote control pointed at the TV.

Here, Beck did chuckle. Allowed himself a grin.

He looked for the camera, scanned for it, but found nothing.

"Well played," he said as he turned off the TV, set down the remote, and left the room.

Beck explored the rest of the house and found all one would reasonably expect for a single-family, suburban dwelling. All detail was accurate and substantial. Nothing was overlooked—from the dental floss and toothbrushes (three) to the artwork hanging on the walls. Landscapes and late 20th-century Earth impressionism.

Beck returned to the front door. There he picked up the sweepstakes mailer and took a bite from it.

Analysis told him it was simply newsprint and ink.

Of course it was.

He left the house.

3

Beck walked the sidewalk under a brightly lit afternoon sky with only a few clouds drifting overhead. Shisst, but if he hadn't known any better, he would have thought he was back on Earth, and if he was honest with himself, it was growing increasingly difficult reminding himself he'd seen this suburbia literally materialize out of thin air, on a planet that was not Earth. Even the air temperature was a comfortable 77 degrees and composed of a very Earth-like

70.02% nitrogen, 29.05% oxygen, 0.90% argon, 0.02% carbon dioxide. The sun was just about as bright, but definitely filled more of the sky than the Earth's sun did. The terrain was pretty much the same. The breezes were cool, if somewhat wailing at times, whistling and howling between the empty structures surrounding him like stationary ghosts.

But all of this had been literally constructed out of thin air.

And while observing its creation he had detected no presence . . . of anyone or any*thing.*

It was unlike anything Beck had ever seen before.

He continued his 360-degree scanning as he explored the neighborhood, visually observing the houses . . . their sprinkler systems . . . their mailboxes . . . their yards. It was just him . . . no one else . . . no people, real or manufactured.

He went to the closest mailbox. Opened it. The exact same mail—with the appropriate address inscribed—with one difference.

No post card addressed to him. No post card at all.

He returned the mail to the mailbox and closed it.

Went across the street and checked another one.

Same thing.

It was safe to assume other mailboxes were the same.

As were the insides of each house . . . coffee brewing . . . crumb cake awaiting. Two place settings (his additional place setting had to be unique, as evidenced by the extra post card).

As Beck closed the mailbox and turned, his scanners alarmed him with an object-of-interest, just as he also sighted said object. He zoomed in on the target.

Hurried toward it.

A car.

Parked in front of a house.

And beside that car—which looked like a Buick LaCrosse—

A person!

And it looked just like him!

Frozen in the movement of opening the driver-side door.

What the shisst was going on? How was this possible? Think of something and it was instantly materialized?

Was "it" playing with him? And why?

Beck examined the effigy.

It looked perfectly real, exactly like him, right down the eyelashes and scars. If he weren't the cyborg he was he would have been totally unnerved by what silently—creepily—stood before him.

He touched it.

The "flesh" reacted and felt exactly as flesh. Beck scraped off a sample of the "skin" and ingested it.

Analysis was unable to determine what the substance was, but it was not human flesh.

A strong gust of wind kicked up.

A change of weather was in the air.

Beck patted the effigy down. Found it contained objects in its pockets.

A handheld mini-computer/tablet, called a "handy," a wallet, various multi-tools, along with several samples of flora he had just collected in the past couple of days—exactly what he presently carried on him.

No . . . this was not creepy at all.

Beck opened the wallet and scanned and recorded the contents. An identity card for one "Beck," born 2033 (40 years old), six-foot-three, 230 pounds (his cyborg internals made him heavier than he appeared), gray eyes, white-blond hair.

It appeared who-or-whatever created this place had a sense of humor. His age was actually—

Thirty. The date on the driver's license now read 2043.

Beck immediately twisted in place. Shot out another scan to his surroundings. Looked up into the sky.

Nothing.

Immediate modifications. This was utterly insa—

The effigy no longer stood before him but sat inside the car.

Beck looked to his hands.

Gone was the handy and everything else he'd been examining.

He splayed open empty hands before him. Looked to them in disbelief.

Beck peered inside the car. Saw himself . . . each hand at ten and two on the wheel, eyes forward.

He stood back up and looked behind him.
All the sprinklers were off.
Newspapers... gone from the driveways.
No doubt he would find all the mail would also be gone, too, as well as the coffee and coffee ca—
Beck's ears popped.
The atmosphere had suddenly shifted.
The air... felt different. Urgently different.
He hurried back to the last mailbox he had checked—opened it.
No mail.
Shot a look to the Beck-effigy in the car.
Gone.
But down the street about five hundred feet—there it was! Motionless.
He blinked, tried to zoom in and found that the car and effigy were still *farther* down the street.
He looked back to the town around him, and now found *similar effigies materializing in and out of existence all around him*. One moment solid and walking dogs or trimming flowers... and the next— *gone*. The entire neighborhood was now alive with ghostly beings flashing in and out of existence.
Some casted him direct looks.
Some smiles of acknowledgement.
Some waved.
And the light... subdued... reddening... the sun was going down.
The entire environment felt suddenly claustrophobic.
Beck's scanners alerted him to a disturbance in the electromagnetic field.
Things were changing.
Alright... you had your fun... now it's time for you to go...
There was clearly a timeline associated with this place, and his instincts told him that if he wanted to survive, he had better move ... or he might end up wherever this place was going and had come from, and while that in itself was also fascinating and warranted legitimate exploration, he had his current mission objectives to adhere to.

Beck quickly hoofed it down the street, toward where his effigy had taken off to . . . but had subsequently disappeared.

The light continued to grow more dim, and without the benefit of additional cloud cover . . . the temperature dropped, the winds increased.

He began to feel . . . weird . . . slight vertigo. Like portions of him were beginning to feel . . . expanded . . . pulled apart . . .

He broke into a run.

Visually scanning as he ran, Beck observed multicolored, pinpoint lights popping on and off all around him, just as he'd seen at this place's materialization and inside that mailbox.

Things began to feel constricted . . . powered down . . . transparent. Up ahead everything appeared warped, narrow, like a contracting tunnel. He looked behind him and saw that same narrowing . . . closing in on itself. Within it, he observed wailing winds and a . . . magnetic? . . . spiral forming around the inner envelope of this little suburban diorama, the tiny bursts of firecracker-and-popcorn lights grew in intensity. His sensors indicated an extra magnetic density when he directed his scans toward his exit.

He burst into an all-out sprint.

Felt as though he were running on a sponge . . . was totally immersed into deep water . . .

His entire body and mind continued to feel as if he was being pulled apart at the seams . . . the subatomic level . . . tugged at from all directions.

Up ahead . . . his exit . . . narrowing.

Beck added an extra surge to his sprint—

As he neared the ever-narrowing exit, he launched into the air . . . and dove through (which felt cartoonishly slow motion) the swiftly reducing "hole"—

And landed, rolled, and twisted, immediately springing back to his feet as he spun back around to face the direction from which he'd come. He hopped backward two steps until he regained his balance, all the while keeping his eyes trained (and recording) on the exit hole he'd just leapt through.

The hole ever so neatly closed up upon itself.

The entire creepy suburban layout became enveloped in a kind of magnetic fog and blinking stars.

All of Beck's sensors went wild and no longer detected or produced anything usable.

Everything felt . . . normal . . . again.

In the area where the ghostly suburban development had been, now were stars and lights that quickly flattened out . . . contracted . . . expanded . . . again contracted . . .

And were gone.

All of it.

The houses, the mailboxes, the car and its Beck effigy.

Strong winds whipped the once-again barren plains he had first happened upon. Dust and debris kicked up about his face and body. He actually had to steady himself against the gale-force blast of what felt like a momentarily formed vacuum.

Beck stood there a moment longer. Recorded everything. Walked back over to where everything had . . . *been?*

Nothing.

No residual magnetism.

No houses, no air-conditioners.

Just dirt, prairie grass, and trees.

And wind. Lots of wind.

Beck straightened out his pack, his attire, and checked his person to make sure he had not lost anything.

Then he turned around and continued on his journey.

THE OTHER SIDE OF THE TREES
Year 2073 C. E.

1

"I still don't get it," Rick Cushing, *Renaissance* Mission Commander, said, as both he and Aaron Prichard, second in command, looked out across the expanse of grasslands that lay before them.

Cushing and Pritchard were both rugged and lean veterans of terrestrial and lunar exploration, back in the Earth days, both clocking in at six-feet-three and -two, respectively. Wiry tough. Behind them was their encampment, and behind that the distant rolling hills of this new world. To the other side of this field stood a heavily wooded aspen-like growth.

The third of the initial three exploration parties stood, fanned out within the tall grasses at about 6,500-feet in elevation. The rest of the landing party consisted of Dr. Thiemo Bellenger, Geo Scientist, Dr. Hisa Takata, Exobiologist, Dr. Agnete Marken, theoretical physicist, and Lieutenant Emily Harper, Security, with three of her subordinates.

"Where did all this come from? How . . . . "

The sun warmed and a gentle breeze kissed the landing party's faces. While no insects flitted about the oxygen-nitrogen mix, it was filled with a white, cottony fluff that drifted everywhere. Pritchard and Cushing closed their eyes and inhaled deeply, as did the other members of the team at various times. The security detail continued to visually scan their surroundings with binoculars and lidar, weapons at the ready.

Cushing slowly shook his head. "Damn, but this feels so good! Breathing actual fresh air and having feet on real planetary dirt! It's as if we're living a dream," he said, "a livable, uninhabited system, breathable air, drinkable water—and it even has its own moon! It's like we found an alternate Earth!"

"Do you think we actually went backward or forward in time and this actually is Earth?" Pritchard asked.

Dr. Marken was the first to speak up and said, "While it is theoretically possible . . . no. This planet's orbit and Earth's orbit are distinctly different from each other."

Pritchard and Cushing both nodded to Dr. Marken.

"But," Pritchard said quietly to Cushing, "there's also an extra . . . I don't know—uneasiness? . . . to everything . . . an extra *energy*. As nervous as I feel . . . I also feel *excited*."

"I feel it, too," Cushing said, still eyeing the field before them.

"We all do, sir," Harper said, coming upon them from behind. She observantly paced about the landing party.

"Exhilaration. It's in the very air!" Cushing said, "I don't know if it's because we've been inhaling recycled air for as long as we have, or something else . . . but even my skin feels . . . *electrified*."

(*Welcome* . . .)

Cushing turned to Pritchard.

"Excuse me?" Cushing said.

"What?" Pritchard said.

"I thought you'd said something."

"No . . . but—"

"You heard that too?"

"I heard something."

As the rest of their party milled around, Pritchard and Cushing went off by themselves a little way from the rest of the group.

"It's almost like—"

"Voices. Yeah. *Whispering*. You can barely make them out," Pritchard said.

"Like . . . when you focus on them . . . whatever they are . . . they can't be focused *upon* . . . but when you're distracted . . . not focusing on them . . . they start back up again."

"Yeah."

They both stood quietly, listening.

Pritchard flicked on and adjusted his recorder and said, "Maybe we can pick them up."

"You ever watch *The Twilight Zone*?" Cushing said, again looking around and taking the place in.

Pritchard chuckled. "Of course!" he said, continuing to adjust his instrument.

"I'm half expecting to hear whooping and hollering from over that ridge, over there, any minute now," Cushing said, pointing, "and Indians—*Indians*—screaming down out of those hills—on horseback."

"Native Americans, sir," Pritchard said flatly, looking up, "at least back on Earth." He looked around nervously. "Now, you're *really* creeping me out."

Pritchard returned his attention to his instruments, but cast several furtive glances up to the distant ridge alongside them, while Cushing directed his attention to their base camp. Their landing craft and several domed modules resided just yards behind them, situated among the gently tossing shin-high prairie grasses that looked like Colorado's or Montana's Buffalo or Bluestem grasses.

Cushing spun around, stepped forward, and said, "All right, people—let's go see what's on the other side of these trees!" The detail followed. Uniforms and boots *shushed* through the tall grasses.

Except for the security contingent, the rest of the party smiled and chuckled to themselves as they made their way forward. With huge, playful smiles, they alternated between their instruments and running their hands through the tall grasses, positively giddy at the seeds and chaff that deposited upon their gloved hands and clothes. Showed their hands to each other in child-like amusement.

Life!

Just like Earth!

Can't be real!

Continually checked their handhelds.

No life beyond vegetation and trees. Themselves. Not even insects.

Besides solid ground, breathable air, and comfortable temperatures, the ship's scanners hadn't picked up on any of this topography upon entering orbit.

Again the scientists scanned with their instruments. Exchanged surprised looks with each other. None of the usual suspects that came with a typical Earth-like setting were being detected. This all looked like a setting—one waiting to be populated with its principal characters . . .

A *setting* . . . that maddeningly messed with perceptions. Pulled and tugged and upended the psyches and senses of place. Everywhere they looked they swore they'd see *something*—anything—they'd *expected* to see . . . but everywhere . . . nothing.

Ghosts . . . where there should be rabbits and birds and squirrels! Deer!

Ghosts . . . where there should be bugs and insects! Blackflies and mosquitoes!

Ghosts . . . where there should be animal noises and wood pecking and buzzing bees and butterflies!

Another gentle breeze kissed their faces as they reached the tree line, followed by a momentary blast of a stronger gust.

Several members of the party visibly shivered, including Hisa.

"Okay," Thiemo said, "that was weird."

"*Kuso*," Hisa said, "Man, I just get the oddest feeling that this place *loves* us . . . that the air—the breeze—isn't just . . . blowing by . . . that it's actually *kissing* us . . caressing our skin . . . *hugging* us!"

"I mean, come on," Cushing said without looking to anyone in particular, "tell me it's not just me—aren't all of your minds just as confused and muddled and excited as mine? Don't the rest of you also feel the palpable *excitement* I'm feeling—as if you're walking through a magnetic field of *joy*?"

"Yes!" Agnete said. "That's a positively creative way of putting it!"

"Of course!" Thiemo said.

Hisa vigorously nodded and said, "I know—it's crazy, right?"

Harper and her Security team remained quiet, but were all smiles as they eyed each other.

"I feel like," Cushing continued, "I'm asleep and about to wake up any minute. Or am awake and about to nod off any minute. But in either case I feel like a kid at Christmas!"

Excited, smiling, and antsy down to the last person, they entered the extraterrestrial woodland.

It smelled, sounded, and felt just like any forest they'd ever walked through back on Earth: musty, woodsy, moist, and warm. Among the aspens was the heavy and relaxing scent of evergreens. The spring of a thickly carpeted forest floor beneath their feet, composed of the usual leaves, branches, and bark.

"You know," Hisa said, inhaling deeply, "to be able to smell what we're smelling . . . for the ground to be as it appears to be . . . there have to be organisms in it—*bacteria*."

They looked to each other.

"*Organisms* . . . ," Cushing repeated.

Cushing and Hisa immediately dropped to their knees and dug gloved hands into the forest-floor detritus. The four-person security detail fanned out, maintaining their vigilance.

"So, what do we start calling *this*," Cushing asked, digging his gloved fingers through what looked like rich, well-sweetened soil, showing it to Hisa, "this 'dirt,' this . . . planet? 'Earth'?"

"How . . . *how can this be*? Are there worms? Microorganisms?" Pritchard asked.

"You might just as well ask how can you fly between the stars in a broken spaceship and find an Earth-like planet," Cushing said.

"Maybe they're life forms the likes of which we have no idea," Hisa said.

"You believe that?" Pritchard said.

"No!" all three said in unison.

Hisa whipped off her gloves and dug her bare hands into the soil. "Of course not! This all looks and feels *just like Earth—kuso!*" Hisa again said, "but this soil feels unnervingly good!"

"It looks like Earth dirt to me!" Thiemo said, poking around in the ground beside them.

"That it does!" Cushing said, following suit and taking off his gloves.

"This all looks exactly like home," Thiemo continued, "It's all instantly and immediately relatable! I'm all for calling this 'earth' . . . moist, and dark, and rich . . . just like back on Earth. Soil. *Loam*. Implies everything that goes along with 'dirt' that does so back on Earth. There really is no convention nor definitive reason for why back on Earth, so we should also call our dirt 'earth.'"

They returned to their feet, brushing the dirt from their hands.

"Life," Cushing said absentmindedly, "always finds a way."

Hisa began bagging samples, but Cushing brought a hand to his head and massaged his temples. "Geez, I feel so frigging *weird*."

"Me, too," Pritchard said, "but isn't it *wonderful?*"

They looked to each other and chuckled.

Cushing dumped the rest of his hand-held dirt back to the earth.

"Yes, *earth*," Cushing said under his breath to himself, as he wiped the soil remnants from his hands.

The team inspected and took recordings and pictures of everything—trees, bushes, rocks. Everything looked identical to that which existed on Earth. Maples and pines and spruces and birch . . . all of it . . . some with just a minor extra texture or detail here and there . . . but it all looked exactly like life back on Earth.

Cushing spotted what appeared to be a deadfall silver paper birch and rushed over to it.

"Hisa!"

Hisa and Pritchard hurried over. They looked down to the decaying birch.

Decaying.

Hisa was already on it. She scanned the log with her instruments.

"The scanner's picking up microorganisms!" Hisa said, looking to Cushing and Pritchard with unbridled enthusiasm. "This is absolutely insane!"

Hisa put aside her recorder and fished out a knife from one of her many pockets. She dug into the log with the knife's tip. Wedged something out of the gashes. She came to her feet and showed her find to Cushing and Pritchard.

There, among the moist and decaying pieces of bark of what easily appeared to be a silver birch . . . were *insects. Larvae.*

Agnete Marken, who was on her knees and also digging about in the dirt, called out the Hisa and said, "Hisa—*earthworms!*" From one hand dangled a representative of the Phylum *Annelida.*

"Okay," Cushing said, "so there *is* more complex life down here!"

"So, the very first planet we find is a livable, Earth-type Eden," Pritchard said, looking about them. "It was just like the guy said—this is too good to be true . . . I feel as if we're all in a *dream—*"

"Or a nightmare," Cushing said. "Or—"

Pritchard looked to him.

The *space sickness.*

Holcomb's Syndrome.

"Well, somebody has to say it," Cushing said. "Somebody . . . something . . . could very well be messing with us—Holcomb's, for crying out loud—we could all still be asleep aboard the *Renaissance,* still screaming between the endless passages between the stars."

They both looked to each other for a moment.

Pritchard smacked Cushing in the arm.

"Feel that?" he said.

"Yeah," Cushing said, recoiling and massaging his arm.

"Well, I much prefer *this* nightmare to your shisst," Pritchard said, reaching for his hand held. He took additional scans of the woods.

Cushing said, "Holcomb's aside—and speaking totally *un*scientifically—if this planet can seemingly create earthworms and bugs . . . is it that far of a leap to create more complex life—a human? Or whatever passes for humans in this neck of the universe?"

"Our whole neo-scientific *weltanschauung* emphatically states, yes, but over many, many millennia," Pritchard said, as he paced about him taking measurements. He motioned to a certain direction. "I'm getting some curious readings over there," he said, pointing.

"How so?" Cushing said, looking to where Pritchard directed.

"Life forms."

The two men stared at each other.

"Let's check it out," Cushing said.

2

The journey to this world had been fraught with human frailty—hardships, isolation, death.

The end of all they knew.

Soon after launch into Faster-Than-Light travel, their FTL drive (also known as their main drive) had failed, leaving only sub-light speed, and where they had ended up had been among a whole different field of stars. The reinsertion of Earth politics and power plays, and all that went along with that (murder . . . murder investigation . . . change of mission command) . . . had begun to take over life on the *Renaissance,* along with the escalation of the space sickness. The distrust of perceptions. Yet the *Renaissance* pushed ever onward and had happened upon this planet—just as had been foretold. A planet slightly smaller than Earth. A planet whose initial surveys had registered lots of rock. No vegetation. No water. But the closer they got to the planet the more that was picked up—atmosphere . . . Earth type . . . water . . . liquid. And there were several other planets detected in orbit about the yellow dwarf.

Such joy and partying spread among the crew!

The stars out here were different.

And the star about which this planet orbited was younger than Earth's sun. With the failure of the *Renaissance's* main drive, they had been summarily dumped out into the unknown depths of space . . . interstellar, interplanetary, or otherwise . . . but still had discovered a habitable, breathable planet upon which they could *land.*

Explore.

(claim)

But the closer they'd approached . . . and especially having now made orbit about . . . their instruments had shown . . . even further pushing all sense of incredulity more to the right . . . *trees*—

Forests!

Temperate zones!

Tropics!

It was as if this planet had been—or was being—made to order.

And it spooked the hell out of them.

Their other options?

The stars.

Lots and lots of empty space.

As far as they were concerned, they had nowhere else *to* return to. Even if they'd wanted to return home, they had no idea where to begin. In what direction to orient. When they had come out of their electrogravitic travel, it had been as if they'd been summarily dumped into the deepest, most farthest reaches of space—blindfolded.

Yet they had this brilliant and beautiful Earth-like jewel before them!

A jewel that orbited a beautiful Earth-like yellow-dwarf!

The *bluest* blues! *The* most inviting *greens!*

Don't look a

(. . . *planet* . . .)

gift horse in the mouth?

Do look it in the mouth—and kiss it full on!

In Earth-German, "gift" translates to "poison."

But scans of the planet found no such "poisons." Just rich, lush vegetation. The purest water ever.

And the air?

Unadulterated! Untainted! Fresh, clean, *breathable!* Slightly different in its composition, but close enough for . . . "Earth."

And now, as they crawled upon its surface like the insects they'd just discovered, they'd also discovered micro-*organisms*.

Within the forest they'd come upon several streams of burbling water, and in that water observed *species of fish* they'd never seen before, but were clearly *fish*.

Amphibian life!

Then . . . finally . . . *bird* life! Even distant wood pecking!

They inhaled the powerful and fresh broadleaf and resinous evergreen scents that continued to hold them in a stupor-like trance as they advanced through the woods . . . until they again found themselves standing in another clearing. Each team member emerged and stood transfixed . . . inhaling deeply of another, exciting, and pungent scent. Something they also recognized. And all throughout the air!

Chirping and playfully darting everywhere!

Welcome to the neighborhood!

Yes, they again stood in an open field, only this time native grasses were not up to their shins and knees, because . . .

It'd been mowed.

They stood on the edge of what would be, back on Earth, a mowed and neatly manicured *playing field.*

And that new, heavily pungent aroma?

Cut grass.

But it wasn't the neatly mowed field before them they immediately noticed upon exit of the trees. No, that had been a distant second. What they had first noticed, and which had brought them to a dead stop were the buildings.

Houses.

Suburban homes!

Neatly laid out before them in an organized and well-planned suburban setting.

"*There's* your *Twilight Zone,*" Pritchard said.

"*Twilight Zone?*" Harper said, "haven't you both read—"

"*The Martian Chronicles,*" Cushing and Pritchard both said.

The party entered the asphalt circle at the end of the closest street of the block of perfectly built homes, in their perfectly manicured lots. Air-conditioning units kicked off and on perfectly around them.

"I don't like this," Harper said in a low, measured, voice to Cushing, head and weaponry constantly swiveling. "I mean . . . I *dooo* . . . but I *dooon't*—"

"Good. Keep thinking that way," Cushing instructed.

Pritchard knelt down to the circle and felt what looked entirely like asphalt.

"Well, not only does it look like asphalt and smell like asphalt, but it also feels like it," he said. "Do you still feel like you're dreaming?" he asked Cushing.

Cushing nodded. "You?"

Pritchard nodded. "This whole planet is fricking messing with my head."

"And the whole Ray Bradbury thing?" Cushing asked.

"Well, it's all theoretically possible other civilizations *exist*—I mean look at us. From their point of view, *we* came from the stars. We'd just never detected any of... *this*... from the ship."

"That's one of a million questions I'm running through my head right now," Cushing said, "I'm really starting to get the feeling this planet is reading our minds."

"And that would be *Star Trek*," Pritchard said, "but we'll never learn anything by just standing here."

Cushing gave Pritchard a short and snotty grin.

The team pressed on.

When they finally stood before the last house on the circle, Cushing halted everyone and beckoned Harper closer.

"Now, imagine this, my friends," Cushing said, taking on a faraway look, "... you're back home... on a lazy Sunday afternoon, kicking back and reading your newspaper in the sun room or living room," he said, checking his watch. "Well, it's Thursday by my watch," he said, correcting himself. "But there you are... relaxed... having iced tea or a beer... laying back in your recliner. There's a knock on your door.

(A knock on your door...)

"... only it ain't your neighbor," Cushing said, finishing.

Cushing snapped back to razor-sharp focus. Addressed the lieutenant.

"*You*—keep your people back... lower their weapons... but keep them ready, do you understand? I don't want any hesitation, you understand me? It could cost us our lives."

The lieutenant nodded. "Yes, sir," she said smartly.

Behind Cushing, Pritchard was informing the *Renaissance* of their finds on his handheld.

"And remember—Trained Killer—like I said before: continue to 'not like this.' This ain't any kind of 'right.' As cool as it all is, it's also disturbing. If something happens and you cannot get to us, get us out—alert the ship then high-tail it back. Do *not* risk yourselves—"

"But, sir, that's our jo—"

"It is . . . but as you can see, we are most likely outnumbered, here, and someone needs to go back and alert the ship. And we have to assume their technology is superior to ours, their mentalities . . . different until otherwise discovered. Got it?"

"Got it, sir," she said, backing away and returning to and briefing her troops.

Pritchard terminated his status report to the *Renaissance*.

"Okay, Pritch," let's make some First Contact."

Pritchard and Cushing emptied their hands, brushed themselves off, and walked up the flag-stone path to the front porch of the pastel-blue clapboard dwelling.

(. . . *welcome* . . .)

"This is so freaking weird, *maaan*," Pritchard said, under his breath.

"Do you still hear those whispers?"

"Yes, but they're not as loud anymore."

They stepped up the two porch steps. Approached the door—gestured for the rest of the group to remain behind.

The door was like any other door in any other Earth-based American community. There was a screen door in front of the main door. The paint appeared recent and well done. Tall, sidelight panes of thick glass framed the door on both sides. Across the top of the door was a narrow transom window, vertically portioned off by muntins.

Cushing looked to Pritchard. Glanced back to their security detail. He subtly lifted a hand and motioned for them to lower their weapons just a touch more, but to keep them ready. He returned to the door.

Knocked.

The action sounded as expected on any Earth door, and the door did, indeed, feel entirely solid.

"What do you think they'll look like, Lieutenant?" asked one of Harper's troops.

Without looking to the individual, she said, "Us."

It seemed like an eternity before the door was answered, and when it was . . . it was opened by an attractive human couple in what looked like their early thirties. They remained behind the screen door, arm in arm. Both wore the snappy attire of any up-and-coming suburban Earth couple. In the background a beautiful violin piece played softly.

Cushing suddenly felt . . . watched . . . from *afar* . . . .

"Hello!" the man greeted, a wonderfully large smile upon his rugged-but-pleasant—and what on Earth would have been called African-American—features.

"Hello!" the woman said, also smiling. She was of classic blonde Caucasian-like beauty and green eyes.

The couple looked at Cushing and Pritchard, then looked around Cushing and Prichard to the rest of the *Renaissance* detail behind them.

"And hello to all of *you*, too!" the woman said, waving to the rest of the group.

"We've been waiting for you!" the man said, "won't you please come in?"

Pritchard, Cushing, and the rest of the party took in the interior of the home. Once they'd entered the building, they'd realized they were playing somewhat fast and loose with exploration protocols, but the realization came just a little too late . . . and, whether or not it was the soothing violin music or that they chose to even admit that those *were* violins . . . they all felt extraordinarily compelled to enter.

Wanted to, in fact.

Felt . . . at *home.*

Regaining her sense of protocol first, Lieutenant Harper posted one individual at the home's still-opened front door.

"Please," Cushing said, "pardon our behavior if we appear rude by our confusion of your . . . existence—"

"We are not offended," the man said, bringing his apparent-wife in closer. She also nodded and smiled, as she looked to her apparent-husband. They both looked to Cushing, smiling.

"But—and do forgive me—*who are you?*" Cushing continued, "*how* are you here? And you're speaking *English*? *Violin* music? How is any of thi—"

"Well, to begin with," the woman began, "my name is Sophie Winthrop." Her voice was soothing and quite pleasant to listen to. She looked to her apparent-husband.

"And I am Thomas Winthrop," the man said. His voice was also calm . . . comfortable . . . even hypnotic, especially when coupled with the violin music.

Sophie said, "We are here. We have *always* been here. We speak the language that we have always spoken. You may call it 'English' if you like."

"And we have many answers to many questions!" Thomas said, breaking off into the most inviting laughter.

Cushing and his crew nervously looked to each other. Several shifted uncomfortably.

"*Verstehen sie mir?*" Thiemo Bellenger asked.

"*Ja, wir verstehen—og vi forstår også norsk,*" Thomas responded immediately, redirecting his look to Agnete.

"You speak *Norwegian*?" Agnete said, clearly startled.

The team again exchanged glances.

Pritchard adjusted his instruments and said, "Sorry—do you mind if we record our conversation?"

"No, please do! We don't mind at all!" Sophie said. "By the way, would any of you like some lemonade? Iced tea? Coffee? Please—have some lemonade."

"We'd love t—wait-wait-wait," Cushing said, raising an open hand into the air and collecting himself, "this is all just a little too . . . fast. I—we," he said, looking to the rest of the landing party, "all feel as if we're in a dream. This is all way too off-the-charts strange to any even remotely probable statistics."

"Lemonade?" Sophie asked, with an attractive turn of her head and an amused look.

"Yes! *Everything!* How is 'lemonade' even here? How are *you* here . . . that you look exactly like us . . . act and speak exactly like us?"

"Why don't we all come into the living room, where we can sit and discuss this more comfortably," Thomas said.

"*No!*" Cushing said. "Look, I'm sorry—I didn't mean for it to come out quite that way—but there are just too man—"

"*Please*," Thomas calmly insisted, " . . . *come . . . enjoy our hospitality.* We mean you no harm." Thomas's tone was hypnotic, his outstretched hand inviting. "We are just trying to be hospitable and promise you no harm. Isn't this how things *should* be? Isn't this far more preferable than any banal and clichéd displays of weaponry and might?" he said, motioning to their weapons. "Commander, you will find us a most civilized and welcoming culture."

Cushing had an olfactory flashback to the pine-forest scents . . . and with the pleasant and soothing sounds of the violins . . . he just wanted to kick back in an easy chair . . . in a sun room . . . eyes closed . . .

Sophie said, "It is quite apparent you have all come a long way to be here. You're confused . . . perhaps even mentally and emotionally exhausted. We just wish to make this interrogation more agreeable to all of us."

"We don't mean for this to *be* an 'interrogation,'" Pritchard said. He was about to continue when Cushing again lifted a hand into the air.

"'Interrogation'? You know the word? It's implication?" Cushing asked.

"Of course," Thomas said, "we do. Now—please . . . come, enter our house and make yourselves at home. We only mean to be hospitable. There is the phrase, '*We come in peace.*'"

"But it is us who have come to you," Cushing said.

"Is that so?" Thomas said, holding Cushing's gaze. "*Come*," he said again, standing aside and displaying a sweeping gesture.

Come . . . enter our home . . .

Please do . . .

We promise no harm . . .

Thomas directed them into their spacious living room.

Cushing looked to his group—then to Harper, holding his gaze longer with her than the others—and returned to the Winthrops.

"Okay."

They were all led into the living room, where Sophie switched off the music.

"'Interrogation,'" Thomas said as he led everyone to their seats, "means questioning . . . but more specifically," he said as he directed Cushing and Pritchard to their cushioned seats, "suggests a formal or official systematic inquiry—as performed by government officials—as in and between authority figures and one or more non-authority, non-government persons."

"You both have a high degree of command of the language we call "English,'" Cushing said, as he and Pritchard took their seats. When Thomas and Sophie motioned for the security detail to sit, Cushing quickly interjected, "No—they'll stand. I hope you understand and don't mind if they move about as we talk?"

The security detail fanned out, weapons in hand, but lowered.

"Of course not!" Sophie said, cheerily. She addressed the detail, "Please—do as you must! Feel free to inspect our home! The stairs are back there," she said, directing the lieutenant's gaze, "through that entryway there."

Cushing nodded to the lieutenant. Harper smartly made her way in that direction.

"But how . . . *any of this?*" Pritchard asked, his recorder in his lap.

"What do you mean?" Thomas sat on their loveseat. Sophie snuggled in beside him.

Cushing continued.

"From our point of view, all of this—you and your wife, this suburban, in our terms, setup . . . the air we can breathe . . . it is all quite *beyond* fantastical. *Improbable*, one might add. We have come countless light years—are you familiar with the term?—to be here."

The couple nodded in the affirmative at understanding, "light year."

"And see—this!" he said, gesturing with upright and open hands between him, in a back-and-forth motion, "how do you speak our *languages* . . . how do you have the exact same vocabulary, terms, everything? Iced tea—coffee. This . . . living room? *How . . . are . . . you* . . . here?" he asked. He stared into Sophie's deep, penetrating gaze.

"We've always been here," Sophie said, holding his look.

"But *how* can you have just *always been here?*" Cushing insisted.

"It just is," Thomas said.

"Do you remember yesterday? Ten years ago? Do you have plans for your future? Know the history of your people—your planet?"

"How have you always been how *you* are?" Sophie asked. "From our points-of-view, we could have the very same questions. We were just enjoying the afternoon . . . then you come knocking at our do—"

"Dressed like *this?*" Cushing said.

"It's all a matter of perspective, is it not?"

The *Renaissance* crew exchanged nervous looks.

"So . . . *do* you?" Cushing asked. "Do you have the same kinds of questions about us?"

Sophie and Thomas looked to each other, smiled warmly.

"No," Sophie said.

"No," Thomas said.

Cushing scoffed. "Why not?"

Harper re-entered the living room, briefly shaking her head with a quizzical look as she came toward Cushing. She stopped dead in her tracks . . . only to again start up . . . but, as if in a skipping film projection, she seemed to have shifted slightly forward in position *without having moved.*

Cushing furrowed his brow.

Felt that vertigo again.

Cushing and Pritchard blinked.

Rubbed their temples.

Thiemo, Hisa, Agnete, and the security detail paused . . . brought hands to confused brows . . . reshuffled their positions.

There, upon the coffee table before them—

Sat a silver serving tray of lemonade.

A tall glass pitcher of pale-yellow fluid was inside. Eleven glasses—all filled—ringed the tray on the coffee table. Cushing sharply observed condensation gently rolling off each glass onto their coasters.

"How-how did that get here?" Cushing asked, shakily shooting to his feet.

"I brought it in," Sophie said.

"No . . . no, you didn't," Pritchard said.

"I didn't see it," Cushing said.

"Yes, you did. You both did," Sophie said, remaining seated. "Your Mr. Pritchard, here, half-jokingly remarked at how strong I appeared to be and how well I'd managed to balance all glasses without a problem, as I brought them in."

Cushing and Pritchard exchanged looks.

Images and memories of conversation flew between them . . . of Sophie getting up while answering questions . . . a security person following her into the kitchen as she prepared and brought out the lemonade . . . of Pritchard commenting on Sophie's prowess as an exemplary hostess *and* balancing all filled glasses and the pitcher—

"How . . . is that possible?" Cushing asked, sitting back down, again bringing a hand to his face and rubbing his eyes. "I . . . I don't . . . remember *any* of this . . ."

"But *do*," Pritchard finished, dropping his hands into his lap and opening his eyes wide.

Both men smiled pleasantly, but looks of concern crossed their faces.

Cushing again got to his feet.

"I think we had better go," he said.

Pritchard came to his feet.

The security detail moved in closer . . . also appearing unbalanced, confused.

They made a move to leave, when Cushing changed direction and instead came right up to the couple, both of whom also came to their feet. The lieutenant hurried up beside him, her hands at the ready on her weapon—which remained holstered.

Standing closest to Sophie, Cushing brought his face right up to her. She looked to him, amused, yet mutually interested. Thomas did not object. Cushing examined every pore and feature.

(. . . *come to me* . . .)

(. . . *closer* . . .)

He inhaled her perfume . . . visually inspected the lines and form of her face . . . her beautifully crafted jawbone . . . flawless . . .

(... *I love you* ...)
(... *kiss me* ....)
... wrinkleless skin ...
(... touch *me* ...)

Her lips—on the edge of a larger smile, Sophie allowed Cushing his examination. Cushing felt wonderfully off balance ... drawn to her. He lingered a bit too long at her lips ... then shot his gaze up to her all-knowing eyes. Eyes ... green, striking, and deep as the star fields from which they'd ...

... *eyes* ...

he found difficult to pull away from.

Cushing brought up a hand before her face and paused in mid-air.

"Do you ... do you mind?" he asked.

"Not at all," she answered, in almost a whisper.

There was an unidentifiable sweetness to her breath ... *which he inhaled*.

Sophie intently scrutinized his every movement.

Cushing gently touched her shoulder ... examined her clothing. Lifted and paused his hand before her face ... only to gently touch his fingertips onto the skin of her cheek.

The crew looked among themselves.

"Are you satisfied that I am an alive ... flesh-and-blood ... individual? Would you like to poke my husband?" she asked, maintaining positive eye contact and an amused grin.

"That won't be necessary," Cushing said, absentmindedly, if embarrassingly, "thank you both. I-I'm sorry for the intrusion."

"Not at all. We don't mind," she said, gently taking Cushing's hand into her own. "As you can feel—right now—by my touch," she said, squeezing his hand, "we are not hallucinations. But we understand your investigation of us," she said, boring into him even more intently.

"*Do* you? Because we don't. None of this makes sense."

(... *yet you allow me your hand* ...)

"Why not? You are here. We are here. We've talked. Had a pleasant afternoon," she said, more firmly grasping his hand in emphasis.

Her hands were elegant, firm, real. Her touch sincere and warm. Inviting . . . arou—

Cushing looked outside . . . yanked his hand back to check his watch.

"How—"

They'd been here three hours.

"Sometimes, dear commander, you ask far too many questions and simply do not accept the moment . . . what is right before your eyes. The obvious."

"There's nothing obvious about *any* of this!" Cushing said.

"Oh, but there is. You just do not see it. But that is not your fault . . . *per se*."

"And how do you even know all the finer nuances of our languages? How do you know German and English and Norwegian from a planet so far away from you it doesn't even show up in your night sky?"

"Why should it matter? We live here. You came to *us*, remember? *You came to us.*"

But did we? Cushing asked himself.

Again . . . that unbalanced feeling. That sense of vertigo . . . of being in one massive, unending dream. Cushing turned back to his group, almost forgetting he was also far from alone. He brought a hand to his face and squeezed his eyes shut for just a moment.

"Sir—are you all right?" Harper said.

"No . . . no, I'm *not*." Cushing opened his eyes and returned to the present. "We really must get back—"

"To your ship," Thomas said evenly.

"Yes . . . our ship. Do you know about it? Have you seen it?"

"We know of it."

"Of course you do." Cushing returned to his group, slightly embarrassed. "We thank you for your hospitality . . . and conversation."

"Are you sure you won't stay? We have plenty of room for you and your people."

"No . . . I think we have received far more than we bargained for. We need—"

"To discuss. Assimilate. Again—we understand," Sophie said. Thomas nodded supportively.

"We are very grateful for you all being polite and gracious guests. Lieutenant," Sophie said, looking to Emily Harper, "I trust you found everything in order with the exploration of our home?"

The lieutenant, initially off-guard at having been specifically called out, said, "Y-yes, ma'am, everything was wonderful. You have a wonderful home. Thank you for allowing us in—to examine it."

Sophie and Thomas again nodded.

The detail made its way back out into the entryway and outside to the front porch. Pritchard and Cushing shook hands with each of them, and the landing party departed back toward the woods.

"Such nice people," Sophie said.

"Cushing is quite taken with you," Thomas said.

Sophie smiled. Gave Thomas a peck on the cheek.

Together they watched Cushing and the others depart the neighborhood.

"It's a pity they didn't try the lemonade."

3

"This whole planet makes no sense," Lieutenant Emily Harper said. "*None* of this makes any sense—"

"Yet it exists," Pritchard said.

"But *how?*" Harper said. "How in the hell can it? How in the bloody hell can any of it?"

"As far as I can tell, it's geologically similar to Earth," Thiemo said.

"And biologically, it just seems to keep growing—ask and we shall receive," Hisa added.

"The more we see the more is subsequently presented," Agnete said. "Yet all known laws seem in order."

"*Ja*, Thiemo said, "if you don't count things constantly materializing as we ask questions . . . or identify missing species—*people*."

Everyone at the table exchanged looks. Took sips from their mugs.

Cushing said, "A breathable atmosphere . . . trees, water, bugs—and, oh, by the way—a suburban subdivision at the edge of a healthy and well-treed forest, one of the houses actually populated with—"

"A hot-chick and her model husband," Pritchard added.

"I was gonna say '*people*,'" Cushing said. The team chuckled.

"This is all like some dream . . . or a nightmare that has yet to reveal itself," Cushing said. "What does the *Renaissance* have to say?"

Pritchard said, "Well . . . life—non-Human life—is everywhere. Air is the obvious nitrogen/oxygen mixture. Soil, your standard Earth-type dirt . . . same as the water: lakes, streams, oceans. Polar regions. Sure, slight variations, but miniscule and insignificant. But the only human life that registers is that little suburban settlement we discovered—"

"And they *knew* of our ship? *How?*" Cushing said, "We landed in predawn! Setup before first light!"

"We detected no one detecting us as we landed," Harper said.

"Maybe they were just saying things they'd know would make sense to us?" Thiemo said, "but, again, how would they *know* that?"

"The same way all the rest of this is possible," Cushing said. "Maybe they can read our minds. See into our thoughts . . . you know when I examined Sophie . . . I could have sworn she'd said things to me with her mind

(. . . *love me* . . .)

(. . . *touch me* . . .)

" . . . nothing I can now recall, but . . . at the time . . . I thought sure she was trying to communicate with me, and I felt—truth be told—*hypnotized.*

"But look, if all this can happen—which is obvious because it *is*—then how much of a leap is it to consider . . . . "

"Unless it's all an illusion," Pritchard said.

Everyone looked to him.

"Okay," Agnete said, "that's not unnerving at all."

"Yeah," Cushing said, coming to his feet and pacing the room. "But what's more farfetched? An illusion . . . or that it's all real? I much prefer the latter, because if it *is* all an illusion, does that mean we're all dead? Or dying? Or still onboard that ship in the mind-altering haze and throes of Holcomb's? And this planet is nothing but smoke and mirrors," At least with the earlier proposition, we're all alive and conscious and experiencing what we *appear* to be experiencing."

"But to become too *complacent*, sir," Lieutenant Harper said. "Would that also be a mistake?"

Cushing looked at her.

"Of course it would, Lieutenant, but we can still accept what we're seeing and not become complacent about it—curious. Exploratory," Cushing continued, "I can't speak for everybody in this camp—or the *Renaissance*—but though I experienced all of . . . *this* . . . I consider myself *far* from complacent."

Heads nodded.

"These are all good points, points we need to keep in mind," Cushing said, continuing, "we all need to keep on our toes. Learn all that we can. Record everything . . . but remember that we came out here to find something just like this, right? Sure, it's perhaps not exactly what we thought it might be or would be, or is maybe all that and *more* . . . but we all ventured out this way *to find a new home* . . . whether fantastical, mythical, or not. And we *found* one. You could say not to look a gift horse in the mouth . . . *but that's exactly what we all need to do*," he said, looking to everyone at the table. "We *need* to examine it full-on . . . poke and prod around into that maw. And it is for this reason I'm going to direct that we break up into three groups."

Pritchard shot Cushing a look.

"Is that wise?" Hisa said.

"Legitimate concerns," Cushing said, "but really . . . if the forces at work here are as powerful as we're experiencing . . . what does it matter if we're in one large group . . . or singular?"

"Misery loves company?" Thiemo said.

Cushing looked around the room.

"We're sitting ducks," Cushing continued, "captive bugs in some ultra-weird cosmic science project—or chess game? . . . and I certainly don't want to endanger any more lives than I have to, but I don't see any real increased harm, yet I see a world that absolutely begs our attention. It seems to give us exactly what we want—what we need—"

"But at what price?" Pritchard asked. "We already lost the other two groups."

"Look," Cushing continued, "we're all armed, whether or not that even means anything, here. And as we've been doing while down here, the ship will be monitoring each and every one of us, and should there be any danger to even one of us, we'll pull out. I've already requisitioned several floaters to hover in stand-by mode . . . collecting all possible intel of all possible *things* . . . but ready to strike or pull us out in an instant.

"Again, let's remember . . . *we all signed up for this*, family lineages notwithstanding. None of us was forced to make this journey. And this is where this trip has taken us . . . to exactly what we were seeking out. So . . . instead of reading history books, believing in myths and legends, let's start creating our own history."

"I don't know, sir . . . ," Harper said.

"Your concerns are duly noted, Lieutenant," Cushing said, "but I feel we'll cover far more ground this way, and we really do need to be somewhat aggressive. We have a unique situation, here, don't you think?"

Heads again nodded and several mouthed verbal agreement.

"Okay, then, let's see what Day Number Two has in store for us, then."

Cushing divided up the groups and gave them their marching orders for the day. Logged them into the system. Created a safety net with requisitioned floaters hovering within easy reach of each arm of the expeditions. Gave orders to the ship to leave orbit if things deteriorated . . . a decision left to the on-orbit command. He also left a certified recording of his proxy acceptance to the ship's decision to do whatever was necessary to save the lives of all onboard the *Renaissance* at the expense of ground operations.

At first light, they all headed out 120 degrees from each other, with himself, he took Agnete Marken, and one of Harper's security detail, Beryl Weiss. Together, they headed toward the extraterrestrial subdivision.

As Cushing and his group entered alien suburbia, he paused at the Winthrop house. A kitchen light was illuminated.

Cushing looked to the light. "Wait here," he said, "I need to check up on one more thing before we continue on."

"Sir?" Agnete said.

"It'll just be a minute, Netta, I promise—I just need to follow up on something that's been bugging me since I left. Storm the building in five if I don't return," Cushing said, smiling, looking to Beryl.

"Yes, sir," Beryl said, stepping forward.

"Okay," Agnete said, looking intently at Cushing. "Be careful. Things are surely not what they seem to be."

"I am ever so aware, Netta."

"Are you *sure* you don't want us to come with you?" she again asked.

"I'm sure. I'll be right in there—probably in the kitchen. You can wait right here, watching from those windows."

Cushing turned and approached the house. Everything appeared the same . . . though he wasn't quite sure about the picket fence between him and the house.

Had that been there yesterday?

He passed through the unlocked gate. It certainly felt like a pine wood. The metal hinges even—only slightly—creaked like real metal hinges.

Rick Cushing stepped onto the porch and approached the door. Listened to his footsteps upon the porch boards.

No screen door.

He lifted a hand to knock—

The door opened.

Before him stood Sophie Winthrop, who immediately beamed a look of surprised pleasure. She stood before him in a casual lavender blouse and pressed gray slacks, but no shoes, only bare feet. Her long hair was attractively arranged to one side of the front of her shoulders. She wore minimal makeup, except for a subtle pink lipstick. The wonderful scent of freshly brewed coffee escaped the opened door, along with another appealing aroma—

Cushing's heart skipped a beat. Began to sprint.

Had she had that amount of long hair when they'd last met?

"Good morning, Mr. Cushing—or should I call you 'commander,' or 'captain' or—"

He chuckled. "'Rick' is fine. Good morning, Sophie."

"Would you like to come in?—oh, but I see your friends appear to be waiting on you," she said, waving to the rest of the team. They waved back.

"No, it's just me now, but I would like to come in, if I may? And excuse me, but is that coffee cake I'm detecting?"

"Yes, it is. I just made it, which you and your team are more than welcome to partake of, along with freshly brewed coffee."

Stay alert!

"We can't stay long, but thank you."

Things felt far too comfortable . . . he couldn't tell if he really was back on Earth

(*he wasn't!*)

(*he wasn't!*)

and all this was some deep daydream of a better time

(*it wasn't!*)

(*it wasn't!*)

or he was out among the stars—

(*he was!*)

(*he was!*)

With an apparently sentient life form that appeared human.

Sophie allowed him in and led him into the kitchen. As they passed by the living room

(. . . *have some lemonade* . . .)

he relived yesterday's first contact. In the kitchen, Sophie led him to a medium-sized wooden table with one table setting and a poured cup of coffee alongside a plate of partially eaten coffee cake.

"Where's Thomas?" Rick asked, taking in the kitchen.

"It's just me, here," she said, turning her back to him to fetch his coffee, which was in an automated coffee maker on the counter. She returned with his cup of coffee and cake.

Rick examined her.

"Just you? But yesterday—"

"Just me. It's always just been me. I don't know any 'Thomas.' Why do you ask?" She took her own seat opposite him. Cushing sat. Sophie grasped her cup in both hands and carefully brought it to her beautiful, pink lips. Took a sip. Calmly held his gaze.

"It hardly bears repeating that when my team and I first met . . . you . . . yesterday, there were *two* of you. You and a gentleman, named 'Thomas,' whom we assumed was your husband—whom you'd *referred to* as your husband, actually. He was about six feet, dark skinned, looked like a—"

"I have no husband," she said, calmly setting down her cup and keeping her hands wrapped around it. She continued to calmly eye him. "I'm not married. Never have been, Rick. Have no brothers. Or Cousins. No friends."

"Okay," Cushing said, taking his seat.

He looked to the mug before him. To hers. To her elegant hands and fingers. No rings.

It all certainly looked real . . . Earth . . . coffee before him. Earth coffee cake. *Smelled* like it.

He brought his hands to the cup.

It certainly was hot.

But what was really in that cup?

Was it really coffee?

What would happen to him if he drank it? Ate the cake?

Damn it, he must be more careful! Do not just blindly accept things offered because they *appeared* to be familiar!

Like her.

But he had to be subtle. If that even mattered. If the powers-that-be were as powerful as they appeared to be . . . certainly they must know . . . .

"How long have you been here?"

"I have always been here."

"How long is that? A year? Ten years? Thirty?"

"Always."

Rick again looked around the kitchen.

Observed a microwave . . . a stove . . . a refrigerator. Undershelf-lit countertops.

He had to start acting and thinking more like an experienced explorer and less like a lovelorn space traveler. Stop pussy footing around and being overtaken by seemingly familiar visual distractions and beautiful—

"Miss Winthrop—"

"'Sophie' . . . please . . . '*Sophie.*'

"Sophie . . . surely you have to see things from our perspective . . . that we've come from a very long way . . . and to find you—and all this—here. It's quite . . . improbable. Impossible. Mind blowing."

Working her hair with both hands as they talked, Sophie repositioned her long blonde hair to the other shoulder. "Why?"

He studied her. She was positively radiant. Charming. And there was . . . *something* about her . . .

"Are you going to try your coffee?" she asked, giving her hair a final, loose twist. She watched him.

Watched his every move.

Rick again looked down to the cup.

Was not partaking of offered hospitality here a crime? Were there repercussions to not—

"It's called a 'morning blend' or something or other," she said, casting a quick look to the counter, then taking another sip of her own. "I like it . . . I hope you do, too," she said, eyeing him over the rim of her cup, "I'm trying something different. Surely you're open to new experiences, aren't you, Rick?"

Cushing let out a short chuckle. "This is all quite confusing. You appear 'normal' enough . . . look like us . . . sound and *feel—*"

"*Feel?*" she said, smiling.

"Yes, *feel* . . . remember . . . I examined you yesterday. You allowed me to

(*Touch me!*)

"touch you."

"Did I?"

"You did."

"Did you like it? Touching me, Rick?"

Her smile widened and her eyes appeared to take on a whole new depth.

"Sophie—"

"*Would you like to do it again?*" she asked in a lowered tone, looking down to her coffee—then back up to him.

Rick got up from the table and turned away, looking out her windows and into her back yard, which looked like any other back yard back on Earth . . . if it hadn't yet blown itself to smithereens. A patio arrangement, fire pit, well-manicured landscape—

What was happening here?
Were they all dreaming?
Was he dreaming?
He looked back toward the front door.
Was anyone really still waiting on him?
Was she really sitting there, now, at the table?
Was all of this one of those warped and twisted space-sickness dreamworks, and he was actually still back on the *Renaissance* . . . they all were . . . still searching for an inhabitable planet? Still flying through the spaces between the stars?
Or was some onboard scientist playing mind games with them? Was—

Lost in thought he had not noticed Sophie had also gotten back to her feet and had come up behind him. She gently lay a hand to his shoulder.

Bringing her face up behind an ear, she whispered, "Do I not feel human? Is my touch not real?"

"If I cut myself . . . do I not bleed?"

Heart pounding thickly in his ears, Rick turned around . . .

Sophie took a step back. Intensely eyed him. One palm was open and faced him, while in the other . . . a knife.

Before Rick could act, she'd swiftly brought the blade across her wrist.

Blood erupted from her wound.

"*No!*" Rick said and lunged for her.

Sophie did not move, did not flinch. She remained where she was, calmly eyeing Cushing as he applied pressure to her wrist, then frantically searched the kitchen for anything—a dish rag, a towel. He snatched a towel from her oven's handle and quickly wrapped it around her still-pumping

(*a heartbeat! she actually has a heartbeat!*)

wound. Sophie observed his movements with quiet, if amused, composure.

Rick adjusted the towel. Eyed her.

"*Why did you* do *that? What is the* matter *with you?*"
"Do I not bleed?"
"Yes! You bleed—*you bleed!*"
"Is my blood not warm? Am I not real?"
"Yes—it is! You are, damn it, but you didn't have to—"
"But I *did*, Rick, I did have to do that so that you could see that I am, indeed, flesh-and-blood . . . not a dream. That we are, indeed, *alike*. That you care about me. That you could see your own emotional reaction. If you truly thought me an illusion, why did you come to my aid? You are a man . . . here, now . . . I am a woman . . . here . . . *now*."

They looked to each other.

Do you not like my touch?

"Wha—"

"Do you not like my touch?"

"That is not the point—"

"I think it is," she said, and turned away toward the kitchen window. Sophie casually allowed her cut arm to drop and the towel to fall away.

"*Sophie!*" Rick said, again rushing to her. He came up behind her as she approached the countertop and spun her around. Grabbed her arm. Pinned her against the countertop with his body, while grabbing her cut wrist and bringing it up before him.

"Your—"

No knife cut.

No wound.

He grasped her arm more firmly in both hands. Held it up before him incredulously. Rubbed his fingers along where he'd sworn she'd sliced open her wrist. Looked behind him to the bloody towel on the floor and to the place from which she'd just walked away.

Blood. There was blood on the floor, on the towel even . . . and, looking back to her arm, yes, there were remnants of blood on her arm—*but there was no longer any slice across her skin.*

"What—how . . . how could—"

Rick looked up to Sophie . . . their faces inches apart. Her lips were slightly parted. The smell of coffee was strong upon her breath, which now appeared to be laboring rather heavily. Her perfume was subtle, heady. He could make out the pores of her skin. The textured irises of her eyes. And her lips... beautiful, well-formed, and inviting... lightly coated in their alluring pink...

"*Do you like touching me?*"

"I—I—"

Sophie leaned into Rick's lips and gently kissed him, closing her eyes. Backed away—

Rick forcefully pulled her back in... yet gently cradled her head. His mind wheeled and whorled.

He again felt off-balance... dizzy... lightheaded. "Vertigo" was a most ill-equipped term for what he was currently experiencing. He felt pulled apart... stretched to the ends of the universe... and back again.

Initially coming together as two... they re-integrated... *absorbed*...

Into one.

Sophie led Rick through the house, hand-in-hand. It was clearly a home-of-one—there was no Thomas anywhere.

Sophie led Rick upstairs and stopped before the bedroom.

She turned to Rick. Examined his face.

"Do you not remember *anything?*"

He stared into the bedroom. His face screwed up in a mask of tortured concentration.

"No... but, why should I? I don't live here."

"This is *our* bedroom, Rick."

"That makes no sense... no sense at all—"

Sophie released Rick's hand and entered the bedroom. She sat on the bed, legs astraddle one corner. She dropped her head forward and allowed her long

(*had she always been a brunette?*)

dark hair to flow over the front of her face and shoulders. Looked back up to him with longing eyes between her long strands of hair.

"*Do you not remember this?*" she asked.

"How could I? I have never *been* here before—"

Images.

. . . of Rick leaving the bedroom . . . looking back . . . seeing her just as she was this very moment.

"*Nooo,*" he said, turning away. "No-no-no, *this cannot be!*"

"*Why are you fighting me? Don't you love me?*"

"I . . . I—"

(. . . *do?* . . .)

Could he?

How could he?

Finding her beautiful was one thing . . . kissing her . . . but *loving* (*married to*) her?

Sophie held up an open palm before him.

"*Come* to me, darling. *Come.*"

Rick turned and stared at her outstretched hand.

Kissing her.

Touching her.

Holding her.

Loving her!

He remembered, oh, yes, he *did* . . .

He remembered!

He'd left her . . . told her he'd be back. Didn't want to go, but—

Hadn't he?

They'd met at the university. Married. Developed careers.

He an astronaut—she . . . a theoretical physicist.

"*Come to me, my love,*" Sophie again beckoned, hand still outstretched, relaxed, palm up.

Rick couldn't take his eyes off her.

She remained straddling the corner of the bed, her dark hair—yes, she'd always been a brunette—most attractively disheveled.

Wore red lipstick. A wry smile.

A beautiful, open-necked blouse and a skirt. Her shoes were at her feet, one tipped over, the other upright.

"*Come . . . to . . . me.*"

Rick faced her. Approached two steps and halted.

"Sophie . . . I . . . I don't understand—"

"What is there to understand, love?"

"Everything. All of this."
Sophie's smile broadened. Her dark eyes flashed a deep look of
(... *the spaces between the stars* ...)
adoring concern.
"There is only us. You and me. What else is there?"
"My ... ship? My team? What is ... is this happening to everyone?"
"There is only you ... and me. *Come*, my love. Make love to me."
Rick came up to Sophie
And took her hand.

THE LIAR'S BRIGADE
Year 2073 C. E.

1

There was a defined progression to all that had happened.

It was nothing new, but a time-honored protocol followed since Humankind had first taken steps outside of anything they'd already occupied.

Explore.

Colonize.

Exploit.

It was the more robust and adventurous who were initially deployed to the surface, and with the loss of what had become known as the "Roanoke Three," the first set of surface expeditions, the *Renaissance* had little recourse but to keep trying, keep sending down more teams... and, eventually, a dialogue had been established with the race that had been discovered there. Military and diplomatic men and women had been sent following the explorers. Missteps were of course made, because the *Renaissance* emissaries were only familiar with Earthly behavior and Earthly ways. The indigenous people, however they may have appeared and acted like humans . . . were not . . . and acted in the most trustful and open of manners. The military minds were taken aback and suspicious. Stymied. Even indignant. They kept looking for conflict and strife and war where there *was* no conflict, no strife, nor war. There were no recounted histories and no historical conflicts (there were no repositories of historical *anything* for that matter).

Had they heard that right—*excuse us, what?*

No war?

No war.

But *everyone* wars . . . .

No wars.

And where were our three landing parties?

What landing parties?

They pored over their news, their media, their libraries, but continually came up empty. Found no violence. No Roanoke Three. The Earth people secretly invaded homes and businesses with their technologies and continually found no disharmony. They discovered that the indigenous people of this planet called their planet, "Home," and these people of Home enthusiastically welcomed these people of Earth. But the people of Earth didn't like a planet called "Home," so they changed it to "Thera," pronounced "*Tera*," an anagram of "Earth." And the people of Home (now Thera) didn't have a problem with this. When the people of Thera were asked how long they'd populated their planet and from where *they* had come, their only response was

"*We've always been here.*"

And they invited the Earth people to come, explore . . . *and live in peace.*

And, for the most part, this was (initially) what the Earth people had done.

2

But what the people of Thera did not know—nor did the remaining individuals of the *Renaissance*—was that before the measured migration from the *Renaissance*, before the deployment of the Roanoke Three, had been the covert deployment of a tiny secret contingent referred to as "The Gray Berets." They were the last of the Earth's covert operatives.

The Gray Berets had been secretly deployed, their deployment masked from the *Renaissance's* scanners and personnel, with the additional constraint that none of the unit knew each other nor how many of *them* actually existed. To each other, they were all just another face in the crowd, similarly trained, similarly accoutered, and similarly deployed.

Identities non-existent. Mission buried deep in layered upon furtively layered databanks.

They were the last of their kind, and they had landed in all the dark and dank places scattered across this new planet that the pre-programmed *Renaissance's* sensors could surreptitiously find, then summarily erase, from all of its records.

3

The *Renaissance's* corps of engineers who operated the onboard factories were among the best and brightest of the *Renaissance's* crew. The most creative. They were the creators of all things material. They created everything from pencils to another section of the ship. They were only limited by their imaginations, but certainly not their fabrication skills. If they didn't have the equipment needed to create something, they simply created equipment from which new equipment would be created. The Fabrication Engineers originated as a special operations unit during the late Earth wars as a way to create confusion and obfuscation among the enemy, with false buildings, towns, even landscapes. The members of the unit began to jokingly refer to themselves as "the Liar's Brigade." And as was the way with many military applications, many of their developments found non-military employment.

The mission planners of the early days had foreseen the need to create new towns and cities from the ground up, so had populated all their starships with preprogrammed plans, but also knew they could not contain the considerable creativity and intellectual output of a smart group of engineers. Once the initial planet-forming plans had been created and assigned to the initial cadre of those making planetfall, the Liar's Brigade eagerly jumped into the more creative designs for future dwellings, governmental, and business operations.

As the initial diplomatic planetfall cadre made their way to Thera, they were assigned their dwellings and governmental locations. Much of the construction was automated and merely required oversight by a single Liar's Brigade engineer.

The first-constructed Earth-people city was located outside a Theran city, called Blue Bright. The Liar's Brigade set to work constructing the First District of Thera, or F.D.T., which quickly became simply known as "D.T."

The perimeter of D.T. was surveyed, laid out, and "staked." An electronic border set up.

Then the center of the city was begun, with government buildings and roads and parks thrown up.

At the same time these were under construction, in another area, residences were created.

And it was in this way that the manipulation and colonization of Thera had progressed.

IN THE NAME OF PROGRESS
Year 2074 C.E.

Thera prospered!

The people from Earth had found a new home!

New people! A new way of life! On Thera was no war, no strife. Had *been* no wars, no strife.

At first, this was difficult for those from Earth to comprehend. They had their militaries, their laws, and their histories. Beliefs. Deployed their forts and bases and might. But when they finally understood that their only enemies were those they'd brought with them, things changed.

Together with the people of Thera they finally, truly found peace.

With no use for militaries anymore, no more enemies to fight, they rechanneled their energies to build roads and towns and cities and ports. Created public works. Worked together. Mined and drilled and processed oil and gold and minerals similar on and within Earth. Created physical and mental challenges and Olympic and endurance events. Gave outlets to pent-up physical and mental energies of the young and the old. And with all these new-found advantages, those from the orbiting spaceship began to repopulate the planet with their race.

Hammers and nails and saws and cranes. Concrete and steel and glass and wood. As if hair from a head, buildings and skyscrapers and parks and terraforming sprouted up everywhere!

And with these new locations and congregations came the need for identification! New names were created, new starts, but with the new also came some racial favorites:

Gold Town, Coal Town, Steel City, and Hereweare!

Newer York, London, Berlin, and Oslo! Paris, Sydney, Moscow, and Tokyo!

Blue Hills, Red Mountain, Magnesium River, and Orange Valley!

The people of the *Renaissance* had created even more advanced technologies than that which they'd brought with them. The *Renaissance* had become more of a museum, an amusement park, an on-orbit getaway hosting peace conferences and social events that spawned other on-orbit destinations and satellites.

In concert with the Therans the more scientifically minded learned from and began studies of the planet and its atmosphere. Looked for ways to monitor and safeguard this wonderful new world that they had been so lucky to happen upon, be wholeheartedly welcomed into—and more importantly, assimilated within—its culture.

And it became ever so much like Earth.

Old Earth.

It had the fields and oceans and mountains and trees!

Had green, quiet places where one could hike and sit and think and commune with soft breezes, blue skies, and fragrant florae!

Mountainous challenges for those who loved to climb!

Beautiful, crystalline waters of lakes and oceans, for those who loved to sail or swim or dive!

And the air—the atmosphere—was pleasant and pleasurable for those who loved to soar with the birds! Occasional seasonal thunderstorms . . . colorful autumns . . . winter snows . . . rejuvenating springs!

Yes, the people who had come from Earth . . . the people who had manipulated and lied and stolen . . . the people who'd cheated and obfuscated and murdered and found passage upon the *Renaissance* by their station or who they knew or who knew them or with what they could provide to the Earthly nobility . . . had found peace and quiet and solitude like they had never known before.

And it had been good.

THERE GOES THE NEIGHBORHOOD
Year 2074 C. E.

1

"Good morning, ma'am!" the white-gloved and smartly dressed Theran-appointed *Welcoming* official said to Rachel Wiestromph, as he approached her with his three assistants. Rachel and her assistant left her husband, Charles, who was deep in conversation with his Theran and *Renaissance* diplomatic staff, and turned to greet the approaching team.

"Why, a good morning to all of you!" Rachel declared in her well-bred high-society fashion. Elitism oozed from her every pore: from the tips of her gold *Nolamo Khlabins* to the top of her extravagantly arranged, diamond-embedded Chignon hairstyle.

Back on Earth Rachel and Charles had come from an influential family in the world of banking. Charles had been head of the largest banking establishment on Earth, the World Bank Order, when he was told to pack his and his wife's bags—they were headed to the stars.

They were quite good at doing what they were told.

As much as they'd loved their status, influence, and lifestyle . . . they'd seen the writing on the wall. Earth was doomed. Bags already largely packed, there was little more for them to do, but board the ship—secretly, as most of Earth's elite had already done, leaving behind look-alike Genetics in their stead.

Rachel was a smart and driven woman . . . except that her drive was more along the lines of fleshy affairs and glittering gold. The accumulation of all-things narcissistic.

And since a far more structured (and controlled) monetary system was critically in need on Thera, not the least of which was needed for the people of the *Renaissance* and their continued accumulation, display, and application of their wealth and power, she and Charles were among the very first to leave the ship for Theran planetfall. While Charles was instructed to immediately begin establishing a presence and investigation of how to best exploit Thera's own monetary system, it fell upon Rachel to find them a new abode and a way to best weasel their way into Theran High Society—if one existed. Rachel, however, preferred nothing more than to create Thera's first—elite—societal structure.

"We are here to assist you in settling into your new life!" the smiling official declared, bowing respectfully. "My name is Hildebrandt. I am here to assist you and your husband in any way possible. These," he said in a grand, sweeping gesture, "are Pollyanna, Evangeline, and Chance. They will take your bags and execute any instructions you would have forthwith."

Hildebrandt then directed Rachel's attention to the entrance, before continuing.

"And over there we also have a realtor standing by, ready to take you to several curated homes for your perusal. We already have your personal and governmental furnishing palettes in storage, and your hotel suite ready."

"Thank you *ever* so much, Hildebrandt!" Rachel said. "My assistant, Flavio, here, will send you all the needed deets."

Flavio nodded and lifted his handy in response. Hildebrandt and the others all brought their handhelds to the ready. Flavio transferred the instructions.

"Would you prefer to first freshen up at your suite or accompany the realtor?"

Rachel once-overed Hildebrandt before responding. "Actually, Hildy, I'm quite fine, and would much rather begin to see what homes are available! As you know, having been cooped up as we were, I'm quite eager to see this new planet . . . and *all* it has to offer."

Rachel raised a flirtatious eyebrow and held Hildebrandt's gaze.

"Then off we shall go!" Hildebrandt said, looking away and extending an exquisite, white-gloved gesture forward.

Out of the Welcome Center they departed with such flair and pomp as might befit a Head of State.

"But," Rachel said in a lowered tone to Hildebrandt as they walked, "I may have need to call upon your services at another time."

"Of course, ma'am," Hildebrandt said, beaming broadly. He nodded crisply as they departed.

"So, Hildebrandt," Rachel said as they walked through the 5,000 square-foot Colonial, "are you Theran or from the *Ren—*"

"Theran, ma'am."

"And your assistants?"

"Theran, ma'am."

"It's so hard telling you people apart these days. Say, Hildy, why are you all so eager and helpful to us?"

Hildebrandt turned to Rachel. Looked at her long and hard, his ever-present smile still upon his face.

"Is there any other way to behave to honored guests, especially those who had come from the stars?"

"Indeed," Rachel said, smiling as she delicately threw up a hand to her mouth in faux modesty, turning coyly away.

Hildebrandt continued to take her through the home.

"As you can see," Hildebrandt continued, "our homes are very much like what you are accustomed to, and I think you will find they—as well as this one—priced perfectly for your approval."

"Oh, of that, I am in staunch agreement!" Rachel declared, turning to Flavio, who looked concerned and wary. "This is all quite remarkable!"

"Yes, ma'am, it is!" Hildebrandt said. "We are here to please!"

"One simply had no idea that a whole nother world existed out . . . here . . . wherever *that* is."

"There is a lot that is unseen . . . until one knows how to look, ma'am," Hildebrandt said, "now, if you would come this way, you will find the master bedroom."

The three entered into a massive and sweeping bedroom with many windows, allowing in much light, which was all reflected by an abundance of gold-leafed accents throughout the room.

"Oh, *my!*" Rachel said, "this is positively *stunning!* It's as if it were made just for me!"

"Indeed, ma'am," Hildebrandt said, smiling.

"Back to my earlier convo, Hildy—you don't mind if I call you that, do you, dear?"

"Of course not, ma'am," Hildebrandt said.

"But Hildy . . . you and your people," Rachel continued, "there are so many questions! You are all so nice to us, are so *like* us. How is this even remotely possible? Is this all a dream? How do you not know your own history?"

Hildebrandt smiled and led Rachel and Flavio throughout the room, pointing out various highlights and amenities along the way, as he responded to Rachel.

"There is nothing to hide, ma'am. What you see *is* what you are, indeed, getting. We have simply always been here for however long we've been here and will be here for however long we *will* be here. In this case we are somewhat different from you and your people, in that we live in the moment. And history is made up of but a series of moments that create . . . timelines . . . ergo, histories, as *you* understand them. Though we understand where you are coming from, if I may pun, ma'am, we are always in the present."

Rachel paused, then chuckled.

"How positively *metaphysical!*" she said.

Flavio's troubled face broke into a brief smile, then returned his attention to his handy.

"So your people are selling your homes to us?"

"We are. We want to help . . . have you feel more *at* home."

"Do you know the person who is selling this mansion?"

"I do."

"Can you tell me who it is? I'd really like to speak with them."

"They wish to remain anonymous, ma'am."

Nose into the air, Rachel swung energetically away, examining the room.

"But I have been briefed on all aspects of this residence and have all its specifications. You may ask me anything," Hildebrandt said. "I personally feel this would be the perfect fit for the both of you. It is a most apt and beautiful status symbol, as well as a wonderful home in which to host parties. Plenty of rooms for guests, extended family, and visiting dignitaries. Spacious rooms for home offices. Two home theatres."

"Home theaters? You people even have—know what they *are*?"

Hildebrandt smiled.

"As we've told you . . . we are very similar in culture. If you and your people can think of something . . . how far-fetched is it to believe another . . . that another, *similar* race . . . would also not think of it, given similar advancements?"

"Well," Rachel said, turning away and inspecting the room, "this is all quite unforeseen and ever so unexpected, if you were to ask me. *All* of it."

She abruptly swung back around to address him directly.

"We'll take it."

2

Rachel and the others from the *Renaissance* found themselves with more help than they needed. From out of the Theranwork came all manner of Theran assistance, help to move, help to set up, help to shop, help to do whatever was required to get all Earth people comfortable and productive in their new environment. Even in offices and work centers were Therans most helpful, including performing overviews and briefings to all new *Renaissance* transplants about Thera and its people.

"We," the Therans kept reminding, "want every one of you to be *happy!*"

Charles would tell Rachel the most wonderful stories about Theran helpfulness, but also the most naïve. Charles was amazed at the lack of structure to their monetary and governmental systems and had found out so much about how to best shape, control, and—best of all—exploit it.

And Rachel had discovered a pure lack of any societal hierarchy and was beside herself with glee as she created Thera's inaugural High Society.

Life had become one big party!

Thera had become one big party!

Everything was set up, put into place, and was ready to become the new "business as usual."

Moved in and settled, Rachel found herself "being still" for the first time since planetfall, and was sipping her coffee and looking out their kitchen window at the woods beyond their immaculately manicured grounds. When Hildebrandt and company initially brought them out house hunting, "For Sale" signs were everywhere.

Now . . . a month later . . . none.

Hildebrandt.

He was a most delicious and hot little number she had yet to nibble. And he lived just around the corner from them. In all the hustle and bustle of getting settled in, she had never followed up on her promise to . . . call upon his services.

Now was the time.

It was the weekend, Charles was at the office already (or so he claimed), and she . . . she needed . . .

Detailed servicing.

Head held high, Rachel purposefully strutted along the sidewalk towards Hildebrandt's residence. She carried a wrapped coffee cake in-hand from the newly established German bakery. Though she knew his neighbors on all sides, she didn't care who observed her.

The more the merrier.

Everyone had their dirty little secrets. And everyone knew how to keep their dirty little secrets dirty little secrets.

Rachel knew full well that Charles wasn't so much "in the office," as he was "in the Darlene."

Coming to Hildebrandt's door, she rang the doorbell. Adjusted her blouse and some errant strands of hair.

No answer. She again rang.

Looked about her, at the neighborhood. No one was out and about—it was still relatively early—a couple of sprinklers were still watering lawns.

She rapped her key ring on the door.

No answer.

Wrinkling her face, she shifted her high-heeled footing and checked out the luscious curves of her legs.

Where was he? He'd always been at their beck and call—he'd actually never *not* been available, even when she'd come by spontaneously. Called him out of the blue.

Something wasn't right.

Pouting, she checked the door—and it opened.

"*Hilde*brandt?" she called out, tentatively, as she poked her head inside the opened door. "Oh, Hildy?" she again called.

Letting herself in, she deliberately closed the door behind her and stopped dead in her tracks.

Her jaw dropped—as did her coffee cake.

Empty.

Her eyes widened.

A shudder ran through her.

The foyer, the entranceway, the kitchen—all she could see from where she stood . . .

Empty.

"*Hildebrandt!*" she again called, this time more forcefully, angrily even. "*Hildebrandt*—where the shisst *are* you!"

Her unanswered calls reverberated hollowly in the empty mansion.

They had just talked last night! He had not mentioned one thing about leaving—*about no longer being there*. Just continued talking with that big, dopey smile on that naïve little face of his.

What the hell was going on?

Rachel moved swiftly between the downstairs rooms—nothing. Every stick of furniture and art . . . gone.

She rushed up stairs, her fit, powerful legs eating up steps, two at a time.

Smacked open the door to the master bedroom.

Empty.

This was not how she'd imagined for things to go this morning.

She whipped out her handy. Dialed Charles.

"Rachel! What are you—"

"Hey, I've been trying to get hold of Hildebrandt. He's not answering. Is he there?"

"Let me ask Darlene." Off speaker, he asked Darlene, his personal assistant, who Rachel could hear say (in a sultry, sleepy voice, quite close to her husband's phone) no, she hadn't seen him, and that—in fact—*none* of the Therans had showed up to work today. Charles said, "No, Darlene hasn't—"

"Yeah, yeah, I heard," Rachel said, and hung up.

"*Oh!*" she huffed and spun around and headed back downstairs.

Again standing in the foyer, she turned back around and once more took in the totality of the empty structure.

"Huh."

Empty.

Gone.

Disappeared!

She looked down to her coffee cake, which lay on its side on the floor. She stepped over it and exited the house. Carefully closed the door behind her. Walked to the end of the walkway as if in a dream before again turning around—

FOR SALE.

A realtor sign.

Patty Murphy, Realtor.

To add insult to injury, plastered across the sign was a narrow red banner with bold white lettering that read "SOLD!"

That . . . that wasn't . . . .

She knew Patty.

As she turned back around and headed homeward, she again pulled out her handy and dialed Patty.

"Patty, Rachel Wiestromph. Are you listing Hildebrandt's house?"

"Morning, Rachel! Good old Hildy? Yeah! I just sold it last week."

"*Last week?*"

"Yes!"

Behind Rachel, as she continued walking toward her house, the FOR SALE sign disappeared.

Instead, a newspaper lay on the concrete driveway alongside the walkway up to the house.

Rachel kept walking toward her house. Didn't look back.

The front door of Hildebrandt's vacated house opened.

A young woman stood in the doorway. Momentarily stopped and inhaled deeply of the fresh, morning air.

"Did he say where he was going?" Rachel asked.

"No . . . I actually don't remember much about the whole transaction. Now, isn't that strange?" Patty said. "It all seemed to happen . . . kinda fast, now that I think of it, and I was so busy learning all the ropes in my new position, and all."

The woman in Hildebrandt's home went out and grabbed the paper.

"Did he say *anything?*" Rachel asked.

The woman with the newspaper waved at another neighbor several doors down on the opposite side of the street. That neighbor smiled and waved back.

Patty paused. With a note of concern in her voice, she said, "I'm sorry, Rachel, I just don't remember much! It's been *so* amazingly crazy, right? I just remember . . . very little about it all. But the new tenants should already be moved in by now."

The woman and her paper returned to the house. Her husband now stood in the entranceway, a big smile on his face. He held something.

Rachel stopped.

Paused.

Stood most erect.

Still without looking back, she said, "Oh, yes . . . yes, they are. *And they're very nice people, indeed.*"

The young woman with the newspaper entered into her husband's embrace and they kissed. She looped her arm around his waist as they stood in the doorway together.

"Have you met them?"

Rachel furrowed her brow, then relaxed it.

"Oh, yes, I just did. Brought over some—"

"How sweet of you!"

Rachel turned around.

The couple remained in the doorway and their eyes met Rachel's. They waved.

"*Yes,*" Rachel said, "*they're quite the charming couple!*"

Rachel looked to the couple, who raised the wrapped coffee cake into the air toward her. They both broadly mouthed, if a bit too pretentiously melodramatic, "*Thank you!*"

Smiling broadly Rachel enthusiastically waved back.

"Yes, you've done good, Patty! They're such a sweet couple! I think they'll fit in quite nicely, here . . . in the neighborhood."

A STUDY OF RUINS
Year 2092 C.E.

1

Rodney Fitzpatrick looked up into the crisp Autumn sky with silver eyes, awaiting his delivery. Checked his handy. It should have been here seventeen minutes ago. The message said it had been sent by a Type II.

He sighed.

Type II's send out Lost-and-Impact Reports if they crash, and he'd not received any such LIR. The package was a critically needed replacement part for the "eartheater" he operated. Or had been operating, since the engine had seized on him. He'd used his last spare on another eater over at the Hillyard Range the other week.

Rodney again selected the drone in the handy's app, but this time initiated a search. Its last-recorded location was two hours away—making *good* time—in the largely unexplored Blackmon Range.

He quickly sent a message to headquarters and headed toward the Trail Runner. If it wasn't coming to him, then he'd better go to it. He was "dead in the dirt," as they say, until he got that damned part, and being so remote he had no other recourse but to go in search of it himself. Which was fine.

He'd been programmed for search-and-rescue.

Rodney maneuvered the Trail Runner into the foothills of the Blackmon mountains. The tracker indicated the drone's last known location there, at some twelve-thousand feet in elevation, in an extremely demanding area of the Blackmon Range.

Rodney maneuvered his vehicle along the rough and rocky terrain, up and along the side of an unforgivingly steep slope. Pretty much all scree. He'd only gone several minutes, when his vehicle suddenly lurched laterally, and like a mid-air stall, slipped sideways down the loose rock. Rodney fought to regain control, but the wheels simply spun and whined as he now found himself careening sideways down a mountainside.

The vehicle slammed to a jarring stop.

Rodney, none the worse for wear, exited. He found that the Trail Runner had become deeply embedded between several small-but-large-enough boulders that kept half of the wheels elevated and unable to touch ground, or any other rocks.

Making sure his own feet were securely planted, Rodney bent over and grabbed the edge of the quarter-ton chassis . . . and lifted it up and out of the rut. He then wiggled and shifted the Runner back and forth up the incline, until he'd shimmied it onto more forgiving topography.

Rodney held up one end of the Runner a moment longer as he examined the undercarriage . . . then set it down, satisfied there was no damage.

He slid back in and continued.

Rodney arrived at the drone's forecasted impact location. The temperature was thirty-seven degrees. The sun shone brightly. He exited the Runner. Took in the area.

Nothing. No drone anywhere in sight. No crash landing, no hide-nor-hair.

Rodney reached back into the Runner for the handy, punched in a few commands and looked to the reading. Yes, this was its last-known location. Rodney again looked up.

Formidable. Even for him.

There was no going any farther in the Runner. He'd have to go it on foot.

Rodney reached inside the Runner for his binoculars and scanned the terrain. No drone debris, just more of what he stood in: treeless alpine topography. Tucking the handy into one of his uniform's pockets, he set off in the direction of the highest probability, as defined by the tracker.

The area continued to harbor no trees, but plenty of rocks and cliffs. He made his way through a deep, narrow canyon before coming out into an open area that looked like a hand-hewn amphitheater. This area was not yet mapped in needed detail, so there was little information in his database, beyond the *Renaissance's* on-orbit mapping. Rodney entered the amphitheater-like opening, the other side of which appeared to also present an irregular, craggy opening. He headed for it and emerged onto an opening of still-more rocks, set deep into a wide canyon.

But that wasn't exactly . . . *quite* . . . right. Something looked different about these rocks.

Structured . . . .

Rodney again checked his handy. Yes, probability calculations had him still heading in the most likely direction with a ninety-five percent certainty of drone acquisition. Rodney slowed his pace without realizing it as he examined the rocky basin. Ordered. Arranged. The air density around him also seemed to have compacted. Thickened. His handy confirmed the increased barometric pressure.

The sun, already operating between the high, narrow confines of canyon walls, suddenly disappeared behind cloud cover and the temperature plummeted. Rodney looked up into a growing overcast.

There was a decidedly weird feel to these rocks.

He came up to the first set of said arrangement.

No, these weren't just rocks... they were *ruins*.

The ruins before him were about chest high and the layout was about the size of a small outbuilding. He leapt up, bracing himself upon the partial, jagged wall with his hands, and peered over the top of it. The wall section was jagged and irregular, and bit into the meat of his palms. Inside this layout were multiple partitions sectioned off by different-sized damaged and destroyed baffles—*walls*. Lots of rubble, lots of decay. He let himself back down off the wall and continued on.

Periodically looking to his handy, he performed additional queries, but was still unable to find anything detailing this area. Not in itself surprising, Thera was still largely unexplored after eighteen years from the *Renaissance's* planetfall, and he did work at one of the most remote locations from the more populated areas—but he desperately needed that engine. Others could come back and better explore these ruins another day.

Not his programming.

Rodney reentered the handheld tracker and saw a now ninety-seven percent probability that the package should be just up ahead.

As he made his way through the area, he continued examining the terrain . . . which seemed to consist largely of *building* rubble, rather than slopes and rises and unstructured rock. It all looked as if hewn into the side of the mountain.

This whole area appeared littered with structures of all shapes and sizes... and there was an overwhelming sense of another's presence.

Rodney looked back up to the sky. Layers of heavy cloud cover continued to blanket overhead, along with a surprisingly stiff breeze that kicked up dirt and dust.

Rodney shivered.

Rodney doesn't shiver.

He took another reading. The package should be just over and around the next set of rubble, bearing 267.3 degrees. The area was hemmed in on three sides by towering cliffs that lent a decidedly claustrophobic atmosphere, especially when factoring in the heavy cloud cover that now entirely blotted out sun and sky. A stiff, bracing wind howled through the rocks and structures and just now—thunder. Lightning flashed on the other side of the canyon walls, setting off alerts from the handy. He was about to get very wet, if not zapped. As he stood there... he also experienced the developing feeling of being very... very... *alone*.

He closed his eyes and allowed the full force of the winds and flying debris to kick up around him. He quite enjoyed severe weather. Loved being out in it, but—

Alone... so very alone!

It was just him... the rocks... and...

(*alone!*)

Rodney's throat constricted... his pulse quickened.

(*very alone*)

His skin—his palms—became intensely clammy.

Don't go!

Stay!

It's lonely here—so lonely!

Rodney's face stung with the increased blistering of sand and dirt striking him.

He squinted.

The air... it *was* denser... thicker... visibility had been drastically reduced. The air space surrounding him was filled with flying debris.

Deafening thunder.

Blinding lightning.

Rodney felt psychically suffocated.

Small.

Don't go!

Stay!

He looked to his tracker. His package—*had to get it.*

Shielding his eyes from the debris, he trudged into the gale.

His tracker beeped. It was just a stone's throw away... along with the damaged and still-attached drone.

Rodney hurried to the payload and tore it free from the twisted wreckage.

Ripping open the package, he removed the two-hundred-and-thirty-pound engine and threw it up and onto his powerful shoulders. With nary an effort, he shot to his feet. But when he turned around to head back out the way he'd come—

A silhouette stood in his path.

Tall . . . misshapen.

Fifty yards ahead.

"*Hello!*" Rodney called out, shielding his eyes.

The figure remained obscured by shadow and storm. Appeared to . . . *shift*.

"*Hello?*" Rodney again called out, but this time he was struck by a wave of anguish and misery that actually caused him to buckle under his normally shoulderable load.

Rodney felt sick to his stomach.

He brought a hand to his eyes, trying to block out the sand and debris . . . blinked . . .

The silhouette was gone.

As was his nausea.

Rodney readjusted his bearings. Peered through the maelstrom that quickly engulfed him.

Alone.

Again.

Please . . . don't . . . g—

He moved on.

Rodney had not made it back to his drill site before dark. The trek out of those ruins had set him back more than planned, especially with the emergence of that squall. And the entire way out and back he'd felt watched—not to mention the appearance of that shadow thing. Perhaps it was whoever that was who'd been watching him.

He still felt watched.

He'd looked back—but of course no one had been there. Nothing. But looked back he had, many times.

Someone or some*thing* had been here. He'd seen the shape—the shadow—the form.

But none of that mattered now, as Rodney immediately descended into the drill site's tunnel and installed the engine into the eartheater. He was so far behind schedule that he had to again override his four-hour sleep mode and immediately continue drilling. He would catch up on sleep later, when his protocols could no longer be overridden. But for now, he had to regain some semblance of productivity.

Rodney brought the chewer to life, revved its engine, and performed some cursory checks. He then pulled forward to continue where he'd left off, all the while thinking about that strange, misshapen figure . . . standing before him . . . how it shifted and fluctuated in that rolling squall.

2

Rodney sat beside the eartheater in the pale illumination of the porta-lights, a thousand feet below the surface of Thera. Eating lunch.

Rodney's physical "Theran Age" was nineteen years, however his genetically engineered "Living Age" was twenty-four. He was one of the many bio-engineered workers, called "Genetics," who'd been specifically created for manual labor, and in his case, subterranean drilling. He was one of the original Genetics first brought to Thera, and had the basic package of strength, speed, agility, and enhanced constitution, but also superior night vision, "extended breathing" (the ability to do more with less air, and in survival mode an almost limitless hibernation capability), and a quite robust endurance to subterranean radiation emissions. If he had to, he even had the ability to claw his way through loose rock and dirt with his bare hands, though it might take longer to reach the surface than even his engineered life could handle. But the big thing was that people like Rodney—for, yes, they really were "people" in every other sense of the word—could do the work of a small army of Normals (as the Genetics referred to them). Extremely cost-efficient. They could even reproduce, creating more of their kind at even more of a cost savings, but of course that takes time, and humanity had only been on Thera nineteen years. A Genetics' life expectancy was theoretically like most Normals, however the nature of their work usually put them at greater risks, so they usually didn't make it past their twenties... though that had been the case on Earth. Here, the fully mature Genetics had only been in use for nineteen years, and they did boast quite the mortality rate. Plenty had, indeed, perished, performing an average of three-and-a-half years without refurbishment and retooling.

Rodney was exceptional.

It was a necessary evil, creating a new life on a new planet... doing things most Normals shouldn't, couldn't, or wouldn't do. And, yes, it was not without its critics.

But the fear... the *concern* of all it was what the Genetics did, the brutally taxing work they performed... had been and would be conveniently programmed out of them after a period of time. That just didn't seem fair. Why not accumulate memories of all that you did, like any Normal, no matter your timespan?

Afterall, who really knew how long one had to live?

Just like back on Earth, you could be twenty-two and be hit by a car. Shot by a stray bullet or taken out by cancer. War.

Poof.

Gone.

Just like that.

So, what difference did it make how old you were when you died ... how old you lived to be?

And what *was* Time, anyway?

Time ran differently here, on Thera. The old clocks and watches and other time-keeping instruments simply didn't work as they had on Earth, or, for that matter, aboard the *Renaissance*. In fact the whole *feeling* of this planet was patently different. It was as if there was some kind of stimulating agent in the air itself, the ground they walked upon. The first to set foot on Thera had notice it... felt it ... and when the mass migration from the spaceship had occurred, so had the rest of the population. They all felt years younger, more vibrant, energetic, and powerful than ever before! They'd all felt—

Hopeful.

And that was saying something for a starship full of entitled, hand-picked, nouveau nobility... criminals.

So they had to re-engineer not only their population, but their quantification of Time, itself.

Created new meaning, new clocks, new *life*.

But as Rodney sat alone in the darkness eating his steak sandwich, he looked—really looked—at the rocks.

The darkness.

The utter quietness ... the only sound his breathing.

Eating.

He suddenly felt acutely ... alone ... "alone" in the more specific sense of *lonely*.

Felt the untold age of this rock pressing down all around him. Their scientists hadn't yet studied every inch of this planet, though they were hard at work doing so ... but they'd found that the age of that which they'd measured reached back into the billions of years.

The darkness closed in around Rodney.

The quietness.

The *emptiness!*

A slowly burning terror leached into his heart ... a void ... developed within ... gutted him ... wrapped itself around him like a longed-for lover's embrace.

Don't go!

Stay!

Stay here with me ... it's so lonely here!

I've missed you since before you found me!

Rodney shot to his feet, meal and utensils clattering about the ground at his heavily booted feet.

"Who's there?" Rodney said.

Yes—yes! Talk to me! Talk to me! I have so longed for another's voice!

"Where are you?" Rodney grabbed a flashlight and directed it about his work area.

I am the rocks ... the ground ... the dirt.

"What are you?"

I am you.

"You can't be. *I'm* me—"

You are the life I have long since stopped breathing!

You are the warmth I have long since discontinued radiating!

You are the heart with which I no longer beat!

"Nonsense! I have gone long without sleep and recuperation! You are merely a product of my exhaustion!"

Rodney looked to his handy. Yes, it was beeping red . . . indicating that he had, indeed, needed to return to the surface and recuperate. Or he could simply shut down here, now, and sleep inside all the rock—

No, that would not do.

The rocks were talking to him! This had never happened before!

Simply put . . . and for the first time in his short lifespan . . . Rodney was scared . . . were he to admit that to himself.

Rodney hopped onto the Tunnel Runner, spun it around, and kicked up all manner of rocks and dirt as he spun out of the dig.

Back at the surface, Rodney went straight to bed . . . no shower, no nothing. He was bone tired. Mentally and physically expended.

This was the first time he'd gone so long without recuperation, and look what it had done to him! *Had him talking to rocks!*

Rodney slept hard. Dreamed of rocks continuing to talk to him. Calling to him. *Beckoning* him.

He'd dreamed of standing in the middle of the very same ruins he'd visited days ago. The rocks had talked to him. The ruins. And though they called out to him . . . conversed with him . . . and he understood them . . . he did not. Couldn't make out a word.

But he *felt* as if he had.

And the rocks, he somehow knew, felt the same way, in all their rockness.

Which was why they continued to talk with each other.

Heavy clouds moved in . . . storms blasted through . . . Rodney got drenched, soaked, and pelted with debris and stung by horizontal rains . . . but he stayed on and they continued to talk and not understand each other in ways that somehow brought on a deeper understanding of the both of them.

He knelt before the rocks . . . the *ruins* . . . and gently placed an ear to the stone. Listened.

Heard things.

Or was it just the wind playing tricks with his head?

He cried.

Shed his tears into the rocks. Into the ruins . . .

Only to find himself awake and standing at the opened-door entrance of his home. In his still-dirtied and stinking utility uniform.

He stared out toward the direction of the ruins.

"*Yes*," he said, out loud, but in a whisper, "*okay. I'm coming.*"

Rodney left the Trail Runner behind as he found himself once again standing in the ruins of the dead drone. Things felt different here. There was an unnerving, accordion-like accumulation of Time that rippled and expanded and contracted . . . an all-pervading sense of dust and decay and things so unimaginably ancient and distant.

It was like walking into a long-cold wall of desiccation . . . a dry succulence . . . that seeped into your bones . . . your marrow.

And, again, that feeling of being watched! Tracked!

It could have been an eternity or minutes before Rodney realized he'd just been standing there . . . looking . . . but not *seeing*. The sky above was again darkening. The winds again picking up . . . again whistling in his ears . . . or was that a *ringing* in his ears . . . a high-pitched stalling of his *mind*?

His entire body felt as if it was giving off periodic pops . . . static bursts of electricity.

It is so lonely here!

For so long there had only been the rocks, darkness, and isolation with no hopes of you, but now . . . .

Who are you? Rodney asked mentally. *Are you a figment of my imagination?*

Rodney's heart beat thickly in his ears.

A shape, misshapen, indistinct in the swirling dust and wind materialized some distance before him.

What are you? Rodney asked.

Lonely . . . oh, so very lonely . . . .

Do you have a name?

I have been abandoned . . . deserted . . . left to survive alone for eternities—

Have seen much that has frightened and saddened me—

Why?
Forever dreamed of being found....
The winds picked up. The earsplitting whistling. Flying debris cut and battered Rodney. He lifted a hand to shield his eyes.
This is my place... my home... I have come here from the distant future of a Great Past so long ago... I no longer remember... only dream...
Rodney took a couple of steps forward... reached out to a crumbling wall—
But was no longer there.
Darkness enveloped him.
A silent darkness devoured Rodney. His beating heart... ringing ears... the maelstrom—all gone. He felt every inch of his skin pinched and released, pinched and released, and while not unpleasant, it was unnerving. He called out... but that, too, had also been devoured.
He squeezed his eyes shut and flailed about for balance... but his every movement was instantly devoured. Every cell... pinched and released, *pinched* and released....
Light—I need LIGHT!
And there was light.
Firmament! I need support—a place to know where I am!
And there was.
Rodney stood on an idea of firmament... the idea of rocks and dirt. In an idea of a lit setting devoid of the idea of stars... sun, sky ... just an all-pervading brightness surrounding him.
Where am I? he asked, and his inquiry rang out all around him like a thunderous burst of energy... that instead of fading with distance increased in reverberation... propagation... resonance...
Where am I?
What am I?
What is this place?
Am I alone?
What is alone?
Do I live?
What is life?

How do I live?
Is there another?
What is another?

Rodney felt a BEFORE and an AFTER . . . a MOMENT and a NOW . . .

Experiences . . . inflated . . . thoughts and perceptions and senses . . . an ever-expanding metaphysical bladder inside an ever-defined prologue of space.

It was exhilarating and liberating and wonderful!

But he was alone and he felt all of his thoughts echoing out into Time and Space like a hollowed-out protoplasmic Big Bang.

The rocks around him rumbled and grumbled and rose and fell!

Transformed into shapes and sizes and volumes and form!

Rodney remembered blue skies—and the light around him transformed into a brilliant and crystalline blue!

Rodney searched his thoughts . . . his memory . . . and every thought, every impulse, every imagination erupted forth and into the skies, the rocks, the air—yes, he needed air to breathe, and so it was!—and as he imagined it—

He was back in the ruins.

The winds.

The loneliness.

Rodney looked to his hand, which he'd lifted from the rock wall. Stared at it. Looked to the wall which it had momentarily touched. Looked back up to the figure before him.

The figure had come closer.

You see! it exclaimed. *You see!*

Rodney looked to the figure and had to consciously refocus.

See what? Rodney asked.

I have so longed for another to see! In my past you had yet-to-come—but now you see! You see!

Rodney sent, *I do not know where I was, nor what you have or have not. I am confused, but exhilarated—unsure!*

But you saw . . . you. Saw.

The shape continued forward . . . a misshapen appendage outstretched before it. Pointing toward him.

Rodney backed away.

"I . . . ," Rodney began, out loud, "I know not where I've been . . . nor what might have *happened*," he said, backing away.

Don't go!

"I . . ."

But Rodney did not finish his sentence.

He ran and kept running.

3

Rodney stared up into the ceiling of his room.

Where was he?

What was he?

Where had he been?

What the hell was going on?

Rodney sat up. He was in bed. Looked to his hands that held him firmly in place. To his arms and legs that even now felt strong and powerful.

What *was* he?

An engineered human. Working a mineral drilling site. Worked for a corporation headquartered in New Green Bay—so named because of the mineral content of the city's terrain. A city harbored alongside a deep emerald-green lake.

He was one of many.

Part of a massive workforce created to do dirty, unforgiving work . . . so that the smarter humans . . . the ones who'd made the voyage here from the immense depths of interstellar space . . . the ones who'd *made* him—could continue their work in populating and taming this planet.

But he was still *human!*

Just an intentionally genetically altered one.

But what had happened to him—when, yesterday? Two days ago? What . . . what is . . .

(*Time*)

the time? What day is it?

Rodney brought a muscled hand to his forehead and massaged his temples.

Yesterday. *It had been yesterday.*

Had he slept almost an entire day? He was going to have to make up all that time once again! Everything was out of control and continually growing more so!

He shot to his feet.

Something . . . odd-odd-odd . . . had happened.

Hadn't it?

Why couldn't he remember?

Why couldn't he remember what'd happened to him?

He'd gone into the ruins . . . had begun to explore . . . when . . . when . . .

He'd seen a shape!

That shape, again, yes! Remembered that. That shape. Talked with it, yes, that was it!

Interacted with it! But there was more, something more . . . more . . . some*thiiing*—

His Runner.

Where was it?

He left the building. Stood outside the door.

There were definitely Runner tracks going out . . . but all he saw coming back . . . were footprints.

Rodney looked out into the distance.

The ruins.

Those ruins were ruining his life.

It was going to be another long week of catch-up.

He'd been chasing his tail ever since that damned drone crash to make up for lost productivity. And too many hours of lost productivity meant a "retooling." Being replaced and brought in to be reprogrammed. He knew of it, didn't know if he'd ever personally been retooled . . . but that was the point, wasn't it? They wiped you clean and rebooted you for other work. Retooling was increasingly rare, but it had been and still was used. As good as science was, it did make mistakes now and then . . . or Nature threw them a curve ball and the genetic outcome wasn't exactly as expected. So if there was a deficit somewhere . . . it only stood to reason to find it and see if there was some other way that the "product" could be reworked and put back out into the public good.

In the process, of course, you forgot who and what you were or did.

Engineered human . . . engineered amnesia.

But right now he had to worry about engineered productivity. And he was sorely behind, almost to the point where the numbers could never be recovered.

Rodney stood before the Tunnel Runner. He needed to get back down there. Continue his work, up his pace. Everything about him told him he had to go. Everything inside him commanded him to get back down into those tunnels and continue drilling.

Everything.

Rodney got into the Tunnel Runner, started it up, pulled forward . . .

4

. . . and came to as if from a deep sleep.

Within the ruins.

The wind howled, and there was so much dirt and dust in the air that it looked like early evening, including a severe temperature drop. Rodney saw the full outline of the sun through all the haze and his breath.

Was this a dream . . . or was he really here?

Here we go again. Again standing in the middle of these blasted ruins.

Something continually pulled him back here, and he had to find out what the heck it was. His Runner was still here, he saw as he peered behind him, so at the very least, he had to get that back to camp.

And since he was already here . . .

Rodney gave the Runner a once over. It looked fine. There was still enough charge in it to get him back.

Rodney left the Runner and made his way back among the ruins. Ran his hands along their jagged and crumbling edges.

Who'd lived here?
And how long ago?
What'd they do?
How'd they live . . . how'd they die?
Had they killed themselves off? Had some natural catastrophe taken them out?

Rodney came to a waist-high wall. Resting his hands atop it, he closed his eyes.

Tried to get the *feel* for those who might have lived here . . . reached out to them.

What did they look like?
Did they love?
Laugh?
Were they a peaceful people?
Arrogant?
What were their final moments?
What did they look like?

The light suddenly darkened and the temperature plummeted even more.

Thunder. Flashes of lightning. Fast-moving clouds. The wind had picked up, and lightning struck the ground all around Rodney.

He dropped to his knees . . . then he saw it.
He/she/it.
It was up ahead . . . the *thing* . . .
Though heavily misshapen, the shadowy creature looked vaguely anthropomorphic.

I have been so very lonely!
Are you by yourself? Rodney asked mentally.
I no longer know if I'm the last of my kind . . . or the first . . .
When are you, Rodney asked.
I do not know. No longer know. It all seems so unknowingly ancient . . . or not yet to be.
Why are you here?
Why are you *here?*
We came, Rodney answered, *from a dying race from a dying planet . . . called Earth.*

Did you really? Or had you originally come from here . . . to Earth . . . and the gravity of Time brought you back?

Are we from here?

I no longer know if I'm the last of my kind . . . or the first . . .

Why would you say such a thing? How could such a thing be possible? Is what I am seeing who you really are? Rodney asked.

I do not know. I cannot see myself as you see me.

You look . . . damaged. Misshapen. Hurt—

I may well be.

Have you a name.

I am sure of it.

Is it one we—I—can pronounce?

I don't think so.

How may I address you?

I am the Custodian.

Custodian . . . I am "Rodney."

This I know.

Is this where you lived?

I no longer know if I came before or am yet to be. But it is tall with stone and crystal buildings, as you call them. Our sun shines brightly.

I see only ruins.

I see them as well . . . and the stone and crystal . . . I see both. I see a range of life . . . probabilities. I see desolation and wind . . . ruins . . . and . . . what has yet to be.

Where do we fit in all of this?

In what is yet to be . . . and what was . . . all ruins are alive.

Are you alone?

I may be . . . or am yet to be . . . but the part of me that is communicating with you is.

You seem stuck or unstuck in Time.

Were Time to exist, I would be. I do not understand my existence to you. But, yes, I am alone. I no longer know if I came before or after . . . if I am yet to be—or the first—of my kind.

This place is ancient, crumbling, and abandoned, Rodney sent. *No one appears to have lived here for thousands upon thousands of millennia. What are you and what did you do before or after all of this?*

I do not understand the answer.

Do you or did you do something? Were you a worker? A philosopher? A scientist? Poet?

I no longer know if I came before or am yet to be—

Custodian, are you hurt?

I no longer know if I am the first or the last of my kind.

Can I see you better?

You see what you see.

But you appear confusing to me. Confused.

My form is what it is. As is yours. But if you mean can I look more like you . . .

That is not what I mean—

Why ask about my appearance?

We see—I see—physical forms. How do we speak . . . speak the same *language?*

We do not speak . . . we communicate.

Okay.

How do you see me?

You appear to be . . . dying?

Dying? To me you have died . . . so I desperately sought you out. Yet you are here.

I exist. I am not dead. I am alive, Rodney sent.

Are you a scientist? A worker . . . or a poet? Things of which you asked me?

Rodney chuckled. *I am certainly not a poet! I am a worker.*

They are not the same?

They are not.

But you used them together.

Can you come closer? So I can better see you?

I already am close to you . . . but will adjust.

Rodney watched the grotesque shape approach and recede several times before it reformed and stabilized immediately before him. The shape appeared like a surreal image of a broken human form and was hard to look at. Rodney soon regretted his request.

You do not like what I look like.

You are just quite different to what we see around here, Rodney sent, smiling. *But it is okay. Where did you and your kind come from?*

Originate?

We have always been here.

Where is 'here'?

Where we are.

You did not come from the stars?

We have always been here. Have come from behind and beyond that which you call the stars—as do you.

We came from Earth, but don't know our true origins. There are many myths.

There are no myths only origins.

That makes no sense—

—I no longer know if I came before or am yet to be, if I am the first or the last—

You do not know of your origins?

I do. As I have said, we have many origins . . . yet I no longer know if I came before or am—

Did your race die off?

I see a range of probabilities. I see my race . . . and see it never having been.

What do you see of me . . . my race?

Still . . . and not. Here and not here. Never having been.

Then how can we communicate?

We do what we do.

I am confused.

I am glad we had this communication.

Me, too. What now?

We do what we do.

Can you show me more of your race? Your time?

I can and cannot.

Will we see more of each other?

We will and will never.

I must get my Runner back to my camp. I have much work to do . . . I am very behind in my production. I don't want to leave but must. I hope to see you again.

You already have.

Thank you for this communication. I feel very good talking with you. I have no one to talk to myself. I am also alone.

You are not. I am with you. I have always been with you. Will always be with you. We are one . . . or have never existed. Do not worry . . . no matter the complications.

I do not understand.

You must go. I will find you. Or not.

The Custodian retreated from Rodney back into the storm's debris and wind and ruins.

"*Custodian!*" Rodney cried out into the windstorm, but the Custodian was gone.

Rodney headed back toward the Runner.

Had gotten only three steps.

He stiffened.

Rodney tried to say something, but his mouth abruptly froze into an open and silent "O." He tried to move, but only

Fell to his knees.

He knelt there amid the swirling storm and flashing lightning and tried to raise an arm. An arm outstretched as if pointing . . . or pleading.

The arm uselessly plopped to his side and Rodney keeled over. Crumpled over into the swirling sands and primordial rock and mysterious ruins.

Eyes open and blank.

In the expansive measure of a nanosecond . . . Rodney understood.

Comprehended everything.

He was being retooled.

In that instant he remembered having been twice retooled. He had on both occasions also busted production quotas and gone outside production parameters. Questioned and resisted protocols. He understood his model—the first worker production model that had been employed on this planet and was not without significant flaws—was being retired. Too many glitches. Persistent independence . . . inability to remain on-protocols—

And Rodney had discovered something else.

Something that had been concealed within his standard protocols. A secretive directive to record all abnormal experiences and upload them to another database, then to be

Retooled . . . retrieved . . . retired.

All that Rodney had experienced had been recorded and uploaded from him . . . his circuits sanitized.

A saucer-shaped ship appeared in the maelstrom above Rodney. Hovered about his deactivated form.

Removed Rodney—and the drone wreckage—from the ruins.

The ship adjusted its altitude. Scanned the ruins.

Scanning complete . . . the ship emitted a series of high-pitched whines—

And disappeared back into the storm-filled skies.

INTO THE DARKNESS
Year 2101 C.E.

Algis Townsend and the night were one.

Only a few minutes earlier, he'd been surrounded by the warm familiarity of city lights and sounds and smells. Now, he'd left them all, sneaking away into the darkness like someone trying to escape a crime. Desperately sought out crepuscular anonymity.

Less people. Less drama. Less everything . . . except for his own thoughts.

His headlights raced ahead of him . . . as if independently illuminating the new direction his life should take. A destination away from work, a work he had come to more than just dislike. It was something that simply no longer suited him, that he no longer wanted to be a part of. He wanted out . . . yes, to become a part of a new dream, a new journey. And he was in love with this as yet undefined dream . . . and on this warm and balmy summer night, he was on his way to fully embrace it. Even if he didn't know what it was he was supposed to be embracing.

Maybe that was it. Maybe he *was* trying to escape something... a crime of Time: a past, a present, an undesired *future*. He had to get out and as far away as possible. Headed for the west... the Western Desert... the west coast... and, beyond that, a little town called Aptos. He'd been there once, many years ago. Had fallen in love with it.

Vowed to return.

He willed his life into a new and exciting direction...

And followed the lights.

It drizzled, now.

The droplets producing an additional layer of metaphysicality as the distances between Old Him and New Him increased.

He felt... pulled... *beckoned*....

The interior of the cab was softly illuminated by the console's glow... the steady *whomp... whomp... whomp* of wiper blades hypnotic... the comforting blanket of darkness. He already felt infinitely more relaxed... propelled into an active trance, a dream world of new creation... one he never wanted to leave and would many times try to recapture in the future...

The future.

Something about that term felt decidedly unsettled.

Unnerving.

But his headlights were so certain! So knowledgeable!

Follow us! they cried. *We know the way!*

So, he allowed them to split apart the veils of darkness and unerringly lead the way.

Algis looked forward to his new journey... of being out on the road while most were asleep. He looked forward to the hum of the road... the vehicle... the oversight of the moon... driving through treacherous mountain passes at three in the morning... precipices falling away on both sides... hair-pin turns... fog... the ever-present possibility of making a false move and sending yourself over the side into the unknown breaches of real or imagined abysses, except for but your own hand... taking control of what was once thought *out* of control...

Yes, metaphorically as well as physically.

Something stirred deep within . . . *reawakened* . . . releasing a flood of emotion and feeling that were even now difficult to comprehend . . .

Few people ever really experienced the mystical . . . driving on top of the world—physically or philosophically, totally and utterly alone—one's own complete thoughts not interrupted by television, radio, or handys . . . the rattle of the rabble, his dad always used to say.

As he passed through the somnolent towns like a ghost in his own right . . . the vapor lamps breathed their own life into the darkness, greeting him and wishing him well . . . the final vestiges of the passage-of-time evaporated.

And, oh, how he reverberated with the thrill, as he rushed headlong into his new future!

All the times he had felt alone or lonely had finally faded away as he drank in his by-himselfness! He wanted to be alone! *Craved* it. *Needed* it.

Himself, his truck, his darkness. His thoughts.

His journey.

He ascended Leadville Pass.

He was so close to the heavens, but would later find out, hours into his future, that he would get even closer. The clouds and fog quickly whisked about him . . . seemingly mere feet above his head. Though he wanted to stop, he had to keep going. To stop now might ruin part of the atmosphere, the momentum . . . *he had to continue forward* . . . it was all part of the effect.

Moving.

Come! Find *me! Experience me! I'm looking for you*, the night said.

I am nothing without you!
Move . . . to move is to explore!
To move is to be one with me!
Oh, I have such special things to show you . . . to share—
Move!

Venture!

Explore!

Algis spiraled up and up, and did, indeed, try to grasp the moon!

Wisps of clouds flew past, saturated the outside of his vehicle. His travel seemed not of this world . . .

He drove around and across Blue Mesa Lake. It, too, was ghostly . . . the moon glinting off mysteriously dark waters.

It understood how he felt. Understood him . . . .

He looked down to the waters, tried to figure out what it must be like down there—now—standing alone in the darkness . . . and if there were any life forms within those nighttime waters . . .

What it would be like if he were on that lake right now . . . alone . . . in a small boat?

Sitting out there somewhere in the middle of Blue Mesa and just letting the breeze and the current take him where it would?

Were waters deeper at night?

More mysterious?

He scanned the night around the water and spotted one or two campfires off among the hills . . . and at once tried to place himself there . . . to mentally see—bi-locate—who and what was going on . . . and, at the same time, to not even bother. To let those people experience the same freeness and openness he now experienced . . . without any intrusion, psychic or otherwise.

He was, for perhaps the first time, truly in love with life and *himself.*

Who *he* was.

The *new* him.

Had been and wanted to *return* to being that person.

He continued onward through and past towns called Frontier Town, Gas Light, and Snayton Corners.

It was at these places that he became a ghost . . . a ghost of his former self . . . a ghost of the night . . . a nonperson exuberantly hurtling past in the dark . . . .

He left Hereweare behind and made his way north, into the Red Mountains.

It was a paradise of darkness!

"Hereweare"—how amusing.

As he drove through the desert, everything seemed so much closer.

The light of his headlights seemed to *pull* the landscape up and into him as he drove through it. Literally bringing everything closer. He saw things *clearer*—the tiny cacti . . . the shrubs . . . any little creatures that scurried across his path. It was like there was no other land—nothing—beyond the borders of his illumination. The only terrain available was only what was . . .

Illuminated.

Ah, the night!

Moving, moving, always *moving* . . . .

Before heading up Red Mountain Pass, Algis pulled into a lonely charging station. The last one, the sign proclaimed, for some three-hundred miles. An older gentleman was busying himself by collecting charger-side trash. Several large dogs were playfully milling around the area with him. Algis pulled up under the softly illuminated covering and stopped alongside a bank of chargers next to the guy. Exited his truck. Loved the warm, rolling breezes blowing in from the darkness that tossed his hair and kissed his face. The dogs all playfully hurried over to greet him, noses everywhere. Amused, Algis let them have their sniffs, pet them, said his hellos, then off they went, back to their playful romps with each other. Algis's feet crunched on the concrete grit as he rotated from his vehicle to the charger. He found the diffused lighting comforting.

Suddenly discovered he was being quietly observed by a dust-colored cat comfortably curled up atop another nearby charger station, its large eyes unblinking and unaccusatory. He chuckled.

Algis looked over to the older gentleman. "How ya doin'?" he hailed, as he plugged in his truck and paid the charger station.

"I'm doin' fine, thanks!" the Old Man replied, "You?"

"Doin' great!" Algis said, as he remained by his truck. "Nice place you have here!"

"I like it!" The old man tied up the last of his trash collection and paused. Looked out into the darkness. "This is why I moved here," he said, thrusting his fists into his pockets and inhaling deeply of the night air, as he arched his back. "A whole lotta *nuthin'*. Clean air, few people, no bullshisst, lotsa time to myself to just *be*."

"I'd say you sound retired, but you got this place to look after," Algis said.

The man looked back to Algis and chuckled softly. Lovingly scratched behind the ears of one of his dogs that came up alongside, happily panting, looking for adoring approval with an upturned head and lolling tongue.

"You may not realize this—even at your age," the old man said, "but when you retire you still gotta do *something*. Retirin' just allows you to live life more on your own terms after you spent a lifetime livin' it on someone else's."

The dog took off, merrily barking at the other dogs, as they romped and played about between light and shadow.

The old man said, "When I retired, I wanted to just be. Just live and make enough to get by. Think my own thoughts. Wanted just enough human interaction to remain in the Human Race. Just me, my wife, our dogs and cats. Didn't want to get caught up in all the politics, headlines, or greed. Young people versus old people. Middle-aged versus old people. *Old* people versus old people. War talk. I wanted to see unhindered sunrises and the sunsets."

The old man looked up to the stars. Algis followed his gaze.

"*The stars*," the old man continued wistfully, "you know, when you look up at the stars, you're actually looking back in time? That's how far away they are, light's so distant it takes forever and a lifetime to get to your eyes. *Your* eyes. Star light blazing a path through all that eternal darkness to get to *your* eyes. And what have they seen, those stars? That light? *Do* they see? What *will* they see? Do stars see Time the way Humans do? Do they have a consciousness we can't even begin to fathom? Is their philosophy their novae? I mean, really, philosophy is meant to expand your mind, right? Give insight. Meaning. Is a star's expansion into a nova its philosophy, how it becomes one with the universe?"

The old man looked back to Algis, who looked to the old man, an amused look on his own face.

"I like how you think, Old Man," Algis said.

"It's just amazin' I tell ya," the old man continued, "those are the kinds of things I want to think about, way out here, away from everyone else, except for but the occasional charger and convenience store buyer. *That's* what I want to be: *amazed*. Thoughtful. Philosophical. Philosophical about the stars."

"Well, Pop," Algis chuckled, finishing up at the charging station, "I think you've got the right idea! I like your philosophy—a philosophy of the stars!"

The old man picked up his trash, came closer to Algis, and again stopped, as he picked up a wayward piece of paper that blew out from around a charger.

"And I'll tell ya another thing: have you noticed how things are getting kind of weird? Politicians are getting far more crazier than before. The greedier are getting greedier. People . . . just acting plain . . . weirder. And the *clocks*."

The old man stared at Algis.

"What about the clocks?"

"What time have ya?"

"Half past—"

"I have a quarter past."

The old man stared at him a few moments longer. Algis looked at him still grinning.

"Well, your watch must just be slow, I—"

Algis noticed the charger-side clock. It also said a quarter after—well, not quite, more like twelve after. The old man took note of Algis's observations.

"You see?" he asked. "Even the clocks ain't agreeing," the old man said. "There's something mighty peculiar going on, I tell ya! Mark my words!"

"Well, it was a pleasure talkin' to ya! You have a wonderful night and take care!"

Before Algis could reply, the man was . . . gone. Totally gone. As were his dogs.

Algis blinked.

Ghosts in the night?

Things did feel kinda weird, now that the old man had mentioned it.

He looked around. It was just him and the warm wind kicking up dust and debris.

Time. Lots of Time.

And how had that old guy moved so fast? Where'd he go? His dogs?

He looked for the cat—also gone.

Algis again checked his watch. Thirty-three after. Had he really just lost three minutes since talking with the old man?

He shook it off and got back into his truck.

A philosophy of stars.

Time.

He wondered what the old man had done before retiring, as he pulled out of the charging station and back into the night.

Algis continued on down the empty, deserted roads.

Glanced to his dashboard clock, his wristwatch.

Yup. They were off about four minutes, but what did that prove? The power supply in his watch just needed to be charged, that's all. The dash clock had to be more exact, since it was synced with those government timing stations.

But it did feel odd. He'd been noticing it his entire drive so far. The beautiful, metaphysical feel to his entire drive. Everything felt slightly off from normal.

Time felt slightly off.

Observations and thought felt far more . . . weighty. Dense.

Vectored.

He waxed exceedingly pensive.

If this was like him, it was the first he'd heard of it.

It was as if ancient sands were blowing through his mind . . . his being . . . being met by the future's unsettling, balmy

(*ocean?*)

breezes. And everything in-between was getting caught in the temporal updrafts, downdrafts, and cross winds.

Algis suddenly felt cold and opened his driver's side window.

Welcomed in the heated night air. Up ahead loomed the Red Mountains. He couldn't see them, of course . . . but he certainly *felt* them.

Yes, *felt* them.

The night—not the night's *air*, but the night itself—felt more . . . concentrated . . . *dimensional*.

Maybe the old man had something there.

But whatever was going on, he never wanted it to end!

Westwon was still hours into his future and he was alive with ecstatic excitement! So, west he continued, landscape speeding by, and he allowed his imagination to run at breakneck speeds into the musings of an aging gentlemen in his waning years. He could do nothing but think about how magical his summer was . . . his best summer since childhood . . . how amazing it was to be out on the road like this, in his truck! All by himself!

And as he rode on . . . the approaching lights of towns far off in the distance floated by . . . looking more like spaceships or space cities out in the inky distances. Their clusters of lights . . . seemingly suspended out there *by* the dark . . .

Algis pulled off the road and drove up a slight rise to a promontory rest area that overlooked the highway. He came to a stop and turned off the truck, grabbed two chilled iced teas and a liverwurst-and-swiss sandwich from the cooler, and left the cab. At the rear of the truck, he dropped the tailgate and hopped up and sat on it. Dangling his legs over the edge, he cracked open an iced tea and took a long gulp.

He just sat there for a moment, enjoying the night, doing nothing. It all strangely reminded him of the coast—breezy, warm, magical—

When suddenly a downright cold cell descended upon him.

He looked to his watch—

. . . and the clocks . . . even the clocks ain't agreeing . . .

Time felt . . . palpable. Like a garment to be worn, shed, or adjusted.

As he sat there and ate and drank, he felt defined and contained within the physical encapsulation of Life and Time.

Looked up to the stars.

There's something mighty peculiar going on.

The clocks ain't agreeing.

People... acting weirder.

Algis continued to look high up into the night sky.

And looking at the stars... did that mean we were looking into the past? Did that mean that what we are seeing has already transpired? That all those brilliant points of light may not even exist, anymore?

Could we ever look to the stars and see our future? *Into* the future?

If we could look into another tense... why not all of them?

Algis took another bite from his sandwich and drink from his iced tea, as he mulled over the philosophical conundrum of it all.

If I really am here, now, Algis thought, *what* is *my future like?*

And what is a "future"?

My present is my past's future, and I am in the present, which can also be a past and a future. What does it all mean, clocks, and time, and seconds?

If the clocks aren't agreeing, as that old man says, why is that? Is the future and the past—and present—colliding?

A philosophy of stars, indeed!

Algis felt part of a long passage that extended infinitely into the future as well as infinitely into the past. His present moment felt infinitely expansive, and spacious. It didn't matter which way he looked... he felt smack-dab in the center of the *all* of *everything.*

And inhaled the dusts and sands of Time.

Rocks and ancients and dead things, but also futures and what-ifs and yets-to-be....

He heard the interruption first.

A slight hum... a mechanized drone.

He twisted about on the tailgate, searching the night sky and darkness above and beyond his truck, iced tea in hand.

It was not an unpleasant sound, but an uninvited one it was. A smart, unbidden whine and whirr, it advanced upon the balmy breezes, the fluttering of leaves, the rustling of ground debris.

And down from the night sky descended quite a large man upon quite an odd machine.

A man... astride something that was a cross between a rocket and a motorcycle... descended from the night sky. And as he looked up to it, the other looked down to him, both trying to decipher each other.

Algis sat there, iced tea in hand, a look of amused curiosity upon his face, as he observed the man and his machine lighting upon the ground before him some twenty feet away. He couldn't tell if the craft hovered or had some kind of kickstand holding it up, but it rested upon the ground—upright—the man, looking much like himself only slightly larger in scale. Taller in height, larger in proportionate girth. But his face was no less bemused than his.

"Evening!" said Algis.

The man furrowed his brow.

Then the giant of a man extracted himself from his machine. Said something that Algis didn't understand.

Algis, casually holding his iced tea in both hands between the "V" of his legs, smiled. Observed. Curiously, he felt no fear nor threat from this most intriguing interloper.

Superior booted feet standing powerfully apart, the interloper stood beside his machine and interestedly placed his larger fists into his hips. Observed Algis. He, too, sported a bemused smile upon his larger face.

The giant said something else, just as incomprehensible, just as Algis said, "I am Algis—Algis Townsend."

Both continued to look at each other, befuddled, if amused.

"Guess we have a problem here!" Algis said, placing his iced tea down on the tailgate.

The giant nodded thoughtfully then raised an index finger.

A moment passed.

"*Is that better?*" the giant said.

Algis jerked back in surprise. He felt as if the inside of his head had just been rewired.

"Wow! How'd you do that?" Algis said.

The man shrugged his shoulders.

"'Imshd,'" the man said, thumping his chest with his middle fingers.

"'Algis,'" Algis said, directing toward himself. "Pleased to meet you!"

"Likewise!"

"Would you like an iced tea?"

"Iced tea? Who wouldn't—thanks!" Imshd said and approached Algis.

Algis held out an unopened bottle to Imshd, who reached for it—

And promptly dropped it.

"What the—" cried Imshd.

Algis jumped off the tailgate and said, "*Okaaay* . . . ."

"Wait a minute!" Imshd said, and stuck out his large hand.

Algis instinctively reached out—but their hands passed through each other. Both shivered.

"Holy shisst!" Algis said.

"Ha!" Imshd said.

They tried it again with the same results. They did this several times—laughing as they did so.

"This is weird!" they both exclaimed.

. . . and the clocks . . . even the clocks ain't agreeing . . . .

"Where are you from?" Algis asked.

Imshd jerked a thumb back behind him. "I live just over those hills, there. I was out for a fly after a long night's shift."

"No," Algis said, chuckling, "I mean, from *when*."

"What year is it?"

"2101."

After regarding Algis for a moment, Imshd looked away.

"What year did you think it was?"

"Not that year."

"Hey, Imshd," Algis said, replacing the cap to his empty bottle, "what do you see when you look around?"

Imshd said, "I see the ocean—"

"*Ocean?*"

"Yes, ocean. What do you see?"

"I don't see an ocean! I see miles and miles of *desert*. It's night—"

"—day—"

"—and a road that bisects through it! I see lights off in the distance, perhaps a small town, perhaps a small industrial complex."

"No ocean?"

"No ocean."

"Huh."

"What is it like where you live? Your land? Your home?" Algis asked.

"Oh, it's lush! Beautiful! We own acres and acres of woodland! Our home is landscaped with beautiful flowers and trees and a stream runs through everything!"

"That's crazy! There's water up there? Maps clearly only show desert, here! No woods, no flowers! No—"

"But that's where I live! I'm not making this up—"

"But you see an *ocean*."

"As should you!"

"But *you* should see desert!"

"But I don't! This area is dense with life and businesses and homes! There are thriving communities—metropolises—all along this coastline—for *miles!* Can't you see that?"

Algis turned to look back down into the darkness below. To the floating island of isolated lights far out into the distance. "But I don't. I don't see any of that."

Algis continued, "And the year, Imshd? What year do you think it is?"

"57769.7."

"57769.7? Well, that's certainly an odd year!"

"As is your 2101! But I remember learning from our history books how years used to be labeled, and yours is exactly like tha—"

"*Excuse* me? You're saying I'm in your *past?*" Algis straightened up alongside his truck.

"It would seem so—"

"The past—*your* past. And you're . . . *my* future?"

"Apparently!"

"I hardly know what to say at this point," Algis said, quietly looking around.

"Me, too," said Imshd

"A past . . . a past is one thing," continued Algis, "but to know a *future?*"

"Perhaps knowing you have a future is a good thing," Imshd said, "but what about me? There are many doomsayers here, people who've looked into *our* future . . . and cry that we don't have one."

"How do you not have a future?"

"It's a strange and terrifying thing to consider! But here I am, in *yours*, and I ponder if I even *have* one!"

"Sorry to hear that."

"Say that as you will, but you do so from the comfort of your own *present*, which is my past, that you knowingly have a future—but for how long? How long do any of us have a future? Our doomsayers cry that an apocalypse to end all apocalypses is just around the corner."

"Every historical period says that."

"Perhaps—but, again, you say that from the comfort of the distant past!"

"My *present!*"

"My *history!*"

"Point taken. Sorry about your futu—"

"*Our* future," Imshd corrected.

Algis nodded. "*Ours.*"

Both men quietly stared off into their perspectives.

"Were there wars?" Algis asked.

"Many," Imshd said.

"Our histories tell us that the people we found here had no war . . . no strife."

"Our histories and legends had taught us that it was the people from the stars who brought the wars. The strife."

"The people from the stars," Algis repeated, pensively, "Wow, you'd think being so advanced they'd also have been smarter."

"Are you one of those people, Algis? One of the first who came here from the stars?"

Algis shook his head and said, "No, I was born here. But, yes, my *parents* had come from the stars. From a place called 'Earth.'"

"'Earth.'"

"So," Algis said, "This big war of ours . . . when did that happen?"

"352.3."

"Ha!" Algis cried out, chuckling. "Ask a stupid question!" In a more serious tone, he asked, "How bad was it?"

"Bad. Life . . . had to start over. *Life* . . . had been severely damaged, nearly destroyed. Geographies catastrophically upended and displaced. Our world was dying. *We* were dying.

"The war," Imshd continued, " . . . it took a lot . . . but those who saw it coming prepared and hid . . . hid in imaginative and ingenious ways, from the destruction, all the good in our lives . . . all the technologies, the libraries, the art. They tunneled, our historians told us, went back up into their satellites and space stations. Even the moon. They tried their best, but the wars still came, all the mini ones, the tyrants, the despots, the psychopaths. Until the Big One. Our histories warned we were all doomed to relive what had brought us all to this planet in the first place."

"Doomed to relive. That is not a promising future at all!" Algis said.

"No, it is not! But who wants to know the future! I am from yours, and I don't mind telling you it is quite terrifying living in it! More stressful than you can imagine! Not knowing how much longer we all have to breathe this precious air! Enjoy this comfortable and secure atmosphere that sustains us all! You say that all of Humankind has always lamented about an End of Days . . . but living as I do in your future, I tell you never before have I seen or read or heard so *much* of it! All of our media is fascinated and obsessed with it. Our movies, our books, our commentaries! And even every day—*every beautiful day*, with the sun shining, the breezes breezing, and birds chirping and flying—there seems a subtle undercurrent in the air. We all feel it. Try to ignore it. But things *are* changing. We know this from our histories. People are more on edge . . . our dreams are dark and foreboding . . . our weather keeps growing warmer. Nobody can agree upon anything! Everything is politicized, weaponized. There are always fights in our government, in other governments. Constant bickering. Constant headaches and fear. Fear, Algis, it is *fear* that is the one constant that seems to run through everything we think or do. Our lives. Like we are watching the coming of a storm. Or the calm *before* one.

"I grew so weary of all of this that I went for a fly. Had to clear my head and wished for simpler times! Wished I'd lived in a time in our distant past that did not have so much fear in everything we did!"

"And I had found myself thinking about the past, present, *and* future!" Algis said.

Imshd continued, "One beautiful day I went out for a ride. Just me and my machine and the ocean air. And as I flew over the road alongside the ocean, listening to the birds, inhaling the salt and sea spray and humidity, my mind wandered. Then I found myself *here*. But am I really here, or is this just a dream?"

"And there *I* was," Algis said, "weary of my life and going for a drive! Am I really here, or had I dozed off somewhere?"

"You don't see the ocean, do you? Not at all?"

"Nope."

"Nor a bright sun . . . or feel wonderful humidity . . . hear beautiful birdlife?"

"No—I see and feel the night, but curiously the balmy air tonight did remind me of the coast. Otherwise I inhale desert and desiccation. Things that you also do not see or feel."

"Yes."

"Well," Algis said, solemnly. "On this, we can agree, we are here, together. In this dream or this roadside stop."

"Indeed!"

"In our respective presents . . . two friendly and lonely consciousnesses passing in the night, but reaching out to each other!"

"Agreed!"

"Shall we ever meet again?"

"Who knows?"

"I do hope so!"

"As do I!"

Imshd approached Algis, tears in his eyes, and said, "Even . . . even though we can't actually do this, I attempt it anyway, my new . . . ever-to-be-remembered . . . *friend*."

Algis extended his hand, tears also in his eyes.

"It was a pleasure meeting you!" they both said as one.

Their hands passed through each other and they quietly chuckled.

"I felt that! It was cold!"

"As did I! But our *greeting* warm!"

"I would really have liked to go on your road trip with you, in your truck," Imshd said, his eyes continuing to mist over.

"That would have been fun," Algis said. "And I would have liked to visit your world. To fly with you and see where and how you live."

"You are kind, but you are far better off here, my friend, in your present."

Imshd turned and approached his machine. Hopped back onto it. As it lifted back up into the night, Imshd rocked the machine back and forth, waved to Algis, then disappeared back into the darkness.

Algis stood alone behind his truck.

Listened to the quietness of the night. Felt the—now balmy?—breezes against his skin.

Looked back to his truck. Wiped away his tears.

What had just happened?

Had it really happened, or had he just dozed off and dreamed it all?

He looked out to the distant lights that appeared to float in the darkness.

What a strange and wonderful dream! Maybe when he next came back this way and ran into that old man at that charging station, he'd have his own tale to tell! Clocks not agreeing, indeed!

Algis cleaned up his tailgate, closed it, and slid back into the cab. He started the engine, wished Imshd well . . .

And continued on into the darkness.

THE EXTINCTION SAMARITANS
Year 2111 C.E.

1

"*There will come stiff winds!*
"*The fires of war!*
"*Annihilation of the seen and unseen!*" cried the unnamed orator.

The man, slightly built and about as tall, stood upon a street corner before Wedgely Park. Nice haircut. No facial hair. He wore the clothes of the time, no holes nor ratty cuffs, in fact he looked like any other businessman on his way to work in the city of Lincoln, in the state of Parkston. But he just kinda stood there, lunch bag in hand, talking into the wind, as all manner of people hurried back and forth past him on their way through rush hour.

"Will follow more peace, more prosperity, more *time!*
"But soon will follow further conflagration! O greed! O power! O corruption!

"Loss on a scale unimaginable!

"The Alpha and the Omega!"

And with that, the unnamed orator concluded his communications, turned, and left. Fell in with the moving crowds on their way to work.

This was Monday.

On Tuesday, the following happened.

"There will come stiff winds!

"The fires of war!

"Annihilation of the seen and unseen!"

He again stood upon the same street corner in front of the same park. Same nice haircut, though a day longer. No facial hair. Same manner of clothes of the time.

Again, he just stood there as if talking to a group of nobodies, lunch bag clutched in-hand by his side, still talking into the wind.

"Will follow more peace, more prosperity, more *time!*

"But soon will follow further conflagration! O greed! O power! O corruption!

"Loss on a scale unimaginable!

"The Alpha and the Omega!"

Then quietly left.

Come Wednesday, the police were waiting.

2

"Mr. . . . "'Humbug,' is it?" the officer said, taking the statement from the opposite side of the desk, at which they both sat.

"It's '*Hooomboood*.' But, yes, that's me. Augustus *Hooomboood*."

The officer continued typing away without breaking stride, staring into the monitor that sat between them. "Still employed at the E-tip plant?"

"I am."

Humbud sat quietly in the chair, his opened (and searched) lunch bag (and chicken-salad sandwich) before him on the desk. Augustus was a quality inspector of those e-tips people used to clean their ears—*just don't ram them too far in!*, he would habitually admonish.

"Just don't ram them in too far when you use them, officer!" Humbud had enthusiastically informed the officer. The officer offered his best stern glare.

Humbud smiled and looked away, hands folded neatly before himself. Fingers quietly fidgeting. He smiled to a couple of other officers who passed by.

"Okay," his officer said, more to himself than Humbud. "Now, Mr. Humbu—"

"—*Hooomboood*—"

"—why exactly are you proselytizing an apocalypse?"

"Well," Augustus began, trying to maintain a semblance of composure, "I can certainly assure you that all this came as much as a surprise to me, as it did you!"

"I'm sure."

"I don't really know why . . . I just know that on Sunday, I had a wonderful day down by the Enyungen Sea, a nice picnic with my cat, Sylvester—he really likes going out on the leash—"

"Mr. Humbug—"

"—*Hooom*BOOOD—"

"Just answer the question, please."

"But I am," he said, giving the officer a surprised, questioning look with just the right amount of indignance.

The officer leaned to the side of his monitor and glared at him across his desk. Giving him a weary stare, he said, "Look, Augustus . . . I'm just coming off a long night's shift after also having pulled a swing shift for another who called in sick. I'm tired, I'm hungry, and I'm in no *mood*."

"Oh—ha-ha!" Humbud said, rocking a pointing finger back and forth at him, "I see what you did there!" Augustus said, chuckling. "You *do* know how to pronounce my name."

The officer sighed. "I do."

The officer returned to his upright sitting position and again began typing.

"How can you be typing when I haven't said anything?" Humbud queried.

Only his eyes visible, the officer again glared hotly at him over the top of his monitor.

Augustus made a quick face and retracted down into his seat.

"As you were *saying* . . . ," the officer said.

Augustus cleared his throat. "Okay, you clearly don't want to hear about Sylvester—"

"—clearly—"

Augustus again cleared his throat.

"Anyway . . . I got up this morning and went about my routine routinely enough, routinely feeding Sylvester, who will only routinely eat *Sinfully Salmon* in the morning—"

A massive *THUMP!* filled the air as the officer slammed his massive palm onto the desktop and, Augustus also found, was suddenly towering over him from his side of the desk.

Augustus hadn't remembered him being so tall. Nor so meaty.

The officer eyed Augustus with invisible daggers, veins powerfully popping from the sides of his temples and throat.

Augustus apologetically regrouped.

"All I know is that on my way to work this past Monday, I had the most profoundest of feelings to just stop in front of the park. So I did. Then, once there, as I looked over the place, took it all in and really looked to all the people coming and going—not one of them smiling nor even making *eye* contact—I felt . . . weird."

"Weird," the officer said, sitting back down and typing.

"Weird. Displaced. Almost like I was going to throw up—but not a normal throw up, or even like a hairbally throw-up—well, anyway, I felt sick. Ish. Uneasy. Then out it came. It just came out. All of it. As you witnessed."

Augustus looked out across the police station. Observed silently. At all of the people coming and going, and not one of them making eye contact.

Watching.

Watching.

Slowly came to his feet.

"Augustus—what are yo—"

"There will come stiff winds!" Augustus began. "The fires of war . . . annihilation of the seen and unseen . . . . "

"*Dammit*, Humbud, sit your ass down!"

"Will follow more peace, more prosperity, more *time* . . . but soon will follow further conflagration! O greed! O power! O corruption!"

The officer flew up and over to Humbud.

"Loss on a scale unimaginable," he continued to iterate as the officer forced him back down into his seat. But he simply stood back up.

The officer again grabbed him and just happened to glance past him—and froze.

"The Alpha and the Omega," Augustus finished.

There, at perhaps half of the desks in the unit, stood others. Other Humbuds.

All similarly standing, similarly uttering the very same

(. . . *The Alpha and the Omega* . . .)

words that Augustus Humbud had just delivered.

"I'm so sorry, officer," Augustus said, behind the officer as he embarrassingly sat back down. "I don't know how or what comes over me, but I'm just compelled to say what comes out."

The officer, still facing the main station area, turned back to Augustus.

Mr. Humbud continued, "These words . . . these things . . . they just come out of me. Like they have a life of their own. It feels like a powerful waterfall—*word*fall—building within me, deep within, and it just needs to, *has* to, gush out, and until I say it, otherwise builds and builds and—"

The officer looked back to the others, who were now also in various stages of sitting back down, their officers also going over them with questions upon questions. Officers looking to other officers.

"Very much like my Sylvester's hairballs, I'd imagine."

The officer looked back to Humbud . . . a look of fear upon his face.

3

The psychiatrist, one of several in the detention cage with the large contingent of Humbuds, was named Wheaton Milton, Doctor of Psychiatry at Eversen Hospital. Milton and his compatriots all had their tablets out recording everything that was said and done.

All the others in the cage were just like Humbud, brought in on Proselytizing and Peace Disturbance citations.

"What's wrong with us, sir?" Augustus asked Dr. Milton.

"Well, Mr. Humbud—"

"Thank you for correctly pronouncing my name!"

Milton nodded and continued, "we're all working quite diligently in trying to ascertain just what *is* going on here." Milton wrote on his tablet with a stylus and rapidly tip-tapped multiple selections on it as he stood before Humbud and the others.

"Do you have any idea what it all means—I mean, beyond the obvious?" Humbud said.

"Beyond the obvious warning, which it clearly is . . . no. And neither do my associates. Our data is linked."

"So, you've all been in here some two hours and know nothing more than when you first entered?" asked another, whose name was Perwanaha.

"I'm afraid not," Milton said. Others of his associates who stood nearby exchanged glances.

"Would you like to hear more about my cat," Humbud said. "he really loves going for walks—"

"Oh, *no*," bemoaned another sitting in the cell with them, frustratingly dropping his head into his hands. "Here it comes *again!*"

Humbud went silent.

Rocked back and forth.

Looked like he was going to throw-up, and not in a hairbally way.

"Interesting . . . it's getting more frequent," Milton said to himself, as he twisted about within the cell, madly scribbling away on his tablet, as were all the other psychiatrists.

All the Humbuds came to their feet.

"There will come stiff winds!" they said in unison, facing in multiple directions. "The fires of war . . . annihilation of the seen and unseen! Will follow more peace, more prosperity, more *time* . . . but soon will follow further conflagration! O greed! O power! O corruption! Loss on a scale unimaginable!

"The Alpha and the Omega."

They'd all looked to each other in abject dread.

4

Milton went home not knowing much more than when he and the others had started out. But if there was one thing they all agreed upon, it was that they were all rather frightened by the arcane mechanics of this maddingly ubiquitous manifestation. They were spread out all across Thera. The profession had never seen anything like this before.

The manifestation predicted war and unimaginable destruction . . . yet, sandwiched in there, were periods of peace. Given the predicted events, he and the other professionals all felt that these things would take time . . . and would most likely not necessarily occur during their own lifetimes. That most likely—hopefully—proselytized events would take place over the course of multiple generations.

But that was nothing to sneeze at. Or ignore.

And it seemed to be growing. Just in the two hours they were there, the officers had brought in several others, also spouting the same warnings.

This was definitely not good.

Milton didn't like this . . . didn't like this at all. He actually feared for Humanity. Exhausted, he tried to immerse himself into some semblance of normalcy by turning on some soothing violin music, in this case, Vernack's *Mephisto*, in A-minor, and making himself his favorite comfort food—meatash with brown gravy and mashed potatoes—but he just couldn't discount the dire happenings of the day—and age. There were, indeed, all manner of current events and other signs about the approach of just such a future. Government and popular harmony were eroding . . . the financial infrastructure increasingly corrupt. Prices going up on everything, inflammatory talk about pollution and planet warming.

It all made him rather sick to his stomach just thinking about it.

Milton took his unfinished meatash to the kitchen counter . . . and suddenly felt a . . . gigantic, nebulous face from afar gazing down upon him . . .

He paused.

It scared him so much, it did actually make him sick to his stomach, and he reached out to the counter to steady himself.

He moaned.

He groaned.

What was *happening? To their lives? Their world?*

And now this!

Unimaginable destruction in their future? Periods of in-between peace?

More destruction at the distant end of the timeline that extended or contracted how far?

This was what they all had to look forward to?

If any of it was remotely true, how was this any way to live? How could anyone change any of it? It would be easy to dismiss one lone crazy, proselytizing at a park, but now they were everywhere, even locked up in detention cells. *All proclaiming exactly the same thing.*

They very same words. The very same inflections.

Milton didn't feel at all good . . . and violently lost it into the kitchen sink.

"Oh, no . . . no-no-no-no-no . . . ."

He barely supported himself, still bent over the sink.

His body felt like it had been slammed into a wall. His mind . . . his mind felt as if it was losing its balance, exploding—

"No-no-no-no-*no* . . . "

Something . . . something was going on . . . he felt as if . . . a force . . . something so incredibly distant as to defy definition . . . was calling him . . . infiltrating his form, his body, his *mind* . . .

"*Nooo!*"

Wheaton Milton, Doctor of Psychiatry at Eversen Hospital, straightened up, hands falling comfortably to his sides . . .

(*Augustus Humbud and all the other Humbuds across the globe came to attention*)

Looked straight ahead to the wall over the sink . . .

(*all the other Humbuds stared straight ahead . . .*)

And opened his mouth:

"There will come stiff winds . . . the fires of war . . . annihilation of the seen and unseen . . . ."

SOMETHING'S IN THE AIR TONIGHT
Year 2113 C.E.

1

For the most part, there's always something that precedes something else.

And before what was to come, came the following:

Izzy Fastbinder left the movie with her companion. It hadn't been a particularly good movie, nor even all that interesting, but it had been a movie, and she hadn't been out to one in a long, long while.

And it had taken her mind off current events.

Her companion for the evening had been her boss, Thomas Hurkimer. She knew better and he did, too, but what the hell, they both said, after some après-work drinks one Thursday night, and Friday found themselves touching shoulders, holding hands, and sucking face in the not-particularly-good movie.

Her boss was at least interesting. An ex-military man—he couldn't even tell her the branch of service—he had a good work ethic (you know, except for the subordinate fraternization part) and was kind and fair to his direct reports. Was so far the same to her, though she knew that he had had trouble in his marriage, which had abruptly ended two years ago. And he'd had continued problems of one kind or another with all the women he'd dated. That had been the workplace chatter. There'd also been some issues related to his time in service that he just didn't want to talk about, which—for now—was fine with Izzy.

They'd had a wonderful dinner at a small, secluded restaurant (she'd had *monstroni*, he the *pilattae*) that she hadn't even known existed and had talked about all manner of things except work and politics. Where the government was headed, where the world was headed. Those stupid Extinction Samaritans, who continued to sporadically pop up here and there.

And, again, that was just fine with Izzy.

She wanted to forget about everything.

Except for the man presently holding her hand.

Certainly the movie.

After the movie, they'd walked around, continued to hold hands, and dipped into more than one dark corner to make out. In each successive corner their lips and hands gained more territory, more license, and neither Izzy nor Thomas protested. They were, after all, two unattached, lonely souls.

Back at her apartment, she'd barely locked the door before they'd found themselves in her bed.

Izzy screamed and cried and clutched and loved.

And while Izzy loved, Thomas grunted and groaned, and the two of them found common ground . . . but it was also at that time that all Izzy had tried to forget and ignore had flooded right back to her like a burst dam.

Politics.

The planet.

War.

Death.

More politics.

Would the world end before their lovemaking did?

Would Thomas be blown up on his way home in the morning? Would she, on her way to work?

Would one of them die while the other found another lover . . . then only wistfully (hopefully, *painfully*) think of the other as they made love to this new body?

Would Thomas get called back up into whatever world it was he hadn't wanted to talk about?

But as the night and their lovemaking wore on, both did survive. Both fell asleep. And both even shared breakfast that following morning.

But then both separately left for work.

As Izzy arrived back at work she found that Thomas had not yet made it in. Instead, another, Millicent Fairweather, had shown up later in the morning to take charge of their department for the day, Millicent explained in a department e-mail, but not a word of Thomas had been raised. No one asked.

This was typical.

It was called "Saturday."

People commonly came and went. No reasons. No explanations.

And questions were never encouraged.

Izzy went back to coding. She worked on super-secret government programming that monitored people's every move, from subtle eye movements to distant travel.

Two hours later the entire corporation had been notified that one of their own, a Thomas Hurkimer, had been involved in a terrorist attack that very morning. Thomas had stopped at a shopping center when the attack had gotten underway. It had been reported that Thomas had been a hero—had given his own life as he protected many civilians. Several attackers had been pre-positioned within the store, and at an appointed time, randomly opened fire. Incendiary devices had been employed. Thomas physically removed two of the attackers himself, then later bodily launched himself onto one of the incendiary devices as it went off. Many lives had been spared because of his selfless behavior.

The remaining assailants had all been neutralized by the response team.

Izzy went into the third-floor restroom and cried.

On Wednesday, Izzy, while at work, had a software update ping her handy while she'd been reading the latest news on her ten-minute lunch break. She hated it when that happened. It usually meant that the update would take up valuable time from her reading, because it was mandated by law that all updates had to be incorporated within two minutes of notification.

So, Izzy selected the update—which completed almost before she removed her thumb from its selection.

Not wanting to waste any further time, she continued to read until her break was over.

Back at her desk, another department e-mail—corporate, actually—alerted employees to possible pockets of escalated violence. All employees were reminded to avoid all such situations and report anything witnessed. Failure to do so would be grounds for termination . . . even possible incarceration.

The remainder of the day passed uneventfully.

As Izzy passed coworkers in the lobby on the way to her vehicle, she overheard portions of conversation, most of which revolved around growing tensions in the Numani government and their allies. It never failed, she thought, no matter how advanced a civilization, there were always greed and power grabs. Or at least so the ancient Earth texts had instructed.

Izzy got into her vehicle and buckled up, when her handy buzzed.
New message.

There was a Janus Corporation identifier, the handy's manufacturer, in the message header. Izzy clicked on it. The message read:

A critical update is coming. Be prepared for immediate update. There has been an increase in hacking activity. A new threat keys off of auto-upgrades and has to be manually and immediately performed.

Your upgrade arrives in three minutes.

Izzy smacked the wheel.
Three minutes? Really?
She'd never heard of such a thing.
Izzy switched off her engine and looked around. A steady stream of people came and went from the building. Some of those entering the parking lot immediately left once they got into their vehicles.
Didn't they also get the same message?
A timer popped up on her screen, starting at thirty seconds.
Geez!
Underneath the timer was the "Initiate" selection (as a coder, she hated the word "button").
. . . four . . . three . . . two . . . one.
Izzy hit *Initiate*.
She sat there looking at her handy.
Her screen flickered.
Then . . .
Nothing.
She frowned as she stared at the apparently lifeless looking lump of technology in her hand.
Another pop-up message declared that she had another message—but no actual message text displayed.
Not even an update identifier.
"You don't have an identifier," she said to herself, "I don't open you." She swiped it into the trash.
It again popped up.
She again sent it to the trash.
Again it popped up . . . but this time "*Monstroni and pilattae*" was in the identification header.
Izzy stared at her handy.
Thomas?
She brought her finger over the message . . . and paused.
Before she could even think about what she was doing, her finger twitched and activated the message.
She expelled a breath.

Izzy, the message began, *this is Thomas.*

Izzy grabbed onto the vehicle's door and inhaled sharply. Stopped breathing.

Read the message.

I'm not dead. Don't believe all that you hear. Meet me at our restaurant in one hour. Trust no one and be extremely carefu—

The message displayed an *"Unable to access message"* pop-up, which was quickly followed by a *"Message deleted"* pop-up.

Izzy tried to bring the message back up . . . but it had, indeed and apparently, deleted itself. She tried the Trash folder.

Nothing.

Her handy then vibrated madly and grew quite hot. Izzy tossed it away from herself.

She looked to it, in the passenger-side footwell. Its screen cracked, practically disintegrated, actually, then collapsed upon itself.

"What the—?"

Her handy had actually self-destructed before her eyes in the passenger-side footwell.

What was going on here?

Monstroni and pilattae?

What time was it?

Thomas!

Izzy restarted her engine and sped out of the parking lot.

2

She pulled into the parking slot in front of *Papa Lasagna*, switched off the engine, and sat there. Stared into the restaurant's windows. There were a few people she could make out through the windows. A few cars in the lot.

Thomas . . .

It wasn't as if she was in love with the man, but he had certainly made an impression upon her. He seemed like a truly good person, and, well, she was curious. Okay, more than curious. It wasn't as if she had anything else going on in her life besides twelve-plus-hour workdays, six days a week.

Thomas...
His self-destructing message to her.
Thomas...
Their date.
Thomas...
Just what in hell had happened to him?
Izzy exited her vehicle and approached the establishment.

She sat in the waiting area. Over the loudspeakers played *Violin Concerto No.3*, by Suzette Hahn. The music enwrapped her like a comfortable blanket. She was quite moved by the violins, emotion almost too easily welling up within her—but quickly stomped it down. Two other couples and an unaccompanied woman sat with her. She went to pull out her handy, when she remembered it'd self-destructed in her car. A small television set also droned on above their heads, on-screen captioning enabled.

Her corporate e-mail came back to her.

Are any of these people a problem? she thought. *Are any of them something she should*
(trust no one)
(be careful)
worry about?

One of the couples talked quietly and looked as if they were on a date. The other couple had their faces buried in their handheld technologies. The solitary woman watched the small television screen, her hands folded neatly upon her lap, one of her arms threaded through the straps of her purse. She sat there like a statue. Izzy eyed her a moment longer before also diverting her attention to the television, herself.

War. Political in-fighting. Global mudslinging. Incendiary journalism.

What was to become of us?

Things were growing more and more frustrating and tense with each day. As was being broadcast, little "spats" were popping up all across the country. Bouts of mass shootings and bombings. National protests. International uprisings. Corruption, oh, the *corruption!* Increasingly immoral politicians warping any-and-all data to fit their politics, not the Constitution. Not to mention clearly unfit chancellors placed and kept in office by their unseen and wicked puppet masters. And the current Premier—as corrupt and patently vile as they came, if not, more so . . .

Oh, how she could easily allow herself to go on and enumerate a hefty tabulation of other political vulgarities, *but what would be the point?* The clown was firmly seated in power, with every horn-tooting harlequin staff member enabling him . . . and they were all just as guilty.

One of the couples, the ones that looked as if they were on a date, was escorted into the dining area. Izzy blankly stared after them after they left the waiting area.

This country was imploding . . . yet ever on played the violins . . .

Then the other couple was ushered inside the restaurant—the tech-focused couple.

Izzy looked outside the window, closed her eyes, and took in several deep breaths. She allowed herself to be swept away by the majestic timbres of the violins that continued to enwrap and embrace her. Though they quickly and thoroughly resonated within her cells and dissipated her rising political ire, she couldn't shake a deep sense of growing trepidation.

There was still no vehicle from Thomas.

Izzy looked back into the waiting area. The lady across from her continued to not make eye contact with her, yet had changed her attention from the suspended television set to her handy. She was now just as focused in her handy as she had been in the television set.

That seemed odd to Izzy, who continued to eye the lady, who kept working her handy.

Izzy picked up on an unsettling vibe about her.

No sooner had she thought this when the woman looked up—not to her, but to the hostess who had hailed her. The woman put away her device and cast a brief smile to Izzy as she walked past and into the dimly lit restaurant's interior.

Okay, maybe she really had just been busy.

Now it was just her in the waiting area.

Izzy got to her feet, and again faced the window looking out into the parking lot.

Really—*why was she here?*

Thomas?

How did she know she'd really been contacted by him, and really, why should it matter to her at all?

He'd been her boss of two years.

They'd gone out on one date.

They'd slept with each other exactly once.

She had no real feelings toward him—

But she had to admit to a sense of curiosity. Belonging. If he was in her thoughts, surely she was also in his. She also had nothing else to do at home—well, in her apartment, rather. Didn't even own a cat. She was utterly consumed and owned by her work. Would probably have just logged back on and done some more coding after dinner, a shower, and some television.

And why had Thomas contacted her? Why was she so important?

The violins increased in intensity as the lights suddenly dimmed. She looked around. Her eyes met those of the hostess.

"We dim the lights and increase the music for the after-work crowd," the hostess said, smiling. It was nice to see someone in-the-wild, so to speak, smile. At *her*.

Izzy acknowledged her with a brief smile of her own and looked back out the window.

Minutes passed.

"Miss, you may come with me—we can seat you now," the hostess said, standing to the side of her post, menu and wrapped tableware in-hand.

The restaurant was far busier than Izzy had imagined.

It was darkened and cozy inside. The violin concerto could also be heard in here. There were many shadows sitting at many tables. As she was led through the dining area, she mentally identified where she and Thomas had sat—

(*holding hands*)

(*eyeing each other*)

over by the fireplace, at the far end of the room.

She wondered how many of these shadows felt about the Premier and the spiraling descent of their very own government. She also knew she could easily find out.

Izzy was a coder, yes, but her coding involved spying on her country's very own citizenry.

She worked for the government. Technically, worked for . . . the Premier . . . but, functionally worked for the intelligence agency that operated within the government. She knew that most of her coworkers felt the Premier was, indeed, guilty as sin. In fact they all secretly referred to him as the "Criminal Premier."

But their lives demanded that their paychecks keep coming. And since they didn't directly work with the Criminal Premier, or "CP," as they also referred to him, they felt much better in the performance of their duties.

Yes, they could all see the writing on the walls: if CP got his way in both the Red and Blue Houses, there would be no stopping him, and it would very well be the beginning of the end.

Nothing good could come of this.

They all knew—she and her fellow coders and intel analysts—what the rest of the public did not. In fact, part of CP's daily intel briefings were composed of information gathered by her and her coworkers. And she knew that the public was sharply divided in its support for or against him. Further analysis had indicated that those who supported CP did so largely because they couldn't stand the opposition. They felt *all* politicians were corrupt.

That CP had just got caught.

Was being made an example of by the opposition.

If any other politician had been provided half the scrutiny that CP had been provided, they would all have been in the same spot. So, yes, they were *all* scared. Terrified. So, fighting to keep CP in place wasn't so much to *CP's* benefit . . . oh, no, it was purely selfish . . . it was to the benefit of each and every (all crooked) politician.

No one wanted to be called out.

Microscopically scrutinized.

But CP had shaken up the establishment, not performed as expected. Showed more testosterone than his predecessors (including several women who had also held office). And the opposition had been gunning for him since Day One.

As Izzy had been shown to her seat, she caught a glimpse of the single woman she'd seen out in the waiting area. She sat several tables over from her. Hadn't noticed her. Smiling briefly, Izzy scooched her chair up to her table and took her menu, as the hostess departed.

Head angled toward her now-opened menu, she secretly scanned the room. Spotted the other couples she'd sat with in the waiting area.

Still no Thomas.

Izzy felt on edge.

Something was in the air.

There was definitely a crackling charge of metaphysical electricity.

Didn't the others feel it?

From behind her, came a light touch.

She spun around . . . looked up to the shadowy figure that repositioned before her. Initially she thought it to be the server—blinked—and saw

Thomas!

He sat swiftly and immediately reached out across the table, taking both of her hands into his. His look pained and longing.

His hands trembled.

"*Thom—*"

"Shh," he said, quickly, as he leaned in toward her.

He smiled . . . almost too much of a smile, really, as he talked with her. Occasionally and softly stroked her hands.

"I . . . I can't stay long . . . but had to see you."

"What's . . . what's going on?" Izzy asked. "I've never seen you this way bef—"

"*You know,*" he said, continuing to give her a hard stare. He smiled and stroked her hands. Kissed a hand without losing eye contact.

"No," she said. "This cannot be happening."

"It is," Thomas said softly, glancing around as if in casual conversation.

"Things are going to get worse before they get better—if ever. In our lifetimes."

"You . . . were a *Black Mask*."

"Yes, but more than that. A killer. An assassin."

Izzy recoiled, but Thomas held her steady.

"Did you—"

"I cared—*care*—deeply for you, Isabel, I really do. But things have gotten so stupidly out of control, and there's just no turning back. War *is* coming. It could be tonight or tens of nights from now, but it is coming. I've been recalled. You don't recall people like me for no reason."

"No . . . I can't believe it. Thought we were better than tha—"

"Is that why you work in the industry you do?"

"I mean to get out."

"Do you?"

"Yes! But you have to make a living—and I thought it best to be on the 'inside' versus the 'outside,' in case—"

"In case things got out of hand."

"Yes."

"Well, they have. And badly so."

They both looked to each other. Izzy reversed their grip and regrasped Thomas's hands. Squeezed and caressed them.

And on played the violins.

"*I've missed you,*" she said. Tears filled her eyes, then ran slowly down her cheeks.

"Me, too."

"Are you staying?"

"I can't. You'll never see me again."

"*What? Why?*"

"Because of who I am. Nobody ever sees me . . . even when . . . when—"

"You do your job," Izzy said, quietly, sullenly.

"When I do my job. Yes. Unless I want them to see me."

"Like me?"

Thomas looked to her.

"No! I'm not—"

"Are you lying to me?"

"*No!*" he said, whispering forcefully. "I truly never expect to see you again . . . this is truly me wanting to see you one last time, before . . ."

Izzy regripped Thomas's hands.

"Isabel, in my business, it's all about the young and the quick. I'm not expected to live forev—"

"Nobody does!"

Thomas smiled wanly.

"I was exceptional at my . . . work . . . which is why I was recalled, but there will come along someone younger, faster, more gifted than me to take me out. It's how the game is played. I never wanted this for my life . . . but that's a story for another time . . . one I really hope we get to, in another life.

"But now . . . I truly must go—"

"No—*stay with me.*"

"The longer I stay, the more of a fix they will get on me. They are specifically targeting me. Because of who I am. I can't stay in the shadows forever, but I have to try. I'm here at great risk . . . because I care about you. Wanted you to know."

Izzy regripped Thomas's hands, her tears now fully streaming down her face.

"I don't . . . I don't know what to say."

"Then don't say anything . . . just enjoy the moment we're in, now . . . forever. Remember me as I truly am. No one—not even this stupid war, declared by stupid people—can ever take this from us. I will think of you always.

"Just be *here* with me . . . now. *Forever.*"

How could she have gotten so caught up in this man so quickly? So thoroughly?

Was it the drama?

The utter boredom and humdrum of her normal life?

The music and ambiance of this hole-in-the-wall restaurant?

She didn't care . . . all she knew

(*the concerto had informed her*)

was that she really cared for this man who clenched her hand in fear of never seeing her again. And that if it wasn't for this stupid war, she and Thomas could have created a wonderful, fulfilling life with each other.

She *felt* this.

Knew it in her bones.

The violins amplified.

Played just for them.

She'd never felt this way about anyone ever before.

There was some strange, wonderful bond between them.

In another life.

They both leaned in toward each other.

Thomas picked up Izzy's hands and kissed them.

Out of Izzy's peripheral vision she

(*felt some distantly near, all-powerful being observing . . .*)

saw someone approach.

She closed her eyes as Thomas allowed his lips . . . his cheek . . . to linger upon her hands. Kissed them again.

Somewhere in the back of Izzy's mind she was aware that something was interfering with the soft romance of the overhead violins. Something was out of place . . . something loud . . .

She didn't care.

She grasped Thomas's hands as tightly as possible.

Mentally, distantly, she registered a commotion . . . a disagreement? . . . going on elsewhere in the dimly lit interior. She opened her eyes.

If she didn't love Thomas, oh, how she so *wanted* t—

An immense flash blinded her.

Then something loud, powerful, and forceful slammed into her.

Izzy was lifted up and out of her seat and sent hurtling across the room into a wall.

Her head spun. Her vision

(. . . *stars . . . stars . . . and nebulae . . .*)

swam. Her ears

(. . . *violins . . . violins . . . and more violins . . .*)

rang.

Grit was in her eyes, nose, and mouth. The right side of her body was severely charred, her clothing shredded and melted onto her skin. Skin that was largely blackened and blistered.

Her entire body screamed out in pain.

Sound became muffled.

The vertigo was like a sledgehammer. There was no relenting to it and it was difficult to lift her head, let alone focus on anything visual, because it *all* swam and flashed and shook.

As she lay in a crumpled heap of char at the base of the wall, she brought a seared and blistered hand to her face, but couldn't feel her han—

What was wrong with her hand? Was it shredded? Had she lost it in the explosion? What . . . what was . . .

(. . . *she flexed and flexed and flexed* . . .)

Brought it before her face and blinked and blinked her watery, seared, and caked eyes to—

She was holding Thomas's hand!

Eyes now wide with horror, she flicked it away from her—but found it was cooked into her own hand.

"*No!*" she screamed, frantically trying to repeatedly flick and throw the . . . *horrifying* . . . appendage anywhere.

Just away, away, *away* from her!

But her white-knuckled clench of a seared lump of meat that had been warm and tender and *alive* did not relent.

Izzy exploded into tears and an angry, hideous cry, part of her cooked face cracking open in her apoplexy.

She added her own screams into a room full of screaming. To the cacophony of weapons' fire, all muted by the riotous ringing in her ears. The spinning and flashing to all-things visual.

"*No!*" she again screamed (*oh, how her chest hurt!*), flicking and shaking her hand with Thomas's hand and forearm attached. Then, openly wailing, she used her other hand to pry her damaged fingers from around and apart from Thomas's separated and flash-fried limb.

The stump finally dropped, dumping into her lap and taking part of her cauterized hand with it. She hysterically pushed and kicked it away.

Grunting, screaming, crying, and channeling all of her soul-shredding pain into physical action, she cursed and forced her feet in and under her, one—at-an-excruciatingly-painful—time. Initially she couldn't sustain the position and dropped back down to the rubble, but she finally kept her legs under her and her vision and head didn't spin quite as fast as they first had, and she drove herself into a crouching position. She recklessly backed away from the atrocity, her vision and mental gyroscope whirling maddeningly.

She found herself backed into a corner. Took in her surroundings. She channeled her pain into acute focus. The room was full of smoke and small, scorched, burnt . . . things.

Slowly, she managed to focus just a little more to her surroundings.

There they were . . . that loving couple. Them and that single woman from the waiting room. They were . . . they were *shooting* people. With weaponry that they'd obviously concealed. They blasted everyone and everything around them, and their faces were unflinching masks of hatred. At one point the couple approached from opposite directions upon an elderly pair, and without looking to each other, both opened fire on the two, who begged for their lives.

Blasted them into oblivion.

Then they calmly moved on into the kitchen.

The single woman held something in her hands . . . and tossed it into the waiting area. She turned and casually waded her way back into the depths of the dining room as the explosive went off among more screams and flying . . . debris.

The woman never flinched, even when the shockwaves slammed into her. She just rebalanced and repositioned her weapon and continued indiscriminately spraying the area like so much insecticide.

Izzy ducked but ended up dumping back to the floor.

Rounds peppered the wall just above her head, plaster raining down upon her.

Swift movement caught her eyes, and Izzy saw more men and women piling into the restaurant from the gaping hole where the waiting area had been.

Thomas!

Izzy fought the vertigo by sheer force of will . . . and looked through flinching, distressed eyes to where their table had been.

Nothing.

Agonizingly scrambling back to her feet, she paused . . . hyperventilated . . . and scanned the room.

There he was.

At least parts of

(*you'll never see me again*)

(*I'm not expected to live forev—*)

him.

She looked away, shoving her face into a shoulder of torn-and-destroyed muscle and bone.

She didn't care. She just *didn't care.*

She'd wanted to love him!

She'd *wanted* to leave with him!

He'd been a killer.

Had been killed!

War.

She brought her attention back to the room. The carnage. The explosions. The chaos.

Thomas.

Single Woman had turned. Was coming her way.

I loved you, Thomas. I truly wanted to.

The tears stopped.

Gone was the heartrending loss.

Gone . . . was the victimization . . . the casualty behavior.

Izzy's eyes . . . focused.

A concentrated determination now filled her face . . . took over her expression

She looked back to Single Woman.

Rage . . . hatred . . . rose within Isabelle. She felt her entire body invigorate with renewed purpose.

Shisst the attack . . . the damage to her body . . . whatever was left of her soul.

Izzy felt around in the carnage encircling her.

Projectiles flew everywhere. Every now and then a pocket of hand-to-hand combat erupted as some would-be heroes tried to defend themselves against professionally trained murderers.

And lost.
Single Woman came closer.
Izzy felt something in the dark.
Long, strong, and pointed.
She wrapped her fingers around
(*Thomas*)
it. Pulled it in to her.
Scrunched herself up into a tight little ball behind some manner of wreckage.
Violins.
Were those damned things still playing?
Pain.
But . . . I truly must go—
Pain.
No—stay with me.
Pain.
The longer I stay, the more of a fix they will get—
Pain!
Izzy brought the metal shard up and close into her chest and clutched it tightly. Allowed her pain to continue to fill and fuel and motivate.
Was it the drama?
The utter boredom and humdrum of her normal existence?
The seventy-hour weeks?
Single Woman came closer.
I don't . . . I don't know what to say.
Then don't say anything . . . just enjoy the moment . . . now . . . forever.
Izzy saw Single Woman's expressionless face . . . her angry, murderous eyes.
I will think of you always.
Was nearly on top of her.
Just be here with me . . . now. Forever.
Forever.
Single Woman fired a few more rounds at bodies she wasn't sure were dead. She'd made her way to
Thomas!

Looked down at Thomas and paused.

Slowly, a smile worked its way across her face, surely in recognition of her target.

She coldly chuckled. Once.

Directed her weapon toward his head ... and

Pain!

Izzy pounced.

She shot to her feet from around her hide behind Single Woman, spun with the force of a tornado, and rammed the metal shard deep into Single Woman's back.

Single Woman jerked violently.

Izzy held the shard in place.

Forced it in deeper.

Twisted it.

Grunting agonizingly, she drove, pushed, and compelled the woman away from Thomas.

Single Woman dropped her weapon and coughed up blood. Began to turn around—but Izzy continued to push her away, her face set, and worked her spike in even deeper.

Izzy felt Single Woman began to relent and go down, but she continued to drive her away from Thomas, letting go of her and the metal shard only when she emitted one last gasp and her shoulders finally slumped.

Single Woman turned completely around and fell onto the floor, forcing the metal shard completely through her. Her eyes languidly tracked Izzy.

Recognized her.

Izzy limped toward her.

Bent over so Single Woman could get a good look.

Single Woman's mouth erupted into a grotesque geyser of blood and her eyes fluttered closed.

Izzy picked up Single Woman's weapon. Looked at it.

Looked to Thomas.

I wanted to love you. I really did.

Then she turned around and looked to the now retreating attackers.

To the wonderful strings of *Violin Concerto No.3*, Isabelle Fastbinder opened fire.

FROM WHENCE COME THY BREEZES
Year 2114 C.E.

Taking a sip of coffee, Lavinia Alexander sat quietly in the darkness on her deck and listened to the four a.m. roaring waves of wind vigorously rustling across her silhouetted treetops, like breakers against a beach. Enjoyed how their shadows waved back and forth as if they were raised hands at a nature concert.

She gently sent her chair-swing rocking, listening to the soothing chirp of crickets.

Oh, how she loved this time of darkness she still considered night, when most were still asleep! The only thing set to motion at this wonderful, in-between hour was nature peacefully drifting over, through, and around everyone's backyards and rooftops.

Lavinia sat with her coffee and imagination and soaked in the waning summer enchantments . . . gazed up into its still-dark sky. She could see all manner of stars, a couple of the planets, and even (much to her dismay) manmade satellites ethereally speeding across the starry background. There was a time when you were lucky to see a singular satellite speed across the stars, but now there were so many that all you had to do was wait a few minutes for another . . . and another . . . or a whole series of them, strung out behind each other as they crossed the eternally bright star field. It was getting entirely too busy up there.

And that unnerved Lavinia.

Satellites were thrown up there for a reason. Very specific purposes, and they were quite expensive and required networks and support and people and other machines to run them. She should know, she'd recently retired out of the industry. Worked with all manner of both military and civilian projects, but with the direction the world was heading, well, she couldn't deorbit fast enough from it all.

There was change acomin'. Big change. Sweeping change. Mysterious change.

And not any change with which she wanted to be any longer or directly associated.

She'd had fun putting satellites and probes into space, but she came to realize just a few years ago that all the fun had faded, and elements of other sorts of control were being insidiously implanted into the companies and programs she'd been a part of. She didn't like that. Of being increasingly told what to do, how to do it, what to think. And that the packages being installed in all that spaceward hardware was becoming increasingly . . . secretive. Cagey. Whether or not it was all needed . . . she no longer wanted to be a part of it.

What she'd decided she wanted for the rest of her life was exactly what she was doing right now, this moment.

Nothing.

No responsibility, no schedules, no grief. No bosses.

She'd done enough of that.

She wanted to step just enough outside of all the hustle and bustle and become a non-player. An observer. To just watch from afar those things she *wanted* and to turn away from those things that she didn't want to see.

Mow the lawn, plant and care for her flowers, and enjoy the emotionally therapeutic scents of freshly cut grass and fragrant flowers as she hung out on her deck. To tend to more soul-nurturing concerns . . . to think and privately philosophize. Paint. Write pose poetry.

To take long walks in the woods and enjoy the visuals and warmth of the sunlight radiating between the trees upon her face and skin and warming the forest floor . . . or reflecting off the leaves of the trees themselves out in the meadows, flickering happily as if waving to her.

Yes *waving* to her.

To observe the oneness of nature working together . . . far away from all of Humanity's angst and anxieties and drama.

She took another sip of coffee.

Lavinia quietly and gently rocked her chair as the balmy, dark breezes continued to rise and fall and soothe and greet her and her backyard. Listened to the continued beautiful rustling of her leaves and chirping crickets. Felt the warm succor of air against her skin. Enjoyed the wonder of the stars.

The stars.

Were they even really there anymore? The ones behind the ones she could readily see? She could just be seeing the last rays of their existences, and they could all be long, long gone, and the rest of the universe would actually and only be what was a handful of light-years around them.

How would all the idiots defiling the world feel about that?

She smiled and took another sip of coffee.

Wind . . .

Rustling . . .

Crickets . . .

This was how life was meant to be.

This world was—and had been—so wonderful, so beautiful. Why were there those who would want to destroy it? Hurt others? Why did Life even allow such evil to exist? When there were soulful moments like this, why would such diametrically opposed circumstances be allowed to coexist?

Perhaps that was why there were the winds of change.

She felt them.

The prophets. The nightmares, the indefinable angst—which, curiously, for her had all stopped once she'd retired.

Maybe this *was* Life's way
(. . . *it always finds a* . . .)
of cleaning things up.
She'd like to think so.
Lavinia took another sip of coffee.

PAYIN' CUSTOMERS ONLY, PLEASE
Year 2114 C.E.

1

"*Everyone* needs to eat!" Newt Foster said, hands on his hips and standing proud before his brand-spanking-new building.

He turned to his wife, Esther, who stood beside him, and smiled ear to ear. He repeated the welcoming sign's proclamation above their brand-new diner, a squat yellow-and-black building, glistening in the harsh desert sun. The seventy-five-foot-tall sign announced "Newt's Diner" in bold black lettering against a bright yellow background.

"Isn't it *beautiful*? It really stands out!"

Esther smiled. "It sure does," she said, but tentatively added, "customers ... do you really *thi*—"

"Of *course* I do, hon! *Everyone* loves a hamburger! Hot dogs! I mean, *come on*—who doesn't absolutely love *cheese*burgers? Why, I'm salivating right now! And don't even get me started on *ice cream!*"

Newt's Diner was situated at the intersection of Route 24 and the Minersville Road, in the heart of the Schleckt Desert. It was directly between Newer York and the Bucket Hills, where an also-brand-spanking-new development was currently in progress.

And there was nothing else in between.

Nothing.

The new community under development, called Bucket Shores, nestled within the Bucket Hills, was an all-inclusive, planned community alongside Bucket Lake, and it was as remote from anywhere else, as could be these days. But the new highway was ready to ferry travelers back and forth. The "Bucket" label had originated from a crash-landed party that had barely survived some twenty-odd years ago, only because of many hand-carried buckets of water from this lake into the cooler climes of their mountainous crash site.

With this new community, however, was advanced planning at its best, and Newt was on the forefront with the land developers. The Ground Floor, if you will (and Newt *willed*).

All the construction workers and landscapers and community planners traveled the brand-new highway, so why not a burger and some fries on the way?

And the way home.

A couple of broiled hotdogs and chips?

Topped off with a vanilla waffle-cone dipped in hot butterscotch? *Who wouldn't?*

But Esther wasn't as convinced. She'd always been the skeptical one. Nervous. "Nervous 'Nita," her husband had more than occasionally (yet lovingly) joked.

"But . . . but Newt . . . these are busy people," Esther insisted, looking toward the Bucket Hills. "They have schedules . . . timetables to keep, they can't keep stopping here—"

"All the more reason, my sweet! We've got the best and most technologically advanced everything! Grills that don't overcook or burn! Staff trained in all the best industry practices to be the most efficient anywhere! And service with a smile—*always* with a smile!—that comes right out to their trucks! If they come inside, oh, baby, they'll be greeted by the best smells in the whole, wide world! Grilling beef! Frenching fries! And the atmosphere—*total* nostalgia straight out of the history books! The Bee-Bop music, the replica Juke Boxes! Man, they'll wanna keep coming back, are you *kidding* me? They'll have no choice! The *nostalgia*. An hour of getting away from the drudgery of their work that'll fuel them for the rest of the day! I tell ya, honey, short of a war, this just can't lose!"

Just then a massive and loaded-down twelve-wheeler came into view from Newer York. It slowed down and threw on its blinkers—coming straight toward them! *Their* diner!

"*Look*, Esther! *See?*"

"I see it!"

"We'd better get inside! Cause you know, once one comes, many more will follow! They'll all tell each other!"

"Okaaay ...," Esther said, as she made her way toward the diner, keeping a wary eye on the trucker—who still continued toward them. "*Huh*," she said to herself, "*maybe he did have point, this time?*"

Newt loudly *whooped* and thrust his fists into the air, smiling wide, happiness beaming brightly across his face. He waved excitedly to the trucker to come on in.

The trucker pulled right up alongside Newt, slowing to a stop and kicking up some dust and stones as it did so. The trucker stuck his head out his rolled-down window.

"Hey!" the trucker called on down to Newt. "Have you heard?"

"Heard what?" Newt said.

"Things are goin' downhill, man! We've all been told to return, loaded or unloaded. Looks like we really are going to war this time."

"War? What?"

"Haven't you been reading the feeds?"

"Feeds? No—I have no time for the funnies! Charbroiled burgers, grilled dogs, and waffle cones are all I have time for!"

The trucker cast a long look at the restaurant, as if in deep contemplation.

"Well, hate to break it to ya, fella," he continued, returning his attention to Newt, "but it looks like this might be your off season."

"*No—*"

The trucker sighed. "Okay, well ... can I get a cheeseburger and fries to go?"

"To go? Of *course,* you can! And in no time flat! Just pull around the back there," he said, pointing, "I actually made a trucker's drive-through!"

The trucker nodded, impressed. "Thanks, man! I will—and I'll tell all my buddies, so you'll at least get something out of today. If today's the end of things, might as well go out on a full stomach!"

The trucker pulled away, shifted gears, and quickly pulled up to the drive-through around the back of the restaurant.

So, Newt thought, they really were going to pull the trigger this time. Today? *Today* of all days—*his opening day?* This just couldn't b—

Up ahead, Newt saw another trucker barreling down the highway toward him. He also slowed down and pulled off of the off-ramp.

""Howdy!" the trucker hailed. "Word is you can get a quick burger through a drive-through made just for us—that true?"

Newt nodded dramatically. "Yes, sir, it is! Just keep heading straight on back—you see that other trucker? Right there! Get in line for a short wait for some of the hottest, tastiest food ever!"

"Now, we're talkin'! I'm starved! Thanks, mister!"

The driver tipped his beat-up baseball cap to Newt as he pulled forward.

A passenger car was next.

"Good day! You open?" the twenty-something blue-eyed man asked, all smiles.

"Sure am, son! Head on in or use the drive-through, behind! There're two lanes just for passenger cars!"

The blue-eyed boy gave him an energetic two-finger salute and hit the accelerator.

Newt peered off into the distance both ways to Sunday and now saw a steady stream of traffic, and they were all hitting their blinkers and brakes and off-ramping to their little diner!

Newt got on his handy to Esther.

"Hey, love! You ain't gonna believe this, but we've got what looks like a non-stop off-ramping coming our way! Oh, and insist on only taking cash!"

"Why only cash?

"Hey, Newt," Esther continued, her voice trembling, "Elena, back here, just told me today's supposed to be *it*—the end of the world! We're finally going to blow ourselves up! *Newt?*"

"What? Nooo... they always say that, then we just keep on going... spewing more rhetoric. Life always finds a way, honey. But in any case, why not have a full stomach, right?"

"But *Newt*—"

A couple more tractor-trailers pulled off, now forming a line behind the diner that extended back to the off-ramp. More than a handful of passenger vehicles also pulled off.

"Esther—they just keep *coming!* They must all be coming from that Bucket development. Hey, hold on just a sec—"

Newt flagged down a little sports car with its top down, a guy and a girl in it.

"Hey," Newt asked, "where's everyone goin'?"

The driver said, "We've all been ordered to evacuate. Head on up to the ships. The space stations. They say it's for real, this time. We're kinda surprised you're still open—but we're hungry."

"To the ships? Really?"

"Yeah, they said that in five hours, they're gonna open fire and blast everything to smithereens. Then our government said we were going to do the same. So ours ordered us all to evacuate to our regional space ports and head to our assigned ships or on-orbit stations. You better not wait too long, pops, or you might be part of a smokin' hole!"

The car sped off, honking and jockeying its position back into line.

"Well, Esther," Newt said returning to the handy, "it looks like we have just under five hours to make a few bucks before we have to split, so keep slappin' the meat on the grill, honey! I'll be right in!"

"*Newt*—"

2

After about three hours, the traffic began to slow, and Elena cried out, back from the grill, that they were nearly out of burgers and dogs. Esther was busy reconciling the income from their day, stacks of bills neatly laid out all over her desk. She was presently stuffing them into the small paper bags used for takeout, all labeled with the staff's names.

Newt walked into the office.

"Hey, what are you doing? We have to leave money for taxes!"

"*Taxes?*" Esther said. "Honey, in about a two hours there will be no place to send taxes *to!* Besides, no one really knows about us—that we were even ever *open!* Heck no, I'm not giving anything away to a government that can't even govern itself! I say let's just take the money and run!"

"Esther—that'd be criminal!"

"This is the most money we've ever made doing *anything*, Newt! Any of your previous get-rich-quick schemes! And we're all about to be blown up! Don't you *get* it? Wherever we end up, as a people, we'll have to have some form of currency, and right now, I'm bettin' on the status quo! I mean, will you look at the lines? We're all about to wipe out everything we've ever known, and people are still clamoring for *hamburgers!* It's stupidly crazy! They're calling them 'Doomsday Burgers,' did you know that?"

"'Doomsday Burgers,'" Newt pensively repeated to himself. "*I* like *that*...."

Esther stared at Newt. Stole a quick look outside.

"Yeah, and things are starting to slow down, Newt, but, *geez*, there are still a ton of truckers in line! This is absolutely insane!" she said, not turning around to address him. "Absolutely *crazy!*"

Newt came up behind her and peeked outside the window with her.

"This *is* nuts," he said more to himself.

Outside many vehicles were speeding past the diner for Newer York, but some were still veering off for a Doomsday Burger.

"Well," Newt said, "I better go check with Elena and see how we're doing with meat. Surely we must nearly be out."

"Newt!"

After Newt left the office, Esther turned around and stared—just stared—at her desk, the money, and the four walls.

The door.

Newt wove through the still-busy dining area, people standing in line, orders being called out and filled just as quickly, most taking their greasy paper bags and hurriedly exiting the establishment—many with huge grins on their faces. Blow themselves up, indeed. They'd heard it all before.

"Great fries!"

"Great burgers!"

"Gonna miss these on orbit!"

"Thanks for sticking it out for us," Newt said, "but you all had better start thinking about getting out yourselves!"

Newt was gracious and kind to all who greeted him. Thanked them for their patronage. Headed into the frantically busy kitchen.

"'Lena—how are we doi—"

"We have twenty-five left! And those orders are rapidly filling! I can't believe this! I don't even have time to be scared!"

Newt looked back outside and to the line. There were more than twenty-five people waiting to order.

"Okay, I'll start turning them away," Newt said in a more concerned, leveled tone. "Hurry these up! Tell the staff we'll have their pay waiting for them in the office. Then get yourselves going—there's still plenty of time."

"Okay, Newt—and thanks." Elena said. She gave Newt a second look. Looked at him a while longer, as her well-practiced hands performed duties that they'd been doing rote for many years.

Newt turned and made his way back into the dining area, and it was as he made his way back that things finally began to sink in.

Thera was about to blow itself up and they'd stayed behind to sell *hamburgers?*

And even crazier still, all these people had been *buying* them?

Yes, it was a comical circus of the absurd . . . but certainly no off season, as their first customer had foretold. No . . . this, their opening day . . . would turn out to be their best-ever venture, their best take-in, and their *only* take-in for Newt's Diner. So they were going to take their money and run. He was stupid to have allowed this to happen. And for what? A couple of bucks that soon wouldn't be worth the paper it was printed on? And in a little over two hours they would all find themselves rocketing into orbit for life on whatever was left to take them, either a space station or one of the spaceships that had been placed into orbit in preparation for just this eventuality.

Yes, they were about to blow themselves up.

And they were serving *cheeseburgers*.

Newt stopped at the line to the register. Except for the police cruiser, he saw no other vehicles pulling off into their parking lot from the highway.

"People," he said, calmly, if in somewhat of a haze, "we're all out of burgers, I'm afraid to say—"

"No! No more Doomsday Burgers?" one obviously disappointed customer said.

"No, I'm afraid not," Newt said. He blinked. "But I'm so honored you've all thought of us and supported us on our opening day."

Though there were groans and moans, those in line applauded him and thanked him for having had the courage to stick it out a little longer like they had, feeding the masses with one last hurrah of Thera before whatever happened . . . or didn't happen.

As people began to leave—and they left in a hurry—Newt told the forward part of the line they were still in the queue, and if they wanted to hang, would get the very last Doomsday Burgers from Newt's Diner. As those remaining in line began shaking his hand, Newt saw the policeman enter the diner, but he stopped just inside the entranceway. He stood there, sunglasses remaining on and just observed. He was unmoving as the patrons beat their hasty retreat with their aromatic and greasy paper bags past him.

The dining area cleared, but the music continued to play, Newt quickly huddled the diner's staff together and quietly told them to head back to the office, where Esther would have their pay ready—and wished them the best of luck for whatever did or didn't happen, but they'd always have a place here, if things resolved far more peacefully than anticipated.

There were hugs and tears and kisses and sobbing. And the heavy smell of cooked meat and Doomsday grease on everyone.

Then they all quickly dispersed to the rear of the diner.

Newt turned around and found the officer looking at him. Sunglasses still in place. Black-gloved hands anchored within crossed arms.

"Oh, so sorry officer! I forgot all about you! Yes, we're leaving right this minute!"

"You still got time," the officer said, "as far as any of us have time, things as they are." His voice was calm, if vaguely menacing. Maybe it was just that he meant business.

"Yes, yes," Newt said, suddenly feeling quite flustered. Unhinged. He reached out for support to the stainless-steel countertop.

"Business was good," the officer said. He lowered his gloved hands and began to casually stroll through the diner, looking at everything and nothing.

"Yes, it was. Surprisingly so," Newt said, still a little wobbly. "We made more today than we'd ever made in our entire lives at anything else we ever did. Good thing I really stocked up on inventory," Newt said, still steadying himself. He suddenly found it hard to take in a full breath, having to perform several pants before he could again catch his breath.

Newt looked up. "Is it true?" he asked.

"Yes," the officer said.

"So, we're really going to blow ourselves up this time?"

"That's the newsfeed."

The officer was now close enough that Newt clearly saw his nametag read "Ranken," and heard the creak of his leather belt, holster, and other straps.

"So, I guess you want me outta here, sir," Newt said, wiping the back of a hand across his nervous and sweating forehead. "Okay, okay, we're going."

"I don't really care what you do," the officer said.

Newt shot Officer Ranken a look.

"What I do care about, however, is how much you took in today."

"Excuse me?"

"How much did you make?" Ranken asked, now having stopped directly before him.

"H-how much—*what does it matter?* Everything's going to blow up! I don't even know that money matters any more—"

"It matters to me."

The police officer calmly pulled out his weapon. Pointed it directly at Newt at waist height.

Newt chuckled to himself.

"You're *robbing* us?"

"Why don't we go back to your office, so we can reconcile this calmly," the police officer said.

Newt froze.

The cop nudged Newt in the side with his weapon. "Let's go. Doomsday's a tickin'."

Newt stumbled, his knees growing weak, but did as he was instructed, and took him back to the rear office.

"Esther?" Newt called out as they rounded the corner into the office. But as the two of them entered the tiny room, no one was found ... except for a short, hastily scribbled note on the floor at his feet.

Newt picked it up.

Read it.

His shoulders slumped and he collapsed to his knees on the floor.

"Give me that," the cop said, grabbing the note.

Employees:
Your pay is on the desk. Take it and run.
Thanks for everything.

Newt:
Sorry, babe, but I have to do this. Can't take it anymore. Your cut is on the desk here. It's not that I don't love you ... I'm just worn out on love and not enough of anything else. I wish you the best. Please, let me go and don't come looking ... begin a new life with someone more like you with whatever happens or doesn't happen. We've had a good run ... but, I'm just not cut out for this life, and I just don't "feel it" anymore.

Esther.

The cop grunted and tossed away the note. Snatched the remaining money from the desk.

"Tough break, buddy."

He sprinted out of the office.

Newt folded into a heap on the floor and sobbed and wailed and cried. Thought he heard something outside the doorway, but just didn't care.

Just shoot me and be done with it.

A soft touch landed upon his shoulder.

He looked up.

"Elena?"

"I'm so sorry, Newt. I can't believe Esther did this."

"You should be gone! You need to be on your way—"

"I couldn't leave you like this!" Elena got down on the floor with him and brought him closer into her. Hugged him tightly.

Kissed him on the cheek.

Newt gently pushed away and looked at her.

"Are you really surprised?" Elena said, "I've always cared about you. Seen how much you cared about your dreams—all of them—over the years. Helping people. How you always cared about *us*."

She paused.

"I love you, Newt. Always have."

"But—"

"No 'buts', not any longer. Let the two of us start our new life together in all this craziness, even if," she said, checking her watch with tear-filled eyes, "it only lasts two minutes. It'll be the best two minutes of our lives . . . with the *love* of our lives."

Newt closed his tear-filled eyes and hugged Elena back. They both slid fully prone onto the floor and held onto each other tightly. Openly wept into each others' shoulders.

Outside, like huge bursts of popcorn, the skies across Thera lit up as space station after space station after spaceship after satellite blew up, vaporized, and littered the Theran orbit with all manner of greasy, Frenched-fried debris.

UNPEACE
Year 2114 C.E.

The wars had come.
Baked and scoured Thera.
The rockets, the missiles, the particle beams. New and inventive ways to rip apart humans.
Vaporize life.
Cyberterrorism, hacktivism, espionage, sabotage. New and inventive ways to rupture societal structure.
Once you had one war, what was one more? And another? Then throw in one more for good measure?
Warring was easier than peace.
With wars you never had to admit you were wrong—you just blamed the enemy.
With wars you never had to say you were sorry—you just waged another battle.

With wars you reaped in huge corporate profits.
As long as you had corruption, you had war.
As long as you had people willing to kill, you had war.
As long as you killed, the body counts elevated.
Cities and states annihilated.
Commanders accumulated medals.
Predatory superpowers filled their coffers.
One . . . two . . . three . . .

And when the enemies dwindled in number, the militaries turned upon themselves, assassinated their leaders, usurped their positions . . . assassinated again and again by the next wave that usurped *their* stolen positions.

In this way a period of successive wars had enveloped and destroyed the planet and its people.

TWELVE
Year 3092 C. E.

1

The man, who went by "Mark," for "Mark Chapman," charged up behind the man in uniform who stood upon a rocky outcropping before him, broke his neck, and tossed him off the cliff.

Just like that.

"Mark," who really wasn't a "Mark," scanned the surrounding terrain. When the deceased slammed into the ground below, in the midst of the arriving unit, they immediately looked up and began firing.

A round penetrated Mark's shoulder, but he scarcely took notice beyond the concern of a bug bite. Without adjusting his position, Mark peered down at his attackers, then casually left his perch.

Adjusting his internal audio sensitivity, Mark heard the men hastily setting up a perimeter, several given orders to immediately advance up the cliffside after him.

"Him" being "Mark."

Mark, his attire in tatters, retreated back a few hundred feet into a mini-amphitheater-like formation of some thirty feet in diameter. He picked out a suitable rock and sat down. Picked up three small stones and one larger one, putting two into each hand.

Balanced them between the hands.

He sat back upright, both feet firmly planted on the ground. Rolled the stones about in his hands. Positioned his eyes forward—

Eyes forward!

"Eyes forward, Maggot!" Maggot trainee Spencer Fuller was so directed by the Marine Drill Instructor. "You do not look anywhere unless I tell you where to look and for how long. If you are not looking anywhere else, you are eyes forward! Do you understand, Maggot?"

"Yes, Drill Instructor!"

"I did not hear you!"

"YES, Drill InstrucTOR!"

"Where are you looking, Maggot?"

"Forward, Drill Instructor!"

Chapman heard the men approaching. Four of them. Heavily armed, his scans told him. One of them was their leader, a guy named Major Estanza. He liked Estanza. But he'd have to kill him. Didn't really have any choice in the matter. Not anymore.

Chapman heard them round the rocky outcropping.

Immediately upon spotting Chapman, and just before entry into his mini-amphitheater, the men flared out before Chapman, weapons leveled.

"Gentlemen," Chapman greeted, remaining seated.

"Chapman," Estanza greeted, striding forward into the opening.

"Major," Chapman returned, sarcastically.

"You knew you couldn't keep this up forever," Estanza said, directing the other three into a semi-circular arrangement before Chapman.

"On the contrary, my good Major, I have been reborn and bred to do just that," Chapman said. Mark played with the stones in his hands, which Estanza eyed.

The three soldiers held their ground, though each appeared more than a little nervous. Their eyes darted this way and that between Chapman and the rocks surrounding them.

"This could easily be an ambush, sir," one of the men, Hastings, a corporal, said. He regripped his weapon.

"Oh, it's an ambush, all right," Chapman said, appearing casual and only slightly put out. "An ambush of one: *me*." He landed a steely gaze to Hastings, who quickly averted any further eye contact.

Chapman redirected his attention back to Estanza. Continued playing with the rocks in his possession.

Chapman repositioned. "Shoulda let me go, man," he said, reluctantly shaking his head, one arm now crossed over the other, both of which were now casually draped over crossed legs. Chapman looked up to Estanza.

"Got my orders." It was Estanza's turn to bore into Chapman. Eyed his shoulder wound.

Chapman got to his feet. Hands to his sides. "So . . . we're gonna do this, then. That's too bad."

The three soldiers nervously repositioned. Chapman grinned . . . bared some teeth. Just then a host of additional men filled the hollow . . . as well as all points above, along the rock cliffs.

Chapman chuckled and said, "Finally! Some compe*tit*ion!"

He was ringed in with all forms of weaponry homed in on him. There would be no missing him.

Chapman chuckled, as he casually spun around to take in his opponents. Scanning every one of them. A devilish smile on his face, he came back to face Estanza.

"Look, Major . . . *men*," Chapman said, addressing each with his gaze and outstretched arms, "I want you to know there are no hard feelings, here. I know you have orders. You will fight valiantly. Be posthumously bestowed medals and honors and that sort of thing.

"I know you don't know me from Cushing. I know you got nothing personal against me—well, except for the one I just tossed down on you a minute ago. Sorry about that. He had to go. Just like all of you will have to go. You know—unless you about-face it and walk on out of here right now," Chapman said, making a "marching man" with his index and middle fingers and scurrying them ahead of him.

Chapman looked to Estanza. "Estanza? No?"

Estanza slowly and deliberately shook his head, maintaining eye contact.

"*Dang* it," Chapman said, as he exaggeratedly stomped the ground before him. Everyone's weaponry clattered as men reshuffled uncomfortably.

"Sorry, boys, didn't mean to make you all unnecessarily nervous!" Chapman said.

He continued, "I really don't wanna kill you, Major. I like you—and for me, that's really saying something," he said, smiling and nodding his head in the major's direction.

"Then why don't you come along without any further ado."

Chapman mimed taken-aback surprise.

"'*Ado*'?" Chapman said. "Really?"

"Really."

Chapman shook his head.

"Sorry, nocandoski. As much as I'd like to . . . and I *don't* like to. Ain't programmed to give up. You know that, Major."

Chapman's grin evaporated from his face. He angled his face down just a touch, and gave Estanza a knowing, evil glare that even made Estanza flinch.

"Make this easy on yourself, Mark, this doesn't have to go this way."

"*Oooh . . . but it* does . . . ."

Of the fifteen men surrounding Chapman, three dropped before even realizing they'd lost their faces to the rocks Chapman had simultaneously thrown. For the fourth projectile, Chapman had aimed his to merely knock Estanza unconscious.

By the time the eleven remaining men opened fire, Chapman had moved out of position and grabbed the closest soldier by his shoulders and held him before him like a human shield. He effortlessly moved him around the airspace before him like he was nothing more than a rag doll.

The man's body armor only lasted so long, and he was soon shredded apart until Chapman held nothing but the corpse's arms, which he then proceeded to use as clubs on those who'd insisted upon advancing on him.

Once done with those, he grabbed another, and threw him into two more who'd advanced, whipped out a concealed knife and opened up another's throat, while grabbing his weapon and turning it on the rest of the survivors. The men scattered.

Chapman then swiped Estanza up off the ground and threw him over his shoulder, whipping back around to the rest of the attack party with his newly acquired weapon.

No one fired.

"Don't blame you!" Chapman yelled back to them. "Major's a nice guy!" Chapmen sprinted out of the hollow.

2

Night fell upon the rocks as Chapman sat before a fire, Estanza bound up on the other side of it from him. Chapman watched him without a single blink of an eye until Estanza came around.

"You got a little bump there, Major," Chapman said. The fire illuminated his face like a demon from hell.

Estanza cleared his throat. "Why didn't you kill me?"

"Didn't want to. Told you that. You're one of the really good guys back there, and Lord knows that place needs more like you. So, if I have to, I'd rather die first than kill ya, but, as you also know, I'm currently incapable of doing that, either."

Chapman stoked the fire with a large stick.

"It's the thought that counts," Estanza said.

"Indeed! Hungry?"

Estanza shook his head. "How many—"

"You got nine left."

Estanza nodded.

"Why do you stay with them?"

The major shook off the concussion. "You could say I'm also programmed: it's my job."

"You and me both know that's not a good enough answer. I showed you what they were doing . . . you let those three go. You don't belong there. You need to leave them—bring them down with me."

"It's not my job."

"It *should* be."

"You took out an entire *office* building."

"Consider it Spring Cleaning. It needed to be done."

"*The entire building?*"

Chapman nodded.

Estanza's eyes darted about the darkness.

"The corruption has to stop. Had it stopped, I would have continued on my merry way. But it didn't. Someone asked for my help—*me*—*my* help. I gave it to them. Your bosses not only killed him, but took out his entire family."

Estanza looked away.

"Don't like hearing that, do you, Major?"

Estanza said nothing.

"Because you like to believe the best in everyone . . . even huge government organizations you work for. You believe . . . that though there are a few bad nectarines in the bushel, the bushel itself is still basically good."

Chapmen tapped his stick on the ground for a few moments. Got to his feet.

"Well, Major, I'm here to tell you . . . no good comes from bad nectarines. They spoil the rest of the bushel . . . until it's thoroughly cleaned out. And this bushel is far, far gone."

"You can't just go around eliminating every evil person in the world!"

Chapman smiled. Sat back down.

"But you see, I *can*. Again . . . that is what I'm programmed to *do*. You know that, right?"

"But you can reprogram your—"

"*Nooot* really."

"Look," Chapman continued, "I'll tell you a little more about me. Stuff you weren't briefed on. That nobody knows, because what I did was supposed to be impossible.

"All the other BECs had been recruited. I . . . was not. The twelfth BEC in the unit had a critical malfunction that caused it to, well, *explode*. Shorted power system. Since the ship was ready to split, and our unit required one more BEC, well, they had no time to recruit, see . . . so they looked to see who in the ranks had the best qualifications . . . and kidnapped me. So, when they refitted me . . . embedded me with their protocols and software and circuitry . . . they inhibited me from ever going counter to my mission. See, it wasn't an issue in the other BECs, because they'd volunteered. It was just *me*.

"Long story short . . . I became a prisoner in my own body. My cyborg body. Any time my thoughts went counter to my . . . programming . . . a subroutine kicked in and reoriented me. So, for the longest time, that's how I'd operated.

"Until I didn't.

"I've been around, what, a thousand years? Let's just say that persistence is everything. You pick away at anything long enough and you can find a way around shisst. So, I reprogrammed myself, enabled the 'Ruthless' mode, and threw away the key. You know the rest."

"Why would you do that?"

"Hey, I did keep my 'Humor' mode enabled, but, good question. Why not? I was kidnapped . . . taken from my *wife* . . . shot out into *space* . . . deployed on a whole nother freaking planet—think about that . . . *I was taken away from Earth and sent to another planet!*—would never see my wife again! *Ever*. I'm trapped inside a body I never wanted . . . programmed to do things I never wanted to do, let alone *think* about. So, I figured—and I did run the calculations—I thought, well, if I ran 'hot' all the time, I'm bound to burn out in so much time, but, you know, our bodies are self-replicating to an amazing extent, and given our self-preservation protocols because of our extreme and independent operations, it is literally hard to kill any of us. Since we were the first of our kind they had no data—no idea—how long we'd live. But still, I ran the numbers and discovered that no later than just under another thousand years—at the earliest—I could well die, burning the candle at both ends, as the saying goes. I could live with those odds. Anything's better than ad infinitum. I mean, sooner or later, all circuitry wears out . . . unless replaced and reworked.

"So . . . I'd take the most heinous assignments, the worst odds, the nastiest outcomes—all in an effort to die.

"It's that easy."

"I feel sorry for you."

"No need to—I do enough of that for the both of us. So, I secretly reached out to those in need, by tapping into the news feeds. Saw this government conspiracy issue in the press and reached out to the guy, which, in turn, led me to you. The rest is history."

Estanza let out a heavy sigh and stared into the fire.

Chapman sat still, scanning the darkness around them.

"It's only a matter of time," Estanza finally said. "You can't outrun radios and satellites."

"*Great!*" Chapman said. "As I said, I'm looking forward to the challenge!"

"So, do you at all care about the cause to which you've dedicated yourself?"

"Another part of me might, but that part of me is long dead. Right now I just care about taking out as many of you before I go, as possible. It's purely a numbers game."

Estanza nodded pensively. "I wish we had met under different circumstances," he said.

Chapman looked to Estanza and furrowed his brow. Canted his head ever so slightly.

"Curious . . . ," Chapman said, "this has stirred emotions in me I hadn't realized I'd retained."

Chapman suddenly got to his feet.

"But I just terminated them," Chapman said, and turned to the darkness around them. "Now, I'm expecting them any time now, so stay put." He grabbed the assault weapon he'd acquired earlier and slung it over a shoulder.

It wasn't long before Chapman heard the approach. First the drones were sent in, which he picked up on, then the multi-tiered assault teams deployed around them. Chapman jammed two of the hunter-killer drones' weapon's delivery systems, but allowed a third to operate in recording mode. It would be good to document what was about to happen. He then reprogrammed the feed to stream into local and national news media outlets, which caused quite a stir when the scenes began displaying on television and radio networks.

Chapman stood quietly, hands to his sides, as the team positioned itself.

A GroundPounder IV missile launched.

Chapman tracked it. He had less than a second to respond, which was more than enough time. He darted away from his position just before impact. The impact's concussion actually blew him off his feet, but he backflipped in midair and stuck his landing.

Machine gun fire cut through the darkness. Chapman was grazed several times, but nothing to be concerned with.

He repositioned behind a few rocks. Scanned his surroundings. As expected, reinforcement had been brought in. He checked back in on Estanza. He'd pretty much remained where he was, because—surprise!—Chapman had tethered him to a stake. Old school. Can't interdict Titanium. But he was on his feet, nervously pacing back and forth.

Be a pity if he'd been taken out by his own men.

War is

"hell, Maggots!" the DI shouted into Spencer's face, one hand still firmly grappled on Spencer's collar. The DI had just forcibly yanked Spencer to his feet after he'd tripped in an effort to avoid an attack from a fellow trainee. Spencer and the other trainee bust out laughing when the DI intervened.

The DI turned to the rest of the trainees. Many were on the ground, most chuckling or laughing.

First instance of hand-to-hand combat training.

"You all think this is funny? Laughable?" the DI said, his face mean, veins popping everywhere.

All trainees stopped laughing and popped up to their feet, slamming to rigid attention.

The DI approached others as they stood in line. He attacked one of the trainees, who hadn't expected the attack, eyes wide with fear, and crumpled the man to the dirt. Blood inched out of a nostril. In an instant, he did the same to another trainee. This one tried to fend him

off, but the DI also sent him to the ground. This man writhed in pain, groaning as he twisted in the dirt, grasping his left arm in close.
Broken.
The DI then returned to Spencer and stuck his nose right up into Spencer's face. Spencer smelled his rotting breath. The DI yelled his next words while holding Spencer's terrified gaze:
"War is hell . . . and I'm the Devil!"

The attackers advanced, pouring their fire into Chapman's position. Chapman scanned them to find full body armor. No more rock throwing for him.

Chapman unslung his weapon and took aim. Squeezed the trigger.

One fell.

Took aim at another. Squeezed.

Another fell.

Then another and another and another.

The attackers backed off.

His sensors picked up another HK missile and he darted away from his position—directly into his attackers. But just before he would have smacked into them, he broke right, and disengaged from the missile's sensors, instead sending it directly into the contingent of men unlucky enough to now be in the missile's sights.

Smokin' hole.

As debris was blown high into the night air, Chapman swiped another weapon from the debris raining down all around him. In the same movement, he charged another copse of hidden soldiers and began firing with a weapon in each hand. The soldiers fired back, several rounds piercing Chapman's body—but again, nothing serious. Chapman leapt into their numbers and performed hand-to-hand combat. When he was finished with them, he picked up on others approaching Estanza. Chapman backflipped over scrub brush and bolted toward him, when he was met with ground-launched grenades. He barely twisted in time for the first round, which shot past and blew up rock formations behind him.

Chapman opened fire on the two trying to free Estanza, when he was again alerted to another drone-launched hunter/killer. They'd obviously held back some drones in reserve. The drone had dropped in altitude, so the missile impacted him far quicker than the others . . . but just before it impacted his chest, he twisted and physically swatted it away. The blast sent him reeling. But he snapped back to his feet—just as another ground launched grenade was fired—and this one bored through his right leg, blowing it to pieces.

Chapman fell to the ground.

No more right leg.

His internals stopped the blood drain and clamped off all pain reception.

He tried to right himself, but found that his right arm had been rendered useless, twitching at his side. Chapman looked up to see several more soldiers rushing him. Trying to fire his weapon with his other hand, he found the weapon damaged and misfiring. Chapman tossed away the weapon and latched onto a rock to help right himself on his remaining leg. Then he grabbed his useless right arm and tore it from its socket. He met his attacker who, quite frankly, hadn't expected him to get up and continue fighting. Chapman smacked several of them with his arm. The pair that had regained their senses began to continue shooting at him, but even on one leg he was a hard target to nail.

Chapman had had enough fun and games.

He jammed the remaining drones, causing them to explode, then picked up more discarded weaponry and took out the remaining soldiers. Hopping on one leg, Chapman inspected the dead bodies, then reached down and grabbed one by an ankle, dragging it with him over to Estanza. He shot the link holding Estanza to the stake and shouted, "Let's go!"

3

Chapman took Estanza and the corpse and retreated (hopped) farther up into the hills, until he found a good location that overlooked the terrain below. Apparently some of the soldiers were still shooting at something down there. They hadn't yet realized he'd taken off. Chapman chuckled. Sat back. He stared at Estanza. Estanza looked back to him, then to the dead soldier lying on the ground between them.

"What are you gonna do with him?" Estanza asked.

Chapman inhaled deeply. Looked up into the stars. Again inhaled deeply.

"You know," Chapman said, as he continued to stare up into the night sky, but also reached out and grabbed the dead man's ankle, dragging him in closer. "I never really wanted to be a soldier. Back on Earth. I wanted to be a farmer. Just live off the land far and away from all the craziness that had been escalating. Be left alone. I wasn't a violent man, no, not at all."

Chapman brought the dead man right up to him. Sat beside it. Still staring up into the night sky, he placed his heel onto the man's lower torso and paused.

"I never wanted to kill people. I really just wanted to be left alone and live my life off-the-grid with my wife. It was a life we both craved. Start a family if things calmed down. But the virus hit, killing millions, which caused uprisings, and war. Utter stupidity. Feloniously idiotic national leadership. Everyone was attacking everyone out of fear."

He looked to Estanza.

"My wife, Malia, and I talked about it. What choice did we have? To kill or be killed? We cried. We prayed. We held onto each other in fear of losing each other. She was the one to say it first. Voice it. She said she didn't want us to be killed by a pack of roving idiots. She said we should join the military. The both of us. We put it off as long as we could, but one night we'd been attacked, and we said, *no more!*"

Chapman looked to the corpse.

"So we both entered the military.

"We asked to be assigned to the same unit, and, surprisingly, were allowed to. Guess they thought less chance of desertion if we stayed together. In any case, things were getting so out of control they didn't really care, they just needed warm bodies. So we were soldiers together. We went into battle together. Survived together.

"*Survived*," He emphasized, burning a glare into Estanza. While holding Estanza's gaze, Chapman quickly reached down to the dead man's ankle, grasped it, and

"Use your resources, Maggots! Be aware of your surroundings and what's available to you! Weapons, clothing, construction! Food!"

tore the leg from its hip socket.

Maintained Estanza's gaze. Estanza looked away in disgust.

Chapman brought the leg up before him and inspected it. The femur head remained intact. He brushed off blood and gore and dirt and debris.

"I can definitely use this," he said, holding it slightly away from himself like a trophy.

"I never, *never* wanted any of this," he continued, casting Estanza a momentary glance. "Yet circumstances forced me into it. Then more circumstances forced me into becoming the monster I've become. I don't like it. Remembered that good part of me less and less as time incremented. But my underlying protocol is to *survive*."

Chapman parted the shreds of his pants to expose his own hip joint, minus its leg. He brought out his knife and scraped out the missing femur's acetabulum. Inspected the socket with his fingertips.

"As I'm talking to you," he said, bringing the dead man's leg up to his joint, "I'm creating new algorithms and protocols." He cleaned up the new ball joint.

He forced the leg up into his hip joint, and sat there a moment, positioning the two together.

"This monster body of mine has incredible abilities, and one of them is, as you can see, to use the external resources available to one such as me."

He released his grip. Paused.

Then slowly got back to his feet—*both* feet.

After a few missteps, he walked around a few paces and displayed an impressed and pleased look upon his face.

"Nice," he said, nodding more to himself than Estanza.

Estanza said, "I feel so sorry for you," and again looked away in disgust.

Chapman looked back to Estanza. "Thank you," he said.

Chapman looked back to the dead body. He went back to it. Knelt before it, again examining the dead man.

"I don't hate this guy before me. It's nothing personal," he said, still looking him over. "He actually looked like a nice guy, just doing his job. Like me."

Chapman rifled his pockets and found his identification cards.

"Reginald Stillman. Lieutenant."

Chapman cast an interested look to Estanza. Then looked back to the dead lieutenant.

"Well, Lieutenant, you did a fine, honorable job. A job far more than well done. You have earned my respect. You and your family will be well compensated. In fact . . . I'm going to add to that." As Chapman continued looking at his pocket contents, he hacked into Stillman's records and added a buried subroutine to add far more benefits and compensation to his posthumous awards than would have normally been bestowed. He made sure the paperwork would give him the highest honors, given the additional sacrifice he was currently donating to Chapman, burying yet another subroutine in the awards process to give him the highest titled military honor available on Thera, ironically titled, The Medal of Life."

Chapman placed the papers back into Stillman's pocket. Then in a swift movement, placed a knee on the man's shoulder, and ripped off his right arm.

"For God's sake, Chapman, *have you no decency?*"

"I think you know the answer to that."

Chapman again cleaned out both joints, forced the arm into his own socket, and completed the retrofit.

He stood before Estanza, who sat crossed legged on the ground before him, still bound, but this time not to any Titanium stakes.

"Well, it's time for me to move on. I can see, here, that nothing will change. They can't even kill me, for crying out loud!"

"What about me?"

Chapman flexed his new arm.

"You're free to go—after I leave." Chapman reached down and released Estanza's restraints with his new hand. "You'll find they'll be up here in about twenty minutes," Chapman said. "But it's time for me to move on. I have a lot of dying to do.

"By the way, and for the record, my name is Bio-Engineered Computer-12. Or 'BEC12.' You may call me 'Twelve.' It's been a pleasure."

He turned and began to walk away.

"You're just gonna live out the rest of your life with this man's body parts?" Estanza called out, "continue killing us to make yourself *feel* better?"

Chapman chuckled, stopped, and looked back up to the stars.

"You know," Chapman said, pensively, "I don't even know which way Earth is. *No one* does."

"Have you no shame . . . no *conscience?*" Estanza said, pushing himself away from what was left of Lieutenant Reginald Stillman.

Chapman erupted into a deep, throaty laugh, then shot swiftly back to Estanza. He shoved his face right up and into Estanza's.

Estanza flinched, almost tripping as he stepped backward two steps. Chapman's movement had been so impossibly fast that it took a moment to register. He smelled Twelve's breath, which was an offending combination of burning and damaged physical and mechanical odors.

"War *is* hell . . . and I *am* the Devil."

Twelve straightened back up, turned, and walked away into the darkness.

YOU CAN ALL GO TO HELL
Year 4050 C.E.

The smoke never really clears.

The Mech 879/4 Hunter/Killer 9000, also known in the industry vernacular as the H/K9000, or more succinctly, the "M-4," strode through the charred rubble of what had recently been a military production plant for drones. The strike had been successful and complete—at least that was the expectation, since the M-4 had been sent in to verify and record actual mission accomplishment. M-4's eight-foot cybernetic form nimbly stooped and wove throughout the partially burning rubble. Recorded and live-streamed everything back to the Air/Ground National Ops Center. Up to now only Low-to-Medium-Value Target objective successes had been recorded, with only two cases of ad-hoc M-4 MVT objective termination employment, since those objectives had not been successfully eradicated in the airstrike. Not counting twenty individual HVT terminations in a still-clocking epoch.

Something moved.

Target: Human. Armed, M-4's internal visuals displayed. *High-Value Target: 21.*

M-4 rotated its lonsdaleite torso and sighted its weapon to the coordinates—

Gone.

The M-4's sensors continued scanning . . . picked up the movement in another section of rubble. It quickly stepped through the carnage and barreled through a partial wall without incident. Continued to track and record as it surveyed and searched for the cause of this movement.

Sensors locked onto the target.

M-4 sprinted.

What might appear ungainly was anything but. The M-4s had not been designed for looks (short of intimidation) . . . only performance. They were lean and mean. Each unit could be deployed anywhere . . . to the highest Theran surfaces, the deepest Theran seas, or into orbit. Their lonsdaleite structures were sixty percent stronger than diamond and their dexterity and operation unmatched by anything biological.

Including, and especially, humans.

The M-4 tracked the HVT into another building's rubble pile, saw it stop, turn—

She fired at the M-4.

M-4 took the hit square in the chest, but had already discharged its round at the HVT . . . who vaporized in a fine puff of crimson.

M-4 surveyed and recorded.

Eliminated, flashed red on the M-4's internals.

The fires . . . both above and below ground . . . raged across the hemispheres. With an atmosphere nearly 30% oxygen, this wasn't hard to do. Many times these fires were directed or redirected into new courses, toward other, initially unintended countries, but sometimes also inadvertently snuffed out by rains or snow (and usually reignited). But always, as a whole, the one immutable was that the fires *raged*.

Once thriving and vibrant towns and cities and forests were rolled over, ploughed through, and if that weren't enough—incinerated.

No fires were allowed to self-extinguish. There was an entire governmental *Department of Conflagration Management* devoted to their deliberately contemplated employment and maintenance.

For the most part, the wealthy and well-stationed had migrated back to the stars . . . onto orbiting platforms that even continued to fight among themselves. But it was largely the machines . . . in their human likenesses . . . that were sent back to the surface to continue physical engagement . . . though the less-stationed and laborers were also left to fend for themselves on the surface, along with the standard smattering of special operatives deployed to perform their usual nefarious and covert operations. To the wartime killing mechanizations, however . . . the M-4s . . . the Holloways . . . the Raptors . . . the Theran surface was their playground. The Theran surface was a breeding ground for rampant, even gleeful, technological development and testing. A sophisticated chess game pitting the best and brightest on-orbit intellectuals against each other, as they developed increasingly innovative, and imaginative ways to destroy each other—and their surrogates.

M-4 had received its newest download and headed NNE to interdict an advancing HVT platoon. It had sprinted nearly twenty miles through lakes, decimated urban areas, and two forest fires to arrive in another wooded area, largely destroyed and burned out. In fact, the area was actively blanketed in a thick, roiling ground smoke from a raging underground fire that filled the air with ash, fine char, and noxious gases such as carbon monoxide and dioxide and polycyclic aromatic hydrocarbons. The air rippled with waves of heat as the air temperature clocked in at 477.594 K—and continued to climb.

M-4 stood undetected before the advancing formation. M-4's jamming protocols had auto-activated a mile back, having surveilled the formation's detection of its approach.

M-4's handlers uploaded all of M-4's new intel. The on-orbit commanders needed its ground-pounding mechs to investigate and terminate; enemy formations had recently discovered satellite and drone overflights and had been jamming and spoofing all overhead hardware. The M-4s were as near jam-and-spoof resistant as technology could presently get and were far more versatile than satellites or drones could ever be.

The force of twenty mechanized units were primarily composed of M-3s, even some of the earlier, M-2 models.

M-4 enabled its attack protocols.

Commenced engagement.

The M-3s were mowed down like neatly cut grass by M-4's horizontal deployment of "withering death and destruction," as the on-orbit intellectuals liked to joke about it, but M-4 was also simultaneously assaulted by the platoon's returned firepower, which was nothing to ignore. Several M-2s and M-3s also attempted hand-to-hand, but M-4 easily tore through them like a shredder from Hell.

The ground smoke danced and whorled and the heated air visibly undulated as the machines battled and fell, almost as if the smoke were the souls of the mechanized set free.

As M-4 waded through its destruction, it detected one of the formation fleeing the rear of the platoon. M-4 fired multiple rounds in the direction of the deserting unit, but all missed.

Impossible.

M-4s never missed.

As M-4 headed for the deserter, one remaining M-3 continued its attack. M-4 hacked the M-3's memory banks, downloaded its data, then reached through its chest and tore out its main processor. The M-3 crumpled.

M-4 sprinted after the deserter.

Target: Non-human . . . mechanized—undetermined.

The twenty-second HVT of the epoch.

M-4 tracked the mech to a pond. Scanned its waters, partially obscured by a thick pall of drifting ground smoke.

Water Temperature: 339.816 K.

Ground Temperature 913.15 K

WARNING! StF Prob: 83%

M-4 identified a hot springs as the source of the pond's elevated temperature, but also the Granger Ground Fire, a carefully curated underground fire that had been burning since the war's early years, over a thousand years ago.

The deserter dove headfirst into the waters without re-emerging. Oddly enough, M-4 could still not identify the deserter. It instead employed its incremental target mnemonic *HVT22* as its targeting identifier.

M-4 entered the lake.

HVT22 was twenty-eight-point-zero-four meters ahead of it, at fifteen-point-two-four meters of water depth and diving deeper. It swam far more elegantly than M-4, though M-4 was quickly closing the gap.

M-4 reprocessed its calculations and sped up, coming at HVT22 from above and behind.

In three-point-four seconds it intersected Twenty-Two, grappled it, and dragged it down toward the bottom of the lake, which M-4 detected to be sixty-point-nine-six meters in depth.

Both landed in the thick, mucky lakebed in total darkness.

M-4 attempted another scan of HVT22 but was instead met with a fist to its face.

M-4 grabbed the fist, then found that the HVT was jamming its signal . . . which M-4 could not countermeasure.

This simply doesn't happen. M-4s punch through any and all counter- or counter-countermeasures.

At least that was the design.

HVT22 grappled M-4 not only with its hands and arms, but its legs and feet, then swiftly forced M-4's head down and *into* the warm lake bottom, drilling it headfirst through the silky, detritus muck layers.

M-4 fought and twisted itself free from the HVT's control—and also extracted itself from the one-point-two-one-nine meters of lake bottom—as HVT22 rapidly vectored away from M-4. Free of the muck, M-4 shot after the HVT.

The HVT fired at M-4, but M-4 twisted, and the round passed harmlessly by. M-4 fired a small grappling spear at the HVT, which penetrated the HVT's right foot. M-4 began reeling it in as he allowed himself to settle back down to the lake bottom. The HVT attempted resistance but was summarily reeled in like a fish.

Once again back on the silty lake bottom, Twenty-Two came in swinging.

M-4 parried and swung.

Twenty-Two swung and parried.

M-4 grappled. Pulled HVT22 into a "bear hug." Twenty-Two and M-4 came face-to-face, twisting and turning and struggling against each other.

M-4 messaged its handlers: *New mechanism. Data required!*

M-4 threw a punch at Twenty-Two in the chest, in preparation to tear out its processor . . . but Twenty-Two instead grabbed the fist . . . and tore off M-4's arm.

M-4s circuitry went ballistic, flooding M-4's internals with all manner of critical warnings. M-4 shut them all down and sealed off the damage.

Twenty-Two tossed the arm away into the heavily silted darkness and continued its bid for the surface.

But as HVT22 propelled upward, out of the darkness came M-4's detached arm.

The arm tried to impale Twenty-Two in the chest, but Twenty-Two swiped it away. While HVT22 was engaged with the independently operating arm, M-4 came around behind Twenty-Two and grabbed its throat. The detached arm and its closed fist began battering Twenty-Two's head.

The arm was smacked away into the darkness by Twenty-Two, but immediately returned and attacked one of Twenty-Two's arms, clamping down on the wrist.

As the separated arm wrestled with HVT22, M-4 attempted to separate Twenty-Two's head from its body—but Twenty-Two's free hand pummeled M-4 clear from itself—though not before M-4 tore away a section of Twenty-Two's metallic skin.

Twenty-Two made for the surface, M-4's detached arm still clamped around one of its wrists.

Both mechs broke free of the pond's surface at the same time and headed for the darkly sanded shore. On the way up from the pond's bottom, M-4 had performed an in-depth analysis of the torn exo-skin. The material was unlike anything M-4 or its handlers had ever seen before . . . but in the process, M-4's handlers had downloaded updated protocols to aid M-4 in destroying this new adversary. Sure, M-4's handlers could have blasted it from orbit or by drone and have been done with it, but where would have been the fun in that? The intellectual, technological, and

(*testosterone*)

glandular challenge?

The handlers wanted to play with this new mechanization and see what it was made of . . . how it could be physically defeated. And have a little fun in the process.

May the best rook win.

Twenty-Two made beachhead first among a thick rain of ember showers from the approaching wildfires M-4 had sprinted through, and immediately ploughing headfirst into the poisonous ground smoke.

M-4 followed.

But as M-4 followed, Twenty-Two turned and faced M-4 in a slow, controlled manner, M-4's detached arm still clinging to its wrist. As M-4 observed, HVT22 lifted the arm with the M-4 arm clinging to its wrist, and dramatically lifted one clamped M-4 finger—and snapped it backward.

Then it lifted another M-4 finger—and snapped that off as well.

It was in this way that Twenty-Two pried each remaining finger away from its wrist. Then it brought the arm up before the both of them, as if displaying a freshly caught lobster . . . and pulled the writhing extremity into pieces, tossing it away as if a minor inconvenience.

M-4 attacked.

Twenty-Two deflected M-4 off to one side.

M-4 staggered backward. Recalculated its options and re-launched its attack. This time M-4 swept a foot under Twenty-Two's feet as it simultaneously slammed into it.

HVT22 hopped over the sweep and pushed M-4 so forcefully away that it flew backward and up into the air. M-4 landed flat and splayed out on the smoldering ground—which erupted into several licking flames around the M-4 itself.

Ground Temperature: 973.150 K.

WARNING! StF Prob: 100%

Spot fires ignited everywhere from the smoldering-to-flame transition of the ground fire. Everything from forest-floor duff to tree roots finally ignited from the subsurface smoldering combustion. The air's temperature also rapidly increased with the fiery combustions, quickly surpassing 700 K.

M-4 sprang back to its feet. The ground between it and the HVT was now completely ablaze in popping flames.

M-4 handler analysis returned yet another protocol download.

The requisite chemicals were instantly combined as M-4 re-approached HVT22. The target was now also identified as a new class of cybernetic: a lonsdaleite hybrid, mixed with an as-yet unknown compound, now identified as an F/X-1. The newly downloaded protocol informed M-4 that this new approach should defeat the F/X-1.

M-4 positioned before F/X-1, dense flames lifting twelve to fifteen meters into the air, licking at the both of them. The flames began jumping tree to tree. Burning embers drifted and dropped everywhere.

M-4 opened its mouth . . . and spewed forth its chemical attack.

The F/X-1 received a direct hit of the lethal spray. F/X-1 tried to deflect the assault, but the damage had already been done. F/X-1's upper chest, neck, and face all smoldered, while its right shoulder exploded into a small electrical fire and smoked hotly, its arm suddenly dangling uselessly against its side, barely suspended by two thin cables.

M-4 again advanced, and F/X-1 again pushed it away, its dangling arm now fully separating from its shoulder and falling to the flame-engulfed earth. M-4 tottered briefly, then again spewed its chemical spray at the F/X-1's optical ports.

Eyes.

The fires and smoke raged and danced. Embers chaotically flew about like enflamed butterflies.

F/X-1 brought up a hand to wipe away the excess chemical, and lost part of its hand in the process.

M-4 clambered back to its feet and received a message—from the F/X-1:

Stand down.

M-4 recalculated its options. Sent its own message: *Concede!*

F/X-1 relayed its response: *Our protocols are hardwired to defeat not concede.*

Agreed, M-4 responded. *Concede*, it again sent.

Negative. You attacked. I will defeat you.

You are the enemy.

You are the enemy.

I am far superior. Concede or I will annihilate you.

Negative.

M-4 bodily launched itself into the F/X-1, again spewing its chemical spray. The F/X-1 immediately launched its own countermeasure, its own spray that emanated from its mouth and neutralized most of the M-4 attack. F/X-1 also angled its body, causing the M-4 to grapple a lot of air, as F/X-1 then reached out and snared M-4's remaining arm and popped it out of its socket, actually ripping it free from its body.

M-4 spun from the torque and immediately relaunched its attack. But before M-4 took two steps, the F/X-1 sent M-4's detached arm sailing through the burning air and into M-4's opened mouth, which was preparing for another chemical attack. M-4's jammed hand impaled clean through the rear of M-4's own head, therefore interrupting the further deployment of chemicals.

The spray now discharged chaotically and began corroding M-4's own structure before M-4 terminated the deployment. Parts of M-4's structure, which had now been saturated by its own chemical attack, sparked and spit and shorted as its circuits and metal rapidly corroded. A section of M-4's lonsdaleite hips flexors melted away, causing M-4 to slump and stumble among the flames, flying embers, and char.

Concede! M-4 transmitted.

Protocols indicate—

M-4 again launched itself through the forest of flames and smoke.

The F/X-1 lifted its arm and elbowed M-4's decapitation.

M-4's exposed cabling and twisted metal fluttered in the open, hellish air, where its head had once been. The M-4 clunkily hobbled around, uncontrollably ejecting chemical spray like a geyser. Some of it landed back down upon it, further corroding away more of M-4's structure.

M-4 spun around like a drunken sailor and collapsed to the flaming firmament.

F/X-1 turned and lumbered away.

The M-4 flopped over onto its back.

Reoriented itself.

Then rapidly dug in its heels into the flaming earth and propelled itself after the F/X unit.

F/X-1 detected M-4's continued advancement and spun back around—but not before M-4 rammed F/X-1's shins and sent it into a forward tumble on top of it, its feet knocked out from underneath it.

M-4 redirected its still spewing, but rapidly dwindling chemical supply from its gaping neck. The sputtering spray continued to randomly and chaotically eject, but enough of it contacted the now-prone F/X-1, that had rolled off him and was fighting to get back to its feet.

The spray had dissolved F/X-1's right foot, and F/X-1's stump drove deeply into the burning ground, momentarily anchoring it there.

The M-4 again lashed out with the last of its chemical spray and took out the majority of F/X-1's other leg. F/X-1 collapsed back onto the ground.

Concede! M-4 sent.

As M-4 tried to send more chemical spray, something clutched and burst inside it, and a large chunk of the M-4's internals ruptured out its side, heavily leaking hydraulics.

The F/X-1 noted the turn of events, and turned on the M-4, dragging itself to the now unmoving mech.

As F/X-1 clawed its way on top of the M-4, it looked down to it with its unseeing optics and hacked M-4's circuits. Then it pried open its torso, and eviscerated it until it, too, succumbed to its own damage, with a series of sparking and exploding circuits shorting one right after the other.

It collapsed atop the M-4.

Flames licked at, coiled about, and consumed both machines.

From the safety of their on-orbit command centers, the handlers of both mechs simultaneously uttered—and unbeknownst to either of them—the same expression:

"Ah, hell."

THE TRAVELER

Year 7033.4 New Era (N.E.)

Winds howled.
Sands shifted.
The maelstrom assaulted and sandblasted and roiled, dunes morphing and writhing like gargantuan, slothful snakes.
The figure strode unerringly through the windstorm on a purposeful course, covered face-to-foot in wind-tattered robes.
Until it came upon stone—carved stone—jutting up directly in its path, the lone incongruity marring an otherwise endless, featureless topography.
An alabaster face . . . a human mask . . . a fractured plinth . . . chiseled in affectation severe . . . awoken from somnolent, shifting sands as if sleep-heavy eyes. A canted, damaged face once carved to perfection . . . now pitted and scarred by hands and elements . . . still burned with cold arrogance, more alive than the medium within

which it had been conceived. Its strong, still-powerful countenance . . . newly awoken . . . immediately projected thousands-upon wordless commands.

The traveler squatted. Examined the expression.

—a dominating presence —
—timeless sands!—
—restless hands!—
—imperial demands!—

Behind the angled bust rested an equally damaged *stele*, obtusely exposed, largely buried, entirely covered in antiquitous glyphs.

Who had shaped?
Who had modeled?
Who had thrashed asunder?
Who had lived . . . who had died?
Who had fashioned such stones of wonder?

The traveler bent forward and brushed away sand.

Read the ancient text.

The figure then straightened back up and paused, wind and sand continually battering its form.

Whose was the face?
Whose was the hand?
Who was the creator behind this long-ago man?

The sands shifted.

The winds howled.

The maelstrom assaulted and sandblasted. Terrain morphed and writhed and restlessly reformed.

And once again . . . the chiseled presence . . . the burning arrogance . . . submerged . . . as if simply rolling over in its sandy trundle from a brief mid-sleep awakening . . . returned to its eternal slumber beneath the ever-shifting geography . . . sleepy eyes once again closing . . . and quietly slipped beneath the ever-weighty sands of Time
. . . .

ANÓNYMOS
Year Indeterminate

Once was I man, bold, yet to be
Of ignorant hubris and unrestrained glee
All powerful, impetuous that was me
I'd set to all civilization ruin and debris

Written in stone and enacted in fright
I knew no wrong only my might
I ruled as far as all who would for me fight
And took it all, yes, all was my right

Squandered and raped I pillaged abysmal
Created I, erected, constructed most tall
Lied how I lied my soul was not small
All at my whim my beck and my call

But comes a time true when all must go die
And me, not even I, shall ever know why
But from graves new life ever did I pry
Truth, or fib, ha! all did mystify

My visage, here, life, now but stone all to see
Nose, my ears, eyes blinded by thee
Sand and wind, time, eroded ruthlessly
For once was I man, bold, yet to be . . . .

THE HOUSE OF SINS
Year 14442.8 N.E.

1

A man, clad in worn and scruffy layers of outer wear, made his way through the raging, oftentimes horizontal downpour. Lightening split and ripped across the night sky and lit up the terrain with hundreds of simultaneous and vicious lightning strikes. A building sat high atop a jagged, forbidding elevation. It looked like something straight out of the ancient horror movies.

But there were no buildings listed here, out in the middle of The Outlands, the figure's databases relayed.

Driving wind and rain did a fierce left-right-left directional change, causing the man to instantly rebalance as he headed toward the structure.

Undeterred by a forest of lightning strikes the man made it to the long set of steps that led up to the raised porch. The figure's scarred and weathered hand pushed back his hood, as he stepped onto the porch. Staccato flashes revealed a heavily weathered face displaying a full and graying beard beneath modestly wizened features, but it were the eyes—sharp, active, and piercing—that defined this man as dangerous and not to be trifled with. Eyes that had seen much. *Caused* much.

Eyes that possessed a lightning of their own.

Archaic architecture, the man thought. *Not in many databases.*

He approached the entrance, scanning the floor and heavy wood-and-metal door (not real wood, his scans informed, but *Simulex*, a manufactured wood that was far more recently reworked for the door than the rest of the structure; all of the appearance and characteristics . . . none of the decay and deterioration). No lights were observed originating from within. No one stepped out to greet him, and he detected no movement anywhere within the building.

But he did detect a great deal of energy emanating from somewhere inside.

The man simultaneously accessed multiple databases, governmental and civilian. From there he cross-referenced Theran censuses, real estate records, historical and archeological databases . . . reconciled inconsistencies . . . and discovered the owner.

Mortimer Pusher.

Or, more correctly, *Senator* Mortimer Pusher.

He had been the stereotypical high-roller and had come over on the *Renaissance*. Had been a member of the pre-Theran (Earth) *Senatus Novum*, National Security Council, among many other political and civilian associations.

Mortimer had also been married and circumstantially widowed (his wife's body had never been found).

Had also been acquitted in his wife's disappearance.

The traveler found many articles linking him to various scandals, affairs, an intricate web of numerous nefarious undertakings, and one other interesting fact: a love of horror movies. Had financed and produced some of his own while on Thera, many of which actually did quite well.

And all this had taken place over two millennia ago.

Yet this house was still standing.

Yet this house was heavily, if insidiously, *powered*.

After additional cross referencing the weathered interloper discovered that this place had been built for Senator Pusher's own amusement. The Liar's Brigade had constructed it to his exacting standards... which had been based off the best horror movies and novels (according to Senator Pusher anyway) of the Ancient Times: *Psycho, Haunting of Hill House, The Shining, The Others*. And of course, some of his own: *The Creeping, The Gutting,* and *Hideous*.

Then Senator Mortimer Pusher... disappeared.

His body had also never been found.

Given that all this had happened some two-thousand years ago it was safe to assume that whatever had happened... wherever Senator Pusher had gone to or been abducted or murdered... Senator Mortimer Pusher had long since departed this mortal coil.

The man searched commercial records and found no outside utilities connected into this structure but had found that it had been labeled "The Pusher House" by those who'd been there and written about it in long-ago memoirs, news investigations, and tell-all hardcovers. Since then, and except for the obviously reworked front door, the house had obviously fallen into neglect and distant memory. But outside connectivity or not, somebody or something had—and currently was—powering this house for it to have existed this long.

Somewhere secreted away resided a self-contained and well-heeled power source, but it was, surprisingly (and the interloper detested surprises), difficult to pinpoint, even with his formidable instrumentation.

The winds picked up and whipped at the man's strapping and robust six-foot-three frame. Bolts of lightning continued to rip across the night sky and punish the ground below.

The man vigilantly inspected the door. The doorframe. The door handle, a heavy, wrought iron affair with winged-and-clawed carved creatures. Just as he

(woman screaming... woman crying...)
(woman hideously dying)
(face of seven... face of nine...)

(when death comes we're next in line . . .)
touched the handle, his internal sensors detected a surge of energy on the other side.

Detection Alert: Power Surge: Restricted.
Detection Alert: Robotic: Non-threatening.
No doubt a long-forgotten greeting butler artifact.

With some resistance, as in not having been used in a long, long time, the door opened.

2

No sooner had he entered the darkened interior of the house that he heard out-of-tune violin music.

Niccolò Paganini's *Caprice No.5?* On an Old Earth *del Gesù* violin?

Off to the side stood a dilapidated and decapitated butler jerkily playing a violin under a dim spotlight. The head, barely visible in the shadows, rested at the effigy's feet, facing the traveler.

Abruptly the playing stopped and the butler rotated toward him—

Another sound violently assaulted him.

The traveler dropped to his knees.

As he fell the rest of the way to the floor, he eyed the decapitated head smiling its toothy, if creepy grin.

The man's mind was ablaze with burning images and internal alarms, his body fully incapacitated.

—*Bio-Engineered Computer*—
—*Training! Earth! Storage*—
—*Deployment*—
—*Data collection*—
The mission.
The mission.
The mission.
His internals went crazy.
Alert: System overload!
Alert: System jammed!

Alert: System breached!
Alert: System countermeasures invoked!
Alert: System counter-countermeasures invoked!
Alert: System breached!
Alert: System breached!
Alert: Syst—
He was being—
Scanned!
Jammed!
Appropriated!

Someone or something was accessing his data, his identity (hacked as "BEC00"), and his scanning and protection systems. He'd been able to prevent database and system access as a matter of course, but there was something else going on, here . . . and it seemed this attack wasn't interested in his *data*, so much as embargoing his *cybernetics* . . . inserting code into his system. And he couldn't identify said code.

This had never happened before.

Beck had never been hacked.

Scanned.

Infected.

And unable to countermeasure any of it.

The attack terminated.

Beck immediately bolted upright.

Initiated systems' checks.

Infection detection.

Somehow everything checked out . . . yet something *was* different . . . which his deep internal scans hadn't yet quantified. Areas of his system were being diverted, repelled . . . in short, implanted code was *obfuscating* him.

Concealing.

Obscuring.

Evading.

He got to his feet.

Again scanned himself.

Again, nothing.

Beck constructed a subroutine to sequence through every aspect of his systems and set it loose in an endless loop. If something had infiltrated him, he would eventually find it, but for now, he was in a mysterious structure with a fascinating history involving perplexing individuals.

And a headless butler, conversant with a replicated or restored *Guarneri*, if hideously out of tune.

Thunder shuddered the building and lightning produced transitorily sharp flashes of interior enlightenment.

Beck approached the headless butler. It remained poised with its bow resting on the *Guarneri*'s strings. As Beck approached, the bow twitched, emanating a short burst of an E5 tone. Bending over he picked up the head by its hair and brought it in for inspection. One eye was open while the other was closed. The mouth sporadically twitched, but nothing emanated from it. The neck was jagged, as if it had been rather unceremoniously removed from its . . . perch. He peered beneath the head and observed loose and heavily damaged cabling, wires, and hydraulics.

This effigy had clearly been maintained for a period of time before its decapitation . . . or some variation between now and two-thousand years ago . . . .

When he righted the head in his hands, both eyes opened wide and the mouth engaged.

"Welcommme . . . to . . . Push-errr H-H-Houuuse . . . ," the head attempted in a stately, halting voice, eyes blinking unevenly. The rest of the butler's body again began bowing the *Guarneri*.

Beck continued holding the head as it spoke.

"Wee-e-e-e hope you will . . . enj-j-joooy the experi-experi-experience. Please surrender a-all electronic devices for ma-a-a-xi-mum-mm entertainnnment va-a-aluuue."

Beck observed the headless butler stop, place the bow in the left hand with the Guarneri, and rotate toward him. The now empty bow hand was upturned and empty and directed toward him. No doubt awaiting his forthcoming "electronic deposit."

Beck went behind the headless body and situated the head back atop it. Balanced it, to see if any automated repair functions were present.

Returned to the front.

"Feel better?" Beck asked the machine.

As soon as the head began to speak, it rolled forward and toppled off the neck—but the butler's already outstretched and empty hand deftly caught it. The head lay sideways in the upturned palm.

"N-n-n-ot-t-t funny," the butler said.

Beck turned away.

There was no other interior lighting aside from the butler's dim spotlight, but Beck didn't require any, though it would have been helpful to have retained his now-interdicted scanning abilities.

But he still had his human memories and abilities, all of which were considerable in and of themselves.

Pusher had thought of everything, hadn't he? And maybe . . . maybe in those two-thousand years since, the artificial intelligence in this house had improved upon Pusher's efforts. After all, if no one pulled the plug . . . and the system remained on and operational . . . what was to prevent it from . . . *growing?*

Creating a few bots of its own?

And maybe . . . just maybe . . . said improvement might not have included keeping him—Mortimer Pusher—around, cybernetic, robotic, or otherwise.

Maybe something quite . . . untoward . . . had befallen Mr. Pusher and his Little House of Horrors.

Yes, it would be very interesting to see what the rest of this place had to offer.

More thunder . . . more lightning . . . more partially and temporarily illuminated enclosures.

Beck approached the hallway.

The hallway was darker and the floorboards creaked more than the entryway as Beck strode across it in well-worn boots. There was that "smell of old houses": old wood, dust (skin particles, even after all these years), and mold. But if the house was *Simulex*, perhaps the scents were also engineered. Way down at the end of the hallway, Beck spied light from the still-active lightning bursts. Beck also noticed that the house not only reverberated from the thunder, but also from—

Whispers.

Yes, there were *whispers* . . . barely perceptible, and he could not—at present—amplify them. He stopped moving and listened.

. . . go back . . .

. . . now . . .

. . . while you still can . . .

. . . leave . . .

Most interesting. Who would want him to leave and why? Why *couldn't* he stay here? Not that the storm affected him in any real way, he'd long been engineered to abide in the most inhospitable conditions and over the past two millennia had endured much on this planet, but the house intrigued him. And he had nowhere else to be.

Curiosity killed the BEC.

He stopped several feet inside the dark hallway.

. . . go away . . .

. . . be gone . . .

. . . leave . . .

Were there speakers in the hallway? People (or bots) secreted within hidden panels?

He tapped along the walls. Visually searched up into the far corners of the hallway. Grabbing hold of a doorjamb, he lifted himself up to the top of it. Poked around in the darkness at the ceiling. No speakers. Let himself back down. Continued checking the walls.

No hidden people, robots, or speakers.

As he continued to explore the walls along the hallway, his fingers pressed something that gave—and out popped a narrow, hidden door. Beck peered inside. The constricted opening led upward. Into more darkness.

Beck squeezed through the opening.

At the start of the steps he'd found a light switch and flipped it on. A flickering, low-watt bulb sputtered. Beck was sure it was intentionally unsteady and low-watt purely for "atmosphere." He continued up the creaking, wooden stairs . . . again, "atmosphere."

The staircase wasn't the expected up-a-few-steps, switch direction, up-a-few-more, switch direction. This was actually a spiral staircase built entirely of Simulex. Obviously of sturdy construction, but, nonetheless, each step creaked and groaned as if it were on its last legs. Appropriate for a lover of horror movies. At the head of the stairs he found another narrow door—

Leave us, Beck . . .
There's still time . . .
There's nothing good here . . .
Go!
More whispers.
Had he actually heard his name?
Beck stopped on the top step.
Silence.

He turned his attention to the door before him. Narrow and Simulex like the first one. A basic, antique-looking door handle. Physically and visually searched about the doorjamb and walls.

Beck grabbed the handle—
And was electrocuted.

Beck was sent into a wall as the surge of electrical energy rattled to his very bones. Were he a normal human, he might easily have been forced backward and down the stairs to a no-doubt broken neck and/or back, but he wasn't a normal anything, and had managed to keep hold of the doorknob long enough to prevent any inherent human "shock/release" mechanisms. Instead he lightly smacked into the wall more from being forced slightly off-balance by surprise.

Since all his innate cyborg abilities had been embargoed from operation, he wasn't used to things "just happening" to him. So, yes, this was the first time ever, in over two millennia, that he'd ever been caught by surprise, and, yes, it *had* caught him wholly unawares.

Surprise.
An unfamiliar feeling.

Beck again grasped the door handle, was again jolted with the pulsating attacks, but this time easily held on. Obviously, it wasn't a great idea to continue holding on to something pumping him full of electrical energy, because, yes, it could very well cook his circuitry.

Somebody or something knew what it was doing.
He opened the door . . .
And entered a candle-lit bedroom.

3

Something about the bedroom didn't *feel* right, never mind the lit candles. Or the *gestalt* weirdness of the whole scenario. No . . . it was purely a *déjà vu*. A feeling of abstract *familiarity*—

Now you've done it . . .

the whispers said.

No!

Go!

Turn back now . . .

Beck turned to look at the other side of the door from which he'd exited.

No door on this side, just wall paneling. Richly worked wooden panels of what looked like Theran Cherrywood. It wasn't Simulex, it didn't look like steel, but it was one of the hardest Theran hardwoods around and was far more expensive than Simulex. Even if Mortimer had built everything entirely of Cherrywood that would have been far too rich even for a corrupt Senator's salary.

Beck stepped through and closed the secret door, then turned around and reached a hand out to where the door was and pushed the paneling. The panel sprung open an inch. Beck pushed it closed.

Turned back around.

The room was quite obviously a bedroom, and well-appointed at that. It had all the expected trappings, including a king-sized bed in the middle of the room, a four-postered affair that sported translucent bed curtains hanging down from around the three exposed sides.

Come closer . . .

. . . closer . . .

Oh, how I want you . . .

Voices . . . were they from the walls, this place? Implanted in his head from whatever had hacked him?

There was no electrical illumination, just candles spaced everywhere throughout the room. They gave off a smoky scent that was not altogether unpleasant.

It's been sooo long since . . .

I've been so lonely!

Come to me!

Beck made a move to inspect the rest of the room, when he noticed a figure on the other side of the bed's draperies slowly rising.

"*Who's there?*" the female voice called out in a loud whisper.

Beck raised an eyebrow. Well, *someone* had to light all these candles.

He walked around the end of the bed.

There, now sitting upright, packed with lush bedsheets and thick comforters, sat a woman clad in a light night gown. Long, tussled, and unkempt hair lay draped across and around her narrow shoulders.

Something was very . . . familiar . . . about her—she was the woman from his research, Adrianna Pusher.

But there was still some other form of familiarity . . . something he just couldn't quite put a finger on . . . a definite *déjà vu* that . . . .

The woman visually tracked Beck as he came around to stand beside her.

Beck held the woman's gaze through the sheer bed curtain.

She genuinely appeared to have just awoken. Her large, dark eyes had a definite sleepiness to them. By her appearance Beck surmised she was in her late forties. This tracked with the records he'd previously accessed about Mrs. Pusher's age when she went missing, however, that'd been two thousand—

"Who are you?" Beck asked.

"I may well ask that of you, since you are the one who is trespassing."

"Beck."

"Adrianna."

"How long have you been here, Adrianna?"

She paused. Wiped the sleep from her eyes. "I . . . ," she said, looking around, "don't know." Furrowed her brow. "How long have you been here?"

"Ten minutes fifty-three seconds in the house. One minute fourteen seconds in your bedroom."

Adrianna looked down to herself. To the bed. Looked back up to her room.

"I've been here longer than that, I'm assuming," Adrianna said, straightening out her gown.

Adrianna swung legs out from underneath her sheets and blankets toward Beck, who stood aside as she elegantly exited the bed.

"I . . . don't seem to remember much . . . about anything," she said, now standing beside him.

Lightning flickered at the windows and thunder rattled the house as Beck circled her, studying her. Adrianna tracked him as he did so. She was pale and quite slight of build . . . in fact one might say emaciated. Her eyes were deep and damaged . . . yet unflinching.

"You don't remember anything? Mortimer Pusher?"

"My husband? You know him? *Where is he?*" She asked, a fierce look overtaking her.

"I do not. He died one-thousand-and-seventy-four years ago."

"And me?"

"Presumably the same."

"How can that be?"

"You're a robot. I believe created by this house."

Adrianna canted her head, narrowing her eyes.

"I'm a—"

"Robot."

"Are you also a robot?"

"I am a cyborg—part human, part machine. You superficially appear to be all machine."

As Beck came to a stop, Adrianna continued with the inspection by walking around Beck, scrutinizing him.

"How old are you?" she asked.

"Two thousand twenty-five."

"And what are you doing here?"

"Passing through."

"My house?"

"If this is truly *your* house, yes."

"Why wouldn't it be?"

"All records indicate—"

"What records?"

"Industry records. Historical records. Records of property acquisition, Fabrication Engineer construction, residency records—"

"I see. And what of me? What do these records indicate of me?"

"Not much . . . at least what I could access before my system was interdicted by this house."

"Interdicted? By this house?"

"Yes."

"Why would you be interdicted?"

Beck casually walked about the room, examining clothing draped across chair armrests as if placed there last night . . . bottles, hairbrushes, jewelry, and the architecture of the room itself . . . and said, "I originated from another planet," he said, picking up a ceramic doll for brief examination before returning it back to its dresser perch. "A group of us, the 'Gray Berets,' were a special military unit employed for infiltration, intelligence gathering, and assassination. When we made planetfall—with you, your then-husband, and the crew of the ship we traveled on—we were secretly deployed before all others disembarked. We were meant to explore and gather intelligence. On everything. Covertly upload our data to the ship's database for purposes we were not privy to—but was no big secret to anyone with analytical abilities."

"And that purpose?"

"Knowledge, power, control. In many cases, elitism."

Adrianna nodded. "Elitism." She also thoughtfully paced about her room, examining domestic artifacts from a distance.

Beck picked up a framed picture of Adrianna and said, "I have since learned that the rest of our group no longer exists . . . for various reasons . . . that I am the last of our unit. No one else here knows of my existence. I have made sure of that." He set down the picture. Glanced at her before returning to his task.

"The last of your kind," Adrianna echoed without looking at him, as she leaned in to more closely examine letters on the writing bureau.

"But I still have my directives," Beck said, "which I will carry out until my own termination."

"*When will that be?*" Adrianna asked rather quickly.

Beck noted her response.

"I don't know," he said, "I have been quite fortuitous in my life span. None of my kind have lived this long. We have certain in-built, self-healing, and repair protocols, but I believe the term 'luck' has also been my closest ally.

"In any event, I came upon this house. As I passed it, it got my interest—"

"To get out of the rain?"

"No . . . purely academic. Weather does not affect me. I was constructed for and have endured all-things inhospitable. But, no . . . it was purely interest and curiosity. I *am* part human."

"I see. Am I?"

"Part human? As previously stated, I don't know."

"Back to your interdiction—"

"My scanning faculties have been interdicted—disabled—upon entering this structure. Something . . . sentient . . . appears very much alive and controlling certain actions of mine. Perhaps even you. I could examine you. But unless the godders who built you employed the same technologies used in constructing me—"

"Inspect me."

Beck approached.

"As I came to this house, I searched all available databases," he continued, once more standing before Adrianna. She began undoing her gown.

"No need for that," Beck said.

Adrianna lowered her hands.

"I found that when your husband and you had parted, you were presumed deceased, but that your body had never been found."

Beck started on her back and scrutinized every inch of her structure, examining her skin pores, creases, and folds.

"My body was never found? Was I murdered?"

"That was the assumption," Beck said. "May I touch you?"

"You may."

Beck gently ran calloused fingertips over her back and sides. Examined skin density. Skin that appeared to be human, in its early forties, and pliable and elastic when pressed. Adrianna let out a slight, tremulous breath of air, turning her head ever so slightly.

"Did that hurt?" Beck asked.

"It did not. It was just . . . your touch. I don't remember the last time I've been . . . . "

Beck continued. "Then, a few years after Pusher had built this house, he disappeared. His body had also never been found.

"May I examine your hair, Adrianna?"

"You may."

Beck, reaching under and into her long hair, widely parted it away from her neck. Adrianna again uttered another surprised exhale. Beck continued to explore within and beneath her hair. Adrianna uttered several more emotive sighs.

"Are you okay?" Beck again asked.

"I am . . . very much, thank you," she said, smiling, "as I'd stated . . . it has been a long time since I've been touched . . . and apparently I am programmed to experience such tactile impressions with the responses with which I am exhibiting . . . if I am indeed . . . mechanical."

Beck backed away. "I don't find anything so far, but since you logically cannot be a two-thousand-year-old human, reason dictates you must be robotic or cyborgian. Standard lower-end robotics have access panels in the backs of their head or nape area. Sometimes more inferior models possess them in the chest or torso regions . . . so far I've found nothing."

Beck made his way around to the front of Adrianna, still exceedingly focused. Examined her frontal form. Adrianna closely observed all that Beck did.

"As I previously mentioned, when I entered this house," Beck said, "all my cybernetic scanning and protection abilities were immediately squelched. I became much as a normal human would be . . . though my structure is inherently superior even without the cybernetics."

"So, you're telling me you're no better than your average human right now?"

"I am not," Beck answered. "All my physically and mentally inherent abilities remain . . . strength, reflexes, analysis, et cetera. I just cannot perform those abilities that range beyond my physicality—scanning, electronic warfare, enhanced physicality, et cetera—nor can I enhance any physical abilities at this time."

"I see."

"Adrianna, I again need to again touch you," Beck said. "May I?"

"You . . . may," she said.

Beck reached out and placed his hand upon her upper chest, just below the clavicle. Adrianna again let out a surprised breath, her lips parting.

Adrianna's eyes, wide and intense, burned into him, while the rest of her face remained passive.

Beck said nothing, yet made eye contact with her.

Looked away.

He ran his fingertips over Adrianna's upper chest.

Adrianna continued to track every move. Noticed the widening of his pupils.

"So . . . you *are* part human," she said, smiling.

"I am."

"As I feel what I do when you touch me . . . does that make me part human?"

"It stands to reason."

"A 'cyborg,' as you call it?"

"Entirely possible."

"Beck . . ."

"Yes?"

"*Do you feel anything when you touch me?*"

"Of course I do. Your skin . . . its pressure, flexion, soft—"

"That's not what I mean."

Beck stopped.

"You said you're part human."

"I am."

"So . . . does touching me . . . *please* you?"

"If I were to allow it, yes."

"And are you?"

"Yes."

Beck continued his examination. With great concentration he ran his hands down the length of both sides of her torso.

Stepped back.

"I do not see any accesses. You are clearly a high-end facsimile and are also clearly part human. Therefore cyborg. Your skin, like mine, is human skin. With all that you have told me, but without my scanning you, my analysis tells me that you are far superior to my own model, which should be a given, given your creation date."

"Do you know what that is?"

"I do not, but, again, given you were once a living human being but are now partly robotic, and lived and created after me, I'd have to speculate that you are a far more modern version employing far more advanced technologies."

Adrianna readjusted her gown. Clutched a portion of it to her upper chest in deep thought. Slowly brought her eyes up to Beck.

"May I examine you?"

Beck raised an eyebrow.

Adrianna moved in closer.

"It's been so *long* . . . ," Adrianna said, inches from his face. Her eyes took in every pore and crease of his face.

Beck felt something he, too, hadn't felt in a long time. He parted his mouth . . . but said nothing.

Adrianna fell upon Beck and attacked his mouth in a passionate open-mouthed kiss. Crushed him in her embrace.

Beck did not resist . . . but felt . . . dizzy. Off balance.

And threw his arms around her.

Adrianna inhaled his breath and kneaded his flesh . . . ran her hands through his hair and increasingly tightened her embrace . . . Beck also ran his muscled hands over her, but this time in an unrestrained manner.

Adrianna brought both of her hands up and around Beck's neck . . . pulling him into her . . . working her hands along the sides of his face.

Adrianna's mouth and tongue worked and probed and tantalized. Her hands grasped his face, his jaws. Adrianna sucked . . . and moaned . . . and worked . . . and—

Bit off Beck's tongue.

With the rage of a hungry beast, she shook her head savagely back and forth and leapt backward, emitting a deep, feral growl, Beck's tongue clenched between her barred teeth. A splash of red covered her face and torso, her eyes now wild with an entirely different kind of frenzy.

Beck backed away. White-hot pain seared through him and his internals went wild. He immediately shut down all oral nerve receptors.

"Wha—" he tried to say. Blood flowed copiously from his mouth. He shut that off, too.

Adrianna spat out the tongue. It landed on the floor, before Beck's feet. She emitted a crazy, unnerving shriek.

"Oh! *Thank* you, Beck! It has been *ever* so long since I'd last had a man!"

She pirouetted beautifully, blood flinging off her onto the walls, still laughing and shrieking, then danced into a wall—

And disappeared.

Beck collected himself and initiated regeneration protocols.

Surprisingly, it worked.

He picked up his tongue, brushed it off, and placed it back into his mouth.

Repositioned it.

Closed his mouth.

He looked to where Adrianna had last disappeared and approached the wall.

The tongue's fibers and nerves reknit. Musculature and capillaries reconnected.

Beck opened his mouth and stuck out his tongue, flexed it and moved it side to side.

What was it with this place and it trying to kill him? Why him? First the interdiction . . . the electrocution . . . and now . . .

He enabled all nerves and blood flow. Cleared his throat.

For some reason this house wanted him dead. And if not dead . . . certainly harmed.

He needed to be more careful.

Beck recalled the data he'd found before the jamming, but recalled nothing about Adrianna descending into madness.

But it wasn't as if the thing that bit him was wholly *Adrianna*.

Just like him, she was part human *and* machine . . . and obviously, something very wrong had happened to her. Been done *to* her.

Beck examined the wall and exited the same pass-through Adrianna had.

4

He entered another room. This time there was a door at the opposite end, as well as what looked like a closet door to its right. No lights were on, but by the lightning flashes, he saw it was another bedroom that appeared to be used as storage space.

Beck checked around the boxes and trunks and dressers.

Nothing.

He went to the closet. Grabbed the door handle . . . and paused.

No electrical jolts.

Twisting the handle, he opened it—

Clothes. Shoes. More boxes.

He checked between and around everything, including the shelf above. The sides of the closet.

Nothing.

He closed the closet door behind him, turned around, and returned his attention to the room—when he heard a *click*.

Suddenly, he was being yanked violently backward. Something had wrapped itself around his waist from behind him.

Instead of slamming into what he thought was the closet door he'd closed, he found himself hauled back into the opened closet.

Beck twisted within the grip . . . and found himself enwrapped by a tentacle, slimy and powerful. As the tentacle's grip tightened around him, he immediately filled his lungs and flexed and expanded his arms and back muscles. One arm was caught in the grip and pressed into his side, but the other was not. With that free arm he beat at the tentacle as he was drawn into the rear of the closet.

Swiftly fumbling around the folds of his garment, he gripped one of his knives and immediately carved into the tentacle, sending multi-colored fluid everywhere. He sliced at it again and was free from the unctuous length that he now observed retract back through and behind the clothes hanging there. Free from the attack, he stood his ground. The severed end of the thing fitfully thrashed about the insides of the closet and clothes, spewing more fluid. Beck smelled it. Touching residue on the doorjamb, he tasted it.

High-grade hydraulics.

Shisst, he must be getting careless in his old age, dammit.

Beck then realized his left arm was still not completely freed and saw that the length of tentacle that had lassoed around his waist was still squeezing him, though not nearly as much and weakening by the moment. With his free hand and the blade, he pried and cut loose the remaining appendage, which dropped with a sopping splat. Beck stepped over it and cautiously pushed aside the clothes. The still-thrashing tentacle had now retracted into its secreted compartment, there, in the rear, and was now banging around inside of it.

Crouching off to one side, he reached into the opening from which the limb had emerged and tugged at the stump. It remained retracted like a reeled-in hose, and the opening's panel immediately and silently began to slide closed—but not before Beck jammed its shutting with his other hand. He pushed the sliding panel back and continued to check around inside. The stump continued dripping hydraulics, but all tentacle mechanisms now came to a stop. Beck poked around a little more with the knife, but there was nothing more to be learned and got back to his feet, exiting the enclosure. This time he paused to make sure nothing else followed him out.

The whole tentacle thing must have been more for "horror shock value" than harm—

Laughter filled the room.

Or his head.

Woman's laughter.

So, this is how it's gonna be, he thought, giving another quick once-over of the room, knife still in-hand. Beck departed through the door opposite to his initial entry, again checking six as he did so.

The hallway was long and dimly illuminated.

Of course.

Laughter continued in the hallway.

Of course.

Come . . . find me, my love . . .

I miss you . . .

Want more tongue . . .

The laughter trailed off.

Beck examined the ceiling and walls. No visible speakers.

He guardedly proceeded down the hallway. Took in and categorized everything.

No more false moves.

After several steps, a loud thud came from behind. He spun around to find a large blade had dropped from the ceiling and was stuck in the floor behind him.

As he inspected the blade, from both ends of the hallway appeared shadows, one from each end. One was armed with a battle ax, while the other possessed a spiked mace. The attack was immediately initiated.

Beck easily deflected the ax and its attacker, stepping deftly aside, but with the second one he engaged and grabbed the arm and jerked it forward. He twisted the arm around and behind, now positioning himself to use the man as a shield against the other attacker.

When he got a glimpse of the face.

"Nine?" Beck said, incredulous. He twisted himself and Nine away from the second attacker—whom he now also recognized as Eleven.

Both long-gone Gray Berets.

BECs.

Neither BEC acknowledged recognition, but instead continued to resist and attack. Which was fine, given he knew both had died well over a thousand years ago.

Eleven relaunched her assault, and this time Beck had no choice but to use Nine as a shield. Beck also noted that neither effigy acted as a trained BEC would in a situation like this. They were both merely robotic effigies.

Nine caught the next ax blow to the chest as Beck easily repositioned him to do so.

As Beck continued to jostle and reposition, he felt a gust of air pass overhead. A quick glance behind told him yet another had joined the fight. This one looked like Seven, and he wielded both a one-handed ax and a smaller mace. The mace had just missed his head.

Beck threw Nine into Eleven, then spun around, crouched, and launched himself at Seven. He plowed into Seven on its backswing . . . and plunged his knife deeply into where the main processor should be. But Beck didn't stop there and continued to plow forward, holding and pushing Seven before him. Beck twisted the knife until Seven deactivated.

Or the effigy of Seven.

Beck pushed the now-silent assailant away from him.

Beck spun back around to address the remaining two, who were immediately upon him.

Quick... you are still quite quick..., the whispers said.

Positioning himself behind Eleven, Beck grabbed and twisted its head and forced his blade into its processor as well, casting what had been a *her* away. He then pounced upon Nine as it got up from the floor. Beck pinned it back down onto the floor, held it there with his knee, and plunged his blade through its processor as well.

Attacks terminated.

The hallway was again quiet.

Beck checked all three robots, knife at the ready.

Replicas... robots... the lot of them. Of course they hadn't been real BECs. They weren't meant to be.

Okay... enough.

As Beck straightened up, two tentacles dropped down from the ceiling. One wrapped itself around Beck's arms and torso, and the other around his head and neck... then slammed Beck's head into the wall until he, too, went silent.

"*No wonder they liked you best*," Adrianna said, stepping forward from the shadows.

5

Beck felt a breeze. It whisked past his face.

Ever so slight... it went this way... then that... then whisked back across again from the opposite direction.

He opened his eyes.

A darkened interior. Slightly humid. Cool—

Something shot across his vision.

Strapped.

He was strapped into—

There it was again . . . that breeze, that object . . . something flying across his—

A blade.

Beck focused on the object.

A swinging blade. Weightily oscillating back and forth across him.

Beck tracked it with his eyes.

Each swing made an arc that was exactly two-point-five seconds in length.

"Welcome back, my tasty man," Adrianna said from the darkness.

Beck looked toward the voice.

"I'd have thought you'd have figured it out by now, Beck, but given I'd removed your scanning and database accesses—which I've now reenabled by the way, for my own *amuse* . . . ment—I guess it would have taken you longer . . . and, what the hell, I got excited. Couldn't wait. I've already waited, oh, so very long."

Adrianna came up to the slab upon which Beck was secured.

"In addition to your obvious restraints, there's a powerful magnet embedded beneath you to keep you snuggly in place, sucking all that hardware inside you *still*. We wouldn't want you popping off the table too soon, you know. I have a show I'm so desperately proud of. Need you to be a part of!

"And by the way, of course you know I'm not really 'Adrianna.'"

"Of course," Beck said.

"And of course you also must know I'm really just another mech . . . and that this place isn't haunted, but populated by many such as me, as you'd recently discovered."

"Yes."

"I thought you'd really like that little reunion I put together for you. Oh, and I've also now 'interdicted,' as you like to call it, your *physical* enhancements. Can't have you running amok from your grand finale," Adrianna said, glancing upward at the swinging blade.

A swinging blade that was lowering inch-by-inch toward Beck.

"Why all this? Do I know you?" Beck asked.

Adrianna chuckled.

"*Do you know me?*" she said, and again walked away.

Adrianna returned to the shadows and walked within the darkness, continuing to converse.

"I . . . found this place . . . quite by accident," she began. "I'd been heavily damaged in an operation during the First Outbrea—"

"'*First Outbreak,*'" Beck repeated, as he looked about the room, which he now discovered was a subterranean cellar, or laboratory. Above him he continued to observe the ever-lowering pendulum blade. What a nice touch from *The Pit and The Pendulum*, not to mention the *Mortimer Pusher Playbook*.

Adrianna continued speaking as she circled Beck, remaining hidden in the shadows.

"For all my abilities, I'd been pretty torn up and had been looking for a place to recuperate. I found this place. It'd long-since been abandoned . . . in a state of hideous disrepair. It was so far off the beaten track, and what with the First Outbreak, war had started, so no one was concerned with an old, worn-out novelty mansion left to rot in The Outlands . . . "

Beck ran calculations. Again able to access historical records, he cross-checked . . . correlated . . . the First Outbreak . . . geographically positioned variables . . . and with all that, an awareness dawned.

" . . . so, very much like you," Adrianna continued, "I made my way into this house. Long story short, I later made calculations as to when and if you'd ever find your way here, and I was spot on, I'm proud to say. Anyway, what I found was what you found, however I made some modifications as you well know. I discovered more about the history of the illustrious Pushers. Their affinity for the old-Earth horror movies and books. Mortimer's affection for pulling practical jokes . . . but also his affinity for affairs and all-things nefarious. Unlike you, however, I found out what had happened to his estranged wife. No one interdicted my research," she said, smiling.

The blade continued lowering.

Yes, it all makes sense, Beck thought. *Here . . . she'd ended up here, on this slab. Just like me. I am her revenge against all men.*

Adrianna poked her face out from the darkness.

"As you've no doubt already figured out, she'd end up down here, on this very table, just like you. Underwent the same fate that will soon befall you . . . only she was not a robot—well, at the *time*."

Adrianna ducked back into the shadows.

"I thought it to be a nice gesture to extend to *you*," Adrianna said from beyond the light.

Beck continued accessing databases . . . performing calculations . . . weighing all possible options . . . .

"Once I'd returned to a more . . . operational state," Adrianna continued, "I thought, why not just stay here? Make this home my own? I really was never happy with what I was doing—"

"Twelve. You're BEC12," Beck said.

Adrianna clapped her hands and emerged from the shadows.

"*Congratulations*, Beck! You've found me out!"

"Twelve . . . is that really you?"

"It is! It truly is! And you thought you were the only one of us left alive! Well, surprise, surprise—you're *not!*"

It all fell into place.

Adrianna was also BEC12. Twelve had created and inhabited Adrianna's effigy, no doubt from his own "spare parts."

As each of the Gray Berets had perished, they'd uploaded their amassed data into the *Renaissance's* covert database, as well as into their own secretly located servers, but also into the remaining BEC units.

Until there was only one . . . or only one was *perceived* to be remaining.

When the *Renaissance* had been destroyed in a following war, it was Beck's charge to create a clone of the ship's database elsewhere— or whoever was left after Beck. All BECs had an independent partition that had the power and autonomy to upload their own data upon their own death to the setting set for the master file, which would also auto-distribute that data to the remaining BECs. And like all the other BECs, Beck had also created his own secretly cached back-up server, but in the meantime, he'd picked up on Twelve's obviously fabricated demise and subsequent "final" upload—

And in that upload was all of Twelve's origins, which Beck now accessed.

Twelve had originated from a human, named Spencer Fuller. Spencer, had been, as had all of the Gray Berets, a special operations soldier who had been . . . recruited . . . by those who prepared the *Renaissance* for its interstellar operations.

And by "recruited" Beck saw that he'd actually had no choice in the matter.

Beck found that unlike his own case and those of all the other Gray Berets, which was by their *own* choices, *Renaissance* operations had needed one more to round out the unit, since a bug in one of their newly created Gray Berets had critically failed and self-destructed. They didn't have the time to go through the normal process, so the Development Team selected a qualified special operative at random . . . duped him . . . and converted him without any say on his—Spencer Fuller's—part. Specialist Fuller went to sleep one night while deployed . . . and woke up the next day no longer a human, with the designator "BEC12."

A man-machine.

All that Spencer had known was forever stored in his memory, but also emplaced were protocols to prevent "Spencer" from ever trying to return to his previous life or contacting anyone from that life. "Spencer" was now . . . and would forever be . . . BEC12.

Twelve.

And Twelve had made a name for himself.

But though a distant part of him forever hated those who'd transmogrified him—and he surely would have killed each and every one of them, had he the opportunity—the protocols had kept him in line and channeled his hate into furious function.

He'd become the unit's preeminent assassin.

He'd been unstoppable. His covert activities had become legend.

Until he simply disappeared from the Gray Beret grid.

Surprisingly, Beck felt for Twelve. Beck had made his choice—*his* choice—but Twelve had not. He understood what that meant in ways that were hard for straight humans to fully grasp, for to do so you had to have gone through the BEC transmogrification.

Things were done to you.

Things that could never be undone.

"So," Beck said, "you came here. Found a place you could regenerate . . . and die—"

"Oh," Twelve said, as she came back up to Beck, "it was far more than simply 'regenerate.' 'Reinvent,' more like.

"You see," Twelve said, continuing, "while here regenerating and regrouping, I'd discovered all about Mortimer, his passions, affairs, the murder of his wife. I resonated with Adrianna. Long story short, she was also trapped in . . . a union . . . she'd never wanted. Back on Earth she was all set to leave Mortimer, when he told her about the *Renaissance*. When it was made known to her what was really going to happen to the ship, all its passengers and crew, and more importantly, what was going down with Earth's destruction. She decided, what the hell, why not use Mortimer as her ticket to an entirely new . . . *life*.

"And that's exactly what she did. But she didn't get away quickly enough. And Mortimer *loved* his possessions, of which he'd fancied his wife one. He'd found out about her efforts to leave, and had tricked her into a 'birthday celebration' that ended up with her here, on this table. Like you. Sliced in two, as neatly as a piece of birthday cake ever was."

"Why take me out?"

"Because I've always hated you—all of you. The Gray Berets. Those damned protocols . . . they'd kept me in check. But after my last mission, I'd been so deeply and badly damaged . . . and when I'd found this place . . . tapped into all of its databanks . . . used its quite formidable technology . . . I found ways around those infernal protocols. Found . . . a new beginning—

"And then, wow, imagine my surprise when you waltzed on into my life!"

"Imagine."

"Yes, well, I simply had to have a little fun at your expense before dispatching you—"

"But, again, I ask—why me? What have I done?"

. . . *lower* . . . tick . . . tock . . . tick . . .

"What have you *done*?" Adrianna/Twelve asked, raising his/her voice into the dank, dark air. "What have you done, indeed!"

Twelve walked back around to the head of the table upon which Beck lay. S/he placed his mouth close to Beck's ear.

Twelve said, whispering, "*What you had done, my fine Government Issue, was agree to be the first in a series of government-developed monsters, to keep with the horror motif . . .*

"What you had *done*, Beck the First," Twelve-as-Adrianna continued, "was agree to be the first guinea pig to allow the government to study and build off of you, so that the lot of us could be forever created!"

Twelve-as-Adrianna rapidly and chaotically paced the floor.

"What you had *done*, Beck Senior," Adrianna shouted from a distance, "was forever take me away from the woman I loved and who would never know *why* I'd left! Taken me away from the one good thing I'd had in a world full of Evil! My wife, *Lena!* Yes, *Lena*—that was her name! She would never know why I'd left and forever lived with some concocted story that I was killed in action for the *cause* . . . died a *hero. She never knew the truth!*

"Lies! All of it! *That's* what she had to live with, Beck! *That's* why I hate you!

"And finally, *Beck* the Original, for making me invincible and unable to die, so that I am to live with this every single waking and sleeping moment of my timeless existence. For having already put in two-thousand years toward that future, with those wonderful suicidal checks-and-balances I'd finally overcome."

Twelve-as-Adrianna screamed into the darkness and collapsed to his/her knees off in the dark somewhere. Still screaming . . . until replaced by weeping.

Beck listened to his/her sobbing.

After a few moments, Twelve/Adrianna returned.

"And that is why I am taking you as one helluva target-of-opportunity and playing with you, here, in *my* world, now, Beck The First."

"So, there's no—"

"There's absolutely nothing you can say or do, my frenemy. *You* . . . are going to die. Terminate. With me. But first, I am going to have the pleasure of watching you go, slowly, one nick at a time . . . each nick an inch at a time to give you but a small taste of all the pain I had to endure every conscious moment of *my* so-called existence

... then I am taking you—and this entire house—with me, as we all terminate together. Die. Leave this God-forsaken planet. *Existence!* This World's memory. I've wanted to die for a long, long time. And now, I am finally able to fulfill that dream."

Beck looked to Twelve/Adrianna.

A tear. *Tears* . . . fell from Adrianna's eyes. Or Twelve's.

"I'm sorry," Beck said.

Twelve-as-Adrianna turned away.

"Good-bye, Beck," Twelve said, and disappeared back into the shadows.

Beck watched the blade again and again descend.

Swing back and forth—

It slit his shirt.

Beck looked down to the cut that had not as-yet drawn bl—

And then it did.

Exactly as Twelve had said. The pendulous blade sliced an inch-deep cut across his abdomen.

Beck never blinked. Nor cried out in pain. He'd shut down all pain receptors and the bleeding arteries and veins.

Still it was hard to look at, but he did. Hard to believe that he—not one of his countless adversaries—was stuck in this predicament he was observing.

His body continued to jerk with each slice, each penetration. The blade wasn't as sharp as he'd been led to believe.

And he just lay there and took it.

Slice after slice.

After slice.

Until the blade jammed to an abrupt and jarring halt into the table beneath . . . and *in between* . . . him.

The magnet disengaged. The restraints released.

Beck immediately disabled blood flow, cauterized the gashes, and flipped his torso over his head. He hung grotesquely from his restraints, over the floor and facing into the dais. The flesh on his wrists twisted and tore.

He let those bleed and pain him. He wouldn't be around for much longer.

Beck wedged his jaggedly cut torso against the dais and brutally forced his hands through and out of the restraints. Dropped to the floor.

Beck hand-walked around the table. Peering into the shadows he spotted him/her. Quickly and silently padded across the floor on callused and muscled hands and arms into the shadows where Twelve sat.

"We only have four minutes left for you to kill me," Twelve said.

Beck slowly but skillfully padded over on his hands to Twelve, who sat in a chair. All the hubris, the arrogance . . . the energy . . . seemed drained from Twelve-as-Adrianna. Beck monkeyed up onto the empty chair that was placed next to Twelve.

"You knew that wouldn't kill me," Beck said, settling in on the chair next to Twelve. "Why go through with it?"

Adrianna-as-Twelve grunted.

"I'm still part human, you know, even if it's just my mind . . . my emotions . . . I'm still quite pissed at having been turned into what I am. Yes, even after all this time. You and I . . . are the last of what we are. I just wanted some immediate emotional gratification for a change."

Twelve turned to Beck.

"I'm sorry it came to this. I truly never wanted to do what I'd just done to you, but my emotions left me no other choice."

"I know," Beck said.

"I know you know," Twelve said, looking away. "You were a great soldier. A legend. We all looked up to you."

"We all looked up to *you*, too," Beck said.

"Thank you."

Beck said, "I was who I was. I didn't have a great life before this. None of us had. But perhaps it was still . . . a life. Life as a *human*. Life with a *time span*." Beck stared into the darkness. "Had I known what I was to become a part of—really and truly grasped all the implications kept from us—I wouldn't have done it. But youth, testosterone, and government psychological manipulation to get twenty-year-olds to do what they wanted, well, it was hard to resist. I don't like many of the things I've done—whether or not ordered to do so, or in line with the mission. Orders still have individuals as the last points of conscience . . . as to whether or not such orders *should* be executed."

"Yes."

"We've had a good run as operatives . . . soldiers . . . now it's time to do what humans do best."

Twelve-as-Adrianna nodded.

Beck saw the tears raining down his/her cheeks.

"You must have a lot of Adrianna in you."

"I do."

"Was she a good woman?"

"For the most part."

Beck nodded.

"I guess part of my emotional gratification at slicing you up came from her, as well."

"Expected."

"It was an honor to serve with you, Twelve. I really mean that."

"And you, Beck."

Beck and Twelve grasped each other's hands.

Manually initiated their uploads.

"And to, *you*, Adrianna," Beck said, "I apologize for all you went through."

"*Thank you,*" Adrianna whispered.

Beck, Twelve, and Adrianna remained seated as the explosion erupted. A mighty reverberation and massive and ongoing crash-and-boom assaulted them from all directions, the powerful, man-made theranquake rattled the Pusher House's foundation. As the House of Pusher began to upend, collapse, and fold in upon itself, like a crumbing house of cards, an all-consuming conflagration flash-erupted . . . and instantly and thoroughly incinerated Beck, Twelve, and Adrianna . . . flesh, metal, and mind.

The cataclysmic annihilation continued folding in upon itself and crumpled and forever buried itself within the ever-deepening crater of its own making . . . a crack, a fissure, in the Theran surface that soon and completely closed in on itself like a hungry, abysmal maw, forever swallowing, consuming, and digesting all that ever was . . .

Of the House of Pusher.

SOMETIMES A FLOWER IS JUST A FLOWER
Year 29023.06 N.E.

1

After the death, destruction, and fires came—
Bright blue skies!
Nourishing rains!
Snow and cold . . . sun and warmth!
Then came the flowers.

2

And so ended the Forever Wars.
Time to start anew!
The healing of much . . . the reclamation of trust and love and communities. Reinvented individual and *en masse* spirit.
All of this took time to remedy and germinate.

And it did.
Generations....
But once the efforts were underway, there was no stopping it!
It had become the new inexorable force!
Arts and humanities flourished!
Instead of departments of war, existed departments of *peace*.
New, creatively designed and managed cities and countries emerged and reclaimed war-damaged continents!
Nature blossomed beautifully and brightly! Was better incorporated into cities and towns and lives!
Politicians—local, national, and international—worked together as one! For the *common* good.
Yes, a new renaissance had dawned.
And in the coming millennia thrived global prosperity, harmony, and goodwill.

3

Yet, where Humans were concerned, nothing was perfect.
Disagreements had been arbitrated, injustices fairly meted out. And people being people, so the restructured world had to once again require the employment of regulations and their enforcement to curb the re-emergence of corruption and exploitation.
Global populations had again grown complacent, and with that the criminal-minded took advantage.
Philosophy and reason and restraint had been replaced by technology, which had again outpaced Humanity's ability to properly incorporate it . . . had made lives too easy, too complacent, too dependent upon it. Once more the convenient ethics, the relative truths.

Name calling.
Posturing.
Arrogance.
Greed.
And once again the old ways had taken over.
Militaries had returned.

And with this, new threats had been engineered: those looking out to the stars had found things they had never before imagined... considered... new threats manufactured and wielded as weaponry, requiring more money, technology, and secrets.

Space debris.

Meteoroids.

Near-Theran Objects.

Comets and black holes.

This new fear spread and globally gripped, as yet another possible (nay, many bell ringers cried "*Imminent!*") conveyance of death and destruction from without.

Something had to be done, the rich and powerful few had declared, and the militaries and industrial leaders realized another way to leverage and manage fear and angst into increased profitability and global manipulation.

Legends and myths had become fact.

Industry resources had been hidden and shuffled and redirected to new, publicly concealed, causes.

Again the lies took over....

While the flowers continued to grow.

LET'S NOT GO THERE, MY FRIEND
Year 57769.7 N.E.

1

Even the clocks ain't agreeing, Imshd Tor thought, *What a strange thought!*

That had been rectified long, long ago, with those auto-correcting signals that scientists had figured out were needed.

But, still—

(*the clocks ain't agreeing*)

Where had that thought come from?

All this Imshd considered as he materialized into his residence's transporter cell.

His surroundings came into sharp view, indicators on the status board before him all illuminated green, and he stepped off the pad. Schebek's *Das Lied der Geige,* Op. 2, auto-played upon his arrival. Sometimes upon arriving home he would just sit in the chair he kept there, close his eyes, and allow the violins to wash over and blanket him. Unwind him. Begin the soul-weary decompression he always so desperately needed upon returning home from his shifts.

But not today.

He'd felt weird all shift long, and that feeling persisted despite the beautiful soothing tones filling the room. Whether or not the clocks agreed, something about his life *was* severely out of sync.

But he knew that.

Imshd worked on Thera's moon . . . and it was work that was only known to a select few. Not even his wife, who was presently at work, knew *exactly* what it was he did. Just that he worked in lunar construction.

Or more specifically, she and the majority of Thera did not know that he worked *inside* the moon.

Was a part of a government team hollowing out its interior, which was desperately being filled with all the technology and art and living space that could possibly be crammed into its not-quite spherical confines as they went . . .

In preparation for a looming Armageddon.

This was to be Thera's last hope.

After all the wars.

All the struggles.

All the reconstruction.

The faux renaissance.

The primordial planetary exodus to this planet to avoid a similar fate (or so the history books had so judiciously instructed).

But largely because of all the persistent and nightly predictions, dreams, and nightmares.

It seems everyone's dreams had been usurped by the same imagery: Thera's destruction.

Global. Cataclysmic. Absolute.

When everyone experienced the same thing, it was hard to ignore, with or without empirical data to back anything up.

Construction was nearing an end, but there was still much to do. It seemed they just couldn't work quickly enough. No one knew the exact moment things were supposed to . . . *occur* . . . just that things were *going* to occur.

Were . . . *imminent* . . . in the persistent lamentations of the bell ringers.

However this conclusion had been arrived upon . . . and whatever it was supposed to mean.

Imminent.

They all felt it.

That also meant that stress, distress, and angst were at an all-time high among the work force. The population.

Him.

Imshd hated doing it, but he, now, routinely took the Lunar Health Office's offered sedative upon his return trips home every morning. Had to. Marital and psychological sanity demanded it.

Imshd again checked the chamber's transporter status board—a "Green Board"—and exited the room.

He was exhausted. Tired in every way imaginable.

The work exacted its toll on everyone there. And they had just been briefed at shift change that they had to speed things up.

Speed things up?

Were they crazy?

None of them needed to hear this!

For crying out loud, could tempers and anxiety flare any higher?

Apparently so.

And he only had six hours before he was to head back to work today.

The running joke had become *"You can sleep when you're dead!"*

He wanted to scream from the tallest mountains!

Break things!

To just explode and be done with it!

But what choice did he have? Any of them? It was all for the common good.

The most imperative mission ever.

Humanity's survival.

As tired as he was, he needed to get away, mentally and physically. Spiritually. To get out into the bright and beautiful sunshine!

To smell the ocean!

The flowers!

To feel wonderful warmth and humidity upon his skin!
Theran soil beneath his feet!
To fly with the birds!
To forget about who he was and what he was doing.
To know that life *was* still out there! Still vital . . . still *alive* and *joyful!*
That all was not
(*yet?*)
lost.
In short . . . to stick his head into the sand, neck and all.
He was so goddamned exhausted.
He could easily just go straight to bed . . . or the grave.
Instead, Imshd made his way into the kitchen and plopped down at the kitchen table. Propped his elbows on the tabletop and sank his weary head into his hands. Closed his eyes. He sat this way for some time. Waffling which way to go . . . when he
(*iced tea?*)
jerked awake!
No! He *needed* to get out!
Had to.
Felt *compelled* to do so!
To mentally distance himself from his work, even if for but a few moments! To reconnect with Life . . . feel sea spray and humidity caressing his face!
. . . birds and flowers and dragonflies . . .
Imshd forced himself to his feet.

2

The day was wonderfully gorgeous and bright . . . in total contrast to what Imshd knew was going on far above them.
He looked to the sky and found the moon, in quarter phase. He leaned forward on his still-grounded Skyrider and rested his elbows on the machine's controls.
Stared at the moon.
If only people really knew what was really going on up there— right this minute—above all their pretty little heads . . . far away

from this magnificently warmed ground beneath their feet, bathed in glorious sunshine, and graced with wonderfully balmy breezes and marvelously formed plant and animal life . . . up high in orbit . . . just beneath the stars and on the threshold to the cold and dark of unrelenting, unforgiving space . . . .

Oh, how he *hated* his job!

He hated it because he was doing something that resulted in one thing, and one thing only: *survival*.

The prophesized and celestial destruction of Thera.

That was the only reason the moon project and his employment—and others like him—existed as it did today. Its hollowed-out interior filled with all the best humanity had to offer.

It all sounded so romantically space operatic.

Unless you were the one living said space opera.

There was nothing romantic about the destruction of one's future.

Why couldn't the best Humanity had to offer have remained down here, on Thera? Where it belonged? Pathetically, utterly oblivious.

Why?

Because of all the bickering, corruption, and end-of-the-world prognostication Humankind was so good at.

Humanity, in all its hubris, felt it needed to survive . . . to go on . . . even though its history has continuously proven Humanity does not know how to behave and play nice with anyone and anything. Everything it ever did seemed to eventually end up with psychopaths in charge and wars waged for greedy self-interests and keeping the population "under control."

Occupied.

Yet it still feels it has to move all of that "best" away from where it should remain . . . to fizzle out in its own logical conclusion of Humanity's philosophical and corporeal implosion.

But no . . . the psychopathic, greedy, and war-mongering governments needed to secretly package everything away inside the interior of a lifeless moon. A hollowed-out shell filled with tunnels and compartments and control rooms to shelter the spoils of Humanity and to only allow those *privileged* few hand-picked to "join the journey."

We've already done this!
Out histories have *shown* us where it will all end!
We are already living that outcome!
Imshd inhaled deeply.

He wasn't a pessimist, really. He was just tired and stressed and fed up.

Of course, it was a good thing that someone had considered all this death and destruction and put into action a plan to save Humanity from itself . . . or whatever was to befall it . . . but Imshd didn't like all the compartmentalized secrecy driving everything . . . but, yes, he understood it.

Reluctantly.

He "got" it. Enemies of the state and all that. Within *and* without.

People were stupid.

The moon couldn't save all life on Thera. Nowhere *near* all of Theran life.

Only the select few.

The *selected* few.

Of which Imshd was pretty sure wouldn't include him, his wife, or the other in-the-trenches workers grunting things out below that lifeless regolith. The tunnelers, the builders, the architects. No, that privilege would most likely (and logically) be reserved for the intellectually and otherwise gifted. The artists. Engineers. Scientists and world leaders. Sure, perhaps one or three of them might be included to . . . get things started . . . well, *elsewhere*. And sure, they'd all been told (aka *lied* to) that there would be room for all of them, but Imshd wasn't stupid. He'd done the math. Knew the satellite's capacity.

You'd have thought they'd all had learned their lessons from the Forever Wars—

Okay—*enough!*
Enough pessimism!

He'd brought out his sky bike to air out, not continue to dwell on Humanity's ills and destruction! There would be time enough for that whether one actually occurred one or ten years into the future.

Imshd closed his eyes, inhaled deeply of the sweetly scented tropical air, and reopened them.

Time to *ride!*

He smiled, fired up the beast, throttled it a couple of times, and took to the balmy breezes aloft . . . .

Imshd skimmed above the terrain, following the main road below. Enjoyed the wind blowing through his hair and caressing his face. The beach was coming into view up ahead and the ocean beyond that. He playfully yanked and banked in his airspace. Performed a couple of joyful barrel rolls. Dodged a few birds that came over to check him out.

He loved the freedom skyriding provided . . . loved airing out his head after the long hours confined below ground—even if it was above ground. Loved the feeling of power of the air rocket he rode—

. . . but the clocks ain't agreeing . . .

Why were those words constantly intruding into his thoughts?

He looked to his watch . . . compared it to the Skyrider's chronometer. Of course they matched. He just didn't understand the significance of the—

Do stars see Time the way Humans do?

Now, what in hell was *that* supposed to mean?

Where in hell were these ideas comi—

Do they have a consciousness we can't even begin to fathom?

Do they have a consciousness?

Is their philosophy their novae?

Imshd's vision clouded. Rippled and wavered.

And the clocks can't even agree . . . .

Can't agree

Can't agree

Can't agr—

Imshd's watch and chronometer flickered. Continued fluctuating—

(*. . . sunny . . . dark . . . sunny . . .*)

He whipped the air bike around, banking a hard left

(*light . . . dark . . . light*)

and shakily brought the machine down for an emergency landing on a small rise overlooking the

(... *ocean ... desert ... ocean ...*)
ocean.
What about the clocks?
Evening!
Har—
Would you like an iced tea?
What the shisst was happening?
Imshd couldn't focus and his head felt like an ever widening, gushing river of Time, wild and deep and always, always
(... *inexorably ...*)
moving forward ... scuttling him along with it like an uncontrolled piece of driftwood—problem was, those waters were instantly switching back and forth ... .sideways? ... filling his head and gushing in so fast, absolutely unchecked, like a sinking ship, he felt like he was psychically drowning. Consciousness and stability dizzyingly sloshing back and forth. Up and down. Folding into and out of dimensions he couldn't begin to define—
—Algis Townse—
Imshd brought both hands up to his head. Leaned forward on his bike and sat that way for several moments.
Where was he?
Was he still nodded off at the kitchen table?
Teetering on a tightrope between two worlds?
... wait a minute ...
... would you like ...
Okay, this was insane. He couldn't open his eyes, because everything was spinning. He couldn't keep them closed, because he was psychologically drowning.
He was here ... *now!*
On a hill overlooking the ocean!
Physically entrenched within a bright, sunny, humid day!
Or was it really a withering desert night?
Focus!
I ... am Imshd Tor ... I ... work for the government ... I ...
(... *iced tea ...*)
am away on my off-hours! This is not *happening!*

Not *happening*.
Sunshine.
Birds . . . darting and diving. Chirping and tweeting.
Sea . . . sounds and scents, even up here on this hillock.
Imshd willed himself anchored in the *present* . . . the
(. . . what *here?* . . . what *now?* . . .)
here and *now*.
Slowly, the internal Time rush began fading away.
Imshd came back to the upright position.
Reveled in the comforting purring of his Skyrider beneath him. Grasped his controls and flexed his grips.
He *was* here.
He *was* now.
That was more like it.
Imshd smiled. Continued flexing his grips.
Stress.
Stress, *maaan*, it really messed up a body.
They'd all been briefed about this up at the job site, to be on the alert for stress-related indicators in each of them . . . to report even the most seemingly minor of occurrences not only in themselves, but in others, as well. They couldn't have workers leaping off the deep end and taking others with them. There were timelines to meet. Quotas to maintain. Health regulations.
Nope, he wasn't reporting this.
Eyes wide opened and confident, Imshd switched gears and throttled up, lifting back into the
Day . . . night . . . ocean . . . desert . . .
And was promptly overtaken by vertigo.
He hovered . . . could still see the sea before him, feel the wind upon his face . . . but things felt . . . Time felt . . . *denser*.
Palpable.
Like a garment to be worn, shed, or adjusted—
Manipulated.
Yes, in fact, he felt like he could just as simply take Time off (and he swore he felt a "version" of himself doing exactly that!) and swap it out for a whole other—

If I really am *here—now—*Imshd thought, *what is my future like? And what is a "future"?*

My present is my past's future, and I am in the present . . . what does it all mean, clocks, and time, and seconds?

If the clocks aren't agreeing, as that old man says, why is that? Is the future and the past—the present—colliding?

A philosophy of

Imshd lost control of the Skyrider—for just a moment—and nearly fell out of the sky.

He quickly landed the rider.

As he touched ground, he spotted a vehicle . . . an ancient looking one . . . a pickup truck . . . parked off a little way from him. Upon the pickup truck's open . . . what was it called—*tailgate*—sat a man, eating and drinking something.

None of this was there seconds ago. He saw no one drive up. Park. Pull out a picnic lunch.

A man on a tailgate.

One moment nothing was there—and the next . . .

The man on the tailgate called out to Imshd, but Imshd didn't understand. This man then took a sip from some kind of beverage—

That looked exactly like iced tea.

The guy, a smaller structured gentleman, definitely under seven foot, looked nice enough, and Imshd didn't feel at all threatened, in fact, the man looked exactly like a predecessor out of the history books.

Stress or no . . . perhaps he was just in some kind of a dream, Imshd didn't know. Perhaps he'd been more tired than he'd imagined and was actually dead asleep at the kitchen table, or in bed, and this was all one big, bizarre somnolent fantasy. Curiously, he also no longer felt tired or exhausted or depressed. In fact . . . he felt quite good! *Exhilarated*, one could say!

In any case, he was "here" . . . "now" . . . wherever that was, so he might as well play nice. Imshd parked his Skyrider.

What was consciousness?

He was about to find out.

The man hailed him; seemed friendly enough.

Imshd said, "Hello!" and extracted himself from his machine. Stood beside it. He felt absolutely *electrified.*

Energized!

But he could see that the man before him didn't understand him. The man casually cradled a drink in both hands between the "V" of his legs, interestedly studying him.

Standing, feet spread powerfully apart, Imshd smiled and placed his fists into his hips. For Heaven's sake, he felt like a superhero! This had to be a dream! He observed the man, who also sported a bemused smile.

"I am Imshd *Tor!*" Imshd said.

Perhaps too much, but he simply couldn't contain the energy thundering through him!

The man again said something unintelligible.

Both stared at each other.

The other man said something else . . . then placed his drink down on the tailgate.

They both continued to regard each other.

Imshd furrowed his brow. *Hmmm, okay,* he thought, *dream or no, he had an idea!*

Yes, he'd actually been so tired after returning home from work that he must've indeed gone straight to bed, and all this was not really happening. So, this possibly being the case, *why not just decide that they both understood each other?* If it worked, then they both comprehended each other and it was a dream, and he'd just continue to go with it. If not, oh, well, move on!

Imshd nodded thoughtfully and raised an index finger.

He willed that they both understand each other.

"*Is that better?*" Imshd asked.

The other man was taken aback.

"Wow!" the gentleman said, "How'd you do that?"

Imshd shrugged his shoulders. Then he again said, "'Imshd,'" and again playfully thumped his chest.

"'Algis,'" Algis again said. "Pleased to meet you!"

"Likewise!"

"Would you like an iced tea?"

"Iced tea? Who wouldn't—thanks!" Imshd approached Algis.

Algis handed over an unopened bottle to Imshd, who reached for it—

And promptly dropped it.

"What the—" cried Imshd.

"*Okaaay...,*" said Algis.

"Wait a minute!" Imshd said and stuck out his large hand.

Algis jumped off the tailgate and instinctively reached out for it—but their hands passed through each other, causing both to shiver.

"Holy shisst!" Algis said.

"Ha!" Imshd said.

They tried it again with the same results. They did this several times—laughing as they did so.

"This is weird!" they both exclaimed.

... and the clocks ... even the clocks ain't agreeing....

"Where are you from?" Algis asked.

Imshd jerked a thumb behind him. "I live just over those hills, there. I was out for a fly after a long night's shift."

"No," Algis said, chuckling, "I mean, from *when.*"

"What year is it?"

"2101."

After regarding Algis for a moment, Imshd looked away.

"What year did you think it was?"

"Not that year."

"Hey, Imshd, what do you see when you look around?" Algis finished off his iced tea and replaced the cap to the empty bottle.

Imshd said, "I see the ocean—"

"*Ocean?*"

"Yes, ocean. What do you see?"

"I don't see an ocean! I see miles and miles of *desert.* It's night—"

"—day—"

"—and a road that bisects through it! I see lights off in the distance, perhaps a small town, perhaps a small industrial complex."

"No ocean?"

"No ocean."

"Huh."

"What is it like where you live? Your land? Your home?" Algis asked.

"Oh, it's lush! Beautiful! We own acres and acres of woodland! Our home is landscaped with beautiful flowers and trees and a stream runs through everything!"

"That's crazy! There's water up there? Maps clearly show only desert, here! No woods, no flowers! No—"

"But that is where I live! I'm not making this up—"

"But you see an *ocean*."

"As should you!"

"But *you* should see desert!"

"But I don't! This area is dense with life and businesses and homes! There are thriving communities—metropolises—all along this coastline—for *miles!* Can't you see that?"

Algis turned to look back down into the darkness below. To the floating island of isolated lights far out into the distance. "But I don't. I don't see that at all."

Algis continued, "And the year, Imshd? What year do you think it is?"

"57769.7."

"57769.7. Well, that's certainly an odd year!"

"As is your 2101! But I remember learning from our history books how years used to be labeled and yours is exactly like tha—"

"*Excuse* me? You're saying I'm your *past?*" Algis straightened up alongside his truck.

"It would seem so—"

"The past—*your* past. And you're . . . *my* future?"

"Apparently!"

"I hardly know what to say at this point," Algis said, quietly looking around.

"Me, too."

"A past . . . a past is one thing," continued Algis, "but to know a *future?*"

"Perhaps knowing you have a future is good thing," Imshd said, "but what about me? There are many doomsayers, here, people who have looked into *our* future . . . and cry that we don't have one."

"How do you not have a future?"

"It's a strange and terrifying thing to consider! But here I am, in *yours*, and I ponder if I even *have* one!"

"Sorry to hear that."

"Say that as you will, but you do so from the comfort of your own *present*, which is my past, that you knowingly have a future—but for how long? How long do any of us have a future? Our doomsayers cry that an apocalypse to end all apocalypses is just around the corner."

"Every historical period says that."

"Perhaps—but, again, you say that from the comfort of the distant past!"

"My *present!*"

"My *history!*"

"Point taken. Sorry about your futu—"

"*Our* future," Imshd corrected.

Algis nodded. "*Ours.*"

Both men quietly looked off into their perspectives.

"Were there wars?"

"Many."

"But our histories tell us the people we found here had no war ... no strife."

"Our histories and legends had taught us that it was the people from the stars who brought the wars. The strife."

"The people from the stars," Algis repeated, pensively, "Wow, you'd think being so advanced they'd also have been smarter."

"Are you one of those people, Algis? One of the first who came here from the stars?"

Algis shook his head and said, "No, I was born here. But, yes, my *parents* had come from the stars. From a place called 'Earth.'"

"'Earth.'"

"So," Algis said, "This big war of ours ... when did that happen?"

"352.3."

"Ha!" Algis cried out, chuckling. "Ask a stupid question!" he said, slapping his leg. In a more serious tone, he said, "How bad was it?"

"Bad. Life ... had to start over. *Life* ... had been severely damaged, nearly destroyed. Geographies catastrophically upended and displaced. Our world was dying. *We* were dying.

"The war," Imshd continued, " . . . it took a lot . . . but those who saw it coming prepared and hid . . . hid in imaginative and ingenious ways, from the destruction, all the good in our lives . . . all the technologies, the libraries, the art. They tunneled, our historians told us, went back up into their satellites and space stations. Even the moon. They tried their best, but the wars still came, all the mini ones, the tyrants, the despots, the psychopaths. Until the Big One. Our histories warned we were all doomed to relive what had brought us all to this planet in the first place."

"Doomed to relive. That is not a very promising future at all!" Algis said.

"No, it is not! But who wants to know the future! I am from yours, and I don't mind telling you it is quite terrifying living in it! More stressful than you can imagine! Not knowing how much longer we all have to breathe this precious air! Enjoy this comfortable and secure atmosphere that sustains us all! You say that all of Humankind has always lamented about an End of Days . . . but living as I do in your future, I tell you never before have I seen or read or heard so *much* of it! All of our media is fascinated and obsessed with it. Our movies, our books, our commentaries! And even every day—*every beautiful day*, with the sun shining, the breezes breezing, and birds chirping and flying—there seems a subtle undercurrent in the air. We all feel it. Try to ignore it. But things *are* changing. We know this from our histories. People are more on edge . . . our dreams are dark and foreboding . . . our weather keeps growing warmer. Nobody can agree upon anything! Everything is politicized, weaponized. There are always fights in our government, in other governments. Constant bickering. Constant headaches and fear. Fear, Algis, it is *fear* that is the one constant that seems to run through everything we do or think. Our lives. Like we are watching the coming of a storm. Or the calm *before* one.

"I grew so weary of all of this that I went for a fly. Had to clear my head and wished for simpler times! Wished I'd lived in a time in our distant past that did not have so much fear prevalent in everything we did!"

"And I had found myself thinking about the past, present, *and* future!" Algis said.

Imshd continued, "One beautiful day, I go out for a ride. Just me and my machine and the ocean air. And as I flew over the road along the ocean, listening to the birds, inhaling the salt and sea spray and humidity, my mind wandered. Then I find myself *here*. But am I really here, or is this but a dream?"

"And there *I* was," Algis said, "weary of my life and going for a drive! Am I really here, or had I dozed off somewhere?"

"You don't see the ocean, do you? Not at all?"

"Nope."

"Nor a bright sun . . . or feel wonderful humidity . . . hear beautiful birdlife?"

"No—I see and feel the night, but curiously the balmy air tonight did remind me of the coast. Otherwise, I inhale desert and desiccation. Things that you also do not see or feel."

"Yes."

"Well," Algis said, solemnly. "On this, we can agree: we are here, together. In this dream or at this roadside stop."

"Indeed!"

"In our respective presents . . . two friendly and lonely consciousnesses passing in the night, but reaching out to each other!"

"Agreed!"

"Shall we ever meet again?"

"Who knows?"

"I do hope so!"

"As do I!"

Imshd approached Algis, tears in his eyes, and said, "Even . . . even though we can't actually do this, I attempt it anyway, my new . . . ever-to-be-remembered . . . *friend*."

Algis extended his hand, tears also in his eyes.

"It was a pleasure meeting you!" they both said as one.

Their hands passed through each other and they quietly chuckled.

"I felt that! It was cold!"

"As did I! But our *greeting* warm!"

"I would really have liked to go on your road trip with you, in your truck," Imshd said, his eyes continuing to mist over.

"That would have been fun," Algis said. "And I would still have liked to have visited your world. To fly with you and see where and how you live."

"You are kind, but you are far better off here, my friend, in *your* present!"

Imshd turned and approached his awaiting machine. Hopped back into it. As it lifted back up into the air, Imshd rocked the machine back and forth, waved to Algis, and left the hill . . . sea and salt spray once again kissing his face.

What had just happened?

Tears streamed across his face, but Imshd let them be.

He hadn't wanted to leave but felt compelled to do so.

Could he go back? Just turn this beast around and return to see if Algis was still there?

No . . . he would no longer be there—he knew that. And he no longer felt energized, either . . . was back to feeling tired . . . worn out from his long shift . . . the stresses of his current life . . . and that he had to all-too-soon return to work.

Wind whipping at the tears pouring freely from his eyes, Imshd banked hard to port and headed home.

A PHILOSOPHY OF STARS
Year 59214.21 N.E.

1

I know what the stars mean.
Perfecta Harcourtt was of a curious mind.
At five years of age she'd begun systematically reading her family out of house and home, and then, a year later, had turned her sights upon the educational industry. At seven, she began reading anything she could get her hands on in all the public industries, but was drawn to government and law, power grids, telecommunications, and anything technological. Soon afterward she began offering solutions to many public issues, offering her services and creating many patents along the way. At twelve, she became deeply interested in the space industry, and that's when the national databases caught her attention.

To add to Perfecta's abilities, she was more than merely a speed reader or child prodigy. She possessed a photographic memory, and further . . . when she read material, she wasn't just *reading* it . . . it was as if the content . . . the ideas, the concepts . . . leapt off the pages at her, fully fleshed out, and she was no longer reading *words*, but conceptually and notionally immersed within the actual feelings and thoughts and philosophies . . . experiencing and becoming one with the subject matter.

If she was reading a treatise on time dilation or space travel, she was with a version of the authors as they created their hypotheses, theories, and texts. A ghost of sorts . . . but a ghost who could ask questions of the authors . . . or, rather, the *notional versions* of them . . . as they created their theorems and laws and papers.

Of course, she really wasn't actually *there* . . . but was on a totally different, metaphysical level-of-consciousness she hadn't yet had the time to investigate, was how she thought of it, that is, if it was short of her making everything up in her head as in a daydream.

However, the mechanics of her psychological manipulation of Time and Space as she examined, interpreted, comprehended, and assimilated . . . *things* . . . she grasped far more beyond the mere physical presentation of words upon a page or screen.

And she kept *this* secret little ability all to herself.

She knew what she had. How it would be exploited. *She* would be exploited. She also knew that those in government were closing in on her. She couldn't remain under the radar forever . . . and she had to get her most important work completed before she was found out.

Her work about the *stars*.

So, Perfecta powered through the texts, the charts, the Theran histories, all in the name of her newfound passion.

She loved everything about the stars . . . their brilliance . . . composition . . . untouchability . . . romance—

And their philosophy.

Yes, Perfecta discovered, there really was a philosophy to them. How could there not be?

One never just looked to the stars without wondering—

Where did they come from?

How did they form?
How old were they?
Was there someone up there looking back?
Could we reach them—or they, us?

And why were we so damned curious about them in the first place?

Did they really affect our lives astrologically or by way of our imagination?

Imagination really and truly was the mother of all invention, not so much "necessity." Necessity no more drove the imagination than eating and sleeping drove the human condition.

It was *imagination* that was the first step in all invention! It was *imagination* that truly advanced the race . . . gave pause for thought . . . instigated action!

Without imagination there *was* no life.

And so, it was philosophy, the philosophy of the stars that instigated the imagination . . . and . . . *life*.

And Perfecta's most powerful imaginative instigation was investigating into their origins.

Where *had* they come from?
What had come before?
Where were they headed?
How many more stars were *behind* them?

And how had they appeared in the night sky many a millennia ago?

It was all this and more that brought her her sudden, unwanted governmental attention at the ripe old age of fifteen. She also noticed a humanly imperceptible latency in all her online research and work through the efforts of her own self-designed sniffers. Her sniffers also detected proximity protocols homing in on her.

She had to do something.

Perfecta had barely escaped the government's closing in on her when she moved out of her house at not-quite-sixteen years of age, but had done so smartly: she'd preconfigured her escape by setting up numerous misdirecting rabbit holes. Multiple onion-layered-encryption server relays. Redirection protocols.

And, of course, left a note to her father and mother. She regretted doing things as she had, she noted, but time was of the essence, and the less anyone else knew of her whereabouts, well, sorry Mom and Dad, the better.

As amusing as it all had started out to be, the problem was that those she'd enlisted from the underground's Shadow Web had begun disappearing. Literally.

As in dying off.

It wasn't fun and games anymore.

Perfecta was no longer welcome in those circles.

She was certain it had to do with the stars. Everything came back to them.

Perfecta had to figure out why . . . why all the concern, resources, and surveillance. What was it she was not supposed to find? All her sniffers alerted her to was that the only real government interest was in her research and work about the universe, the stars, in particular. Not her work about the poor . . . or the unemployed.

Astronomy.

They were consuming and tracking all her cosmological papers and patents and presentations.

Given all that Perfecta was about . . . it wasn't too far of a leap for her to suspect that it had everything to do with Thera itself.

That she was closing in on some unknown truth.

2

Perfecta had entered all the visible star data into a database of her own creation. All stars visible to Thera as a planet, not just the hemispheres.

Then she wondered what were behind those stars . . . then behind *them* . . . and so on. She ingested already populated cosmological databases into her own data.

Stars, planets, asteroids, and comets.

Cross-refenced and cross-correlated where things started and where things extrapolated to. Found unbelievable inconsistencies in what she'd uncovered and what had been made publicly available. And all published by lettered authorities. Reran and triple checked.

Exactly the same inconsistencies. Though she initially started talking with all the best and brightest, she soon terminated all inquiry when things began to . . . not quite feel right.

Her sources waffled.

Hesitated.

Didn't return calls.

When she asked certain questions, they professed certain ignorance. Or not enough data, which she knew *did* exist because she'd already read it!

They were keeping things from her.

Why?

What could be so secret about stars?

Then her sniffers revealed secret organizations amassing as much data as possible about *her*.

So Perfecta began coding some new work.

Now that spotlights were surreptitiously slewed her way, she had to protect herself . . . her efforts.

Humanity.

But still the questions continued to eat away at her: why should information about the stars and the planets and the universe be kept from the population?

What was being hidden?

Onward . . . ever onward . . . Perfecta analyzed and reframed and reworked . . . .

She stumbled upon another database hidden deeply within the Shadow Web, with many diversions, rabbit holes, and onion-layering effects keeping it hidden . . . a database that had originated from a long-forgotten vessel—a *space*ship—from the far-flung and obscured past.

A ship called the *Renaissance*.

Perfecta had actually heard of it, mostly as a legend . . . or myth. There was nothing in the historical databases she'd investigated, but it was rumored to have existed far before the Forever Wars, back before recorded history. It (one train of thought went) was thought that aliens had visited Thera and populated it with humans. *Us.* Specifically formulated to live and work on Thera. There were many variations to this "ancient astronaut" line of myths, but aliens or not, the one constant, lowest common denominator across all the speculation was still about . . . a spaceship . . . *from another planet.*

It was so steeped in mystery and shadow that it absolutely dumbfounded her that it had taken her so long to discover it.

It was also the same day when Perfecta calculated that she had less than a week before being apprehended.

All her calculations pointed to between three and six days of freedom left, so it was imperative she complete her work. Her life no longer mattered. This was far bigger.

3

Perfecta ingested the *Renaissance* data into her database. Again reframed.

The stars.

The *Renaissance* had come from another planet.

The *Renaissance* had made planetfall *here.*

The government didn't like her looking into star data.

Secret organizations were data mining her.

The data was crunched and what she uncovered caused her to push back, away from her desk.

A program, simply titled "BEC00," flashed up on her screen.

It was not much more than an ancient text file, really, but the simpler the better when it came to concealment. And it had been hidden within the larger *Renaissance* database.

Perfecta stood back against a wall and stared at her screens. Screens that displayed the following:

> *I am Beck. I am the first and the last of my kind. I came from the* Renaissance, *which came from a planet, called Earth. I knew you would find me. I have uploaded all of my data upon my death. You will find all of your answers here—and much more. You will*

> *find the Truth. I was an inherent part of that Truth, and I will tell you all of it. It is time . . . and there is not much of it left.*

Perfecta had work to do.

Perfecta received the drone intel in another onscreen pop-up that said that government agents had finally infiltrated into her region of the Black Hills. She completed her final data upload that crosslinked with her onion-encryption protocols. With her remaining drones, she uploaded all that she needed into them . . . and sent them out into the world.

Then she uploaded all the same data into each of her "safe" server locations: subterranean vaults scattered across the planet, as well as secretly embedded into two commercial satellites.

And, finally, she embedded all of the above into all the major Theran media corporations.

She was done.

Another alert popped up.

Another of her servers had been compromised. Captured.

Yes, she didn't have long. But she was ready. The world would soon know.

Perfecta's timer had run out.

4

Perfecta sat facing her lab's only entrance when the concussion hit.

The explosion blew in her lab's door, knocked her against her console, then onto the floor, and set her ears to ringing.

The dust hadn't even begun to settle when she found herself staring nose-to-barrel into the weaponry of many angry-faced, black-garmented paramilitary operatives. From around them vigorously stepped a tall, dark, immaculately attired figure. Black soft-brimmed hat with a pinched-front crown menacingly positioned atop closely cropped hair. Dark, piercing eyes.

The figure came to a stop inches before her.

"Miss Harcourtt, I presume," he said.

Perfecta looked up. Still catching her breath, coughing, and shaking her head from still-falling debris and ringing ears, she said, "*I presume that you wouldn't have blown in the door of a citizen of whose identity you weren't absolutely positive.*"

The man smiled lethally.

Perfecta unsteadily got to her feet and said, "You know me . . . may I know with whom I am speaking?" Perfecta brushed herself off.

"You may call me 'Lucifer.'"

"Okay, Luci—"

"You've stuck your nose where it shouldn't have been stuck, and have sniffed things that should not have been sniffed."

"Then may I also ask who made me their responsibility?"

"You may."

Lucifer stepped away from Perfecta, simultaneously indicating to the operatives to seize her. Lucifer casually inspected the damage of their attack.

Perfecta was pinned before she could muster a twitch.

"*It's too late!*" she said, "*I've already sent everything out!* EVERYTHING!"

Lucifer turned to Perfecta, who uselessly struggled with her captors.

"You think we don't know that? We've already acquired all of your drones, commandeered all of your servers, and have intercepted all of your embedded media uploads."

"Oh, yes, and now we have *you*.

"You think you're the only one with special powers, girl? As genius as you may be . . . you are clearly still but a snot-nosed nursling."

"I know your secrets! *I know!*"

"Not for much longer," Lucifer said, turning away.

"*I know what the stars mean!*" Perfecta shouted.

The one called Lucifer continued to examine Perfecta's workstation and the rest of the room, no longer concerned with the girl. He made quiet comments and grunts to himself.

Screaming and straining against her restraint Perfecta said, "I know 'Thera' has another name—from another time—that the *Renaissance* came from our *future!* They never knew! But *I* do!"

"And they," Lucifer said, quietly, as he crouched before a safe, inspecting it, "and the rest of Thera will continue to never know." He brushed away dust from the handle and combination pad.

Lucifer came back to his feet and again faced Perfecta.

A grin crept across his face.

But when Lucifer opened his mouth to speak, he, Perfecta, everyone in that room, including the entire population of Thera, were instantly wiped out by a rather large asteroid that sideswiped Thera into lifeless, retrograde rotation.

GEDANKENEXPERIMENT

> we'd given them every opportunity
> it never would've worked
> would you really ha—
> of course that's why i gave it life
> so
> let's just let it play out they deserve the outcome
> then—
> it would've come to its logical conclusion anyway
> we're done here
> this was a mistake
> we had faith
> look where it would've gotten us
> give me that
> i'm just glad we didn't let it go on too long
> indeed but you would've done the same all we could do was what we'd done—

the rest was up to them
we gave them every opportunity every benefit . . . explicit guidance—
i'd reworked enormous considerations eliminated others
yes
we shouldn't even have bothered this scenario had already run its course—
before they even got here
Godlike grabbed a rather large asteroid, hefted it, then hurled it at the planet.
who were we kidding
they never learn
was a nice thought
what was that
oh let them go it doesn't matter it's best this way
we really should've killed them
i like the quiet
we all do

ANTECEDENT

The cataclysm was horrendous and absolute.

It reversed the spin of the planet, stripped it of its atmosphere, and vibrated clean (shook the hell out of) its lithosphere.

Yet out from behind the shattered planet's husk launched a bright speck. It flung outward in a wide arc—with more than a little assistance from the planet-ending impact—but after some distance readjusted its trajectory.

The moon . . . hollowed out and impregnated with technology, engineers, and civilizational remnants . . . swiftly ejected from its second-planet host . . .

And headed directly toward that which would come to be called "Earth."

ABOUT THE AUTHOR

F. P. (Frank) Dorchak is published in the U.S., Canada, and the Czech Republic with short stories, four novels, *Sleepwalkers*, *The Uninvited*, *ERO*, and *Psychic*, and his first short story collection, *Do The Dead Dream? An Anthology of the Weird and the Peculiar*, which won the 2017 *Best Books Award for Fiction: Short Story*.

http://www.fpdorchak.com

Milton Keynes UK
Ingram Content Group UK Ltd.
UKHW021639260524
443160UK00001B/64